One Moment, One Morning

One Moment, One Morning

Sarah Rayner

PICADOR

First published 2010 by Picador
an imprint of Pan Macmillan, a division of Macmillan Publishers Limited
Pan Macmillan, 20 New Wharf Road, London N1 9RR
Basingstoke and Oxford
Associated companies throughout the world
www.panmacmillan.com

ISBN 978-0-330-51882-6

9 8 7 6 5 4 3 2 1

A CIP catalogue record for this book is available
from the British Library.

Typeset by Ellipsis Books Limited, Glasgow
Printed and bound by CPI Mackays, Chatham ME5 8TD

Visit **www.picador.com** to read more about all our books and to
buy them. You will also find features, author interviews and news
of any author events, and you can sign up for e-newsletters
so that you're always first to hear about our new releases.

Monday

07:58

Lou is pretending to be asleep, but out of the corner of her eye she is watching the woman opposite put on her make-up. She always finds it fascinating, watching other women do this, constructing themselves, on the train. Lou never wears make-up, really, other than for very special occasions, and although she can understand it saves time, she finds it odd – choosing to make the transformation from private to public persona whilst commuting. It takes away the mystery, covering the blemishes, thickening the lashes, widening the eyes, plumping the cheeks, surrounded by people. And on the seven forty-four to Victoria, Lou is surrounded by people: most of them silent; many of them asleep, or at least dozing; some of them reading, and a few, a minority, chatting.

The woman on the seat adjacent to her, separated by the aisle, is one such person. Lou has her iPod on, softly, so she can't hear what she is saying, although from the tilt of the woman's head, it's clear she is talking to a man to her right. Lou shifts in her seat, adjusts her parka hood, damp from a cycle ride through drizzle to the station, so as to view them better round the fur lining. They are married. Matching rings, circling fingers circling cardboard coffee cups, betray this. The woman, Lou decides, is around forty.

Lou can't observe her full on, but she appears to have the sort of face Lou likes. Her profile is interesting, attractive, if with faint traces of a jowl; her hair a thick curtain of chestnut brown. From what Lou can see of him, her husband is not quite as good looking; he is heavyset, greying – Lou reckons he is ten years his wife's senior, maybe more – but his face is kind. There is a gentleness in his expression and the lines around his mouth, deep crevices, suggest he likes to laugh. The woman leans affectionately against his shoulder. Before him is a thick paperback, the latest best-seller, but he's not reading it; instead he strokes her hand, slowly, softly. Lou has a small pang of jealousy. She envies their tenderness and the way they show it without a second thought.

The train pulls into Burgess Hill. It is pouring now, and weary commuters shake and close their umbrellas as they board. There is the sharp blow of a whistle to hurry them, and as the doors slide shut, Lou returns her gaze to the young woman opposite. Now she has finished applying shadow to her eyes, they have more emphasis: it is as if her whole face has acquired definition, an edge. Except the lips, still pale, appear bereft. Lou thinks she looked just as good without make-up: sweeter somehow, more vulnerable. Either way, though, she is pretty. And her hair, a mass of Fusilli blonde curls, is so ebullient, so springy, so different in texture from her own spiked and mousy crop, that Lou wants to reach out and touch it.

Lou watches as the young woman turns attention to her lips. Suddenly, the young woman stops, Cupid's bow comically half pinked in, like an unfinished china doll. Lou follows her gaze back to the couple; the man has unexpectedly, embarrassingly, vomited. All down his jacket, his shirt, his tie, there's a stream of frothy, phlegmy milk, and bits of half-digested croissant, like baby's sick.

Lou unhooks one earphone, surreptitiously.

'Oh, Lord!' the woman is saying, frantically wiping the mess with the too-small napkin that's come with her coffee. To no avail: with an infant gurgle, the man pukes again. This time it goes all over his wife's wrist, splashes her chiffon blouse; even, horror, lands in the curtain of her hair.

'I don't know—' he says, gasping, and Lou sees he is sweating, profusely, repugnantly, not normally at all. Then he adds, 'I'm sorry . . .'

Lou is just thinking she knows what it is – the man is clutching his chest now – and she sits bolt upright, any pretence of discretion gone, when, *boof!* A thud and he lands, face down, on the table. And then he is still. Utterly still. For a few seconds – or so it seems – no one does anything. Lou simply watches his spilt coffee, follows the beige trail, drip drip drip, along the window ledge, down the side of the cream Formica table and onto the floor. Outside, rain-drenched trees and fields still whoosh by.

Then, pandemonium.

'Simon! Simon!' His wife has jumped up, is shouting.

Simon does not respond.

As his spouse shakes him, Lou catches a glimpse of his face, mouth open, sick still damp on his cheek, before he falls back, head lolling. She is sure she recognizes him; she's seen him on this train before.

'Jesus!' says a disgruntled man opposite, shaking out his

copy of the *Telegraph*. 'What the devil's wrong with him? He drunk or something?' He harrumphs, judgement plain.

It's as though his disapproval galvanizes Lou. 'He's having a heart attack, for fuck's sake!' She leaps to her feet, ancient Health & Safety training, Girl Guide badges, episodes of *ER*, all coming back in a rush. 'Call the guard, somebody!'

Another man, young, scruffy, goatee-bearded, next to the woman who has been putting on her make-up, flings down his plastic bag, gets to his feet. 'Which way?' he asks Lou, as if she knows everything.

'Middle carriage!' cries the wife.

The young man looks unsure.

'That way,' says Lou, pointing to the front end of the train, and off he runs.

* * *

Three carriages along, Anna is treating herself to her favourite glossy magazine. In two stops she has devoured the lead article about a pop princess in rehab, and now she's onto the 'Most Wanted' section, where she spies a jacket she hopes might suit her, from a chain store, new in for spring, very reasonably priced. She is just folding over the page as a reminder to check it out in her lunch hour when a young man with a goatee knocks her elbow as he rushes past.

'Thanks,' she mutters sarcastically. Annoying Brighton hippies, she thinks.

A few seconds later he returns at speed, the guard following closely. She reassesses the situation – both look anxious. Perhaps something is up.

6

Then the driver's voice can be heard over the speakers: 'Are there any doctors or nurses aboard? If so, please contact the guard in carriage E.'

How will people know where carriage E is? Anna thinks. But apparently they do know – barely ten seconds later two women charge past her, handbags flying behind. Anna raises her eyebrows at the passengers opposite. Such consternation is a rarity on the seven forty-four, where there is an unspoken rule of quietness and consideration. It is a bit alarming.

Shortly, the train pulls into Wivelsfield. Why are we stopping here? Anna worries. We normally speed straight through. She hopes it is just a signal, but fears it is something more sinister. Five minutes later, her disquiet has grown, and she is not alone: all about her people are getting impatient and shifting restlessly in their seats. Anna needs the train to be on time if she is not to be late for the office. She works freelance, and although she is on a long-term contract, her employers are pedantic about timekeeping. They run a tight ship, and the boss has been known to wait scowling in reception, checking for tardy arrivals.

There is a 'fuff fuff' of exhaling air into a microphone and another announcement: 'I'm sorry but a passenger has been taken seriously ill on board. We're going to be here for a few minutes while we wait for an ambulance.'

Her heart sinks and she thinks, why can't they take whoever it is off the train and wait for an ambulance there? Then she berates herself for being uncharitable: one glance at the rain-soaked platform answers her question. It is February, chilly.

She is too distracted to read, so looks out of the window, watching the rain hit grey paving and gathering in pools where the surface is uneven. Wivelsfield, she thinks, where the hell is that? It is not somewhere she has ever visited; she has only been through it on the train.

Ten minutes turn to fifteen, twenty, with no further announcement. By this time, people are texting on their mobiles, or calling strings of unidentifiable numbers, most with voices low. Some, less neighbourly, loudly state their lack of sympathy – 'Not sure what's wrong, someone taken "ill", apparently, probably a bloody drug addict . . .' – whilst others seem to enjoy the opportunity to convey a sense of their own importance – 'Sorry, Jane, Ian here, going to be late for the Board. Get them to hold off, will you, till I get there?' and so on.

Then, at last, Anna sees three figures in Day-Glo anoraks rushing past the window, guiding a stretcher. Thank heavens: shouldn't be long now.

She keeps her eyes fixed on the platform, expecting to see the stretcher returning with a body strapped to it, pushed at speed. But instead the tired concrete wall just stares back at her, the rain keeps falling, filling the hollows of the yellow 'Mind the Gap' warnings with more water.

Finally, a tap, a splutter, then: 'I apologize again, ladies and gentlemen, it looks as if we're going to be here for an unforeseeable duration. We're unable to move the passenger. If I could just ask you to be patient, we'll let you know as soon as we have news.'

There is a collective sigh, more shuffling.

How annoying, thinks Anna before she can stop herself,

then, more benignly: how very odd. She certainly doesn't buy the drug addict theory – Brighton's smack-heads are hardly known for catching the morning commuter train, for goodness' sake. So obviously someone is genuinely ill. Yet she is worried about her boss, her colleagues; she has heaps on that day. Her thoughts – a tangle of self-interest and altruism – seem in sync with the passengers opposite: frowns mixing exasperation and concern.

'Why can't they be moved?' says the man opposite eventually, breaking taboo by speaking to strangers on the train. He is tall, bespectacled, with closely shaven hair and an immaculately starched collar, a Norman Rockwell painting made manifest.

'Perhaps whoever it is has got a spinal injury,' says the passenger next to him, an apple-shaped elderly woman. The way she adjusts her posture to create space between the two of them as she speaks suggests she's not travelling with him. 'They wouldn't be able to move the neck.'

He nods. 'Possibly.'

Anna is not so sure. 'Bit strange, though: how would you get a spinal injury on a train?'

'Perhaps someone's *died*.' Anna turns, sees a young girl next to her. Lank black hair, facial piercings. Gothic.

'Ooh, goodness, no,' gasps the elderly woman, worried. 'Surely not?'

'Could be,' agrees Norman Rockwell. 'Would explain why we have to stay here. They'll have to get the police.'

'Certify death,' says the Goth.

Suddenly Anna's magazine doesn't seem quite the same. It usually provides her weekly fix of fun, fashion, style and gossip; she knows it's shallow but reckons she deserves it, and anyway, it covers wider issues too. Then, as if to mirror her thoughts, she turns the page and sees just such an article: a picture of a young Afghan woman, whose body has been horrifically scarred by burns.

Anna shudders.

* * *

For Lou the sight of passengers ducking their heads as two men hoist a stretcher up and over the seats is almost farcical. The stretcher is an awkward shape, even with the crossbar and wheels removed – bigger than any suitcase – and the whole experience seems unreal, filmic, or, more precisely, like an episode of a television drama. Only TV you can turn off, whereas here she's forced to watch – how can she not, with it all happening inches away?

For the last ten minutes, two young women – nurses, apparently on their way to work at a hospital in Haywards Heath – have been trying to resuscitate the man, with increasing desperation. They have checked if he is breathing, felt for a pulse in his neck and then, with the help of the guard, pulled him onto the floor so as to get him horizontal. All this right by Lou's feet, before she had time to move, so she has been pinned in, witnessing the horror unfurl. They've taken it in turns, one nurse pumping pumping pumping with her palms flat on his chest, the movements so deliberate and assertive as to seem vicious, while the other has been breathing into his mouth, perhaps every thirty pumps or so. When the nurse pumping has tired, they've swapped over.

Through it all, the man's wife stands in the aisle, help-less. She is utterly silent, her attention flipping from one nurse to the other and back to her husband, her face contorted with worry.

It all happens so fast in the end. The paramedics arrive, the nurse at his mouth stops, looks up and shakes her head – a tiny gesture but significant. No joy.

The paramedics manage to tilt the stretcher sideways, slide him onto it and swiftly propel him to the much wider space by the train doors. The few passengers standing there shift hurriedly to create room. Lou sees oxygen, a defibrillator, drugs – an injection – there's a cry of 'Stand clear!' and they shock him.

Nothing.

And again.

Nothing.

Again.

Still nothing.

Everyone in the train carriage is transfixed. It is not just morbid fascination – it is an inability to comprehend what is happening, shock. What are they going to do? But the guard misinterprets the slack jaws, the wide eyes – whether out of sympathy for the man and his wife or a desire to take control, it doesn't really matter – the upshot is the same. He barks an order, loud enough for everybody to hear: 'Can you all please leave the carriage at once.'

So Lou gathers up her things – her mobile, her iPod, her rucksack – in many ways thankful to be given permission to move. On the adjacent table the man's book remains; not that he will need it, now. Lou zips her coat, pulls up the hood and heads out of the doors into the rain.

Another announcement follows, this time a request over the speaker system that *all* passengers disembark from the train, and soon Lou is surrounded by people, mystified, looking in confusion for the exit at a station they do not know.

* * *

Anna has to fight to create the space to raise her umbrella. The platform is heaving, but she is damned if she's going to get her hair wet as well as everything else – she hates it when it goes even slightly wavy, which it will if she is not careful. Today it would be especially galling as she got up early, whilst it was still pitch black outside, to wash and blow-dry it for a meeting. Thankfully, Anna is tall and her brolly has one of those automatic buttons that makes it open with an efficient 'poof!' She raises it safely above the throng and bingo, she is sheltered from the worst.

Next to her is the rotund elderly woman and inching along just in front is Norman Rockwell.

'What the devil are we supposed to do now?' he asks.

'They'll lay on buses,' says the elderly woman.

Anna doesn't know how the woman knows – it is not as if this sort of thing happens every day – but takes her word for it. 'Where on earth will they get enough buses for everyone?' Her mind is only just catching up with events.

'I guess they'll have to bring them from Brighton,' says Norman.

'Fuck that,' says a fourth voice – it is the Goth girl, wedged behind Anna. 'They'll be hours. I give up. I'm going home.'

I can't, thinks Anna. If only she could. But she has clients coming in for a presentation, plus if she doesn't make it into the office, she simply doesn't get paid, and she is the main breadwinner.

Regardless of whether they are heading for the buses or back to Brighton, they all have to shuffle the same way. The exit and the opposite platform are beyond the covered area of the platform with its worn walls and peeling advertisements, down some steps at the far end of the station. Shoulders jostle and elbows nudge – some people insist on talking and texting on their mobiles, which only slows matters further, so it seems to take an age before they are down the stairs, past the ticket office, and outside.

Here Anna pauses for a moment to take stock. It is an incongruous sight – several hundred people in so small a space. The place is tiny – there is not even a proper station building, just a little ticket office halfway down the stairs. Although there are probably a thousand stations like it up and down the country, it is hardly designed for the mass exodus of all bar two of the passengers from a packed ten-carriage commuter train. There is not even a proper car park. And no bus stop that Anna can see, let alone any buses.

Shit.

But at that very moment, with a swoosh through the puddles, a white Ford Mondeo pulls up and stops beside her. A taxi. For a brief moment, Anna thinks, impressed: blimey, someone's ordered that, how organized, before she realizes that maybe no one has, that this is a station, albeit a small one, so there might well be taxis anyway. The light on its roof is on; it is for hire. The crowd lurches forward – competition is fierce. But the back passenger door is right at her side – it is now or never. She opens it, leans in, and asks the driver: 'Are you free?'

The opposite door opens simultaneously. She sees a fur-trimmed hood, an anxious face. 'Haywards Heath?' asks the other woman.

'I'm happy to share,' suggests Anna.

'Whatever,' the taxi driver grunts in approbation. It's all in a morning's work for him. A fare is a fare.

Before he has time to renege on the offer, the two women get in.

08:30

Anna exhales, 'Phew.'

Rain is thundering on the car roof, as if to underline their good fortune.

'That was a stroke of luck,' says the woman in the parka, pushing down her hood and wriggling out of her rucksack. She is compactly built and supple and seems practised at the manoeuvre. 'That poor guy,' she says, sitting back.

'What was it?' asks Anna.

'Heart attack,' says the parka woman.

'Did he die, do you think?'

'I'm afraid so.'

'Oh, Lord.'

'I know, awful. He was travelling with his wife, too.'

'How do you know?'

'I was sitting next to them. The other side of the aisle.'

'Gosh. That must have been a horrible thing to witness.'

'Yes,' nods the parka woman.

And there I was, complaining that all this was just inconvenient, Anna castigates herself. The Goth was obviously right. What does it matter, really, if I'm a bit late for work? She voices her thoughts: 'It's not exactly how you'd choose to go, is it? You'd rather die flying a kite with your grandchildren, or at a great party or something. Not on the seven forty-four.'

'Oi, ladies,' the driver interrupts before she has a chance to continue. He is listening to a crackling and distorted voice over his radio. 'No point going to Haywards Heath. Apparently the trains from there are at a standstill. Whole lot's buggered.'

'They can't do that, surely?' asks Anna.

'Ooh, they can, believe me,' says the driver. 'You know what it's like on the Brighton line – it's a single track each way from Haywards Heath to the coast. Only takes one train to scupper it.'

The two women look at each other.

The driver chivvies, 'So where do you want me to take you?'

'Home?' suggests the parka woman.

'Where's home?' asks the other.

'Brighton,' says the parka woman, then clarifies, 'Kemptown.'

Anna's mind whirrs. Anorak, boyish face, cropped and gelled hair, no make-up, jeans, rucksack, Kemptown address: she's gay. Kemptown is not that far from Anna's house: it's *so* tempting, but – 'I can't,' she explains. 'I have to get to London.'

'I guess I should go too,' agrees the parka woman. 'Just quite nice to have an excuse for once.'

'I've got a meeting,' says Anna.

'What time's it at?'

'Ten.'

Anna looks at her watch. It's eight thirty-five now. 'Typical, isn't it?' she says. 'Normally the seven forty-four gets me to work fine.'

'But they'll understand, won't they?' says the parka woman. 'Someone has just died on board.' She laughs, but it doesn't seem unkind; rather it is a comment on the ludicrousness of their situation. She pauses, assessing. 'Can't you just ring and explain you'll be late?'

Anna imagines the bulldog stance of her boss in reception and isn't so sure.

'Ladies,' the driver cuts in again. They are approaching traffic lights at a crossroads. 'I need a decision. Where are you going?'

Anna catches his eye in the mirror. She is sure he is smirking, enjoying this. 'I really need to get to London,' she reiterates. She doesn't want to leave her colleagues in the lurch. Not to make it would compel one of them to present in her place – no fun at short notice, Anna knows. She leans forward, close to his ear. 'How much to take us there?'

'Depends where.'

She wonders: where would suit her and hopefully the other woman, and not be too difficult in terms of rush hour traffic? 'Clapham Junction?'

'Where's your meeting?' asks the parka woman.

'Cheyne Walk off the King's Road – I can get lots of buses from the station.'

'Fine by me,' agrees the parka woman. 'I'll get a train from Clapham up to Victoria.'

'I'll do it for seventy quid,' says the driver. They're stopped at traffic lights.

Anna does a rapid calculation. It's not unreasonable for sixty miles or so. On her daily rate it is worth it – she will lose much more than that if she doesn't show. She glances at the parka woman. She looks hesitant – Anna is aware that not everyone earns as much as she does.

'I'm happy to pay fifty quid of it,' she offers. 'I really do need to get there.'

'Oh, that wouldn't be fair.'

'I get paid by the day,' she explains. 'So I'm fine to, honestly.'

'Are you sure?'

'Yes.'

'Um . . .'

'Really, it's fine. I'd be paying it on my own otherwise.'

'OK then. Thank you,' the parka woman smiles, appreciative.

'Great.' Anna leans forward to the driver again. 'Do it.'

So he flicks up the indicator, turns left and heads towards the motorway.

*   *   *

'I guess I might as well introduce myself. I'm Lou.' Lou turns to face the other woman and thrusts out her hand.

Her fellow passenger is not conventionally pretty, but she is striking nonetheless. She must be in her early forties – whereas Lou is ten years younger – and she has a strong, angular face with Cleopatra dark hair, styled poker-straight. Her make-up is bold: a gash of lipstick, dark shadow that makes no apology for deliberately intensifying brown eyes. It signals confidence, an effect compounded by her height and long limbs. She is slim and well dressed, in a smart navy trench coat, and her large snakeskin handbag looks expensive. The overall effect is of someone intelligent yet daunting.

'I'm Anna,' she returns. Her hand is cold, bony; her grasp assured and firm. But she is generous and empathetic, Lou has noticed already; clearly she is not *that* hard.

'Where are you going?' Lou asks.

'I work in Chelsea. My meeting is at the office. You?'

'I'm on my way to Hammersmith.' There is a moment's silence. 'I'm a youth worker,' Lou adds.

'Ah,' Anna nods.

Though she loves her job, Lou is conscious her profession is not particularly glamorous or well remunerated. Whilst she has no idea exactly what this woman who works off the King's Road does, she supposes it's far more high-flying, and somehow wants her approval. But she doesn't get the chance to elaborate on why she does what she does because next Anna swivels her hips and tucks her left foot under her, so as to face Lou as fully as possible.

'So tell me,' she urges. 'What happened on the train?'

Lou recounts the events as best she can remember.

'There simply wasn't time for anyone to resuscitate him,' Lou finishes. 'The nurses were there in next to no time, and they tried . . . God knows they tried.' She shivers, recollecting. 'But it was over so fast. One minute he was drinking his coffee, the next, so it seems – gone.'

'The poor woman he was with!' Anna says, aghast. 'Just imagine that, leaving for work with your husband, thinking it was just a normal day, and then suddenly he keels over and dies. Right beside you. Oh, I *really* feel sorry for her.'

*   *   *

'So do you live in Brighton too, then?' asks Lou, once they're on the motorway. The driver puts his foot down and soon they're doing a steady seventy miles per hour. Gorse bushes just beginning to bud yellow flash by on the embankment.

'Yes.'

'Where are you?'

'Seven Dials. You know it?'

'Of course,' retorts Lou. 'I've lived in Brighton for nearly ten years.'

'Ah, well.' This makes it worthwhile to be more precise. 'I'm on Charminster Street.' Lou looks blank. 'Between Old Shoreham Road and Dyke Road.'

'Oh, yeah!' Lou exclaims. 'Lovely little white Victorian houses, office block at the end of the street.'

'That's it. It's a bit scruffy, but I like it.'

'Is it just you?'

She sounds genuinely interested and Anna sees her glance at her finger – presumably to check if she is married. How funny, Anna thinks, we're both looking for signals, assessing. Nonetheless, she pauses. It is not a subject on which she likes to be drawn. 'Um, no . . . I live with my partner.'

Lou picks up her cue, and changes the subject. 'So, do you always work in London?'

'Mostly, yes. You?'

'Four days a week. I wouldn't want to commute the full five.'

'No, it does get tiring.' Anna experiences a flush of resentment: if Steve earned more, she wouldn't need to travel so much. But she doesn't say this. Instead she takes a deep breath and says, more positively: 'I love being in Brighton though. So it is worth it.' She smiles, thinking affectionately of the terraced home she has put so much time and energy into decorating, with its patio garden and views out over the Downs. Then there is her handful of close friends conveniently nearby; the Lanes, jostling with one-off shops and equally eclectic people; the steep shingle of the beach and beyond it, the sea . . . That, perhaps above all else, makes the commute worthwhile: the grey, the green and the blue of it; the crashing, the calm and the choppiness of it; the never-the-same-two-days-in-a-row of it: ah, the sea . . .

Lou interrupts her thoughts. 'I like being in Brighton too.'

'So where are you in Kemptown?' Anna asks. 'I do hope you're not going to tell me you've got a whole house on the seafront there!' She is joking, of course: the Regency houses overlooking the beach in Kemptown are huge. Not merely that, they are magnificent; elegant cream stucco frontages, giant windows rising floor to ceiling, rooms of breathtaking proportions with marble fireplaces and elaborate plaster cornices – to own a whole one would be a dream.

Lou laughs. 'Hardly. I live in a little attic flat – it's not much bigger than a studio really.'

Something about the way she uses 'I', not 'we', suggests Lou is living alone. Anna clarifies, 'So I presume you don't share?'

Lou laughs again. She has an infectious laugh: deep, throaty, uninhibited. 'God no, there's barely room to swing a cat.'

'And where is it, if you don't mind my asking?'

'On Magdalene Street.'

'Ooh. Does that mean you can see the sea?'

'Yes, from the living-room bay, down the bottom of the road. I think estate agents call it "an oblique sea view". And I've got a tiny roof terrace where you can see the sea *and* the pier.'

'How lovely.' Anna is wistful. She has always fantasized about having her own garret. Fleetingly, she imagines a different life for herself: one where she doesn't have so many commitments; where there is no mortgage to pay, no Steve, and she is free to pursue her own creativity . . .

Enough of that: she can't change it, and anyway, she wants to know more about Lou. 'It must be great for nightlife round there,' she says, hoping to prompt revelations. Lou lives in the heart of Brighton's gay district and there are dozens of pubs and clubs at hand where Anna imagines all sorts of exciting things happen.

'Sometimes a bit *too* good,' replies Lou. 'It can get a bit noisy.'

That's a bit tame, thinks Anna. She'd wanted tales of wild drug-taking and lesbian threesomes. If her own existence is circumscribed these days, she can at least live vicariously. Then again, if there are interesting aspects to Lou's life, she is hardly likely to confess all to a stranger in a taxi.

*   *   *

Half an hour into the journey, Lou has decided that Anna seems OK, but is still unsure if they have much in common. Lou is a good judge of character on the whole; years of working as a counsellor have honed an innate skill, so she tends to assess individuals well. She is perhaps less shrewd when it comes to judging women she fancies, when sexual attraction can get in the way. But she has seen many straight women – and men too, come to that – make poor judgements when lust muddies perception, so at least she is not alone.

Anyhow, Anna is clearly straight, and not Lou's type physically. Nonetheless, she is intrigued. She loves nothing more than delving into people's psyches; it is the same curiosity that has her watching strangers on the train, mapping out lives for them, piecing together the evidence. And it is also what drives her professionally; she loves getting to the bottom of what makes complex – though often tragically self-destructive – young people tick.

In spite of Anna's polished exterior, which suggests a more materialistic bent than Lou herself, Lou reckons there might be more to her than her travelling companion's unruffled presentation suggests. There have been little signals, along the way. She has made no mention of any offspring, and most women would do, given the nature of the conversation they have been having about their respective homes. So Lou reckons she doesn't have children, which is relatively unusual for a woman of her age. But more interesting is the way Anna hesitated before mentioning her partner; Lou reckons there is a story there. She is quick to pick up when someone is hiding something – not least because in certain situations, she does it herself. Plus there is the way Anna is sensitive to the needs of others, even when she is taking control. They did what Anna wanted ultimately, after all, yet she offered to pay Lou's share. It hints at a sharp mind and a complex character, and Lou's curiosity is piqued.

I wonder, she muses, as they pull off the M23 and onto the dual carriageway into the drab outskirts of Coulsdon, whether we'll ever see each other after today? She's used to journeying up to London on her own in the morning, using the space to gather her thoughts. Still, it would be nice to have someone to chat to from time to time, when she is in the mood. Maybe, if Anna is on the seven forty-four as often as she says she is, they will see each other on board. That said, it is a long train and always packed with people. Being on it at the same time is no guarantee their paths will cross again.

09:45

Karen is standing in a car park. Exactly how she has got here or how long she has been here, she is not sure. It is only when, fingers trembling, she tries to light a cigarette that she realizes it is raining. The white paper becomes peppered with droplets that expand and turn it soggy. She looks up; grey clouds skid across the sky. She tilts her head right back. Her face is rapidly covered in water. She should be able to feel it, cool and wet on her skin, but she can't. She opens her mouth to see if she can taste it, but though her mouth fills with raindrops, she can't. She is shivering, but she can't sense the cold.

She tries to locate herself. A large sign, white type out of blue, announces:

ROYAL SUSSEX COUNTY HOSPITAL

Seems to make some kind of sense. What is she supposed to do now?

Simon is dead.

Dead.

Even though she repeats the word to herself, even though she has seen him die, right in front of her, it is not real.

Even though she has watched as two nurses tried to revive him on a train and some paramedics tried to shock his heart into working – they tried again and again, and in the ambulance too. Even though a doctor confirmed he was dead a few minutes ago and recorded the time of death; it is still not real, not at all.

They let her be with Simon in A&E – there were tubes everywhere. Now they are moving him to the mortuary – to the viewing room, apparently, where they've suggested she might like to spend some more time with his body. But she wanted a cigarette, first, so somehow she has ended up out here, bewildered, numb.

'Numb.'

She repeats this word too, aloud this time. She has a weird recollection. Don't they say that feeling numb is the first stage of grief?

She supposes she ought to do something about the children. What time is it? Where are they? Ah, yes, of course, today they are with the childminder: Tracy.

Tracy's number, yes, right – it is on her mobile.

Oh dear, it is raining; so it is, of course. She had best move out of the rain; her phone will get wet.

Karen sees there is a big glass awning at the entrance to the hospital, a few paces away. There are people beneath it, chatting. She joins them. Briefly, now she is under cover, she is conscious she is drenched. Her fringe is sticking to her forehead in rats' tails and there are rivulets of cold water running down the back of her neck; even her suede pumps are soaked – how horrible.

She gets the phone out of her Liberty-print shopper – the

bag she uses to carry paperwork when she has it, and which today also contains the March issue of *Good Housekeeping*, her purse, lipstick and a comb, a bottle of water and her cigarettes. Her mobile, a basic model with a worn leather case, which her children have covered in ghastly sparkly stickers, has Tracy's number listed in the address book. She is sure there's a quicker way to find it – speed dial or something – but can't remember how it works. So she scrolls down the alphabetic list and is just about to press the green button and dial when she stops.

What on earth is she doing? What is she planning to say? 'Luke, Molly, Daddy's dead. Come to the hospital and see the body'? They're five and *three*, for God's sake. They won't understand. She doesn't understand.

Jesus. *Jesus*.

No, what Karen needs is to speak to her friend, her best friend. *She* will know what to do: she always does. This is one number she knows automatically without having to think. Fingers still shaking, Karen punches in the digits.

*   *   *

Not far from Clapham Junction, the taxi is stuck in traffic. The driver has made excellent time up the M23, wound through the depressing suburban sprawl of Croydon, Norbury and Streatham at an impressive rate despite dozens of sets of lights, but so far it has taken them about twenty minutes to get down St John's Hill.

Anna is just beginning to feel twinges of impatience, when there is a vibrating against her hip: her phone. Soon it is ringing increasingly loudly from the depths of her snakeskin bag. She rummages around. Damn – where is it? Finally she feels smooth metal and pulls out a neat, clam-shaped device.

Hurriedly she flicks it open, knowing she only has seconds before voicemail clicks in.

'Hiya!' she says, happy to see the name that comes up on the screen.

'Anna?' checks a voice, thin, plaintive.

'Yes, it's me. That you?'

The voice on the other end cracks. 'Yes.'

It sounds as if there is something the matter. 'Hey, hey,' says Anna, adopting a gentler tone and leaning into the mouthpiece to make herself heard. 'What's happened?'

'It's – it's – Simon.' The voice – so familiar to Anna – is strangely small.

'What about him?' Anna is confused.

'He's—' There is a pause. A long pause.

'*What?*' Anna is insistent – now she is worried.

'He's . . .' Then everything rushes through Anna's head at once. She has a terrible premonition: she knows what's coming next, but it can't be, no, it can't – then, finally, dreadfully, confirmation; the word is there, out, in the cab, real. '. . . dead.'

'Oh, my God!' cries Anna. Thoughts hurtle. What is this – some kind of sick joke?

'What is it?' says Lou, immediately grabbing Anna's knee.

Anna shakes her hand, motioning that quiet is called for. 'What – when – ?'

'Just now – this morning – on the train –'

'What? The seven forty-four to Victoria? No!'

'Yes.' The voice is barely audible. 'How did you know?'

'But I was on that train!' exclaims Anna. 'Christ, I don't believe it! Oh, oh, Karen—' Instinctively, she starts to cry; giant tears plop forth before she can stop herself. It is not even sorrow, really; the information hasn't even sunk in. It is shock. Karen and Simon are her friends. Karen is her *best* friend. Still, she has to get the facts straight. 'But what were you doing on that train? You never normally get that train – that's the one *I* get.'

'Yes, I suppose it must be,' says Karen. 'I didn't think.'

'Shit.' All at once Anna realizes this is no joke. It makes sense. 'You had to sign the mortgage papers today, no?'

'Yes,' says Karen, scarcely above a whisper. 'We were going up to London together, to the solicitors, before Simon went on to work. It seemed to make sense to do it like that. And then I had some shopping to do. I was going to Hamleys to get a birthday present for Luke.'

At this point, the taxi driver interrupts. 'I'm sorry, love,' he says, his manner less brusque this time. 'But we're here.'

'What?' Anna looks out of the window; sees a flower stall, a splash of colours and foliage, and up above it, a large red sign:

CLAPHAM JUNCTION

'Oh, oh, right.' She gathers up her bag. 'Hang on a minute, Karen, hang on, just need to pay for this taxi. Stay there, right there – I'll be with you in a tick.'

'It's OK,' says Lou. 'You get out – carry on – I'll get this, don't worry. You're all right, we'll sort it in a sec.'

Anna nods her head, grateful. 'Thanks.' She opens the taxi

door and somehow manoeuvres herself from the car onto the pavement, still holding her phone open precariously so as not to lose Karen. Lou pays the driver – luckily she seems to have enough cash – and follows her.

'You still there?' Anna checks.

'Yes,' says Karen.

'Just a second.' Despite everything, Anna wants to settle up. She digs deep into her bag for her purse but just as she pulls it out, she drops it.

Lou retrieves it. 'I can wait,' she says, handing it back. 'Please. You just carry on.'

'Are you sure?'

Lou nods and diplomatically steps to one side so as not to be intrusive.

Anna returns to Karen. 'Where are you?'

'At the hospital,' says Karen.

'Which hospital? Haywards Heath?'

'No, Brighton. For some reason they brought us here – I suppose it's because they have a cardiac ward or something.'

'Oh, right. So, tell me, what happened, exactly?' Although she's heard the story from Lou already, Anna has to hear it again from Karen to make sure the experiences tally and to grasp the fact that it's real.

'We were sitting on the train, together, this morning, you know, everything was normal, when – I don't know – we were chatting, we had a coffee each, and – suddenly – he had a heart attack.'

'What? Just from nowhere?'

'Well, the funny thing is, he had been complaining of indigestion on the way to the station. But you know Simon, he's always getting heartburn, he gets so wound up about stuff, and – well, to be honest, I thought it was nothing. Just nerves, about the new house, signing the papers.'

Anna nods, although there's no way Karen can see her. 'So, what—' Anna hesitates, unsure if she's being insensitive, but ploughs on anyway. There have never been many barriers between herself and Karen. 'Did it just come on all of a sudden, or what?'

'Yeah. He was right beside me. It all happened in minutes . . . He was sick, fell forward, knocked over his coffee. Then nurses came running, tried to resuscitate him, and everyone had to get off the train, then there was an ambulance and we were taken to hospital. They took him to A&E . . . Then I had to talk to the police, and the hospital chaplain – there were so many people. But the doctor said there was nothing anyone could have done.' Karen's voice tails off to a whisper again. 'Apparently he died immediately. Just like that.'

Anna is reeling. She leans against the pillar of the flower stall for support. 'Er – er . . . Let me think . . . Where did you say you were?'

'The Royal Sussex.'

'What, in Kemptown?'

'Yes.'

'Oh, right.'

'The children?'

'They're at Tracy's.'

'Luke's not at school?'

'No, it's half-term in Brighton this week. We took them both there, so we could go on to London.'

'I see. When are you supposed to be picking them up?'

'Oh, um . . . half three.'

That's good – it gives us a bit of time, Anna thinks, her mind whizzing. 'You told them?'

'No.'

'Tracy?'

'No, no, not yet. You were the first person I called.'

'And where's Simon?'

'Um . . .' Karen sounds fazed, as if she doesn't know what Anna means. 'He's here, too. At the hospital. They're moving him to a special room. I'm to go back in a while. I suppose to A&E. Where are you?'

'Clapham Junction. The station. I got a taxi—' Anna thinks about explaining that she has just been sitting next to a woman who witnessed Simon's death, but then decides not to. Now is not the time, and it is not relevant. 'Look . . .' She tries to formulate a plan. 'I'll come back. I've got a meeting, but someone else can go. It's not that important, really. I'll call them. They'll understand, and if they don't, well, sod it. So, I dunno . . . wait there. I'll be—' She checks her watch. It's five to ten. 'I think the trains go at twelve minutes past the hour. As long as they're still running the other way, I can be back in Brighton by eleven, and get a taxi, be with you as soon as I can.'

'Can you really?' Karen's voice cracks again. 'Are you sure you don't mind?'

'Mind?' Anna is incredulous she should even ask. 'Of course I don't mind. Where are you going to wait? Are you going to go home?'

'I don't know.' Karen is obviously in no state to make a

decision. 'Later, yes, but I want to be with Simon now . . .'

'Of course. I'll be on the phone again anyway, in a minute. I just want to make sure I get the next train and ring work, so I'm going to go now. OK? I'll call you again, in a bit.'

'OK,' so quietly. 'Thanks.'

A few seconds later Anna feels a squeeze on her shoulder. It's Lou. 'You all right?'

'Yes, I guess,' though she's far from it.

'Do you want to go for a coffee or something? You're white as a sheet. I think you ought to sit down.'

'No. I have to go. That was my friend, Karen. It was her husband on the train. I've got to get back and see her. But thanks anyway.'

'Are you sure? You really look as though you could do with sitting down. There's a coffee shop right here . . .'

Lou is right: Anna has been gazing at the familiar blue logo whilst on the phone without really seeing it. 'No.' She is definite. 'I need to get the next train, I promised.'

'I understand.'

Anna smiles, weakly, then recalls, 'Oh, gosh, I owe you fifty quid, don't I? Or is it more than that? Did we give him a tip?' She rummages in her purse. 'Damn! I've only got three twenties.'

'Two's plenty. Really. You don't want to leave yourself short or you won't be able to get a cab at the other end.'

'No, no,' insists Anna. 'I'm sure I can change one.'

'Don't be silly! Forty is fine.'

'I hate owing money.'

'All right, then, but tell you what: rather than worrying about that now, here, take this.' Now it's Lou's turn to open her wallet: she takes out a functional-looking white business card headed *Hammersmith & Fulham Education Services*. 'Pop it in the post to me at some point. Or better still, give me a call or text me one day when you're on the train. Well, you know.'

'Yeah, sure,' says Anna.

'I work Mondays to Thursdays. Or give me a ring any time. If you just want to talk.'

Lou's expression is so sympathetic Anna doesn't know what to say. She mutters 'Thanks', but it seems quite inadequate.

'It's nothing.'

'No, well, still, I appreciate it.'

'Really, don't give it any thought. And please, when it's appropriate – if it ever is – tell your friend, I really am very sorry.'

'Um, yes, sure, I will,' says Anna.

11:00

Anna is fingering Lou's card, absently using the edges to clean beneath her nails, when the train halts at a signal just before its final stop. To her left the city sprawls up and over the Downs, row upon row of terraced houses getting smaller into the distance. The sign at the end of the carriage is scrolling in orange dots: *The next station is Brighton.* Although she is nearly there, she feels completely disoriented, emotions all over the place. She has travelled from Brighton to Wivelsfield to Clapham up the motorway and back, and it's only eleven. She feels as if she has left pieces of her mind scattered along the way and is no longer herself as a result.

She attempts to reassemble her thoughts into a more coherent stream, so as to help Karen. But how are they ever going to get through this? There's the issue of Luke and Molly: how does one tell two small children their father has died? It is not just a question of telling them; it is how it will impact on their lives. What will this do to them, losing their father? They are so young; they have so much of their childhood to go. Then there is the rest of Simon's family – his mother is still alive, for instance, and he has a brother too, Alan. Anna has met him many times, and he and Simon are close. He lives nearby and they play football together, down on the lawns on the seafront, with some other local dads.

And there is Karen herself. She and Simon have been together since Karen's first job after college. Simon was living with another woman when they met – what a drama that caused. But that was aeons ago; they've been together for nearly twenty years. And while they have had a few bleak periods – there was the time when Simon lost his job, for example, and when Luke was very ill just after he was born – these ultimately didn't threaten them as a couple. In fact, nothing has ever truly rocked their relationship . . . until today.

Anna shivers. She is aware this is just the beginning, the very beginning; and already she feels so much of Karen's pain that she's not sure where her own feelings end and Karen's start. She is sure it hasn't sunk in fully yet, because she still can't believe what's happened, that Simon is really gone. And although she shed a few tears an hour or so ago, it feels too soon to cry.

Maybe he isn't dead, she allows herself to think, just for a split second. Maybe Karen has gone mad, got it wrong, or someone else has.

Anna shakes her head, suddenly angry. Of course no one's got it wrong. But couldn't someone, somewhere, have done more for him? A fifty-one-year-old man doesn't just keel over: there had to be some signs, surely? Didn't Simon himself know something was up? What about when he was playing football? Didn't he feel a twinge, or anything, then? Why didn't he have a check-up, get himself examined? He was a father, for heaven's sake, with responsibilities. Failing that, the medical profession should have pre-empted it. Why didn't his GP warn him? (Though she can't imagine that Simon would readily go to the doctor; lots of men don't. Anna's own partner, Steve, hasn't been to a doctor in years.) But what about those nurses Karen mentioned, on the train – why couldn't they do anything? Or the bloody paramedics, or the doctors in Brighton's precious cardiac ward? Doubtless it was because they were understaffed and unequipped. It was the government's fault, then, too. Bunch of idiots. Fuck the lot of them.

Then, another thought, less enraging, but more distressing. Anna is sure Karen will blame herself – it would be typical of her to do so. Karen can be a worrier, and always puts other people first. The children, Simon, often Anna too. And of course it's not her fault, but Anna is sure she will think it is, will believe she has failed Simon.

This leads Anna to touch, for the first time, on her own guilt. Perhaps *she* is the one who's failed Simon. Karen not spotting his condition is understandable when she lived with him, and when she looks after so many people. Anna can comprehend how she could easily miss a gradual change in his health. But she, Anna, had the benefit of more objectivity. *She* should have noticed something. Been less wrapped up in her work and the demands of her own relationship. She had seen Simon pretty much every week, hadn't she, for God knows how long? She should have noticed that he was breathless, faint or dizzy, or had indi-gestion more than was normal, or was really pink in the face, or whatever symptoms there are that act as a forewarning to a heart attack, if she had been less self-absorbed.

Oh dear, she thinks, coming back to the present with a jolt. The other passengers have gone ahead of her, and she is alone in her seat. She had better get off the train. The cleaner is making her way down the aisle, using gloved hands to put cups and discarded newspapers into a big clear plastic bag. So Anna pulls on her coat, picks up her handbag from the table and, for the second time that day, makes her way through Brighton station.

*　*　*

Karen is sitting in the cafe opposite the hospital, watching the clock on the wall. Only a few more minutes until Anna arrives. She wants to wait for her, she needs her help, guidance, before going back. Karen has never in her life needed rescuing, not from anything serious; she has always been the one to take care of others. Even when she was a little girl, she was the elder sister or bossy friend taking charge. But today has made up for forty years with one catastrophic event. She seems caught in a nightmare she cannot escape; she wants someone to wake her up, tell her it is all a mistake, it is not happening, she can go home. She feels completely disconnected from the world about her. The room she is sitting in looks unreal, the proportions all wrong for a cafe: it is too big, there is too much space between the tables, the strip fluorescent lights are eerily bright, the counter from which she collected her tea looks oddly one-dimensional, flat. And though she can hear voices – the cafe is sadly empty but still there are people, an elderly couple, for instance, and a woman cooing at her baby nearby – they sound distant, echoing, distorted.

When she was an undergraduate, she dropped acid once, with Anna. She hated the experience; she felt so out of control. This is like that, but worse, because somehow even then, through her fear, she knew she was hallucinating, that it would end; that it was just a trick of the mind. Plus she'd had Anna with her, who was also tripping, but who had done it before and was rather enjoying it. She had helped ground Karen, talk her down.

But here she is alone, and now she has no idea what to do. The person she would normally ask is Simon, so in her head she asks him, yet at the same time a voice in her head – the doctor's from earlier – reminds her: he is dead. The two thoughts can't co-exist: it is all very confusing. She can't believe he has gone. She feels numbness, and suffused through the numbness, stabs of panic, like shards of glass. The panic is horrible, horrible – she feels she can't control it; the numbness is better. It is the panic she wants to go away.

Perhaps she should make a list. She is good at lists.

She's got all those legal papers in her bag; that's good, she can write on the back of one of the sheets of A4. And yes, there's a pen. She remembers putting it in the front pocket earlier; she's been caught without a pen before on the train and it has irritated her. Though to feel mere irritation – she can't imagine that will ever happen again. It was a lifetime ago.

Still, at an utter loss what else to do, she forces herself to draw upon her memories; she can use the experience they had with Simon's father to help. Five years ago he'd died, also unexpectedly. He had an aneurysm and one day it popped. And if she'd told Simon to get himself checked out afterwards, in case it was heriditary, she had told him a dozen times, but did he? Of course not. Among the shards of glass comes a tidal wave of fury. She almost likes it though; it feels sort of normal. She has been cross with Simon before and she recognizes the sensation – this is the same, just more powerful, and she wants to scream. But in a split second it has gone, and she is back to the shards of glass, the numbness and panic.

When Simon's dad died, she and Simon helped Simon's mother to make a list of what to do. Karen puts all her focus into the task, and slowly, automatically, she begins to formulate the words.

1. *Phone Tracy. Collect the children.*

How odd, her writing looks pretty much the same as usual, slanting loops of black ink. She had expected it to look different.

2. *Tell the children.*

She has no idea how she is going to do this, but before she has a chance to feel any pain she adds,

Bring them to the hospital to say goodbye?

Next she puts:

3. *Go home. Phone:*
  - *Simon's Mum*
  - *Alan*
  - *Simon's work*

Oh gosh, Simon's work. She should phone them at once. They will have been expecting him. Lord, and the solicitor. They have missed the appointment. These people can't wait until later, till she is home. They all need to know right now.

She reaches for her phone again. The little stickers glitter and twinkle at her and she has a pang of affection for her daughter, Molly, who insisted on putting them there, so deliberately, in places that presumably mean something to Molly but appear random to anyone else. There is a star covering the circle of the logo, for instance, and tiny flowers round the screen. Karen starts to dial Simon's work. But again she stops. She just can't manage it. She can't find it in herself to explain what has happened. Perhaps she can wait till Anna gets there. Anna can help. She puts the phone down, berating herself for not being able to cope. She always copes with everything.

'Karen, hello.'

She looks up. Thank God, a familiar coat, bag, face: it is her friend.

* * *

Before Anna does anything else, she steps forward and wraps her arms around her friend's shoulders. Karen gets up and hugs Anna too, and they hold each other for a moment like

41

that, in silence. Karen sits down again and Anna takes a seat opposite, but instantly feels too far away, so shifts the chair round and leans forward to take both her friend's hands in hers.

She is struck by how Karen's face has been transformed by the morning's events. Usually her friend looks healthy and vibrant, but the flush in her cheeks has vanished. She looks wan, grey; her long hair, generally shiny as a conker, is soaking wet, drab; and her hazel eyes, which normally sparkle with warmth and feeling, are glazed, unseeing. The joy and energy have been replaced by fear and confusion. And it is not just her face that has changed – it is her whole body. It is as if she has literally been gutted, or had the wind sucked out of her by some giant vacuum cleaner. She is bowed, deflated. She is also shaking badly, her hands especially. Although – bless her – Karen has clearly been trying to write. Anna can see from the piece of paper opposite her.

Anna wishes she could lift her up and take her back to her cosy living room, dry her off then ease her into her most comfortable armchair, wrap her in a blanket and light the fire. She would make her a hot chocolate and give her biscuits, too. Instead they are here – she glances around – in a place that would be bleak at the best of times, let alone on a rainy day in late February. It is utterly charmless; a big room lit by strip lights with ugly, battered metal furnishings, as far from consoling as a cafe can get.

'I'm so sorry,' she says, gently, and gives Karen a small, utterly half-hearted smile. She is sorry; she has probably never been as sorry about anything in her life. She can feel tears pricking, but she must not, *must not* cry.

Karen shakes her head. 'I don't know what happened.'

Anna exhales. 'No.'

'I think I'm in shock.'

'Yes, sweetheart, I think we both are.' She looks down at her friend's hands in hers. We both have the faint beginnings of liver spots, Anna notices. We are getting old.

'Heart attack, they said.'

'Right.'

Karen takes a deep breath. 'I guess we could go now – I was waiting for you.'

'Where is he?'

'This special room; they were sorting it out.'

'Sure,' nods Anna. She wonders if they are going to do a post-mortem. She thinks it will mean waiting longer for a funeral. But it also might provide some answers. She has many questions herself; doubtless Karen has more. Then again, maybe Karen won't want one. It won't bring Simon back.

'But before we go, I wondered; could you make a couple of calls for me?'

'Of course. Who to?'

'It's just I really can't face it.'

Anna smiles sympathetically. 'It's OK – that's fine. Who do you want me to ring?'

'The solicitors, if that's all right. It's just they were expecting us. And Simon's work . . .' She trails off.

Anna takes control. 'No problem. Have you got the numbers?'

'Yes, here. Or it might be easier to ring on my phone, I guess.'

'Sure.' Anna picks up Karen's mobile, with its familiar leather case and peeling stickers, from the table. 'So, let's ring the solicitors first.' In one way she hates to be so down to earth and practical; in another it is a relief to be able to help with something relatively mundane. 'Just tell me, had you exchanged on the house yet?'

Karen shakes her head. 'No . . . We were signing the papers today.'

Phew, thinks Anna. This means there is room for manoeuvre. She switches into let's-do-it mode. 'Right. I'm going to ring the solicitors. Tell them you're putting it on hold.'

'They'll be very cross,' says Karen, suddenly engaging with other people's reality.

'I don't give a bugger about that! And nor should you. Let's not worry about that, shall we?'

'No.'

'So, where's the number?'

'The vendors will be upset too . . .' adds Karen. It's typical of her to be preoccupied with other people.

'Never mind them either.' Anna is brisk. 'They can wait. At this moment we're looking after you.'

Karen nods.

'Number . . .?' she coaxes.

'Here you are.' Karen, whose mind clicks back into gear with Anna to steer her, locates it.

'OK,' says Anna, getting to her feet. 'But I'm going to do this outside, the signal in here is crap. You all right, waiting here for a bit?'

'Mm.'

As Anna pushes open the door of the cafe, the cold air and rain hit her. The signal is actually just as strong inside as it is out here; she has told a white lie. She thought it diplomatic Karen didn't hear her go through the whole explanation of Simon's death — it will only cause unnecessary pain. Given that it is sure to be the first call of many, it seems kind to soften the experience wherever and however she can.

11:35

'So, Miss, you one of them lesbians then?'

'Sorry?' Lou is having a one-to-one session with fourteen-year-old Aaron, and although she comes across a broad spectrum of issues in her line of work – drugs, abandonment, poverty, rape – the question catches her off guard. She counsels pupils who've been excluded from so many schools – 'expelled', her mother still insists on calling it – that there is nowhere else in the state system for them to go. Instead, they continue their education in a special establishment with a much higher staff/pupil ratio, where Lou is a recent fixture. In addition to lessons, the children can opt to have a once-weekly session with her. She sees fifteen pupils in total, and all, without exception, have had it tough.

'You heard me, Miss.' Although Lou likes to be addressed by her first name, Aaron can't shake the habit of 'Miss', which he associates with those in authority – though in his case it hardly denotes respect, more of a challenge. He continues, crossing skinny legs draped in baggy low-slung jeans and leaning back in his chair with practised nonchalance: 'One of them, you know, *lesbians*? You fancy women? You a dyke? Or what?'

Lou's personal life is strictly off bounds to Aaron, something he well knows. He is being deliberately provocative, and she refuses to rise to it. Yet she also knows this is not an area to avoid completely: as an adolescent, Aaron is exploring his own sexuality. She strives to handle their dialogue with care.

He shifts in his chair, eyes her. 'Why won't you tell me, Miss? You ashamed?'

She is not going to be drawn on herself, but his attitude is revealing. She wonders where he has learnt to associate being gay with shame. 'You think it's something to be ashamed of, Aaron?'

He sits back, gratified. 'So you are, then.' Again Lou says nothing. 'Why not tell me, Miss?'

She is firm. 'We're here to talk about you, Aaron, not me.'

'How can you expect me to talk about me when you won't talk about you?'

Reasonable point, thinks Lou, but that is not how it works, and Aaron is using the subject to deflect attention from himself. Were she not his counsellor, she *might* let Aaron know she is gay. But telling him goes against the therapeutic dynamic and may not be useful, especially if he is asking chiefly to satisfy his voyeuristic needs. Nonetheless, it is enlightening that he has latched on to the subject at this particular moment; he had been talking about his drug use – skunk, to be specific – and Lou knows this is an evasion tactic. She smiles inwardly, appreciating. Evasion: they are both at it.

'Kyra thinks you're gay, too,' Aaron adds.

Oh, great, Lou thinks. So they have been discussing me behind my back. That means other students probably have, too. Lou wants to keep her sexuality out of her counselling sessions, not just because confession isn't befitting to her role, but because the kids she deals with can be belligerent; some are extremely intolerant of difference. She has heard it first hand – the mickey-taking of one of the teachers deemed 'posh', the bullying of pupils who work too hard, the cruel laughter at the overweight caretaker. She has no intention of letting her personal life provide similar ammunition. She has only been at the school just over a term, and hasn't told the head or any of the other teachers that she is gay. After all, she thinks indignantly, why should any of them need to know?

She is adamant Aaron must focus on himself. 'We both know we're not here to discuss Kyra, or what Kyra thinks of me,' she says. Then she pauses, and asks, 'I am interested, though. How would it help you to know if I'm gay or not?'

'So you *are* gay then.' Aaron grins with satisfaction. 'That's what I reckon.'

For the moment he seems content to leave it there, and Lou decides not to push him. But intuitively she knows this won't be the last of it. Aaron will provoke her again, she feels sure.

* * *

Having rung the solicitor and Simon's work, Anna wants to make one more call before she returns to Karen. She needs to keep it brief, as she is concerned Karen is sitting alone in the cafe, but she must bring Steve, her partner, up to speed. She has tried him twice already, from the train, but he is not picking up his phone and it is not the kind of thing you leave a message about. This time, however, he answers.

'Hello?' He sounds bleary.

'Ah, at last. I've been trying you for ages. Where were you?'

'Oh, sorry, I was asleep.'

Typical, thinks Anna, glancing at her watch. It is nearly midday. She knows Steve has got no work lined up – he is a painter and decorator and sometimes has periods of inactivity. Nonetheless, it is a Monday and she finds it irritating that he chooses to waste half the day. It would gall her under normal circumstances when she has to be up at six thirty, but the fact that he has slept through such a major crisis means she finds it hard to break the news as tactfully as she could.

'I need you to wake up.'

'Yeah, yeah. OK, I'm awake.'

'Something's happened.'

'Oh, what?'

'It's Simon.'

'Simon as in Karen and Simon?'

'Yes.'

'What's he done?'

'He's not *done* anything.' Anna's annoyance increases. Steve and Simon aren't especially good friends, but how inappropriate that Steve should assume Simon has done something deserving blame. She delivers the information bluntly, with no softening. 'He's dead.'

'You're joking.'

'No, Steve, I'm not.' She pauses to allow him to assimilate. 'He died on the train. Of a heart attack.'

'Oh, Christ.' Steve can obviously tell from her tone that she is serious. 'How?'

'I don't know exactly, I guess he just had a massive coronary. They tried to revive him, apparently, to no avail.'

'Jesus. Poor Karen.'

'I know.'

'Where are you now?'

'I'm with her.'

'You didn't go to work, then?'

Anna sighs, her anger subsiding. Most of her rage is projection at what's happened, anyway, nothing to do with Steve. 'I did, actually. It's a long story. I'll explain it fully later. I just needed you to know, that's all.'

'Yes, well, blimey, sorry, I'm a bit shocked.' Anna can hear the rustle of sheets as he sits up in bed. 'Where are you exactly?'

'In a cafe in Kemptown, opposite the hospital.'

'What are you going to do now?'

'I'm not sure. Spend some time with Karen, I guess. She needs me. She's in a total state, understandably.'

'Of course.'

'They're moving Simon to a viewing room or something, so we're going back inside in a minute.'

'Right. Er . . . what about the kids?'

'They're with the childminder.'

'Do they know?'

'No, not yet. I guess we'll deal with that later.'

'Do you need me to come down?'

Anna pauses to consider. She would like his support, but isn't one hundred per cent confident he'll help the situation. Steve can be a bit blundering when it comes to emotional issues – not always, but sometimes, and she is never sure which way it will go. He doesn't know Karen nearly as well as she does. Plus she imagines Karen would rather not be with a couple at present. 'No, no, it's probably best not.'

'Is there anything I can do?'

Again she reflects. She doesn't find it easy asking for help. 'Not at the moment, that I can think of.'

'You sure?'

He is trying his best, she can tell. She softens further. 'No, don't worry. I'll call you later. Just be there when I get in.' She does not want him out at the pub when she returns: she is sure of that at least. 'Perhaps you can make me dinner?'

'Of course I will.'

At once Anna feels a rush of affection. Steve might not be perfect, but he is still alive; she is thankful. No, more than thankful: she is *lucky*. 'I do love you, honey,' she says.

'Love you too, babe. You know I do.'

This is true. When he is on form, and sober, Steve is one of the most loving men Anna has ever met.

* * *

At eleven fifty-five, when Lou is between clients, her mother rings. Her mother knows she has a few minutes between each session and has a maddening habit of timing it so as to catch her daughter for the full slot. She even rings on the landline so Lou can't vet the call. It might, after all, be one of the other members of staff, who also know she has this time free, so Lou is obligated to answer. Lou really hates this habit of her mother's, as she needs the space to clear her head, and her mother's calls tend to be all-consuming, even three-minute ones. Her mother talks fast, and – it seems to Lou – manages to squeeze more neurosis into one hundred and eighty seconds than any other human being she has ever encountered. Today Lou's head is especially full as she is still trying to process the experience on the seven forty-four. Right now though, there's a fat chance.

'Darling,' says her mum. 'I know it's short notice, but I'm calling to see if you might come up this weekend. Uncle Pat and Auntie Audrey are going to be here and they'd love to see you.'

Oh, no, thinks Lou. She quite likes Aunt Audrey, her mum's sister, but Uncle Pat is nearly as hard work as her mother. Anyway, she has plans.

But her mother hurtles on before she can get a word in. 'Now you know Uncle Pat's not been too good of late—' Lou does know this; how could she not? Her Uncle Pat has suffered from Crohn's disease almost ever since she can remember, and recently his condition has been particularly bad. She also knows her mum will use Uncle Pat's illness to manipulate her daughter into doing what she wants: but her mother is like a steamroller when she gets going; she flattens all in her path.

'Well, he's good again now, having been laid up for several weeks. So you can imagine, Auntie Audrey is desperate to get away. She's been cooped up in that little bungalow for ages' – Lou shudders; what a ghastly thought. She feels for Aunt Audrey – 'and of course I suggested that they come here. So they're coming as soon as they can, as I've a room free this weekend.' Lou's mum lives in the country, in a large house outside Hitchin, which she runs as a bed and breakfast. 'The thing is' – Lou braces herself, though she already knows what the punchline is going to be. Sure enough – 'I can't really manage them both, on my own.' Then she delivers another blow to ensure Lou is well and truly beaten. 'With my hip, it's just too difficult for me to get to the shops, show them round, entertain them all the time.' Rubbish, thinks Lou. When she chooses to let rooms, her hip has never stopped her. Cooking a full English, making beds, putting on a brave face – surely it is harder work with strangers than with Lou's uncle and aunt. Peculiar, that: where money is involved, Lou's mother will be brave as anything. Still, on her mum rolls: 'So I thought you could come up – it's not too far for you, is it darling, if you come after work on Thursday? You can get the train to King's Cross from Hammersmith, then on up here.' If she were not used to this, Lou would not believe it – her mother is actually roping her into three days, not two. What about my sister? she thinks furiously. Can't Georgia help? She knows there is no point in arguing. Lou's younger sister has a husband and children, and her mother never asks her to do even a quarter of what is required of Lou.

'Mum,' she says finally, aware the spiel is drawing to a close now her mother has made her demand, 'it's very short notice and I have made arrangements already, you know.' It is true: she plays tennis first thing every Friday morning, then she helps out at a local hostel for the homeless, and she has been invited to a party on Saturday.

'Really? I'm so sorry. Oh, well, if you're too busy . . .' There is a pause, which Lou's mother fills with silent disappointment.

'Let me have a think. I'll see what I can do.'

More silence. Lou knows her mum is waiting for her to speak again – an ingenious tactic designed to further her own cause.

'I may be able to come for some of it,' she relents, eventually. The guilt, the guilt! She is livid. She knew she would give in; she always does.

'OK, darling, of course the whole weekend would be best, obviously. So let me leave it with you.'

That's big of you, thinks Lou.

Just then, there is a tap on her door. It is her next student.

'Listen, Mum, I have to go.'

'Sure, that's fine. But Lou—?'

'Yeees . . .' Lou tries not to sound impatient.

'Will you let me know tonight? It's just, if you can't come, well, I'll have to cancel them. And I don't think it's fair to do that *too* late in the day.'

FUCK OFF! thinks Lou. But instead she just mutters, 'Sure, of course,' and puts the phone down. She is so angry and feeling so bullied, that she is shaking. With a mother like hers – so controlling, so self-obsessed, so tunnel-visioned – is it any wonder Lou has never been honest with her about her own sexuality?

12:06

The hospital is a maze of corridors and wards, annexes and Portakabins, and neither Karen nor Anna is in the right frame of mind to work out the signs. They head to A&E, but when they arrive and ask at reception, they are told to wait, and eventually a kindly-faced nurse emerges.

'Is one of you Mrs Finnegan?' she asks.

Karen nods.

'Your husband has been put in the viewing room. I'll show you the way if you like.'

'Please,' says Anna.

They follow her clicking heels down several linoleum flights of stairs and along even more corridors. They end up outside some double doors and a sign saying MORTUARY. It all seems terribly brutal.

The nurse buzzes and they are let in.

'It's Mrs Finnegan,' she says to a man in a white coat.

'Mr Finnegan is in the viewing room,' he says. 'But hold on a second.' He goes to a locker, opens it and gets out a large bin bag.

'Which one of you is Mrs Finnegan?' he asks.

'Me,' says Karen.

'These are your husband's personal effects.'

'Oh,' says Karen. 'Thank you.' She glances inside.

'It's mainly his clothes,' says the man. 'And his briefcase.'

'Right.'

'I'll show you where to go if you like,' says the nurse, and leads them to a second door. She opens it and they step inside.

Simon is lying on his back with his arms placed neatly over a white cotton blanket. He has been dressed in a hospital gown, Anna notices. The only light comes from a window, which is partially covered by a Venetian blind, its slats turned at an angle so they can see but it is not too bright.

'Please feel free to be here however long you want, Mrs Finnegan,' the nurse says.

'Really?'

Anna is surprised. She had assumed time would be limited.

'Yes,' assures the nurse. 'I understand your husband's death was very sudden?'

Karen nods again.

'A lot of people find it helpful to stay with a relative's body for a while. There really is no need to rush. We'll leave you with him here a few hours if you like.'

'Thank you,' says Karen.

The nurse turns to Anna. 'Are you a friend?'

'Yes.'

'I wonder if I might have a quick word outside?'

'Of course.'

They step back into the corridor.

'You might like to give Mrs Finnegan some time with her husband alone,' suggests the nurse, her voice low. 'It can help people accept what's happened. It must be a terrible, terrible shock.'

'Yes, sure.' Anna was going to do this anyway. 'Er . . . before you go, can I ask you something?'

'Fire ahead.'

'My friend, Karen, has two small children.'

'Right.' The nurse sighs, empathizing.

'I just wondered, whether, well, what we should do about them? What should we tell them?'

The nurse takes a deep breath. 'In my experience, it's best not to protect them too much. So, once your friend has had some time to take in what's happened, it would be good if you could encourage her to be as honest with them as she can. Within reason, obviously, if they are very small.'

'Do you think we should bring them here to say goodbye?'

'How old are they, exactly?'

Anna considers, then says, 'Three and five.'

The nurse pauses. 'It's a really tough one and not everyone would say so, no. But personally – and we do see a number of deaths in cardiac – I would say yes, if they want to come, bring them. Though later today it's likely that Mr Finnegan's body will have to be moved.'

'To where?'

'As his was a sudden death, there will have to be a post-mortem.'

'When will that be?'

'Depends on the schedule, but as soon as they can fit it in. Then he'll be taken to the funeral parlour.'

'Will it still be possible to see him there?'

'Yes, of course. And don't worry, we can explain all this properly to Mrs Finnegan in due course. The doctor will have told her most of it already, but often people do need to hear it more than just the once.'

'I see. And thanks,' Anna smiles. 'You've been really helpful.'

'It's my job,' says the nurse, and Anna is struck by how mundane her own profession seems in comparison.

*   *   *

While Anna is outside talking to the nurse, Karen walks slowly over to the bed where Simon is lying. The rain is clearing outside and the day brightening, so the light filtering through the blind at the window creates stripes on the blanket, which loop in semicircles over his arms. Over his chest the loops are big and broad, and for a fleeting moment Karen is sure she sees the blanket rising and falling; that he is breathing, ever so gently, just as he does when he is asleep.

'Simon?' she whispers.

But he doesn't reply.

She can't believe he is dead. They've told her he is, but to her he still seems to be here. She looks at his face for clues. There is something different about it, but the details are the same. His eyes are shut, the lashes are dark and familiar against his cheeks, his brows still need a trim, just as they did last night. He is close shaven – it is relatively early in the day, after all, but by nightfall his beard will be coming through again, won't it? His hairline is the same; he is proud of his hair, Simon – it is one of the few things he is vain about. It is thick and dark and lustrous, if streaked with grey. 'Very distinguished,' she heard him mutter into the mirror once, and several times he has swanked to her that he has got more hair than his younger brother Alan, who is receding badly. She had smiled to herself at the time, amused at the way men compete over signs of youth in middle age.

She recognizes without thought or question the substantial barrel shape of Simon's chest, broad beneath the blanket. His arms, too, faintly freckled and veined; the hairs on the back of his hands glint in the sun; his hands are still big and square and so much stronger than hers.

Yet . . .

He is no longer wearing the shirt he ironed that morning while she was feeding the children breakfast, with the cufflinks she gave him two Christmases back. It has been removed, replaced by an eerie ice-blue gown. And his wedding band has been removed too; it is the one thing Simon never took off. Instead there is a dent where it was tight around his finger; he had put on weight in the last few years, Karen knows.

The pain that comes from seeing these changes is overwhelming, frightening. Karen can feel her breath getting short, and a tightness in her throat, as if someone is choking her.

There is a chair by the bed; she sits down, quickly.

That's better.

She pulls the chair up closer, takes Simon's hand. How strange. It feels similar, in many ways, just as his face looks the same. But it's cold. Simon's hands are never cold, even when he's chilly. She, Karen, has bad circulation – she gets chilblains on her toes from time to time – and her hands are quite often cold to the touch. But his never are.

Perhaps they are right, then.

She looks again at his face. It is not that his cheeks are pale: sometimes he's quite grey, anyway; he's not got the healthy colour that she and the children have, never has had. No, it's that he looks flat, diminished, as if a part of him isn't here, has vanished. The life has gone; there is no spirit in him. Bizarrely – or not so bizarrely, perhaps – Karen is reminded of when Charlie, their cat, died. He was very old, and one day he'd crawled under the kitchen table, somewhere he felt safe. When she'd found him later, it was as if his body was there, but somehow he wasn't; he had stopped looking like Charlie – he just looked like any old dead cat, flat, his fur a bit matted, his mouth all rigid and dry. It was as if his spirit, his Charlieness, had disappeared.

And she can see the same with Simon now; part of him has disappeared.

'Simon?' she says again.

Again he doesn't answer.

'Where have you gone?'

Silence.

In a flash she recalls the scene on the train. The small bursting noise as he is sick next to her, the '*boof!*' as his head lands on the table. The realization that something awful is happening when he doesn't respond to her cries, the people rushing, the nurses . . .

Again she feels an awful surge of anxiety.

She looks down at his hand in hers, hoping it will ground her. It is a hand that has held hers countless times, stroked her hair, brought her to orgasm. A hand that has written notes, birthday cards, drawn endless landscape designs. A hand that has signed cheques, held hammers, sawn wood, even – though not as often as she would have liked – hung washing. A hand she grasped tight – so tight – when she was in labour, as if it was all that could keep the pain at bay. And a hand that held one of Molly's while Karen held the other, only yesterday, so together they could swing her along the pavement as they walked up from the beach. 'One, two, three . . . wheeee!' she can hear Simon say. She can still hear Molly's wild whoops of laughter as she flies high in the air and then lands with small feet safely on the paving stones.

He wouldn't leave Molly, would he? She's so little. 'Give me a Daddy cuddle!' is one of her frequent cries. And Luke, too. He might have outgrown Daddy cuddles a bit; both she and Simon have to ask him for hugs now, but nonetheless he is an affectionate boy who loves nothing more than to play rough and tumble with his father.

No, Karen can't believe Simon isn't coming back.

Just then, the door opens with a soft click. There is a few seconds' pause and for those brief moments Karen thinks it is him: that he's heard her; that he has returned. Her heart lifts, soars . . .

But Simon is in the bed at her side.

She turns to check.

It is Anna.

Of course. Karen now realizes the pause was because she is carrying two polystyrene cups; she had to open the door first, then pick them up and carry them through.

'Hi,' she says. 'I brought us another cup of tea.'

*　*　*

Tea, that's what Lou needs with her lunch today. She's been busier than usual this morning, having been on half-term the week before, and normally she'd have had a cup when she got to work, but what with arriving late, this is the first time she's been able to stop. After all that has happened, she needs something warm and comforting; she'll even have sugar in it, a treat she usually reserves for when she is ill.

Lou has a kettle in her therapy room. There is no fridge, so she takes a handful of miniature long-life milk cartons from the school kitchen every morning. As a result her tea has an unpleasant aftertaste, but it is better than traipsing to the other end of the building every time she wants one. Plus she likes to offer the students a cup of tea or coffee when they come to a session; she feels it helps them distinguish her interaction with them from the rest of their activities and makes them feel more adult and responsible.

As she stands waiting for the kettle to boil, she looks around her, contemplating. In the few months that she has been at the school, she has tried to make the space her own, or the students' own, to be precise. Many of her clients find it hard to sit and focus one-to-one, so she has various toys and accessories for them to play with as they talk. Against the wall leans a giant bamboo filled with beans; a rain-stick – one boy seems to find it easier to confide with its gentle patter as a backdrop, and will repeatedly pick it up during their sessions and turn it to and fro. In the corner is a large plastic box of Play-Doh; several of the younger students – they start at eleven – seem better able to relax if they can twist and pull and thump it with their hands as they talk. There are a number of posters on the wall: printouts from the net she thought interesting, abstract patterns she hopes are restful on the eye, a 'twentieth-century wonders of the world' illustration that came with one of the Sunday papers. Last but not least, there is a giant pop-art print she has had framed over the sofa.

I KNOW WHO I AM

it proclaims in black and white.

I wonder if that man who died this morning – what did Anna call him? Simon? – knew who he was, she thinks. Not that it mattered if he did, really, now, but Lou sure as hell believes it matters when you're alive. She sees so much damage wrought by parents who don't know who they are, and whose lack of self-knowledge gets translated into violence or abuse, which is in turn reflected in their kids' dysfunction.

And what about the man's wife, Karen? What would it do to a relatively young woman to lose a partner so suddenly? Will she know who she is, with her husband gone? Lou believes that part of how people define themselves is through their loved ones, and she is profoundly touched by Karen's circumstance, having experienced it at first hand; emotions compounded by having then met Anna in the taxi. A sudden death like that cuts right across the priorities and sensitivities of the living: one minute Karen was drinking coffee and engrossed in conversation with her husband; the next she was witnessing his last moments. Lou cannot shake the image of Simon, his head lolling, mouth gaping. Did he know what was happening, that he was dying? How dreadful to have no warning, no chance to say he loved his wife, no time to say goodbye. And if it is dreadful for him, it is even more so for Karen, left behind with a thousand unanswered questions, a million unspoken words.

The kettle has come to the boil. Absently Lou fishes for a tea bag, puts it in a mug, pours the water. As she does so, she considers: how do these events cast light on the way she herself lives? Does she know who she is? Do others? The poster reminds her of Aaron's jibes earlier. While she's entitled to privacy from the pupils, is she being totally honest with herself as to why she has told no other members of staff? She knows there have been moments when she could easily have said, and chose not to. And although there are many benefits to being a blank page as a counsellor, does she *have* to maintain such anonymity with her peers? She is relatively happy with how she dealt with Aaron, but might he – in some small way – have a point? After all, how can she be asking these young people to explore who they are, if she is practising concealment in some areas of her own life? How can she invite them to open up, when she is still closed – 'in the closet' – to everyone she works with?

Until now it has been easy for her to rationalize discretion. She has simply wanted to protect herself from discrimination or rejection. But then again, isn't she, more than the other members of staff, supposed to be in touch with her identity, her feelings? And most of them seem to talk about their partners freely; inevitably their relationships come up, even if just in passing.

Perhaps she should at least let the head know; certainly she will bring up Aaron's jibes with her counselling supervisor.

As for the rest of the staff, it is a tough one. The subject feels so intimate, so complex, like a giant knot of barbed wire, impossible to unravel without causing pain.

No wonder she needs sugar in her tea.

15:10

Anna is driving to the hospital in Karen's car. She was worried that her friend was too shaky to get behind the wheel, and although Anna is wobbly too, she is less so. Collecting the children in her own vehicle would have meant moving their car seats from Karen's battered Citroën, so this seemed the best option. Working it out took a while as neither of them is in a fit state for logistics, but at least it has allowed Anna to give Karen some more time alone with Simon, without making a big deal of it.

She parks in the hospital car park and heads inside to find her friend. Under normal circumstances Anna has a good sense of direction, and she knows Karen is depending on her, so she allows instinct to take over, and manages to locate the viewing room again despite her frame of mind.

The room is hot and stuffy, and Karen is still sitting exactly where she was when Anna left. Her polystyrene cup of tea is half drunk on the wheeled table by the bed; in her right palm she holds Simon's hand.

'Hello, sweetheart,' says Anna.

'Oh, hello.'

'Do you think we'd better go?'

'Go?' Karen turns to Anna, mystified. If anything she looks even more shell-shocked than she did earlier. Her eyes are bloodshot, though Anna is not sure she's actually been crying – she seems too overwhelmed for tears.

'To collect the children,' Anna reminds her. 'It's nearly half past three.'

'Oh . . . yes . . . of course . . .'

'So are you ready?' Anna hates this. It seems so cruel to make her leave.

'I don't know . . .' There is a long pause; Anna just waits. 'I don't know whether I can come. I don't think he'll be OK without me.'

Anna feels Karen's heart breaking; her own is in smithereens too. 'Oh, my love.'

'He doesn't like sleeping alone.'

'No, I know.' Karen has told Anna this before. Anna has always found it surprising; it is so at odds with such a big bear of a man.

'I can collect the children if you want,' she offers. 'If you need some more time.' Though how long Karen will need and how Anna is going to entertain Luke and Molly in the interim is worrying.

The suggestion jolts Karen. 'Oh, no. I can't ask you to do that. No, no, I must come. You're right. The children need me.' Slowly, still clutching Simon's hand, she stands up.

'He'll still be here if you want to come back later,' suggests Anna.

'Will he?'

'For a while . . . yes . . .' As she says it, Anna remembers the nurse said there will have to be a post-mortem before

Simon is moved to an undertaker's; she can sense Karen making the same connection.

Karen sighs, deeply. 'I guess I can see him again at the funeral place.' Reluctantly, she lets go of Simon's hand and picks up her bag. 'OK.' She half smiles, though Anna can see tears welling. 'Let's go.'

Anna takes the black bin bag – Simon's briefcase makes it heavy. They leave the room and the hospital and locate the car. Anna puts the bin bag in the boot and they get in, clicking seat belts.

'It's weird seeing you drive this,' Karen comments, as Anna turns the key in the ignition.

'It's weird driving it. It's so much bigger than mine.'

'It's filthy,' observes Karen. 'Sorry.'

And Anna's heart twists: through all this trauma, she is still thinking of others – still behaving like Karen. Which makes it worse, somehow.

They drive in silence the rest of the way.

Tracy lives in Portslade, three miles or so west of the hospital. It is a straight road along the seafront, a drive that Anna normally enjoys. Even on a grey February day like today, it encapsulates what she loves about living on the south coast: the architectural variety as modern buildings jostle alongside old; the holiday spirit, even in winter; the chance to feel close to the elements. The rain has passed, but clouds still hang heavy over the Palace Pier, making its gaudy fairground attractions and flashing lights seem all the more defiant. There is a wind up too; the sea is rough, white horses run right to the horizon, a reminder of the power of nature. Then it is along past a battered row of Regency hotels, with their empty hanging baskets and peeling balustrades, and the clumsy 1970s concrete of the Brighton Centre, host to party conferences and countless comedy shows and rock concerts. Next are the ruins of the West Pier, its black, skeletal columns threaded by a lattice of ties and girders; gulls plummeting and soaring in the gusts over-head. Then it's the ancient bandstand with its pretty filigree at last renovated by the council, and finally they're in Hove, with its grandiose buttermilk parades of houses and pastel-coloured beach huts.

Finally they pull up outside Tracy's house. A tired-looking 1930s mock Tudor fronted by leylandii, it is not beautiful or especially elegant, but with generously sized rooms and a long stretch of lawn at the back, it is practical for a woman with older children of her own and a cluster of toddlers in her care.

Anna stops the engine and turns to face Karen before they get out. Karen's face is ashen; she is gripping tightly onto the straps of her Liberty shopper, knuckles white with the effort. Anna reaches over and gives one of her hands a squeeze.

'Courage,' she says.

Anna has already called and told Tracy, wanting to save Karen the upset of having to do so when they arrive. But obviously Tracy will not have broken the news to Molly and Luke. She has been looking after both children a couple of days a week since they were only a year or so old (although she looks after Luke only occasionally now he is full time at school). Still, brilliant carer though she is, no childminder can be expected to do that. Besides, Karen has wanted to prolong the children's happiness for a few hours more.

The result is that two innocent faces peer excitedly through the window at them as they walk up the garden path. 'Mummy!' Molly and Luke cry, then scoot down from the back of the sofa on which they are perched and round to the front door.

Before Karen has a chance to rat-a-tat-tat, the chrome letterbox pops open and a familiar set of eyes can be seen.

'That you, Molly?' says Anna, leaning down and looking through.

'It's Godmother Anna!' squeals Molly.

There is a scuffle, and another pair of eyes takes the place of the first. 'What are you doing here?' asks Luke.

'Out of the way, children,' says a voice; it is Tracy. There is the sound of a chain being unhooked and the door opens.

'Hello, poppets,' Karen crouches down at once and takes both children in her arms. She hugs them close to her, squeezing them tight tight tighter, as if her life depends on it.

Anna watches from the porch. It's unbearable.

'Ow!' says Luke, after a few seconds. He pulls away and Molly follows suit.

'Look what we've done, Mummy!' she orders, yanking the bottom of Karen's blouse and dragging her down the hall.

Anna follows the three of them into the kitchen, Tracy close behind. On the table is a tray of gingerbread men, some rather badly burnt.

'Wow!' says Karen.

'Do you want one?' asks Molly, picking one out.

'Um, can I have it in a minute?'

'Aw.'

'It's just I'm not that hungry right now, I'd like to have it when we get home, with a nice cup of tea. Is that OK?'

Molly nods.

'Can I have one?' asks Anna.

'Can she?' Molly checks with Tracy.

Tracy's appearance is a little like her home. She was clearly never a beauty; now, approaching fifty, she is generously proportioned and her clothing is more practical than modish. Yet her unprepossessing style is reassuring in crisis: she is what Anna thinks of as a salt-of-the-earth type and her whole demeanour exudes capability and generosity of spirit. 'Of course!' she smiles.

'Thank you.' Anna takes one of the less burnt ones. Like Karen, she wants to protract this moment for Molly and Luke: these few last minutes while they believe their father is alive. 'Mm.' She takes a generous bite. 'Aren't you both clever? Did you make these on your own?'

'Tracy helped us,' admits Luke.

'And Austin,' says Molly. Austin is a little boy whom Tracy also looks after.

'Well, they are very delicious. Yum!'

'Right then, children, have you got your bags?' Karen urges. Both obediently run back into the living room to pick them up. 'I think we'd better go home.'

* * *

Karen turns the key in the front door and steps into the hall, the children and Anna following. Everywhere, everywhere, there is the presence of Simon. Simon's anorak slung over the banister from when they went out the weekend just gone, Simon's football boots, covered in mud and left at the bottom of the stairs, from his game yesterday. The photos of Simon with his father in a frame on the hall table, a handful of Simon's CDs scattered beside it. She's even trodden on Simon's post on the doormat.

Another wave of panic; but somehow she draws upon a reserve of strength she never knew she had, and forces it back. She goes into the kitchen to put on the kettle. She doesn't know how she is going to tell Molly and Luke, but she knows she has to. And as she puts down her bag on the work surface by the sink, there is a little mew and there's Toby, coming out from a space he has squeezed into behind the vegetable rack, and he gives her an idea.

'Hello, Toby,' she says, picking up the kitten. He is a tabby, only ten weeks old, and one of Luke's Christmas presents. The offspring of one of their neighbours' cats, Luke was allowed him on the condition he waited until the middle of January; quite a challenge for a small boy.

'Give him to me!' says Luke immediately.

'Aren't I allowed to say hello too?' says Karen. She tickles Toby behind his ears. The fur there is exceptionally soft, warm and fluffy and after the horrors of the day she finds it briefly, oh-so-fleetingly, comforting.

'OK.' Luke is gruff.

'Now, children,' continues Karen, whilst Anna busies herself making them both yet more tea. 'Do either of you want a drink?'

'Yes,' says Molly.

Luke shakes his head.

Karen hands over Toby to Luke, and fetches Molly some juice in her plastic cup with a spout.

Molly tips it up and starts sucking immediately.

'OK,' she says, assertively. 'I want you both – you can bring Toby if you want, Luke, that's fine – to come with me into the living room, so I can tell you something.'

'Do you want me?' asks Anna. 'I'll wait here if it's easier.'

'No, it's all right,' says Karen.

So, bearing the tea, Anna follows. She opts for an armchair in the bay window; it is a big room, and Karen senses she does not want to be too intrusive.

Karen takes a seat on the settee and leans forward. 'Come here,' she says, and pulls both children, plus the kitten, towards her. 'Now, listen to me. What I am going to tell you is very, very sad. And it will be a big shock to you both. But I want you to know that whatever you are feeling, both your Mummy and your Daddy love you very, very much.' She can hardly bear to watch the children's expressions. Luke is scowling, mystified; Molly is sucking on her juice, instinctively seeking solace.

'What's happened, Mummy?' asks Luke.

'Well.' She takes a deep, deep breath. 'You remember our old cat, Charlie?' She gives Toby, who is in Luke's arms, another little stroke, hoping to glean strength from him. He lifts his chin to encourage her to tickle beneath it, blissfully oblivious to anything other than pleasure.

Both children nod, very seriously.

'And you remember when Charlie died, and I told you he'd gone to be with other cats, up in the sky?'

'So that he could fight whenever he wanted to,' remembers

Luke. Although Charlie had been neutered, he was very territorial; he was always having scraps with the neighbours' animals – including the cat that gave birth to Toby. He even liked to provoke the poodle next door from time to time.

'That's right,' continues Karen. 'And I also told you that Charlie wouldn't ever be coming back, but that he is very happy, fighting all the other cats, up in the sky.'

'Yes,' says Luke.

Molly is saying nothing.

Although both children are standing right by her, Karen reaches over and scoops up her daughter onto her knee. She pulls Luke, and Toby, even closer, and drops her voice even lower. 'Well, today your Daddy's heart suddenly stopped working, just like Charlie's did. Charlie was old, though, and your Daddy wasn't, so it's a big shock. But it means your Daddy's gone too, just like Charlie.'

'What, to play with Charlie?' asks Luke.

'Yes,' says Karen, at once liking his thinking. 'To help Charlie win as many fights as he can.'

'Oh.' Luke is puzzled.

'But Daddy is not just going to play with Charlie. Daddy is going to do all those things that Daddy loves.'

'Is Daddy up in the sky?' asks Luke.

'Yes,' says Karen. She really cannot think of a better explanation. The accuracy is hardly important. The main thing is the emotional truth, surely, and delivering the news as kindly and clearly as she can. 'Do you understand, honey?' she asks Molly.

Molly is busy sucking sucking sucking on her juice, even though Karen can hear all that's left in the container is air.

Karen looks into her face. Eyebrows furrowed, bottom lip protruding; she knows her daughter has understood something of it. 'Anyway, where Daddy has gone, he can do all the things he likes doing, ALL the time. He'll be able to play football . . . there are lots of people there who love playing football. He'll be able to drink beer . . . I'm sure he can find plenty of men who like to have a nice cold beer up there. He'll be able to chat with friends; have a snooze in the afternoon – every afternoon if he wants to; and listen to his music, *really* loud! And you know what's really nice? He won't have to go to work, in London, ever. He'll be able to do his designs, just the ones he likes, whenever he wants. He'll have a lovely time!' As she says all this, Karen feels disconnected from her words; her speaking voice is far more jovial and upbeat than she is inside.

'But doesn't Daddy like being with us, Mummy?' asks Luke.

Karen has not seen this one coming. 'Of *course* he does, sweetheart.'

'But I thought you said Daddy could do all the things he likes doing?'

'Well—' Karen searches for an answer. He is right, of course. 'It's just that up there, there are people who need Daddy's advice and help. You know how good Daddy is at that. And right now they need it more than we do, so he's gone to help them work some stuff out.'

Luke frowns. 'So when he's helped them, will he be coming back?'

Oh, Lord, she is making a right mess of this. 'No, my love, he won't.'

Luke begins to cry.

'My baby boy.' She hugs him tight and rests her cheek on his brown mop of hair. 'I'm so sorry.' His tears release her; she begins to weep too. 'It's very sad, and it's not very fair. Daddy didn't really *want* to go, but he had to. You know how sometimes you have to do things you don't want to, but you have to? Like brushing your teeth and eating your vegetables?'

Luke nods through his tears.

'Well, dying is a bit like that, in some ways. You don't want it to happen, it just does.'

'Oh.'

Now Molly is crying too. Karen is aware that Anna is sitting on the chair on the other side of the room, witnessing it from feet away.

'Hey, Anna,' she says, 'come and give us a hug.'

And Anna, clearly grateful to be of use, comes and puts her arms round the three of them, and then all four cry, giant gulping wails, together.

*   *   *

Lou's sessions finish at half past three, and then she has a staff meeting, so it's gone four by the time she leaves. It's a few minutes' walk to the Tube, and as she makes her way there, she spies Aaron and Kyra sitting on a wall outside the newsagent. It is impossible to avoid them; they will see if she turns back to take another route. So she carries on walking. As she approaches she can see they are smoking; her immediate fear is that it is weed, as Aaron smokes far too much of it, so she is actually relieved to see the brown filter ends of cigarettes. They are not supposed to smoke tobacco either, being underage, but Lou considers it the lesser of two evils. She is just wondering whether she should involve herself in a situation she can't be sure won't escalate, when they see her coming and rapidly stub the cigarettes out on the wall beside them, leaving black charcoal smears on the red brick. Given that they are out of school and she doesn't like to come across as too authoritarian, it's best to ignore it, she decides.

'Hello, Miss,' says Aaron, squinting as she approaches.

'Hello, Aaron. Hello, Kyra. How are you both doing?'

'I'm all right, Miss,' says Aaron. 'How are you?'

'Tired, actually,' says Lou as she draws up alongside. It is true: the shock of that morning has been compounded by the demands of her job and having to perform as a counsellor so immediately after the incident. Now the adrenaline rush has passed, what she really wants to do is sleep.

'Up all night, then, Miss?' asks Aaron.

Lou frowns. She can see where this is headed.

'No,' she says categorically. 'Yesterday was Sunday.'

'Doesn't stop some people,' says Aaron.

'Were you with a woman?' asks Kyra. Her tone is a blend of disgust and curiosity.

Lou could just walk on at this point, but intuitively feels they will read that as avoidance and it will provoke them further. She looks them, first one and then the other, in the eyes. Aaron's are deep brown, challenging. Kyra's are pale blue, narrowed aggressively. Aaron is scuffing the ground with his trainer; Kyra is twiddling her long hair; both displacing surplus energy.

'I watched *Coronation Street*,' Lou states. 'Then a costume drama on ITV. Then I went to bed.'

'There's a gay man in *Coronation Street*,' says Kyra.

Jesus, these two are quick.

'Indeed there is,' Lou nods. She notes to herself that this seems worth exploring in their individual counselling sessions; both seem preoccupied with homosexuality.

Kyra continues, 'Are you gay, Miss?'

It is at moments like these that Lou wishes she had chosen a less gruelling arena to work as a counsellor; one where it would be unlikely she would come across clients outside their sessions. Compared to where Lou last worked, counselling in a school makes the boundaries more blurred.

'Aaron says you are.' Today of all days, Lou hasn't the energy. There's no let-up, however: 'Apparently you good as said so.'

'Guys, guys. If you want to discuss this further, I would appreciate it if we could do it at the appropriate time.'

'What's wrong with now?'

Lou takes a deep breath. This is getting close to bullying. 'I think you know, Kyra. Whilst I respect your interest in my personal life, you know the rules: if I want to keep something private, then that's up to me. If there's anything else you wish to discuss then please bring it to our session – this is a public place. Let's chat when you see me tomorrow, OK?'

'But how come you asks us to share stuff with you, and then you won't share this with us?'

'Because our roles are different.'

'Sounds like bullshit, Miss,' challenges Aaron.

She can't help but admire his savvy. Lou talks a lot to the students about being straight and honest in their sessions, and she appreciates his perspective. 'I am sorry you feel that way,' she concedes, 'but you need to respect my feelings too, and right now I am exhausted, so I'm going home.' She walks away.

'But we still think you're a lesbian, Miss,' Kyra calls after her.

19:57

Anna steps through her front door that evening and there is no post on the doormat, no waft of stale air, no silence. Steve has scooped up her letters and put them on the hall table, the house is warm but not stuffy, there is the smell of cooking and the sound of the radio filters towards her.

'Hello,' calls a voice from the back of the house. 'You must be bushed.'

Anna feels a whoosh of gratitude – what a contrast to Karen's homecoming. She goes into the kitchen and Steve is standing at the cooker, wearing her apron. Whilst it is not actually frilly – that is hardly Anna's style – it is pastel green and gingham, so clearly a woman's garment, and there is something endearing about seeing it on such a macho male. Perversely, it makes him appear more handsome. And Steve, without doubt, is handsome. Tall, broad-shouldered, with dishevelled straw-coloured hair, he is the kind of man that women turn and stare at in the street – and some men, too, come to that, given that this is Brighton. Anna is fully aware much of Steve's success as a painter and decorator stems from the fact he is eye candy – she fell for it herself, after all, when she moved to the house and needed work doing. She has noticed his looks don't seem to threaten straight men either – probably because he is also good at the male bonding thing; he loves pubs and outdoor sports and cars.

'I'm making spag Bol,' he says, putting down a wooden spoon.

Anna's heart lifts further. She had feared his reaction to the day's events would be to knock back several drinks before she got home; it wouldn't be the first time he had reacted to other people's emotional dramas that way. But she can tell that he is sober. Really, truly, she could not have coped with him being anything other than supportive today, and she is grateful.

'Ooh, yum.' She can smell tomato, minced beef, onion, mushroom and garlic. It is *just* what she feels like eating: homely, comforting, full of carbs, and one of Steve's best dishes. He is an accomplished cook; Steve is good at most things that involve using his hands. ('So he must be good in bed, then,' Karen had joked when he and Anna met.)

'Come here.' He turns down the radio and opens his arms. Anna steps into the space and leans against his chest, inhaling his scent, feeling the heat of his body, his strength, his solidity. There is nothing she needs more than this, and she breathes out, long and hard, trying to exorcise some of what she has been through.

'Must have been quite a day.' He kisses the top of her head. 'So, what can I get you?'

Anna would dearly love a large glass of red wine at this moment, but she says, 'A cup of tea,' though she's had plenty already.

'You sure?'

She nods. 'If I start drinking I won't stop.' This isn't true and she knows it, but if she has one he will too, and she can limit herself to just one or two drinks far more easily than he can.

'OK. One tea coming up. Now, you sit down, here.'

Relieved, Anna takes a seat at the kitchen table, and without her having to ask, Steve massages her shoulders. Instinctively he knows where she is holding tension and gently eases away the strain. She rotates her head, relaxing. 'That's nice.' He finds a knot of muscle in the nape of her neck, intensifies the pressure with his thumbs. 'Mm, just there . . . Thank you . . .'

She leans back and kisses the nearest bit of him: her lips brush the front of his shirt and she can feel the muscles of his chest through the cotton. She is almost getting turned on, but not quite: she is still too raw from all that has happened.

'So, tell me,' he says.

She sighs, again. 'God, it's absolutely awful.' And, as if the movement of his hands is channelling it from her, out it pours, in one long rush: the train, the taxi, Karen's call, the hospital, Simon's body, the children.

When she has finished, Steve asks, 'Was there anyone with Karen when you left?'

'Yes, Simon's mum came over pretty much at once, and his brother, Alan, was coming straight from work. He left early so he'll be there by now. Do you remember him?'

Steve nods. 'Sure – nice guy. Oh, well, that's something, I guess.'

'They were going to have to choose some clothes for Simon to be laid to rest in, the three of them. That'll be fun.' Anna winces. 'Still, at least Phyllis is going to stay over, by the sound of it.'

'Good idea. I don't think Karen should be on her own tonight.' He stops massaging, and returns to the stove to the stir the Bolognese. It's on a low heat; Anna can hear it softly bubbling. Then he comes to the table, and with a scrape of wood on ceramic, pulls back a chair and sits down. It is his turn to exhale. 'Poor bloody Karen.' He rubs his eyes, runs his hands through his hair. 'Jesus. I guess there's no way she can afford the new house now.'

Anna nods: he's voicing something she and Karen haven't broached yet – money.

Steve continues, 'Did Simon have any life assurance?'

'I expect he did. He was kind of good like that, Simon.'

'Not like me, you mean,' Steve laughs, but there is a touch of bitterness in his voice. He feels his lack of wealth keenly.

'No, not like you,' Anna agrees, but her tone is forgiving, affectionate. At this juncture she is so glad to have Steve there by her side, pulsing with life and energy, that she has no urge to jibe whatsoever.

Awareness of Steve's physicality thrusts her back to the hospital with a jerk. The sight of Simon is one she will never forget. She's not seen a dead body before and she doesn't know what she expected, but it wasn't that. In life, Simon was bigger even than Steve – a real tank of a man – yet that afternoon he seemed so much smaller, so grey, so still.

She leans in, closer to Steve, and takes his palm in hers. She is struck by the contrast again; here she is holding her partner's hand, just as Karen held Simon's earlier. And here is Steve's hand, filled with warm blood and pumping veins

and firm bones and working tendons, with its chipped finger-
nails and hardened skin from years of manual labour. She
grips it, she grips tight. For that brief moment it feels as if
it is all that is keeping her from being swept away.

*   *   *

'Again, Mummy, again!'

Karen closes the picture book and puts it down. 'Twice
is enough, Molly.'

'And Mummy is pretty tired today,' says Simon's mum,
Phyllis.

This is an understatement, Karen is near catatonic with
exhaustion, but sleep will not cure it.

Alan has come and gone, taking Simon's clothes for the
undertaker with him. She could hardly see straight to choose
something for her husband to wear, but she did her best,
and with Phyllis and Alan to help, they've selected a dark
grey work suit, clean white shirt and Simon's favourite silk
tie.

Now she and Phyllis are putting Molly and Luke to bed.
Together they've managed to feed them – fish fingers and
baked beans were simplest – and bath them, get them into
their pyjamas and upstairs, without too much protest, to
their room. Karen is thankful for her mother-in-law's assis-
tance and presence; left alone, she fears she might just have
sat in the living room clutching the children, the three of
them weeping all night. But for the last hour or so the adults
have distracted Molly and Luke with normality. Nonetheless,
Karen is aware that Phyllis is in severe shock too. To lose a

child is awful under any circumstance; to lose one so late in one's own life, and so unexpectedly, is a blow from which she may never recover.

Luke interrupts her thoughts. 'Where's Blue Crocodile?' Blue Crocodile is his favourite toy, worn, gaping in places and with stuffing coming out at the seams. Incongruously for a crocodile, he is very furry, though the fur is matted now from years of attention. Luke has been less interested in him of late, but he still asks for him when he's in need of comfort.

'He's here,' says Karen, locating the toy at the foot of the bed. Luke grabs and squeezes him tight. 'Shall I tuck you in?'

Luke shakes his head, obstinate. 'I want Daddy to tuck me in when he gets home.'

Phyllis and Karen glance at each other. Has he not understood? Karen thought he had. But maybe it's too much for him, beyond his comprehension. And under usual circumstances, of course, this would be exactly what would happen: when Simon got home from work he would bound up the stairs, two at a time, just in time to say goodnight.

'No, my little one, do you remember, I told you? Daddy's not coming back tonight, I'm afraid.'

'Oh. Is he coming tomorrow?'

'No, I'm so sorry.' Karen doesn't want him to start crying again – it'll set her off too. She changes tack. For the moment all she can offer is herself, so she says, 'But I tell you what, why don't I just sit with you here, till you go to sleep? We can turn the light out, but I'll just be here, on the chair, until you both drift off.'

'Yes,' Luke agrees.

'I'll go downstairs, I think,' says Phyllis, getting to her feet. 'I'll be with you in a bit.'

'There's no hurry.' Phyllis turns off the switch. 'Shall I leave the door open a little?'

'Wider,' says Molly. They both like to see there is nothing to be frightened of.

Karen can hear Phyllis softly padding down the carpeted stairs. She reaches over to stroke Molly's golden curls away from her face and then adjusts herself in the wooden chair. It's not very comfortable, but she's not bothered. What she needs now is to be with her children as they fall asleep. Then, as they slumber, she finds she can't tear herself away. She sits for hours in the semi-darkness, just to hear them breathing, still alive.

*   *   *

It is nearly midnight. The lights are off, the curtains drawn, the alarm set. Anna lies snug under the duvet, conscious of Steve's body wrapped in a large curl around hers. She usually loves this; it gives her a feeling of freedom, facing out, combined with the security of being held. Steve drifts off at once, but tonight her mind is still churning.

For the first time she has the space to think of her own relationship with Simon, how much she will miss him. After all these years, she has grown to love him, platonically, but deeply. He has been a root in Anna's life, someone she can rely upon. He's shored up Karen; Karen's shored up Anna. There is more, too; she will miss his humour, his kindness, his intelligence, his generosity. Even when she was at their house and she and Karen were chatting, just the two of them, over coffee in the kitchen, there was something about knowing he was there in the background, watching telly, playing with the children, doing DIY; just being. Even if he was out at work, Anna was conscious of his presence. He gave every moment she shared with her friend something indefinable, something extra. Not just security, but a sense of reality, groundedness, sheer *humanity*. She respected Simon; he had principles, morals. He was a landscape architect, often dealt with councils, or worked on large housing projects. There were people he refused to do business with if he felt their politics or aesthetics were at odds with his own. Simon was a moral measure by which she judged her own life, in many ways.

It all means that the prospect of living without him is scarier, less certain. Anna feels like a tent without enough guy ropes, caught in a wind, vulnerable, flailing, as if she will blow away easily. And though she is aware it is only a touch of what Karen must be feeling, it is horrible nonetheless.

Why Simon? she wonders, tucking herself more closely into the hollow of Steve's C-shape for solace. Why Karen? Why now? She knows it's supposed to be part of a bigger picture; all things happen for a reason, blah blah blah . . . but she just doesn't get it. Karen and Simon are such good people, so kind and loving. They haven't hurt anyone she knows of, they don't deserve such punishment, it is so unfair.

Then she hears her mother's voice, from decades back, when she herself was small, explaining: 'But, dear, the *world* is unfair.' Then the phrase was used to justify other children having more than Anna did: guests having bigger helpings of pudding, friends with nicer toys, classmates getting more pocket money. A simple philosophy, for sure, but the only one that seems to make any sense of everything that has happened.

* * *

In her house a few streets away, Karen is alone, lying on her back, eyes wide open, looking at the ceiling through the darkness. In twenty years she and Simon have spent very few nights away from each other; she still cannot remotely grasp how her life has changed from the way it was twenty-four hours ago. The king-sized bed is a yawning gulf of Simon's absence. Normally, she sleeps easily, deeply. Out in seconds, awake a neat eight hours later. She doesn't get up to go to the loo, or anything. Only if one of the children cries does she stir, and even then Simon normally surfaces sooner, so he often deals with the problem. But tonight he's not there and Karen can't sleep, and she knows she won't. She can't cry, she can't move. All she can do is be. And wait for morning.

She is still lying there when, two hours later, there is a pit-pat of small feet across the landing, the sound of the door handle turning, and the room is flooded by a stripe of light in the centre of which stands a familiar silhouette.

Luke. He is trailing Blue Crocodile.

'Can't sleep, poppet?'

'No.'

'Me neither. Would you like to come in for a cuddle?'

Luke nods, and she holds up the sheet in a giant triangle to make room.

He curls up next to her, and she strokes the back of his neck gently, where downy hair meets pyjama collar. Within minutes his breathing steadies and he sleeps.

She lies there a few moments, then remembers: Molly. If Molly were to wake and discover she's without Luke, she might well get frightened.

As quietly as she can, so as not to disturb Luke, Karen lifts the sheet on her side of the bed, and tiptoes across the landing. Molly is slumbering soundly in her cot, a tangle of sheet, blanket and cotton nightdress rucked around her knees.

Karen leans over the cot, gently unravels the tangle and lifts Molly clear.

Molly makes a small snuffling noise as Karen carries her through. She lowers Molly onto the bed, and edges herself in carefully from the foot, between the two children, pulling the covers over them all.

Suddenly, 'Where's Daddy?' Molly asks.

'Daddy isn't here, love,' says Karen.

But Molly is barely awake; she snuffles again and swiftly resumes her slumber.

Then, oh-so-quietly, Karen says, 'Daddy's gone.'

It is more a reminder to herself than anything.

* * *

Less than two miles away in her attic studio, Lou is asleep on her futon. She is dreaming; a dream so vivid it seems real. She has to catch a train. She is in a dreadful hurry –

it is about to leave – but there are crowds and crowds of people getting in her way. Some are facing her, blocking her path, leering, propelling her in the wrong direction, away from the train. Others have their backs turned, and are lugging big suitcases or pushing pushchairs and wheeling bicycles. They are moving too slowly, oblivious to Lou's needs. She has got to be somewhere important, it is really urgent, and she is not going to make it. Although she doesn't know where she has got to be or why, she knows it is a matter of life or death.

She wakes with a jerk, pouring sweat, gasping for breath.

She is disoriented, panicked, but then sees the familiar panes of her little window outlined through the blind, and is thankful.

She is here, at home. She is not at the station, after all.

Then memories of her day flood back and as she lies there, tears start to fall silently, in sympathy with a woman she doesn't know and one she met only briefly, until there is a patch next to her cheek on the pillow, cold and damp and salty.

Tuesday

05:34

It is still dark outside, but Karen can hear the faint rumble of trains in the distance, signalling it is early morning. The warmth of Molly and Luke has offered some comfort throughout the night, but nothing can ease the tumult in her mind. She has been over and over events, thoughts tumbling like clothes in a frenetic washing machine.

Simon's 'I've got a touch of indigestion,' as they walked swiftly down the hill through the rain to the station.

Her 'Let's get a coffee, then,' as she checked her watch, 'we've got time.'

'A coffee?'

'A nice milky latte might help settle it,' she had argued, but it was because she fancied a drink herself. Then, as they arrived in the concourse, her dictate: 'I'll go and get them, you get my ticket.'

She had left him to queue, while she went to the coffee stand. What if she had not done that? What if she had waited with him? Would he have told her that he was not just uncomfortable, but in more serious pain? Then they might have sat down on the circle of benches outside WHSmith, waited a few minutes, maybe even decided to catch the next train. And if they'd been at the station – so much nearer the hospital – when he'd had the heart attack, the outcome could have been very different . . .

Instead she had said, 'You probably need to eat,' when he'd joined her just as the barista was sprinkling her cappuccino with chocolate.

'Not sure I fancy anything,' he had replied, eyeing the crumbling pastries behind the glass counter. She had been surprised; Simon rarely turned down food. So why had she not pressed him then, asked if he was feeling OK?

But instead she had persisted, 'I'm having a croissant,' so he had gone along with her.

What if that one coffee was the cause? It boosts your heart rate, Karen knows. She can picture the boiling water seeping through deep, dark granules of pure espresso into the cardboard container. How sinister, with hindsight. And she was the one who had hankered after caffeine, not him. She knew that without her, his daily ritual was to pick up a paper and avoid the faff of waiting in line. He'd simply buy a cup of tea from the girl with the trolley on board as she passed. So if it was the coffee, then it was her fault, for sure . . .

And what about when Simon collapsed? The crucial seconds before help arrived, when she could have, *should* have tried to revive him. Why didn't she? It wasn't like her at all. OK, she didn't know how to give the kiss of life properly, but she had an idea. Yet she had not even attempted it . . .

Then there was their last conversation, on the train. It had been banal beyond belief; all about her. She had been moaning about her job, complaining that her supervisor had moved her desk without asking her, so she no longer had a seat by the window. She only worked part time at the local council; she didn't really like it, and had begun to look for something else, scouring the *Argus*. What did the position of her desk matter? But she had been banging on sourly, as if it was important . . .

She never said goodbye; she even hadn't told him she loved him for ages – she can't remember the last time she'd said it. In every likelihood it was 'lots of love Karen', scrawled on the tag of his Christmas present. Before the arrival of the children she used to tell him she loved him frequently. And it's not like she loved him any less after Luke was born – if anything she loved him more – so why had she let it go unsaid? It would only have taken a moment to have said it that morning.

If only. If only. If only. Instead, he is gone; Karen is lying here, alone.

The red LED of the clock by the bed declares it is 06.01. Strange that all the clocks in the world continue when her world seems to have stopped. Yet she can see light beginning to creep through the gap in the curtains, gulls are screeching and there is a scuttling downstairs. It's Toby – though Luke would like it otherwise, he sleeps in the kitchen – and he will want breakfast, and so, soon, will the children. She could lie here forever, but she has to get up. Then she can start to do things. There are arrangements to be made, people to be told, decisions to be made about the house purchase. And first thing this morning there's to be a post-mortem. The hospital has to do one as a matter of course, to establish the cause of death, officially. She is not sure what good it will do, and the idea of slicing open her beloved Simon . . .

She cannot bear to think of it.

Then, of course, there is a funeral to be organized.

This last thought does it: before she has time to change her mind, Karen eases herself out from the covers and lifts her legs up and over Molly, who, curled into a tight little ball, is not taking up much space.

Once upright, Karen automatically reaches for her dressing gown on the back of the door. But to get to it, she has to unhook Simon's. It is navy, thick towelling, shin-length, and, even though it is several years old, still luxurious; she can't resist pulling it to her, inhaling . . .

Sure enough, it is suffused with his scent: a combination of deodorant and aftershave – it's what he pulled on most mornings as he stepped out of the shower – and Simon's own, natural smell. Unique as he is; was. One of her favourite smells in the whole world. Still she cannot believe he will never give off that scent again.

*

An October morning, a hotel in Manchester. Grey clouds billow across the sky outside the bedroom window, doubtless there is a chill in the air, but no matter, Karen and Simon are inside, snug.

'Oh, look,' says Karen, opening the wardrobe. 'Dressing gowns. How posh.'

'What, darling?' Simon comes from the bathroom; he has a white towel wrapped round his waist, another in his hands;

he is drying his hair. He stops and says, 'Sorry, I missed that.'

'Look,' she repeats, unhooking one of the gowns and holding it out. They are matching, navy, enormous, stitched on the breast with a curly 'M' to represent the name of the hotel.

He unhooks the towel from his waist and flings it on the bed. 'Perfect.' Then he takes the dressing gown from Karen and puts it on, tying the belt round his middle.

'It suits you,' observes Karen. It does. The navy brings out the blue of his eyes, but it is more than that: it fits him so well. He is big and the luxury of the fabric and the generosity of the cut does him justice in a way many clothes don't, emphasizing the breadth of his shoulders and creating a pleasing 'V' to his waist.

'Mm,' she smiles. 'It makes you look really manly.'

'Don't sound so surprised,' he laughs. 'I *am* manly.'

'Of course you are,' she laughs, too.

Karen is enjoying herself. It is fun being in this hotel, all the more so because it is on expenses. Anna recommended it, and she is always spot on when it comes to matters of taste. The decor is elegant yet not stuffy, modern yet far from minimal. Whilst it's not overly expensive (or Simon's work would complain), the whole place has a sense of opulence, makes her feel spoiled. The night before, the bed was blissfully comfortable, the evening meal a series of sumptuous and spectacular delights – they even indulged in candlelit cocktails beforehand at the panelled oak bar. There are pleasing details too – the bath foam is not the usual hotel fare reminiscent of old ladies, but some heady concoction that allows Karen to imagine, just for this brief time, that she's someone incredibly glamorous and successful. And while Simon has come up for a conference, she has just come along for the ride, and is free to spend that day as she wants. Never mind sightseeing, she plans to go shopping – Anna has told her Manchester is great for that.

She takes a seat on the stool at the dressing table and reaches into the drawer for the hairdryer. As she does so, Simon comes over and slips his hands around her waist from behind.

'And you, my lady, are very womanly.'

She arches her back, tilts her head up and kisses him. She is only wearing her underwear and at once she feels aroused: it is the combination of the surroundings, sense of freedom from her usual routine, moisturizing lotion tingling on her skin, and, above all, Simon himself. He smells so clean, so fresh, and at this moment he looks particularly physically attractive.

'Mm,' it is his turn to mutter as he picks up on her mood. He slips a hand into her knickers and down.

'Ooh . . .'

His fingers find their destination fast, yet he is gentle with her: he knows her body well, how to gauge it.

She swivels to face him. 'Don't start anything you can't finish,' she teases. 'Don't you have to go?'

He glances at the clock by the bed. 'I should,' he grins. 'But it's only some boring seminar first thing. If I don't turn up till afterwards, I dare say no one will notice.'

'So how long have you got?' She undoes the ties of his dressing gown. He has an erection. 'Mm,' she laughs again. 'I'd say well over six inches.'

He chuckles; it is an obvious joke, but that is its humour. 'I'd say, oh, forty minutes . . .'

'Only forty minutes?' Slowly, she traces the line of hair from his belly down with her fingertip then looks up at him.

'Well, maybe an hour . . .' He raises an eyebrow at her. 'If that's what my girl needs.'

'She does,' says Karen. 'If she's to take time to do everything properly . . . .' She takes his cock in her hand and starts to move it in the way she knows he finds impossible to resist.

Minutes later, she straddles him on the dressing-table stool. They make love there, prolonging it, both feeling naughtier than they have in ages because they are somewhere different, decadent, delicious, and Simon should be at work.

Later that day, when Karen is still purring and happy, she discovers they sell the dressing gowns at the hotel as memorabilia. So she buys one from the hotel reception, and gives it to him once they are home, as a surprise. A few weeks later still, she discovers she is pregnant. Whether it was that morning, or the night before, she is never sure. But she works out from her cycle that at some point on that trip, Luke was conceived. Her baby boy, now five years old, lying asleep in her bed, all slight and small and sucking his thumb, in the spot where usually Simon himself would lie; her Simon, all big and broad and manly.

06:30

Anna's alarm goes off; she wakes with a lurch. She had finally fallen asleep around 3 a.m.; now she is launched straight into the world by the radio, tuned permanently to Radio 4. Even though Steve would prefer music, it is a battle Anna has won, arguing that she is the one who has to be up and out first. Anyway, Anna has the final say, although she has never had to articulate it: this is her house – Steve contributes to the mortgage, with sporadic payments of rent or else in DIY, but she is the one whose name is on the deeds. Anna is specific – even truculent – about her tastes. She doesn't like music first thing, she can't be doing with DJs. She finds their determined perkiness too much; it often clashes with her mood. Moreover, she finds music – pop songs especially – too loose, too vague. They leave her hanging, emotionally unsettled, and she doesn't like that, not first thing, at any rate. Under normal circumstances she finds there is something about the spoken voice and news – however grim – that places her in reality, somewhere specific in time. It gives her a sense of stability, grounds her.

Today, however, everything is different. Almost before she has even opened her eyes, Anna is conscious of the events

of the day before: Simon, Karen. The presenter is inter-
viewing a politician – one gravelly voiced Scot versus another
– but she doesn't take in a word; her head is jostling with
sadness and worry and anger and feelings she cannot even
define.

Before she gets sucked in, she focuses: today she is going
to work. Karen has assured her she'll be OK with Phyllis
there; that she and Phyllis can support each other. Anna will
go over that evening. So she must get up. Now.

Steve is still fast asleep, snoring slightly. It never ceases
to amaze Anna how he can slumber in spite of the radio,
but four years together have proved that he can, perhaps
because when he works it's physically exhausting. In some
ways Anna resents it, as it serves to underline how brutally
early she has to be up and out of the house. But in others
she likes it because it allows her to get ready without any
interruption.

In the night Steve has flung his arm around her, and it
is resting on her shoulder. Gently she lifts it up, slides herself
out from under the duvet and slips her feet into worn suede
slippers. Then she pads over to the far side of the room and
turns on the little fluorescent light above her dressing table.
It is not that bright and Steve rolls over, mutters vaguely,
and resumes snoring.

After showering, Anna dresses. Normally she likes to plan
her outfit; assemble shoes, tights, separates and jewellery so
they complement each other, before she goes to bed. She
has done this since her university days, when she and Karen
shared a house. Karen has always thought her incredibly
organized, and, as Anna rummages for clean underwear, she

hears her friend teasing: 'You are such a control freak!' Karen is one to pull on whatever is nearest, if it is an average day, or if she is going somewhere special, whatever takes her fancy that moment.

Anna sighs. Today, of all days, deciding what to wear won't be top of Karen's list.

Because she wasn't up to laying anything out the previous night, now Anna behaves like Karen and reaches for what is easiest: yesterday's skirt and top.

Next, she does her make-up. But as she opens her eyes wide to put on mascara, she is overwhelmed by an urge to cry. It takes her aback; until now she has been fine, or fine-ish, operating on automatic pilot. The tears spring forth before she can stop them, smudging her eyeliner and leaving pale trails through her blusher. She wants to howl like a baby, but gulps and blinks back the tears.

Blast, she'll have to apply some of her make-up again; she'll miss the seven forty-four if she carries on like this. She forces herself to concentrate, and, a few minutes later than usual, she is ready.

Outside the morning is cold but crisp. It is getting light, and as she heads down the steep hill to the station, legs juddering as the incline propels her forwards, her breath billows white, like steam from a train in an old movie.

* * *

Lou loves her sleep, and has her morning routine down to a fine art so she can maximize her time in bed. She lives a mile from the station, but her alarm goes off later than Anna's.

Her priorities are: get clean, dress, eat, drink, all as fast as possible.

Her studio doesn't have a bath; there is not room, but a brisk power shower is a daily pleasure. She loves the way the water blows away the blurry feel of night: a sensation she compounds with a peppermint shampoo called 'Invigorate' which makes her scalp tingle. A quick blast with the dryer – she doesn't even need to see what she is doing, so familiar is the routine – a touch of gel and her hair is ready; she clips on a cotton bra with equal dexterity, then it is clean knickers and T-shirt, jeans, zip-up top. Next, breakfast. A bowl of muesli and sliced banana, eaten standing at her little attic window, watching the rising sun transform the sky in the east. Barely has she swallowed the last mouthful and had a couple of slurps of tea before she is pulling on her parka, tucking one leg of her jeans into her sock, wiggling into her rucksack and bounding down the stairs.

She keeps her bicycle in the narrow communal hall – an agreement she has come to after much wrangling with her neighbours. She pushes on the light – it's on a timer – to see, knowing it will go out just before she has turned the key in the lock; the landlord is tight about any expense, including electricity. No matter: after several years Lou knows the layout in the dark. All she needs to do now is open the front door, edge the bicycle down the steps (banging her shins as she goes – ouch) and with a swing of her left leg over the crossbar, she is off.

It is a much nicer day today, she thinks as she speeds along the promenade; chilly, but fresh – perhaps it will be sunny later. She is concentrating so hard, head down, focusing on the motion of the pedals, that – oops – she has to swerve sharply to stop herself from going into the back of a large vehicle. It is an ambulance, double-parked across the inside lane of the road by the Palace Pier, blocking her way. Its lights aren't on, but there is a police car too. Something is happening.

She slows to look, and sees paramedics carrying a stretcher up the slope from the beach. At once she knows the reason for the lack of flashing lights – a cover is pulled over the body's face; the emergency has passed.

Oh, dear, she thinks. Not again.

But she has not got time to stop, and anyway, that would seem prurient. So she sticks out her right arm at a mini-roundabout and turns up towards the ornate domes of the Pavilion and Theatre Royal.

The rhythm of pedalling acts like a sieve, sorting her thoughts.

I need to deal with Aaron, she thinks. That's something I cannot leave to fester. I need to ring my mother, and – damn it – let Vic know I won't be able to make her party.

Her mother. Hmm . . . The furthest Lou has been able to push rebellion is to hold off on calling the night before as requested, but she is going to agree to the visit itself.

She cuts along the back streets of the North Laine to the station, switching down a gear as she goes. It is uphill, but Lou is fit and used to it. Rows of white terraces flank her on either side; houses with doors that open straight on to the pavement. Here there are no front gardens, merely window boxes or clusters of pots by doorsteps. A century ago these dwellings used to belong to railway workers and fishermen.

They have long since been taken over by boho families with small children called names like Apollo and Atlas, students with multiple piercings and dreadlocks, and artists of sometimes questionable talent struggling to pay the rent.

Lou gets off her bike and wheels it through the station to the cycle stands at the back. She locks it, removes her helmet and heads for platform 4.

How strange, she thinks, recalling the previous morning, that everything is totally back to normal; everyone is behaving as if nothing has happened. It makes her feel sad, that one person's life has so little impact. And what about that body on the beach just now? Perhaps it was one of the people who sleep on the beach; Brighton has a lot of homeless people, and winter is hard for them. If so, chances are their death will impact on an even smaller circle – many people prefer not to think too deeply about them, let alone get involved.

Lou sighs and checks her watch. Oh, well. She makes for the front of the train so as to be near the exit at Victoria, scouring the windows as she walks for a glimpse of Anna.

She would like to see her again; she feels connected to her by shared experience. But either Anna is not here yet or she is not working today. Although Lou has given Anna her card, she has no way of initiating contact herself.

I do hope she is OK, she thinks, and her friend Karen, too.

*　*　*

Anna buys her breakfast at Marks & Spencer in the station forecourt as she always does, and heads for platform 4 and the seven forty-four. She has cut it much finer than usual, but manages to find a carriage where there is still space – it's an advantage that Brighton is the start of the line. She takes off her coat and puts it on the shelf overhead and settles into a window seat, facing forwards, her usual choice. Briefly, she thinks of Lou, wonders whether to call her or send a text. But she's not up to holding a conversation with anyone today, she decides, not unless she has to. Another time, maybe, when she is less raw.

A couple of minutes later there is a blast of a whistle and the train sets off. They stop at Preston Park, someone takes the seat next to her, and her journey is going just as it has done for months on end, until they pull out of Burgess Hill and she is overwhelmed.

This is where it happened. Twenty-four hours ago exactly. At this place, Simon had a heart attack.

Inexplicably, the tears burst forth before she can stop them. Miniature rivers and rivers, smudging her eye make-up all over again.

What is happening?

The people next to her and opposite, whom she doesn't recognize from yesterday, were probably on the train, but have no idea she knew the man who died.

They will think she is mad, crying. It is ghastly, these unexpected bursts of emotion. They seem to come from nowhere. She reaches in her bag for a tissue.

She can see the man opposite eyeing her, so struggles to smile at him, stop herself from weeping. It doesn't really work; all she does is grimace.

Then, through the tears, comes a fresh realization. She

betrayed Karen in many ways, being on the same train, a few carriages apart.

What if I'd known Karen and Simon were on board? she thinks. What if we had bumped into each other at the station? Or if by chance we had been in the same carriage, and I'd seen them when I got on? If they were sitting down before I did, I must have walked straight past. If we had been together, I could have helped, altered the course of events, done *something*. But instead I was here, almost in this very spot, reading my magazine. Oblivious.

She remembers folding over the page with the jacket she wanted to buy on it. How materialistic, how shallow she is.

08:56

Lolloping walk, low-slung jeans revealing underpants elastic, giant trainers: Lou sees Aaron a few paces ahead of her. She also smells him. Wafting behind, sweet, sickly, heavy: skunk. They are less than two hundred yards from school; it is not even nine in the morning. Her heart sinks.

Should she catch up with him and confront him, or let it go? He is not on school grounds; strictly, it is beyond her remit. Especially as she is his counsellor, not his teacher, so his relationship with her is unlike his with other members of staff. She doesn't want to seem pompous or dictatorial and the situation between them is already sticky. Plus she has not got a session scheduled with him today, so his being stoned won't affect her directly. To ignore it would be far easier. Still, he won't function properly if he is stoned, and that's not in Aaron's interests. Long term, he needs to get back into conventional education – be deemed able to return to a regular school. Skunk before lessons is not the way forward.

So she ups her pace and within seconds is alongside. 'Aaron, hi.'

He is caught unawares, with no time to jettison the joint. His manner is lazy, nonchalant. 'Oh, hello, Miss.' He turns his gaze to her. Eyes sleepy, narrowed, bloodshot. 'Want some?' He holds out the reefer with a practised finger and thumb, roach end towards her.

'No, thanks.'

He stubs it on a concrete lamp post, but instead of throwing it away, slips it into his pocket to finish later, defiant.

Lou takes a deep breath. 'It's interesting you're smoking before school.'

He looks down. Mutters, 'What's it to you? You're not seeing me today.'

'It's not me that I'm bothered about. It's you. I'm wondering why you need to be stoned for lessons.'

He turns to her, smiles, audacious: 'Makes them more fun, Miss.'

'But how can you focus when you're stoned?'

'Don't find it a problem.'

'I think you could concentrate more if you weren't.'

'So you've been stoned, then?'

She has to hand it to him; once more he is swift, even in this state. 'Aaron, this isn't about me, this is about you. Isn't smoking weed what landed you here in the first place?'

His eyes narrow further. He is angry. 'You gonna report me, then?'

'I'm not sure.' Lou considers it his teachers' role to instil discipline, not necessarily hers. If she is to gain his confidence, she can't betray all his misdemeanours.

A few beats' silence. They continue walking side by side. They are nearly at the school.

Eventually, he breaks it. 'Strikes me you have your secrets, and I has mine.'

She knows what he's alluding to; the remark is loaded, threatening. And his argument has a certain logic, impressive for someone who is stoned. Then again, he is adept at functioning through a haze.

'You know the ground rules,' she reminds him, as they enter the building. 'Your relationship with me isn't about my life. I'm here to help and support you.'

'If you say so.' But he grins, confident he has disarmed her, for the moment at least. 'See ya.' He turns and heads down the corridor.

Lou mounts the stairs to her room, brow furrowed. However long he and Kyra prolong this dance, even if they intimidate her further, the outcome must be the same – she will not reveal herself to them; they must learn respectful social skills. Nonetheless these incidents have brought one thing home to her. She would like the support of a colleague; she wants the head to know. She'll have a chat with her as soon as they both have a moment.

*　*　*

Just after nine o'clock, Anna steps out of the elevator and into the Chelsea marketing agency where she freelances as a writer. Most people will not know anything out of the ordinary has happened, she reminds herself, pushing thoughts of Karen and Simon aside. Probably only her boss, whom she'd phoned the morning before, and Petra, the woman who schedules her workload, will have any idea. And they have their own preoccupations; it will be of passing interest to them, no more.

Sure enough, a 'Feeling better?' is all her entrance prompts from the receptionist. Anna doesn't correct her. If her colleagues think she has been off sick, it is fine by her.

'Yes, thanks,' she says, and pushes open the double doors into the noisy office where she spends her working day.

Anna's desk is sectioned off from Finance by a shoulder-high partition: through it she can hear the young woman who sits just the other side thumping on her keyboard with a clickity-clack of her nail extensions.

In the Creative Department her colleagues are behaving just as they always do: to her left is Colin, the new boy fresh from college, mumbling to himself, reading radio ad scripts aloud so he can time them with a stopwatch. She can see from the wodge of A4 he is clutching that he has written up several different ideas; he is so keen, his mere existence makes Anna feel guilty. To her right are Bill, an art director, and Ian, another copywriter, talking about last night's telly. They are more like she is: very experienced at what they do, middle-aged, world-weary, sardonic. She likes them both.

But before she has a chance to indulge in some morning banter, she is collared by Petra.

'Anna, hi,' she says briskly. 'Feeling better?'

So her boss hasn't even told Petra what was up. Anna doesn't know whether to read this as discretion or disinterest on his part, but no matter, it makes it easier. If someone is too kind, she might cry again.

'Yes, thank you,' she nods, and Petra gives her some letters to draft for an insurance company. Initially stalled by fear that she can't do the work, Anna forces her brain into gear and, minutes later, starts typing. Within half an hour she is feeling more normal; it is good to focus on the familiar. Eventually she has the strength to step out into the corridor for privacy, and phone Karen.

* * *

Karen is standing in the kitchen, looking out of the French windows but not really seeing anything, while Phyllis is sitting at the breakfast bar, pen in hand. The children are watching *Dora the Explorer* in the living room: not something Karen would normally advocate at this hour, but today nothing is normal.

She might have managed to put on some clothes – though if someone had asked her to shut her eyes and say what she is wearing she wouldn't remember – and she might have managed to give the children breakfast, but she has not been able to eat anything. She feels very strange physically. Even though she is not moving, her legs seem light, as though her feet aren't quite on the floor. She is like one of those figures in a Chagall painting, floating around the room, limbs in limbo, defying gravity. Worse, she keeps having terrifying whooshes of panic that leave her breathless, heart palpitating.

She and Phyllis are struggling to make a list of other friends and relatives they need to tell about Simon. Phyllis is in charge of writing; Karen's job is to remember names. If only it were that easy. Everything is upside down, not as it should be, including her memory.

Get a grip, she tells herself. People need to know what has happened.

She looks at the clock. 'I could do some phoning now, I guess. It's a perfectly reasonable time.'

Phyllis nods. 'Before you do, though, I was wondering. I think I'd like to go to the undertaker's and see Simon.'

'Sure,' says Karen. 'Of course you would.'

Phyllis's voice cracks. 'It just doesn't seem real.' She starts weeping. 'My boy.'

Poor Phyllis. Even through her own grief, Karen feels it: the longing of a mother for her son. What would it do to her to lose Luke? Age makes no odds, surely. Karen goes over, puts her hands on the back of her mother-in-law's shoulders, bowed these days with old age, rests her head on her soft grey pillow of hair. They remain like that a while, quiet save for Phyllis's tears; the physical connection says it all.

'Let's ring them, then,' suggests Karen, eventually. 'See when Simon is likely to be released from the post-mortem. I think it was due first thing this morning.'

'Do you want to come with me?'

Karen hesitates. She wants to grasp every opportunity there is to be with Simon – she would have gone back to the hospital yesterday afternoon if it had not been for Molly and Luke. But that is the point: she has to think of them. 'I'd better stay here. It would be a bit much for the children.'

'Whatever you think best. But I would like to say goodbye to him.'

Just then, a small voice interrupts them. 'Who are you going to say goodbye to?'

They both turn to see Luke standing at the kitchen door.

'Your Daddy,' says Karen, before she has a chance to stop herself.

'But I thought you said Daddy wasn't coming back.'

Oh, no, she's made a mess of it *again*. 'Poppet, I'm sorry, he's not.'

'So how come Granny is going to talk to him?'

'She's going to say goodbye to his body, not Daddy himself.'

'I don't understand.'

'Daddy's body has stopped working.' She takes a deep breath. 'It's very sad and we will miss him very much.' But Luke just appears confused, so Karen continues, 'You remember how I told you yesterday, he's a bit like Charlie? Do you remember how Charlie's body was still here, when he died, and how we buried it in the garden, but Charlie himself was gone?'

'Are we going to bury Daddy in the garden?'

Karen can't resist laughing gently. 'No, honey, we're not. What we'll do, because Daddy is a very special person, is have what's called a funeral in a few days' time. It is a kind of party, though people will be a bit sad and some of them might cry. That's when you and I and Molly can say goodbye to Daddy properly.'

'But I want to talk to Daddy today!' He stamps his foot. 'Can't I go with Granny?'

Karen and Phyllis look at each other. Neither is sure what to say or do.

Phyllis scoops him onto her knee and mutters, her voice low, over his head, 'Might not be a bad idea, you know, if he wants to. I saw my grandfather when I was not that much older.'

Karen is unsure. On the one hand she wants to protect Luke; on the other she has never been one to cosset her children, and it did help her to spend time with Simon's body.

What would Simon want? she wonders. Would he want his children to see him in a coffin, all cold and lifeless? She can't be sure. Yet when his own father died, she recalls the two of them had talked about how much death is hidden these days and she knows Simon thought that a bad thing. He was conscious of his father's background – he was an Irish Catholic and regular churchgoer – and when he died, Simon and Phyllis had tried to respect his faith as best they could. 'The tradition is different – it's more open,' Simon had said about having the coffin at his parents' home before the funeral. 'Dad would have wanted it like this.' But while Simon might have thought that appropriate for his dad, they were a generation apart. Would he actively choose the same for himself?

Round and round go Karen's thoughts, spin cycle on over-drive. Nonetheless, she is conscious Luke is standing there, waiting. This is not the time for procrastination.

Perhaps what is best in this situation is whatever Luke wants. She crouches down to his level on Phyllis's lap, gently grasps his shoulders and looks into his eyes. 'Luke, sweetie. If you'd like to go and say goodbye to your Daddy, then of course you can go with Granny. But Daddy will look different.'

Luke looks a touch afraid. 'Different how?'

'It's nothing to be scared of or worried about,' she assures him.

'You'll see,' says Phyllis. 'He'll be very still.'

'Like he's asleep?'

'A bit. But stiller even than that.'

He nods, looks up at Phyllis and declares: 'I'll come with you.'

Karen is so proud of his bravery she wants to burst.

It is at that moment the phone rings. Karen jumps, and is then relieved: it is Anna.

* * *

There is no need for niceties. 'How are you today?' Anna asks.

'Terrible,' says Karen, but laughs wryly.

Anna is thankful; it is good to hear Karen laugh.

'Actually, you caught us trying to decide something,' she says. 'Hang on a minute while I just take this outside, I could do with your advice.'

As Anna waits she can hear the French windows sliding open and then shut again.

'It's just that Phyllis wants to go and see Simon.' Karen has dropped her voice.

'Ah, right.' Anna frowns, not sure why this is an issue. 'Is he still in the hospital?'

'He's being brought to the undertaker's – it's not far from here, towards Hove. They're moving him after the post-mortem this morning.'

'So she can get herself there, surely? I thought she drove.'

'Yes, yes, she does. That's not the problem. It's just that Luke wants to go.'

'Luke?' Anna struggles to keep up. Somehow she can't picture little Luke at Simon's side. Instinctively she wants to safeguard him from the trauma. Seeing Simon was gruelling enough for her, let alone a five-year-old.

Karen explains, 'He overheard us talking about Phyllis going, and now he wants to go to say goodbye too.'

'Ah.'

'What do you think?'

'Gosh, Karen, they're your children, I really don't know. What about Molly?'

'I was thinking she and I would stay here.'

'Hmm, I'm not sure about that.' Anna calls on all her emotional understanding. Gradually, she comes up with what she feels is the right solution. 'If you're going to give Luke that opportunity, I think maybe you ought to give it to Molly too.'

'But she's only three, don't you think that it would be a bit much for her?'

Then Anna remembers. 'Actually, that nice nurse yesterday suggested to me that you took them to see him. If they want to go.'

'Really?'

'Yes, she did. I'm so sorry, I should have mentioned it.' Anna feels guilty: she's failed Karen again.

'Oh, don't worry. We were all of a dither yesterday. Well, we're all of a dither today too . . .'

'You could always ring her and ask her, but she did say that, yes.' Anna stops, then adds, 'It's not as if Simon's all bashed up or anything, is it? He's not been in an accident or anything, in which case I'd say not; it might upset them to see him like that. But he looks at peace, really.'

'Yes, he does. . . Mm, maybe you're right. . . I wouldn't want to force her, though . . .'

'No, of course.'

'I know what I'll do. I'll ask her too.'

'That sounds very sensible,' agrees Anna. 'I'm sure you'll

put it in a way that she understands, so see what she says. But my guess is that in years to come she might be thankful.'

Goodness me, she thinks, putting down the phone a few minutes later. Who am I to encourage such openness? I keep half of my domestic life under cover. None of my colleagues know much about my troubles, do they? Imagine what Bill and Ian would say if I revealed what Steve is capable of when he's drunk. They'd be horrified, surely.

Anna sighs. Bottling all this stuff up isn't good. In the wake of Simon's death it seems even unhealthier. She returns to her desk and her letters, attempting to put her thoughts on hold once more. Still, they are there, eating away at her. Secrets. Lies. Simon lived with such straightforward honesty that his departure casts an uncomfortable light on how much she keeps under wraps.

She is not sure how much longer she can carry on like this, now she's seeing things from a different perspective.

10:51

'Is that you, Lou?'

Blast. Lou was going to call, yet her mother has gazumped her. She feigns enthusiasm. 'Yes, Mum, hi!'

'I thought you were going to ring me last night.'

Barely a sentence spoken and Lou is made to feel bad. 'Sorry, yes, I know – I, er . . . I had to phone a friend before I got back to you. I did mention that I had to cancel something if I was to come.' Ha! Fight guilt with guilt, Lou: that is the tactic.

But her mother seems interested only in whether Lou is doing what she wants. 'So you are coming, then?'

'Yes, yes, I am.'

'On the Thursday?'

Aargh! 'No. I'll come on Saturday morning.'

'Oh, really? Not sooner?'

'I'm afraid I can't,' she says abruptly. This is a lie; she *could* go on Friday after tennis, but can't face the prospect of that long with her mother. 'I'm not going to a party on Saturday night as it is.' This bit is true, and to salvage some of her plans is only reasonable. She is damned if she's going to surrender to her mother completely.

'That's good, darling, thank you.' Lou's mother has clearly

picked up on her tone, and realized this is the most she's going to get. 'Uncle Pat and Auntie Audrey will be so pleased to see you.'

Yeah, right, thinks Lou, furiously twiddling the phone cable to contain her irritation. She decides to cut her mother short. 'Is that all, Mum? It's just I've a couple of other calls to make and I only have a few minutes before my next student.'

'Oh, OK.' Her mother sounds disappointed, but Lou ignores her. Do as you would be done by, after all.

'Bye, then!' Lou is ludicrously upbeat, and puts the phone down. She can't resist kicking her filing cabinet, though, once she's in the clear.

I'd better phone Vic, then, she concludes. Vic is an old friend, whom Lou has known since school. She's still got a few minutes.

'Vic, it's Lou.'

'Hello.'

'I'm afraid I've got some really annoying news.'

'Oh, what?'

'I can't make your party.'

'Bugger. Why?'

'It's my mum.'

'Not again.'

'Yes, *again*.'

'What this time?'

'She wants me to go and help with my Auntie Audrey and Uncle Pat. Uncle Pat's not been well and she's asked them to hers as they've barely been out of their house for months.'

'Why does she need you there?'

'To look after them. They are quite hard work.'

'Can't she do that?'

'She says not. Her hip's bad, you know.'

'But you *always* go. Can't your sister Georgia help?'

'You know she won't be able to. She might be able to drop by, but she's got kids and things – she's bound to have stuff arranged already.'

'But so have you! I've had this party planned for *ages*.'

'I know, I know, I'm sorry.' There's guilt wherever Lou turns. And it's not as if she isn't disappointed anyway. Vic knows so many colourful people that her parties are usually a riot.

'It's my birthday on Sunday. It's rare it falls on a weekend.'

More guilt. 'Vic, honestly, I'd so much rather be with you – it goes without saying, surely. But I can't say no. You know what my mother is like. She'll be a nightmare for months if I don't go.'

Vic sighs. 'I suppose so. It's a shame, though. There was another reason I wanted you to come.'

'Oh, yeah?'

'I had someone I wanted you to meet.'

Lou stops twiddling the phone cable. 'Really?'

'Indeedy.'

'Who?'

Vic isn't gay herself, but she works in the theatre and has heaps of gay friends, although most of them tend to be men. 'This lovely woman I met recently backstage.'

'Oh?'

'Yes. A friend of one of the actors. She's just your type.'

'What's her name?'

'Sofia.'

'Is she Italian or Spanish or something?'

'Yes, Spanish, but she's lived here for years.'

'What's she like, then?'

'She seems like a very nice person. Funny and intelligent and, well, just lovely.'

'What does she look like?'

'I said, she's just your type. Pretty.'

'Pretty in what way?'

'Short dark curly hair, brown eyes; honestly, she's really attractive. I'd fancy her myself if I was gay.'

'Mm, she sounds great. What does she do?'

'She works for a web company. She's a director, I think.'

So, bright too, and seemingly capable. Lou has had it with needy types. It is all most appealing. 'How old is she?'

'Thirtyish, I'd say.'

That's a couple of years younger than Lou, but not too young. 'Where does she live?'

'Acton, at the moment. But she works in East Croydon.'

Lou races ahead. She's at her happy ending already: 'Ooh, so if we got together she could commute!'

'My thoughts exactly.'

Lou remembers her obligations. She kicks the cabinet again. 'Damn!'

'Well, it's your loss . . .'

'Can't I meet her some other time?'

Vic exhales theatrically. Her profession is no coincidence – there's more than a little drama queen in her. 'I suppose so, if you must.'

'Aw, Vic, go on, you know I haven't had any sex for months. Set us up.'

'What, on a blind date?'

'Oh, no, that's a bit embarrassing. Can't we go out, you, me and her or something?'

'I'm not introducing you if this is all just going to be about sex.'

'You're a fine one to talk!'

'No, I know, but still, I'm not. She's a nice girl, Sofia. I'm not having you break her heart.'

'Of course I'm not going to break her heart!' Lou protests. Though in some ways she is flattered Vic would think her capable of such a thing; treating women mean is hardly her style. In truth, she's usually the one who gets hurt, not the other way round.

'All right,' Vic relents. 'I'll see what I can do. You'd better tell me when you're free, then.'

'Friday night?' says Lou hopefully. She doubts Vic will be around at such short notice.

'Hmm, as a matter of fact, I might be available . . .' Vic is toying with her, Lou can tell from her tone. She's loving it.

Thank goodness Lou told her mother she couldn't go to hers until Saturday. 'Why don't you come down to Brighton?' she suggests, eager. 'We could go out.'

'Well . . . I was supposed to be painting my flat – I want it to look nice for the party. And as you've let me down, I'm not sure I should be quite so accommodating . . .'

'Oh, Vic, honestly! Since when did decorating ever take precedence over anything?' Vic's flat is a tip; she has lived there nearly ten years and has barely cleaned it in that time, let alone decorated. 'Anyway, aren't you better off painting it after the party? It might get damaged.'

'Maybe you have a point,' Vic concurs. 'I'm not getting drunk, though – I'll have to host the next day.'

'No, no, we won't,' assures Lou, though she knows Vic will.

'And you'll have to invite someone else too. I'm not going out in my prickly green suit with just the two of you. That won't be much fun for me.'

'OK.' Lou racks her brains. A suitable candidate is not that simple: a lot of her friends are paired up; another couple could exacerbate Vic's sense of exclusion. Plus Vic's a strong character; some of her quieter single friends might find her overwhelming. 'What about Howie? You met him before – at that Murder Mystery gathering, remember?' Howie lives locally and there's the chance he might be available, especially as he's just dumped his boyfriend of several years and is up for socializing at the moment.

'Let me ask Sofia before you speak to him. Even if she is free, she may not want to come all the way to Brighton.'

On this score, Lou appreciates she is being truthful. 'Sure, fine. I'll keep it open until you let me know. I must get on now, anyway – my next student's due any second.'

* * *

'Right, children,' says Karen, going over to the television. Luke and Molly are sitting on the sofa, legs swinging as they don't yet reach the floor, mesmerized by the closing credits of *Dora*. 'That episode is finished, so there will be no more telly for a bit.'

She switches it off. 'Aw,' says Luke.

'Now, Molster, in a while, Luke and Granny are going to say goodbye to Daddy. And we can go too, but only if you'd like that. So you need to listen to me very carefully before you make up your mind.'

But Molly just sits there wide-eyed. Her face – so heart-wrenchingly reminiscent of Simon's – has borne the same perplexed expression for most of the morning. Karen is not sure if she understands or if it is all simply too much.

'Daddy is going to be buried soon,' Karen explains.

'But not in the garden,' remembers Luke, soberly.

'No, not in the garden. And when he is buried, he'll be in a special box, called a "coffin".'

'Like Charlie's?' They'd buried the cat in a large shoebox.

'Yes, I suppose you're right. A coffin is a bit like that. Anyway, when we see Daddy in his special box, he won't be the same as you're used to. He will be like Charlie was, when Charlie died. So although you can say things to Daddy and tell him goodbye, he won't be able to say anything back to you, because Daddy is gone to—' – she flounders and then uses the only word that seems appropriate – 'heaven.'

'Up in the sky,' nods Luke.

'Yes. So what we'll be seeing is only part of Daddy, not all of him.'

Molly looks anxious. 'Is he missing some bits? Like Princess Aurora?' Princess Aurora is Molly's favourite toy. But the doll long ago lost the ball in her hip joint, so only has one leg.

'No, no,' Karen corrects her. 'He's all there, nothing like that. It's just his body will be there, but not his *character*.'

As soon as she's uttered this, she knows it's too big a word for Molly.

But somehow Molly seems to have understood the essence. 'I want to say goodbye too,' she proclaims.

'Are you sure? We don't have to go. You and I could just stay here and – oh, I don't know,' – Karen plucks an idea from the air – 'make biscuits. Then Luke and Granny can have them when they get back.'

Molly shakes her head. 'I want to go with Luke and Granny.'

So far as Karen can tell, she has grasped it. 'Right, that's settled then. Who's my gorgeous girl?' She picks her up from the sofa and gives her a hug and a kiss.

But then, as she leans to ruffle Luke's chestnut hair, she sees it's his turn to look troubled. 'What's the matter? You worried about going now?'

'Mummy, will Daddy be all right in a shoebox?'

She understands his thinking. The thought of Simon alone in hard, frosted earth upsets her too.

Luke continues, 'When we buried Charlie, we gave him his favourite blanket.'

'Ah, yes.' Bless him; he's following the Charlie parallel right through to its conclusion. 'Are you thinking it would be nice to give Daddy something to cuddle, sweetheart?' They can hardly bury Simon with a rug matted with fur, however. She tries to think what might work instead.

But before Karen can come up with a solution, Luke jumps up from the sofa: 'I know!' and runs out of the room.

Molly wriggles out of Karen's arms, slides down her leg and follows her older brother. There is a thump thump thump up the stairs to their room. She can hear Luke saying something to Molly, and her replying. A minute or two later, and they are both back down. When she sees what they have in their hands, Karen has to force herself not to cry.

It is Blue Crocodile and Princess Aurora.

12:26

'The undertaker says to give them another hour,' says Phyllis, replacing the phone.

'Oh?'

Luke is struggling into his lace-ups at Karen's feet; Molly is all buttoned up and duffel-coated, arms scarcely able to bend for padding, waiting to go.

Phyllis lowers her voice so the children can't hear. 'They've only just got the body after the post-mortem. I presume they have to dress it.'

'Ah,' says Karen. They must have sliced Simon's beautiful barrel chest, and maybe more besides. She reels. The thought makes her sick, giddy.

'Love,' Phyllis touches her shoulder, 'I know, it's horrid. Here. Sit down.' She pulls back a chair.

'Thanks. Sorry.' Karen puts her head in her hands, waiting for the dizziness to pass. When she lifts her head she sees Molly watching her, alarmed.

'I'm all right, darling,' she smiles.

Molly is clutching Princess Aurora close to her chest, tight, for comfort.

Immediately it strikes Karen: Molly *needs* Princess Aurora. Luke, too, needs Blue Crocodile, though right now the toy is discarded, felt legs in the air, on the kitchen floor. Now is not the time to take away these sources of comfort. They need – *she* needs – all the tools of support they can get.

'I've been thinking, children,' she says at once. 'Maybe Princess Aurora and Blue Crocodile might like to stay here, with you.'

'But I thought you said to get something for Daddy to cuddle?'

'I did.' Not for the first time, Karen is perturbed at the mixed messages she's giving. 'It's just . . . wouldn't you miss Blue Crocodile an awful lot, if you weren't to have him to cuddle yourself?'

'I'd be all right,' says Luke, confidently. But Karen knows it's because he doesn't want to be seen as a baby.

'Well, *I* would miss him,' says Karen. 'And I think you might too, just a little. Don't you remember how sad you were when we thought we'd lost him at Gatwick Airport?' Sad is an understatement: Luke's wails of distress cut through the entire South Terminal.

'Yes, but I was only four then.'

Phyllis chuckles at him. 'I know!' she exclaims. 'I've got an idea. Molly, my dear, take off your coat.' She swings into action, unbuttoning her granddaughter's duffel, and Molly frowns, not keeping up. 'We're not going anywhere right now. They're not quite ready for us to see Daddy yet. So we're going to take a little while, and you can each do your dad a drawing.'

What an excellent solution, thinks Karen.

Phyllis briskly opens the drawer in the table where Karen

keeps the children's drawing materials. 'Do you want to use crayons, or felt-tip pens?'

'Pens!' says Molly, obediently shifting focus.

'But I want to give Daddy Blue Crocodile!' Luke, however, is unyielding.

'I tell you what,' suggests Phyllis. 'Why don't we take Blue Crocodile and Princess Aurora with us, so they can say goodbye to Daddy too? How about that?'

Karen is grateful – Phyllis is doing a magnificent job. 'That's a great plan,' she agrees.

Nonetheless, Luke gives each of them a black look. He can be awfully determined at times.

Karen truly doesn't think it wise that Luke part with Blue Crocodile. She struggles for an alternative. Eventually – 'You know the great thing about Charlie's blanket . . .' she cajoles.

'What?' Luke growls.

'. . . It kept Charlie really snuggly and warm.'

'Mm?'

'Well, I'm not sure Blue Crocodile and Princess Aurora are going to keep Daddy that warm, are they? I mean, they're very nice to cuddle, but they're not as good as Charlie's blanket when you want to be all snug, tucked up in a special box. So I'm thinking . . . why don't we take Daddy his lovely blue dressing gown? Then if he gets cold, it'll keep him really cosy.'

Luke is silent, assimilating. Eventually he nods, cautiously.

'I'll get it,' says Karen, and before he can change his mind, she goes up to the bedroom and unhooks it from the door.

* * *

There is a rap of nails on wood.

'Yes?'

A face peers round the door of Lou's room. Glasses, a frame of frizzy grey hair. 'Can I come in?' It is Shirley, the School Head. 'Thought it might be easier if we had a chat in here.'

'Sure,' says Lou, getting to her feet and then immediately sitting again. Although she has scheduled the meeting and knows she is doing the right thing, she is nervous.

'Mind if I eat my salad while we talk?' asks Shirley. She doesn't wait for an answer, pulling up a chair opposite Lou, unclipping her Tupperware lunch box and forking a pile of couscous, sweetcorn and red peppers into her mouth.

'Not at all,' Lou nods. She reaches for her sandwich, peels back the cellophane wrapper, pulls out a triangle and takes a bite. But the bread feels gluey, sticks to the roof of her mouth. She doesn't want to eat; she won't enjoy it. She'd rather get this over with. So she puts the sandwich down and braces herself.

'It's to do with Aaron.'

'Ah, Aaron,' nods Shirley. The 'ah' implies a lot: 'we both know Aaron is trouble', 'I understand where you're coming from' and 'why does this not surprise me?' It's remarkable how much a single syllable can convey.

But it pulls Lou up short. She can see them headed down the wrong path. 'Actually,' she corrects herself, 'it's not just about Aaron: it's about me.'

Shirley's fork, en route to her mouth, stops in midair. 'Oh?'

'It's to do with something Aaron has worked out about

me.' The words are clumsy, the phraseology not quite right. Lou's heart is pounding, her hands are clammy, she can feel colour rising in her cheeks. For all her professionalism, she is still a human being: vulnerable, sometimes shy.

'Ah,' says Shirley, slowly. The word conveys something different this time.

Lou knows Shirley has pre-empted what is coming, but she is compelled to explain nonetheless. They can't skip the difficult bit, although she'd like to.

'I'm gay,' she blurts.

There is another pause. Lou's heart beats faster; her cheeks are flaming.

'You didn't have to tell me that, you know.'

'I know.'

'It's not really my business.'

'I appreciate that.' Lou feels the colour subside: the worst is over.

'How you live your life in your spare time is truly nothing to do with the school.'

'No, I realize.' She understands that this is the right answer; the one Shirley must give so as not to cause offence, or get herself into trouble. She also knows Shirley probably means what she says; she wants to believe Lou's sexuality has nothing to do with her work. Shirley is a good woman, and her views are liberal.

Nonetheless, it isn't true: Lou's private life *does* have something to do with her professional life – a great deal, in fact – and not just in her relationships with Kyra and Aaron, but on a deeper, wider level. In actuality, Lou might not be here, if it weren't for her sexuality. Her identity is so bound up with being gay that it forms a huge – nay, *crucial* – part of her. From a very early age, she had a sense that she was different, even before she even really knew why. Wrestling with her sexuality has coloured her views of life, people and relationships. And working it out, with all the excitement, pain and fear that went with it, has given her a strong sense of herself, as the black and white of her poster declares: she knows who she is because of it. Not only that: it has given her a strong bond to those who are also, in different ways and for different reasons, disconnected from society. Ironically, she is connected to the Aarons and Kyras of this world by the fact that they are each of them disconnected.

Still, this isn't the time or the place to go into these nuances with Shirley. It will confuse things, and is beyond what is called for.

'I wouldn't usually have brought it up,' Lou continues. 'I would have just assumed you knew. But the problem is Aaron has worked it out, and so has Kyra.'

'I see.' Shirley is still chewing.

'I wouldn't have troubled you with that either, under normal circumstances. Except that now their behaviour's become rather intimidating. And obviously that's not good or healthy, for Aaron or Kyra, or me. So far, obviously, I've kept my private life private, and I'm going to continue to do that – with them, at least. But I wanted to bring you in on the loop.'

'I'm glad you did.' Shirley gives a kind, supportive smile. 'In fact, I'm honoured you've told me, thank you.'

'Oh.' Lou is surprised, and relieved. So far this is proving easier than she'd feared.

'I don't want my staff to feel they have to undertake every-thing single-handed. That's not what this school is about – the kids are hard enough work as it is. We all need as much backup as we can get.'

'Right.' It takes Lou a few moments to process this; it's a warmer response than she'd anticipated.

'So where do you think we should go from here?' asks Shirley.

Deciding to be honest with Shirley is as far as Lou has got. She thinks hard. 'I'd rather you didn't tell the other members of staff, if you don't mind.' She's not ready for some great public announcement. That would feel overly dramatic, embarrass her.

Shirley scrapes the last vestiges of couscous from her container. 'I don't see why I need to. It's none of their busi-ness. As for Aaron and Kyra, how can I help? Would you like me to talk to them?'

Lou thinks again. 'It wasn't anything specific I wanted; I think it's better I deal with them personally, in our sessions. It's just I realized no one here knew about it, and, well—'

' – you felt bullied,' nods Shirley.

'Close to it, yes. And I'm always advocating the kids are open and honest about their emotions, and I encourage them to tell someone in authority if they feel intimidated. So I felt I wasn't practising what I preach.'

'Well, now you are,' assures Shirley. 'And please, don't hesitate to talk to me again if you need to.'

'No, I won't.' Lou smiles; she feels lighter already. It all seems surprisingly simple.

'Great.' Shirley rises from her chair. 'I'd best get on.'

'Thanks.' Lou also gets to her feet. As she closes the door

behind Shirley, she wishes coming out to everyone could be that painless.

*

Lou is at her parents' house, in Hitchin; she has her own place, locally, but has returned to the family home because her father is very, very ill. Cancer, which started in his lungs, has spread rapidly. He was only diagnosed six months previously and it has been a horrible time. Though no one has uttered the words, his spectral figure says everything: he has been sent home from hospital to die. Today he has requested that he see his two daughters, in private. Her younger sister, Georgia, is in the kitchen, red-eyed; he has spoken to her already. Now it is Lou's turn.

'Hello, Dad,' she says, entering the room. Her father is propped up, pillows behind his head. A tube drips morphine slowly into a vein in the back of his hand.

'Hello, love,' he rasps. He has little energy, he has had a tracheotomy; it is tough to speak. His fingers are frail, bird-like, shaky. He reaches to hold the hole in his neck shut. 'Sit,' he orders.

She pulls an armchair close to him.

'My Loulou,' he says, using her childhood name. It tears her up. Sharing many of the same passions as Lou – sport, the outdoors, making things – he seems to have found her, more than her sister, a kindred spirit as they were growing up. In fact, Lou has often wondered if, secretly, she is his favourite. Certainly she loves him unconditionally, whereas her relationship with her mother is more strained.

'Dad.'

'I know you've not had it easy,' he continues.

She is surprised; this is not what she had expected him to say.

'With your mother, especially.' He is forcing the words out; they are slow, painful. She almost wishes he wouldn't, yet she is keen – desperate – to hear him speak. 'Let's face it,' he laughs, but his laughter causes him to start coughing. Lou gets up and bends him over gently, patting his back until he stops. He slips back onto the pillows. 'Sorry.'

'Don't worry.'

'She is not an easy woman . . . Lord knows, I know.'

Lou nods. She's long realized her parents' relationship is far from smooth: they are very different. Her father is an optimist, humorous, freethinking. Her mother is more suspicious of the world, constantly comparing herself to others, nervy, brittle. Her father has sublimated a lot of himself to stay with her, Lou believes. He is a good man, of a generation imbued with a sense of duty; he'd never leave her, however incompatible they are. Instead he's bent himself, like the wood of a bow, to accommodate her tautness, the string. One day, Lou has felt for years, something will snap.

Instead, what has happened is that his body has given way. He is only sixty, but years of smoking – a habit doubtless worsened by the tensions of living with his wife – have come back to haunt him.

It seems unjust, somehow, that her father should be the one to pay the price of such compromise, especially when her mother is the one to bottle up her feelings. Though then again, her father must have stifled his emotions, too, in order to remain married. Nonetheless, more than once of late Lou has wished they could swap places, that her mother could be the one who was ill; then she has pushed the thoughts to the back of her mind, feeling terrible.

'You always seem to rub each other up the wrong way,' continues her father.

Lou nods. 'I know.'

He takes a deep breath, reaches for her with his one free hand. She places her palm in his. He is colder than usual.

'You may not think so, but she does love you, you know.'

Again Lou is surprised. She has never believed her mother loves her, fully, but she didn't think her father guessed how she felt. It has always seemed to Lou as if there were conditions attached to her mother's affection: conditions she has no idea how to satisfy.

'There are lots of things about you, though, that she'll never understand.'

You're telling me, thinks Lou. But she says nothing.

'You appreciate what I'm talking about.' He looks at her directly. His eyes are watery and bloodshot, but behind the sickness there is recognition. Immediately, she knows that he knows. How long has he been aware? She is twenty-three and out to her friends, but she has never told him. She hasn't wanted to put him in that position: to force him to lie to his wife. She is sure her mother couldn't handle it. She couldn't handle an erotic chapter in a literary novel Lou's sister recently lent her, for instance – it incensed her so much she never picked up the book again. She is that not comfortable talking about sex.

'I just wanted to say to you, it's best not to tell her.' His eyes are pleading. 'I know it's tough for you, I really do. But it would kill her.'

Lou nods. She is hot, emotions all over the place: anger, grief, relief her father is aware of the truth.

'But I want you to know that I know, and whatever you choose to do, is all right by me.'

Lou gulps.

'I can't pretend to understand, and it's not my way, but honestly, what you do in your bedroom is totally down to you. The main thing I want is for my Loulou to be happy.'

'Oh, Dad.' Lou starts to weep. 'Thank you.'

'Don't cry now.' He pats her hand. 'It'll be all right.'

'Really?'

'Yes,' he smiles. 'Somewhere out there, there's someone for everyone, I'm sure.'

She smiles back at him. Of course, it is not the prospect of being single that has made her cry; it is losing him.

'That's all I wanted to say,' he says, gesturing her to go. 'I'm tired now. I'm going to go to sleep.' He closes his eyes.

She rises to her feet, quietly leaves the room.

Within twenty-four hours, her father has passed away.

14.05

'Gosh, a lady undertaker,' says Phyllis, looking up at the sign above the window.

FUNERAL DIRECTOR
BARBARA REED AND SONS

'Yes,' says Karen. 'Frankly, they are the nearest, but I've passed here a few times, and thought they look OK. I've often wondered what goes on behind those curtains, but I never thought I would find out.'

The window display, in front of net curtains, is a bizarre assortment. The centrepiece is a large mottled grey marble cross, sombre, ugly. On either side are two matching floral arrangements – Karen has noticed they change them regularly, and this week lilies, ivy and palms burst forth from two giant urn-shaped vases. They are more life-affirming, but nonetheless, so far, so traditional. What made Karen decide to use this particular undertaker is the remainder of the display. Because scattered all around are shells of every shape and size, pebbles smoothed by the sea and giant starfish. And last but certainly not least, on each side of the vases – clearly symmetry is important – there are two miniature replicas: on the left, the Brighton Pavilion, in all its mad baroque glory, and on the right, the Palace Pier, complete with fairground attractions and flashing lights. The overall effect is utterly daft, but better that than grim.

'Ooh, are we going in *here*?' asks Luke. He and Molly have stood noses pressed to glass many times.

'Yes,' says Karen, and pushes open the door. A bell tinkles, and they are in a world of pink pastel chintz and polished mahogany – kitsch is clearly not confined to the exterior. Every table has a doily-like cloth; every chair a lace antimacassar. Even the light shades are frilly, like Victorian bloomers.

'Ah, Mrs Finnegan.' A woman in apricot blouse and tight black pencil skirt steps forward to greet them. She is tanned, plump and with hair dyed too bright a red for her age, so the overall effect is part pumpkin, part tomato, but it is not entirely unattractive – her face is warm, smiley, and Karen is grateful that she is not ghoulish.

'Yes,' says Karen.

'I'm Barbara Reed, the Funeral Director. I spoke to your brother-in-law late yesterday.' Alan had got in touch the night before, just before they closed. 'He dropped off the clothes for your husband first thing this morning.'

'Call me Karen,' she says, shaking her hand. 'And this is Phyllis Finnegan, my mother-in-law.'

'Hello,' says Barbara. 'I am very sorry for your loss.'

'Thank you,' says Phyllis. She is extremely close to tears.

'So these must be the children?' Barbara smiles at them. 'What are your names?'

'Luke,' says Luke.

Molly doesn't say anything; instead she edges herself behind the fullness of Karen's skirt, and puts her thumb in her mouth.

'Sorry, this is Molly. She's a bit shy sometimes,' apologizes Karen. 'You can say hello, Molly.'

'That's all right,' says Barbara. 'I'm sure it's all a bit overwhelming.'

'Can I go and look at the Pier?' asks Luke.

'Of course,' says Barbara. 'Would you like me to pull back the curtain so you can see it better?'

'Yes, please.'

'Don't touch anything, though,' Karen warns him.

Whilst he is distracted, Barbara continues, 'Your husband's body arrived here a couple of hours ago.'

'Right.'

'And I've arranged it so he's in one of our chapels for you.'

'Thank you.'

'At some point we do need to discuss the arrangements for the service, but perhaps now is not the time.'

'I'd prefer it if the children weren't around.'

'Sure. So,' – Barbara glances at each of them in turn, and leans round Karen's skirt to catch Molly's eye – 'I gather you've come to see your Daddy.'

'Yes,' says Luke, stepping away from the Pier. 'We've brought him a drawing.'

'May I see?' asks Barbara.

Karen reaches into her bag and gives Luke his drawing. He brandishes it proudly.

'That's fantastic!' says Barbara. 'Is that you?'

'Yes. That's me, and that's Mummy, and that's Daddy, and that's Molly.'

'I can see that,' says Barbara. She turns to Karen. 'He's very good.'

Karen smiles. Barbara's not the first to notice it: Luke has inherited his father's talent. What's particularly endearing is that he seems to have a design bent too; his drawings are painstakingly detailed, he fixates on pattern and line. She recognizes exactly which top he has drawn her in, for instance, by its tiny purple flowers, and he has put patches on the knees of Simon's jeans, just like in reality.

'Have you done one too?' Barbara asks Molly.

Molly emerges from behind Karen's skirt. Karen hands her the other sheet of paper so she can hold it up herself. 'It's Toby,' Molly explains.

'Toby is our kitten,' adds Karen. In contrast to Luke's, the roundy-roundy scribble does need clarifying.

'That's splendid,' says Barbara. 'I'm sure your Daddy will love them. So, are you ready?' She turns to Karen. 'You have told them a bit of what to expect?'

'Yes,' says Karen.

'Right then, follow me.'

And she leads the way through a door and into the chapel.

The casket is at the front, on a bier. From where they are standing they can't yet see inside.

'I'm frightened,' says Luke. He's been so fearless until now that Karen is taken by surprise. Nonetheless she knows what to do. 'Would you like me to carry you?'

'Yes,' nods Luke.

Karen puts down her bags, and scoops him into her arms.

'I'm scared as well,' says Molly.

'Would you like me to carry you?' offers Phyllis.

'Yes,' says Molly, so Phyllis picks her up.

Together the four of them approach the casket. Karen thinks she knows what to expect, yet the combination of floral arrangements and chemicals – presumably embalming fluids – is sickly sweet, cloying. Combined with her anxiety on behalf of the children, the smell is overwhelming, and she has a violent surge of nausea. She swallows to overcome it: she needs to be strong.

Simon is lying on cream silk-satin, and his face looks greyer than it did before. There's no sign of the post-mortem at all, yet it is as if the real Simon is further removed from his body, somehow. Though it's odd, as he still looks like her Simon too. God, how she wishes he could speak! He is wearing the suit, white shirt and tie that she, Phyllis and Alan picked out the night before. It makes him appear very sober and formal; not a look she is used to. The first thing he would do when he got home from work would be to undo his top shirt button and loosen his tie – he couldn't bear to be constricted. She imagines him longing to do it right now.

Karen had considered dropping off a different outfit this morning, instead, but what would she have brought? The suit that she, Phyllis and Alan opted for is very respectable, and they chose it together, and though personally she always liked him better in casual clothes, the idea of him being buried in a big chunky jumper or sweatshirt just doesn't seem right. Anyway, she has his dressing gown now: something of the less formal Simon.

Next to her, Phyllis gasps, unable to conceal her upset.

This must be awful for her, thinks Karen. She hoists Luke onto her hip so she can hold him up with just one arm, and reaches over to give Phyllis's shoulder a squeeze.

The four of them remain there a moment in silence, taking it in.

'Can I touch him?' asks Luke.

Karen looks at Phyllis for advice; she nods.

'OK. Why don't you just stroke his cheek?'

She edges forward so Luke can lean over the casket.

'Does he feel cold?' asks Karen.

'Yes. Why?'

'That's because the blood has stopped flowing through Daddy's body. You know like when you cut yourself and blood comes out? That's because your heart is pumping it round. Right along your arms here' – Karen strokes along his arms, down to the ends of his fingers – 'to here . . . and all the way back. And all the way down your legs' – she strokes down to the top of his shoes – 'and back. But Daddy's heart stopped working, so it stopped pumping blood and that's why Daddy feels cold.'

'Can I feel him?' asks Molly.

'Of course you can,' says Phyllis. Molly reaches over and touches Simon's cheek too, tiny plump fingers meeting older male skin.

'So is Daddy dead, then?' asks Luke.

'Yes. This is just your Daddy's body. Daddy is up in

heaven now.' She endeavours to be as straight as she can. Surely wishy-washy answers will only confuse and upset them both?

'But how did he get up there if he's here?'

Karen tries to make it simple. 'His body is here, but his spirit is up there.' She takes a deep breath. 'So ... would you like to put your pictures in Daddy's special box?'

They nod – each is still clutching their drawing.

'OK. So why don't we put them in here?' she suggests, taking Luke's and tucking it just under the casket lid to secure it. She takes Molly's, and does the same with that. 'Now, would you like to get your toys so they can say goodbye? They're in the big shopping bag by the door if you can manage it, Luke.'

Luke gets down and fetches it. Karen takes Blue Crocodile and hands him to her son.

Luke chews his lip, hesitant.

'Me!' Molly reaches out for Princess Aurora.

Karen passes her daughter the doll. 'Why don't you lean over with Aurora here, so she can give Daddy a little kiss? Daddy likes kisses, you know that.' Karen knows she's mixing up the notion of Simon's body and spirit being separate, but she is making it up as she goes along; nothing has prepared her for this.

Phyllis edges the two of them near. Solemnly Molly taps Aurora against Simon's cheek, accompanying the gesture with a kiss from her own mouth.

'What about letting Blue Crocodile kiss his other cheek now, Luke?'

Karen gently guides Luke by the shoulder to the coffin. He is still tentative, but loath to be seen as hesitant compared to his younger sister, so follows suit.

'Now, let's give Daddy his dressing gown,' she says, pulling it from the bag. 'I think we'll just put it here for the moment, round him, like this.' She wraps the dressing gown loosely over Simon, tucks it around the suit. It might not be appropriate for it to stay like that, but she'll discuss it with Barbara separately.

'Will he be cosy?' asks Molly.

Karen nods. 'Yes, honey. Look, Daddy's lovely and snug.' Her voice cracks. Memories of Simon come rushing in . . . Countless mornings of him pulling on his dressing gown when he went to make the tea; weekends when he'd stand in the kitchen cooking breakfast in it; nights when he'd yank it on hurriedly because he'd heard one of the children crying and wanted to check.

If the drawings are the children's gift, here, today, the dressing gown is hers, surely. It seems so little to give him in some ways, so significant, so intimate in others. Certainly it's at odds with his surroundings: the shiny satin of the coffin interior, the respectable grey wool of his work suit. She's not even had the chance to wash it, either. That's a shame.

'Karen?' Phyllis interrupts her thoughts.

'Oh, sorry, yes.' Karen lets out a breath, slowly, and struggles to concentrate on the present. 'So, children, is there anything more you would like to say?' Both of them look at a loss, so she prompts: 'Would you like to say goodbye?'

'Goodbye,' they say in unison.

Again Karen's heart lurches. It's a lot for them to deal with.

'I tell you what,' she says. She is finding it unbearable herself. 'I think Granny might like a little while with Daddy on her own. So why don't we go back home, and maybe she can meet us there?'

She looks at Phyllis to check if this is in fact what she would like.

Phyllis, who is still hugging Molly, is weeping noiselessly into her granddaughter's blonde curls. She nods quickly.

'We'll see you back at the house, then. I'm sure Barbara can get you a cab, if that's OK.'

A few minutes later, Karen is clipping Luke into his car seat.

'Mummy?' he says.

'Yes?'

'Are you going to die too?'

So many questions! Still, it helps to focus on their needs, not her own. She pauses to consider and then tells him, 'Everything and everybody that lives will die some day, sweetheart. But most people can expect to live much longer than your Daddy. What happened to him was very, very sad because Daddy was still very young – he was fifty-one years old – and we didn't know he was ill, so it has been a great big shock to us all. But most people live until they are seventy or eighty, so it is very, very unlikely that I will die for years and years and years. I promise.' She thinks of how she can back this up. 'I'm younger than Daddy, remember?'

'How old are you?'

'I'm only forty-two. So you'll be *very* big and grown up by the time I am eighty.'

'What about Granny?'

This is more awkward. Nonetheless, 'I don't think she was planning on dying right now.'

'Good.' Luke frowns. 'So why *did* Daddy die?'

Jesus, thinks Karen, if only I knew.

21:33

The children are asleep. Phyllis has gone. It is just Karen and Anna, a glass of red wine apiece, sharing the sofa, end to end, just as they have shared sofas for over twenty years.

Sitting here in Karen's home makes Anna remember: the house purchase. They still haven't finalized what to do about it, but she's worried it's even more for Karen to consider, so broaches the subject with caution.

'Let me get something straight, honey,' she says. 'We've put the place in Hove on hold for the moment, but you hadn't signed the actual contracts yet?'

A pause, and then Karen says, 'That's what we were going to do yesterday morning.'

'I see.' Anna exhales. The next question is tough. 'I was wondering . . . Do you still want to go ahead?'

'I had been thinking about that.' Karen frowns. Anna can feel her trying to assimilate. Big house, on the outskirts of Hove: large mortgage. Versus smaller house – but not that small – nearer to Brighton station: manageable – or at least not totally unmanageable – mortgage. The answer is clear, really – even if Simon did have life assurance, Karen may find it hard to afford it alone. But she is still in such shock it takes her longer than usual to make the connections. 'I guess not,' she says.

'No.' Anna shakes her head, feeling Karen's grief at this second, more minor, loss so soon after the first. She knows one of the big appeals of the new house to Karen was the outside space; like many houses in central Brighton, their patio is tiny. She had wanted somewhere for the children to play and the chance to grow flowers and vegetables. Simon loved plants, planning; he had wanted a bigger garden too, and the house in Hove has a glorious hundred-foot one at the back. Saying goodbye to this would be tough under any circumstance. But truly, moving now isn't practical. She's got far too much to deal with – there is no way she could take on the stress. The house she is in at the moment is fine, all things considered.

Again, silence, save for the gentle swoosh of the gas fire in the grate. The kitten is stretched out on the hearth, basking in its warmth.

Eventually: 'One of the main reasons we were buying that house was so Simon could have an office and work from home and stop that beastly commute.' Karen snorts, derisive. 'How ironic is that?'

Anna sighs. 'I know.' She and Karen had spent ages weighing up the pros and cons of Simon setting up his own landscape architectural practice. Karen had had one or two misgivings – 'It's hardly a good time, the economy the way it is, and he might drive me nuts around the house all day' – but overall was keen for him to be able to spend more time with her and the children. 'He's an old Dad, Anna, with two little ones, but he hardly ever gets to see them. He wastes twenty hours a week on those damn trains.'

Ironic, indeed.

Anna reaches over, gives Karen's hand a squeeze. Her heart contracts with the gesture. She so feels for Karen it is as if they are one being at this moment, sharing legs but with separate heads, like the Pushmi-Pullyu in *Doctor Dolittle*.

And as they sit, in silence, nursing their glasses, Anna thinks of Steve. What would she do without him? How would she cope? She imagines her bed, empty of his presence, a life devoid of sexual intimacy. What would it be like never to chat to him, laugh with him, share jokes and tease him again? She shudders. She is *so* glad he is alive.

Then, fleetingly, perversely, she wonders if it might have caused less pain if it *had* been Steve who'd died. It would be awful, yes, but primarily for her, whereas Simon's death has impacted on so very many people. Certainly Steve would be missed; he has parents in New Zealand who love him, sisters, friends too. And she, of course, adores him, doesn't she? Or she wouldn't endure the behaviour he puts her through. But they've been together far less time than Karen and Simon; they are less rooted. She had a life before she met him – her home, friends, work; she could resume it all without such trauma.

But for two decades Karen and Simon's lives have been intertwined; she has been able to depend on him, and vice versa; her identity is bound to his. He has fulfilled so many roles for her: he has not just been her lover, friend and confidant; he's been her holiday companion, finance manager, handyman, gardener, playmate, car mechanic, sometime supermarket shopper . . . the list is endless. He's been like the RSJ that holds up the living-come-dining room she and Karen are sitting in at that very moment.

And Karen is not the only one bereft. There is Phyllis, and Alan too. Simon's work colleagues and friends. And there are Molly and Luke, who will never see their father again.

Anna thinks of her own father, now in his early seventies. She has had over forty years with him, and for the first twenty his role in her life was central. Her head is chockfull of memories – the Easter egg hunts he arranged for her and her brothers, the doll's house he built for her, the arguments over which subjects she should study, the outfits he preferred her not to wear, the boyfriends he resented. Molly and Luke will have none of this.

Karen breaks the quiet. 'It was my fault,' she says, for the third time that evening. 'I should have known.'

'Dearest friend, you're not Mystic Meg,' says Anna, attempting to make her smile. It works, though all too briefly. 'You did not know. I did not know. Phyllis did not know. Simon did not know. Even Simon's bloody doctor did not know.'

'But I'm his *wife!*' Karen protests, as if berating herself more means that Anna, at last, will accept she *is* to blame.

'Of course, of course.' Anna picks at a loose thread on one of the cushions, struggling to find words of comfort. She knows guilt is inevitable – hasn't she felt it herself? Yet she wishes she could ease the torture of wrestling with it.

'I should have given him the kiss of life,' says Karen. 'I was in such a fluster . . .'

'I wouldn't know how. Do you?'

'No, not really . . . Though I should do. Anyway, I could have given it a go.'

'So could anyone else in the carriage,' Anna points out. 'But they didn't. And anyway, from what I gather it was seconds – a minute or two at most – afterwards that those nurses arrived.' At once, this makes her think of Lou. She's not told Karen about their encounter in the taxi; yesterday she'd feared it would cause more distress. But she's useless at secrets, as is Karen – or at least in terms of their friendship they're useless – frankness and confession being the dynamic that's evolved over the years. The last thing Anna wants now is the distance caused by unspoken truths.

So she says, carefully, 'I didn't tell you something yesterday. When the train stopped at Wivelsfield, I shared a taxi up to London with this woman.'

'Ah, right.' Karen looks uninterested, as if Anna is trying to distract her with irrelevancies, and it won't succeed.

Anna plunges straight to it. 'She was sitting next to you and Simon. Across the aisle.'

'Oh.' Karen pales. Then she says, 'That must have been awful for her.'

Typical Karen: thinking of others and putting them first. 'That's not why I was telling you. She – Lou – was lovely, really lovely. You might remember her – short brown hair, parka, sort of pointy face, not that tall, slim.'

Karen shakes her head. 'I don't think so.'

Anna realizes this is a foolish thing to have said; of course Karen is unlikely to remember her. Anyway, this is not the point Anna wishes to make. 'Lou told me in the taxi, before

I knew it was Simon, what happened,' she continues gently, not sure how Karen will react. 'I can't remember every word she said, obviously, and she didn't go into every tiny detail, but nonetheless I do remember her saying there was absolutely nothing that she, you, or anyone, could have done.'

'Oh,' says Karen, gradually assimilating. 'Maybe you're right . . .' she concludes eventually.

But Anna can tell that she is not convinced.

*　*　*

Gently, Karen closes the front door behind Anna. Now her friend has gone, she is without company for the first time that day. Anna had offered to stay, but Karen knew this would inconvenience her. Sharing a house for several years during and after college means Karen knows Anna's likes and dislikes almost as well as she knows her own. Anna likes to look good, and she would miss the comforts of her own toiletries and clothes, not to mention bed. And Steve. So Karen has shooed her off home at a reasonable hour.

She returns to the living room. The real-flame-effect gas fire burns in the grate; it reminds her of Simon. Impressed by the fireplace at Anna's house on Charminster Street, he had opened up the chimney breast and installed it himself, choosing a clean, simple, square surround with pebbles in a polished chrome metal basket. As flames lick rounded shades of pale grey, they make Karen want a cigarette. She locates a packet in her bag on the coffee table – she is not a heavy smoker, at all. She only ever indulges in one or two when she's out without the children, which is very rarely these days, or when she's exceptionally stressed. Simplest is to lean past Toby, who still slumbers, free from any anxieties, and light it from the fire, though it chars the white paper doing so.

She opens the window, inhales deeply, allowing the smoke to fill her lungs. Who gives a damn if it's bad for her? Normally she suppresses the knowledge that her habit is lethal, but tonight she positively relishes it. She feels the poison curling its way round the alveoli, get drawn into the bloodstream and hit the receptors of her brain. She senses it bringing her closer to death, to Simon . . .

All at once, Karen feels wobbly. Maybe it's the nicotine; more likely it's because she's alone. It's as if she is a rag doll who's been propped up by those around her – Molly, Luke, Phyllis, Anna – and now there is nothing to support her. Her legs are merely soft cream canvas filled with stuffing, her feet useless rounded ends of black felt, and stitched seams at the hips and knees mean that she cannot remain upright on her own. She sits down on the sofa before she falls.

What Karen wants to do – needs to do – is cry, but she can't. For some reason the tears come when she is with others, as if then has she permission to weep. But here, alone, when she could howl, beat the sofa cushions, scream; now, somehow, she is unable. It is not even because she is worried about waking the children. It's for fear that if she gives in to it, she'll lose all sense of who she is. She is afraid that if she falls apart in private, then she'll fall apart completely, and won't be able to look after Molly and Luke, or organize a funeral, or care for Phyllis, or anyone else. That if she crumbles, like a house in an earthquake, she will disappear down some deep, dark crevasse, and never be able to pull herself out and put herself back together again.

* * *

The door is double-locked when Anna gets back: Steve is not home. Moreover, he has not told her where he's going, which means she knows exactly where he is. The pub. Probably the one down the road – not that it makes much difference. Odds are, this means trouble. If she is lucky she'll get away with it – if he's drunk enough to be near comatose when he returns, he'll crash out on the sofa, snoring, fully clothed. More worrying is if he has drunk marginally less; then he'll be lairy, energized, wanting to talk.

She is just unclipping her bra when the door slams. She pauses mid action, waiting to hear where he goes. Thump. Pause. Thump. Pause. Thump. Here he comes, up the stairs, footsteps so much heavier, more cumbersome than when he is sober.

Rapidly, she pulls on her nightdress – she is vulnerable enough, without being naked too.

Within moments he has flung open the bedroom door; the brass handle bangs against the wall, where there is already a dent in the plaster. Such force is unnecessary, but bevvied up, Steve can't gauge his own strength.

He won't start off angry, Anna knows that. She has been through this before; she has learnt the pattern. The descent is usually rapid, and there's something so much worse about the fact she can feel it coming.

She is braced, every sinew in her arms rigid, legs taut;

even her stomach muscles are tense. She knows what's on its way: verbal abuse, fierce, vitriolic, self-righteous. Then again, maybe, for once, she'll be lucky. Hasn't she been through enough today? Doesn't God, Steve, Fate, whoever, owe her this small favour? She's drawn on so many emotional resources already with Karen. She hasn't the strength for another ordeal. Maybe, just maybe, Steve will appreciate this.

Tentatively, persuasively, hoping to appeal to his better, sober, nature, she ventures, 'I just got back from seeing Karen.' She thinks the mention of her friend might jolt his memory and understanding.

'Ah . . . right.' Clearly he had forgotten. His visage clouds. It is astonishing how Steve's features transform when he is intoxicated. Gone are the handsome proportions, the heroic cheekbones, the sensual yet masculine mouth, the kind, thoughtful eyes. Instead, his face seems soft, unformed, his lips full and blubbery, his eyes unfocused, misty, small. His body too, is different; his stance is less upright, his paunch more noticeable, his shoulders hunched.

He sits down on the bed, leaden, clumsy. But then he surprises her. Instead of inconsequential burble, followed by recriminations, accusations, criticism, he is quiet. His mouth is a cartoon of upset, an upside-down semicircle. Then his eyes spring giant drops. He is crying.

Anna is surprised, touched, and more than a little relieved. She sits down next to him. 'What's the matter?'

He wipes away the tears with the back of his fist, toddler-like. 'I'm useless,' he shrugs.

'No, you're not!' she insists, indignant. However much she

hates his excess drinking, she knows it stems from self-loathing.

'I am,' he retorts. 'Look at me!' He lifts his hands up, turns them this way then that, despairing. 'Covered in paint. What am I? Just a bloody decorator.'

'You're a very good one,' she says, and it's true. Steve is a perfectionist. Yet he's also a fast worker, a rare combination. Clients often ask him back and frequently recommend him to friends.

'Yes, but . . . not a career, is it?' Though addled with booze, he is strangely coherent, and, actually, right. His job doesn't bother Anna – she is not the type of woman who likes to bask in the reflected glory of a successful man. But that is not the point. What matters is that he is not fulfilled by what he is doing; he considers himself too bright, worth more. 'Simon had a career,' he adds, his voice mournful.

He starts crying again, and although she has seen him weep before, Anna can't get over how disconcerting it is to see a grown man shed tears. Then, finally, out it comes, the thought that's troubling him through the fog of beer and spirits. He bangs his head with his fist. Hard. It must hurt. 'It should have been me.'

'Sorry?' This is unexpected.

'Me. ME!' He thumps his chest, now furious. 'It should have been me who died.'

'Hey, hey, hey . . .' Anna placates him, puts an arm around his shoulders. 'Don't be silly.'

'That's what you all want, isn't it?' He throws off her arm. The anger is mounting and turning outward; the direction Anna dreads.

'What do you mean – what we all want?' Though as she says it, she knows this is the wrong tack. Not that there is a right one.

'You'd rather it had been me. You. Karen.' He turns to her, eyes cold and narrowed, full of hatred.

'No, we wouldn't!' This is ridiculous, and not a conversation she wants to have, particularly at this moment. It's even more unnerving because his observation is accurate: he's picked up on her own thoughts, earlier, and she's filled with remorse for having contemplated such a thing, however briefly. But for Steve to pursue this tack is not constructive. It's certainly not helping her – or him, come to that – feel better. This is what she can never get her head around: whatever is eating away at him, it is only made worse by alcohol; heightened rather than eased or numbed.

'You'd rather I was dead.'

'Stevie Babe.' Anna's voice is firm; she uses her nickname for him to further placate. 'We would not. You're being ridiculous.'

Then, curiously, as if God, or Fate, or whoever, has – belatedly – heard her plea, he seems to listen, to reflect. 'Am I?'

'Yes,' she whispers.

'Oh.'

'I love you, babe.'

'I love you too.' And with that he propels himself – almost gracefully – lengthways onto the mattress. Within seconds he's flaked out, snoring.

Tenderly, Anna pulls off his shoes, undoes his belt, eases his jeans down his legs. He rolls over, murmuring but not waking, as she pulls the duvet out from under him, then tucks him beneath. He's still in his underpants, shirt and socks, but no matter.

Relieved, she sits back on her haunches.

In slumber, the warm arc of light from the bedside lamp casts Steve's features differently again. The curl of his lips seems sweet and guileless; his eyelashes brush his cheeks angelically; she can see the glistening trail of tears on his cheek, like a small child who's fallen asleep exhausted by his own outburst. Now she can see the boy that predated the man, when his rebellious spirit was innocent and playful, not damaging and self-destructive. She wonders when the balance shifted; when, like a see-saw, he tipped from merely being a naughty youngster – for she knows he was; he has told her – and became first troublesome, then troubled, and then turned to drink.

Nonetheless, she can smell the alcohol on him. It is not just on his breath; it emanates from every pore. It is vodka, she knows. Whoever said vodka was odourless, was wrong. It smells acrid, deadly, is redolent of clandestine binges and lies. She loathes it. It repulses her. She appreciates she likes a drink too; she shared a much-needed bottle with Karen earlier, for example. But Steve's consumption is in a different league; she can stop when he can't, because for him it serves a different purpose. Sometimes she wonders if it is obliteration not just of circumstance he is after, but of his whole personality.

Had she known this when she met him, would he be here now? She is unsure. It is like being tugged in half by two separate Steves. The seductive, capable, charming Steve –

the sober Steve: and the hostile, resentful, offensive Steve
– the drunken Steve, the addict. So she feels torn, beholden
to him on the one hand, fearful of change on the other. She
worries about what would happen if she were to finish it;
and not just to him, but to her. He might go off the rails:
she doesn't want to be alone. She's over forty; someone said
a colleague was 'past her sell-by date' only today at the office,
and Anna is a few years older. And she does love Steve; she
even still fancies him. Irrationally, the chemistry between
Anna and the sober Steve is electric. She loves the smell of
that Steve, too. It turns her on, Steve's natural scent: primal,
delicious, other.

She smiles to herself, remembering.

*

'Come and meet our painter,' Karen says one afternoon when
Anna pops round on the off-chance she is in. 'I got his
number from a woman in my post-natal class.' She winks
knowingly, and as she leads the way upstairs, mouths so he
doesn't overhear, 'He's gorgeous.'

Steve is standing at the window.

Painty cut-off jeans, big painty canvas trainers, painty T-
shirt, painty arms, painty sun-bleached hair. He turns as they
enter the room, brush of white emulsion poised.

'Steven, this is my friend, Anna,' Karen says.

'Hello,' he grins. 'Nice to meet you.' His voice is deep and
attractive with an Antipodean twang; Anna wonders if he is
Australian. Later she learns he is from a well-off family in
New Zealand. 'So you're posh,' she had observed. 'You mean

for a painter,' he had said, and yes, in all honesty, she probably did mean that. Compared to decorators she has met in
the past, he is distinctly well-to-do.

With hindsight she might have questioned why a man
with relative social advantages ended up just doing odd
jobs. But her initial take is just to note that he looks a
few years younger than her and Karen, and assume he is
still finding his feet, career-wise. She wonders if he is a
writer or something artistic, decorating to earn extra cash.
There are lots of creative people in Brighton; it wouldn't
be unusual.

'Anna's got loads of work she needs doing,' says Karen.

Have I? thinks Anna. She's just moved into her new house,
true, but she'd been planning on doing it herself. 'Ah, yes,'
she says, cottoning on. 'Perhaps you could come round and
give me a quote.'

'I'd love to,' he grins again, eyes full of mischief. Then he
holds her gaze a second too long. Anna's stomach lurches
with excitement – the attraction is clearly mutual.

It is that simple. A quote leads to a drink that same
evening – when, revealingly, he does *not* get drunk; obviously he is incredibly keen to impress her – which leads to
a late-night dinner when she hardly eats anything because
she is relishing their conversation; which leads to a night of
'non-stop shagging'.

Or that's how Karen puts it the next day.

'It wasn't like that,' Anna protests.

'Pardon me,' Karen teases. 'Making love.'

'Ooh, no, not that either.' Anna cringes. After just one
encounter this sounds too serious, embarrassing.

Soon, however, they are making love, and within a few weeks he's moved in with her.

*

Ah well, Anna thinks, edging under the duvet alongside him. Good times, bad times – aren't all relationships like that? She is too tired to contemplate any further. Minutes later she, too, is asleep, more soundly than the night before, just plain worn out by emotion.

Wednesday

07:37

Lou is just locking up her bicycle when her phone bleeps, once, then again. She rummages in her rucksack and flips open the top.

You have 2 messages, it says.

One is from Vic, the second from a number she does not recognize, so she opens Vic's first.

You're on, she reads. *I've lured the wench to Brighton for you. Friday night out on the tiles, celebrate my birthday a bit early, crash at yours. Just promise you won't do it with me in earshot. You owe me. Big style. V x*

Lou laughs to herself. Vic is straight to the point as ever, and it hardly sounds as if she is intent on staying sober. But she does have a point about the smallness of the venue: Lou can hardly put her oldest friend in the bathroom to sleep. Never mind; that's detail at this stage – she might not even fancy this woman, or vice versa. Nonetheless, the prospect of meeting her is exciting. Now she will invite Howie, too – it could be a really good evening. Lou slings her rucksack over her shoulder and makes her way rapidly across the station concourse, a decided spring in her step, reading the second message as she goes.

Hope this reaches you, it says. *It's Anna here. You on the*

7.44 today? I'm middle carriage, just past the clock. Can give you that tenner.

Lou is pleased. She has been thinking about Anna, and Karen, her friend, and, buoyed by news of Sofia, feels like a chat. She hits the green phone symbol and soon hears ringing.

'Just coming up the platform now,' she says.

'I'll try to save you a seat.'

Seconds later Anna is rapping on the window to get her attention; shortly after that Lou is settled next to her in the aisle chair, rucksack on the shelf overhead, mobile and iPod on the table.

Lou turns to her. 'So how are you?' Anna appears tired, she observes, and her hair is less immaculate than it was forty-eight hours ago. It is not surprising.

'I'm all right, I guess. Anyway, before I forget, that money.'

'Don't worry about that.' Lou brushes the air to indicate it's OK.

'No, really, I want to.' Anna opens her purse – Lou notices it's quality leather with a chunky brass zip – pulls out a battered note and puts it on the table in front of Lou.

'Thank you.' Lou can tell there is no point arguing. She is grateful, not for the cash, but because it has provided an excuse for contact again. Lou likes the idea of having a travelling companion from time to time, and Anna has broken with custom – the unspoken law of commuters is to stick to companionable privacy. The train is not the normal place to get acquainted. 'How's, um, Karen, she's called, isn't she, your friend?'

'Crap,' says Anna.

Lou nods: few other words will do in the circumstance.

Anna sighs. 'I guess she's in shock. But it's such a bloody mess.' She looks out of the window. Lou can see she is holding back tears.

'Had she and her husband been together long?' Lou doesn't want to seem nosy, but it is not her way to be coolly polite.

'Nearly twenty years.'

'So you must have known him well too, then.'

Anna nods and reaches into her bag for a tissue. She dabs the corner of her eyes.

'I'm so sorry,' says Lou.

'Thank you.' Anna tries to smile.

'It's, well, such a horrible thing to have happened to anyone.'

'They've got two children,' Anna blurts. It's this that opens the wound: she croaks and the tears fall freely.

'Oh, Lord,' Lou winces. For some reason she'd not second-guessed this, though with hindsight it was likely. 'How old are they?'

'Molly's three. Luke's five. I'm their godmother,' Anna adds.

Lou feels for her, for them all. She reaches over and puts an arm around Anna's shoulder. Even though she hardly knows her, it seems appropriate, and badly needed. Anna shifts forward to allow her to do so. The people opposite are vaguely watching, but one has earphones on, so can't hear; the other is tip-tapping his laptop, and doesn't seem that interested. Outside the window the Sussex landscape lays itself before them: green fields, rolling Downs, postcard-perfect.

'I guess they all really need you right now,' observes Lou. 'Have you got someone to look after you?'

'Yes . . .' Anna nods. 'I guess.'

Again Lou has the impression Anna's home life has complications: her reaction is not that of someone with a hundred-per-cent-responsive partner. Lou is quick to recognize the signs and has been there herself in a different guise; her mother is far from supportive of her. But now is not the time to probe too deep.

'I'm sorry,' sniffs Anna, relaxing a little.

Lou removes her arm. 'Please don't be sorry. As you say, it's crap.'

Anna continues, 'It's just Karen feels so guilty.'

'Oh, dear.'

'She thinks she should have done more to help. That she could have saved Simon. She believes if she'd given him the kiss of life at once, he would have survived – that sort of thing. I keep telling her it wouldn't have made any difference, but she won't listen.'

Lou frowns. 'There was nothing she could have done, I'm sure. I saw: he died immediately.'

'I know, that's what I keep telling her. But you know what it's like. You always think "if only . . ." And Karen's especially like that. Often taking on other people's problems. Feeling responsible for the world.'

'She sounds a good person,' observes Lou.

'She's lovely.'

'But I guess all that guilt is not very helpful now.'

'No.'

'Though it's very common.'

'Is it?'

'Oh, yes.'

'I don't know that much about grief,' admits Anna.

Lou makes herself clear. 'I've not lost someone suddenly like your friend has. But my Dad died several years ago.'

'I'm sorry.'

'Don't worry, it was a long time back. And, well, since then, I've explored it a bit through my work, too.'

'So what do you do, exactly?'

'I'm a counsellor. I work with kids who have been excluded from school.'

'How interesting. Tell me more.'

So Lou does just that. Anna is clearly grateful to have a shift of focus.

* * *

The children are at Tracy's. Karen doesn't want them to overhear the ins and outs of funeral arrangements, or every phone call she must make to friends, colleagues and family. Moreover, she is trying to maintain some sense, however fragile, of normality for Molly and Luke through this, and Tracy, with her long-standing relationship with both children, seems a good person for them to be with.

So the half of Karen's mind that was functioning normally put the children in the back of the car, did up the seat belts and drove them at a careful thirty miles an hour to Portslade. They were there, as arranged, at nine o'clock exactly. Karen then drove herself back, locked the car and put the kettle on. It is coming to the boil any second.

Yet Karen is aware of a dichotomy, as if her head has split into two. One side is able to walk, talk, make tea and, yes, drive Molly and Luke to Tracy's. It is this side that has put on respectable clothes and combed her hair. It is this same side that is seeing to everything that needs seeing to: talking to a vicar she's never met and emailing people she doesn't know, using the address book in Outlook Express on Simon's laptop. Karen recognizes this half of herself – it is the effective administrator for the council, the organized mother who is hardly ever late for Tracy or for Luke's school, the woman who goes round the supermarket in Hove with the children in a double-seated trolley and a list.

But the other half of Karen isn't functioning properly at all, or that's how it feels. This half is a manic tangle, like one of Molly's drawings: pens and colours everywhere, directionless, knotted. But whereas her daughter's pictures are exuberant expressions of fun and life and happiness – or so Karen has always fondly thought – this is a dark, sinister hell of a place, all deep blues, reds, purples and black. It is a crazed muddle of emotions: there is the feeling she can't shake, that she was responsible, of guilt turning in on itself, impossible to unravel. There is the sense of loss whose force she fears she has yet to feel fully – a gigantic, overwhelming sense of sorrow and gloom. Then, in the very centre of the snarl-up, there's the bright red of searing pain, excruciating, burning, unrelenting, as if her skull has been sawn off and acid is being poured directly inside, onto the nerves of her grey matter.

Karen tries to keep this hellish half of herself away: to squash and bury these thoughts, beat them into submission.

She would rather organize, focus. She succeeds surprisingly well for long periods of time.

She supposes she must be in shock, that she is able to suppress her emotions like this. She has seen Simon's body, she has told other people, absorbed sympathy, witnessed and shed tears. Yet she feels she can remove herself from the whole experience, sever herself from reality, as if it is not really happening.

She still expects Simon to come back. She keeps thinking she can hear his key in the lock, his call 'hello!', his footsteps in the hall. Or that she has caught a glimpse of him, working at his computer, sitting at the kitchen table, watching telly with his feet up on the sofa.

But no.

So, instead, the funeral.

It is to be a church one, she and Phyllis have agreed. Having never discussed with Simon what he'd want, they can only go on instinct, gleaned from what they know of him. They go through the decisions in a daze. Who should be notified? What would be best for him? How can they make these decisions when they have barely accepted his death as reality?

Yet somehow, together, they do.

The initial post-mortem showed that he'd had a *'total occlusion of his left coronary artery causing infarction and rupture of his left ventricle'*. In other words, it was a heart attack, plain and simple.

'But it doesn't really answer our questions,' says Phyllis. And she is right: what they both really want to know is why is life so unfair – why their Simon? No amount of medical paperwork can resolve that for them.

As for the funeral, Karen briefly suggested a less traditional ritual – this is Brighton, after all – but somehow being buried in the woods or a biodegradable basket – or both – just seems too alternative, too pagan, too plain *daft* for Simon. It is not as if he was a green campaigner or anything. Yes, he helped recycle bottles and paper and tins, though that was hardly difficult as they were collected from the house, and they bought organic vegetables – but that is the sum of his credentials. In reality, Karen cares more about these issues than he does and she wouldn't want a woven casket, so why should he?

They could have him cremated; he'd probably not mind that – he liked bonfires and barbecues and he built the living-room hearth. But somehow this didn't seem right to Karen or Phyllis either; the idea of having such a big man reduced to a small pile of dust is too inconsequential, too transient. Simon weighed over sixteen stone, for goodness' sake.

So, they have agreed. No arguments, no dissension: he will be buried, with a proper headstone, in Brighton cemetery. It has gravitas, people have been buried for centuries, including Simon's own father, not so long ago. But principally, it is because both Karen and Phyllis want the solidity of a grave. Insofar as Karen can envisage anything at the moment, she can picture visiting it in the future, with the children, and she prefers this notion to any other. Plus she is worried Molly and Luke won't recall scattering the ashes in years to come. They are so small, and she wants to have somewhere they can go to remember.

There it is, again: the searing pain that comes with

imagining the future. With a mental shove she pushes it away. Then she picks up her pen, and begins to write a list of food she needs to buy. People will need something to eat after the funeral, won't they?

15:04

The moment Karen turns off the car engine she can hear the screams.

'I WANT DADDY CUDDLE! **I WANT DADDY CUDDLE!**'

Her stomach turns over. Her daughter has not had a full-blown tantrum for months – she and Simon have noted this development with a mixture of pride and relief only the weekend just gone, but immediately she understands what Molly is communicating with such urgency. Often it's a Mummy Cuddle she yells for; now she wants her father. Such a simple request: how Karen wishes she could grant it – she wishes it more than *anything*.

Molly's voice is getting louder. '*I WANT DADDY CUDDLE!*'

Oh, Lord, thinks Karen, heading up the garden path, poor Tracy. If Molly is audible from here, it must be ear-piercing inside the house. She rings on the doorbell.

Tracy opens the door immediately.

'I'm sorry,' says Karen. 'How long has this been going on?'

Tracy raises her eyes to the sky. 'Since lunch,' she confesses.

'Oh, Tracy! You should have called.' Tracy normally feeds the children at half past twelve.

'I wanted you to have some time to yourself.' She runs her fingers through her hair.

'I know, and thank you – I did get heaps done, but still, you're a saint, putting up with this for such hours.'

'**I WANT DADDY CUDDLE! I WANT DADDY CUDDLE!**' Molly is screaming so loud she has not heard that Karen has arrived.

'Normally I can stop her,' says Tracy, raising her voice to make herself heard. 'Or rather, I ignore her, and eventually she runs out of steam, as you know.'

'***I WANT DADDY CUDDLE! I WANT DADDY CUDDLE!***'

Karen nods. 'Usually the best way.'

Momentarily Tracy guides Karen into the living room so as not to have to bellow so hard. 'But today she's just gone on and on.'

Karen sighs heavily and bites her lip. 'Where is she?'

'In the kitchen, under the table.'

Ordinarily, Karen would be hardened to her cries; she's learnt to let them almost wash over her. But the sound of Molly's pain is excruciating: '. . . DADDY CUDDLE! . . . DADDY CUDDLE!' Karen relates totally; she is longing for a Daddy cuddle herself.

'I'm afraid she's had an accident too.'

'Oh, no.' Molly has been using the loo pretty successfully since the previous autumn and hasn't had any mishaps since before Christmas. 'Pee, I hope?'

'Both.'

Karen winces.

'It's all right.' Tracy smiles, but Karen can tell she is worn out.

'I didn't even give you a change of clothes,' she castigates herself. This hasn't been necessary for a while, so it didn't occur to her that morning. She has not been thinking remotely straight.

'I put her in some old stuff of Lola's,' says Tracy. Lola is her own daughter, now seven. 'I kept bits and bobs of the children's for emergencies.'

'Bless you.'

'Really, don't worry. Though they are a bit big.'

Karen hurries through to the kitchen. Molly is under the wooden table, scrunched up in a tight ball of fury and upset.

'Your mummy is here,' says Tracy, her voice raised.

Karen crouches down. 'Hello, sweetie.' She crawls in.

But Molly is a lorry speeding down the motorway in the rain, so energized it is impossible to stop. She carries on in spite of Karen's presence: 'I want Daddy cuddle! I want Daddy cuddle!', pummelling her fists on the linoleum floor.

Karen feels powerless, but sits down, cross-legged, touches Molly's hunched back and ventures, 'Daddy's not here,' her own soul crying out for him as she says it. 'Will a Mummy cuddle do?'

At least Molly doesn't bat her away. Gradually her cries drop to a less desperate level and at last she edges, maintaining her beetle-like shape, over to Karen's lap and collapses into it.

They sit like that together for several minutes. A waxed tablecloth encloses them; Karen is aware of the darkness and warmth of their location, the smell of pine: no wonder Molly elected to retreat here. They are in their own private safe haven.

'There, there. It's OK. It's OK. I'm sorry I'm not Daddy. But I'm here, Molster, I'm here.' Karen wraps her arms around her daughter, stroking her hair softly, until finally Molly gulps down the last of her sobs, her breathing slows and she is quiet.

Eventually Karen asks, 'Are you feeling better?'

'Everything ache,' says Molly, lifting her head.

'Where does it hurt?'

'Here.' Molly sits up and rubs her tummy.

'Aah, poor tummy.' Karen rubs it.

'And here.' Molly touches her forehead.

'Poor head.' Karen kisses her brow.

'And here.' Molly returns to her torso, her chest this time. 'All hurty.'

Karen knows this exterior pain is a manifestation of interior suffering. She feels all hurty too. As she strokes Molly's chest, she looks up and sees Luke standing there. He's pulled back the tablecloth and is peering at both of them.

'Hello, love,' she says, reaching out for him. She wonders how long he has been watching. 'Do you want to come in?'

Luke shakes his head.

'I guess we'd better get up, then.' She shifts position. 'Come on, Molly, time to go.'

Molly squeaks like a distressed baby animal and snuggles in more tightly.

'Now come on, Molster. We do need to get back.' Before Molly can argue or revert back to tears, Karen carefully manoeuvres them both up and out from under the table.

'Luke, poppet,' she smiles as she stands, conscious she's barely acknowledged him.

Luke says nothing.

'You all right?'

Luke just stares at her, bottom lip protruding, silent. It's uncharacteristic; usually he would at least nod or shake his head. But he doesn't even acknowledge her question.

'Let's get you both home,' she says. 'And then we'll have a drink and biscuits, and if you're very good, I might let you choose a DVD to watch on telly. How about *Shrek*? Would you like that?'

'Yes,' says Molly without hesitation.

Luke remains uncommunicative. Maybe he will say more when they are back.

She would never customarily let them watch a DVD at this time and doesn't want to break all the rules, but they both seem so distressed that she wants to comfort them in any way she can. And in the general scheme of things, what does it matter? It's hardly as if excess TV is going to be as psychologically traumatizing as the sudden death of their father.

'Don't forget these,' says Tracy, handing her a bag of Molly's clothes. 'I've run them through the wash but they're still damp.'

'You're an angel.' Karen shoves the carrier up her arm and onto her shoulder. Then with a palm on each head, she guides both children down the hall, Molly looking faintly clown-like in a dress several sizes too big for her; Luke dragging his heels, grumpy and disconsolate.

* * *

On the edges of the Firth, where the rich mineral waters flow and the sea breezes blow, stands the distillery. It's here we go about our daily tasks to bring you one of Scotland's finest Single Malts, just as we have for over two hundred years. Pour yourself a glass, look at the colour against the light. From the palest gold to the darkest hue, every shade is a reflection of our Highland home.

Not for the first time, Anna is glad of the distraction of her work. It is an effort to focus, but she is used to that. How many times has she had to repress memories from the evening before in order to write after a row with Steve? She has become adept at ignoring racing thoughts, telling herself that she'll deal with her own problems later. And although now it is not Steve who is in the back of her mind – it's Karen and the children – the ability to channel her energies is like a well-exercised muscle; Anna can do it with almost disloyal ease.

'Tea?' says Bill, pushing back his chair next to her.

'Ooh, yes please.' Anna looks up. Around her the office is buzzing. There's music on low volume, mobiles ringing, colleagues chatting. But Anna has been in a world of her own, far north of the border, surrounded by mists and sea air and the scent of seaweed. She enjoys writing descriptive copy like this. It allows her to whisk herself away to another place, almost like magic.

As Bill puts down her cup of tea, there is a bleep. It's a good time to take a break and check her texts – she has lost her flow already.

All really getting on top of me, it says. *Be nice to chat but I appreciate you're busy. K xxx*

Anna feels bad. There she was, congratulating herself on being able to blot out the very circumstances Karen cannot escape from.

She goes into the corridor and rings at once.

'Hello?' says Karen.

Anna can tell from that one word that she is crying. How long has she been weeping like this, alone? 'Oh, my love. You should have called me earlier.'

'I didn't want to interrupt you.'

'I wouldn't answer if I was that busy, but it's rare I can't speak for just a few moments. So next time, just ring me, please. Though I should have called *you*. I am so sorry.'

Karen gulps, trying to stem the tears. 'I'm sorry, I'm sorry. I find it so hard to cry most of the time, too. And now there seems to be no stopping me. The kids are in the other room watching *Shrek* and I just – I dunno – I was supposed to be calling the funeral parlour about flowers and whether we wanted them or what and I couldn't face it, I just crumbled. Molly had the most dreadful, dreadful tantrum this afternoon at Tracy's; I've never known her have one quite that bad, it must have been nearly three hours altogether, and all she wanted was her Daddy, and Luke won't talk to me, he just seems to have clammed up, won't say a word, yet yesterday he was fine, well not fine, but you know, he talked and he cried and I felt I could help, but I can't be their Daddy, I never will be able to be and – oh, Anna – why has this happened to me? I just want Simon back! I just want him here, with us! I want him to help me deal with all this!' She starts to cry even harder. 'I came home just now and I was trying to do things, but when I opened the tumble dryer, there were some clothes of his he'd put in there on Monday morning – shirts for work – I've not thought of washing since so I didn't know they were there. I just started sobbing, and Luke came in; the expression on his face – it was awful – he looked so aghast.'

Anna just listens, then after a while Karen calms down a little, and says, 'I'm so sorry, you're at work. It's just today, I'm finding it really hard to cope. Sorry, sorry.'

'Sweetheart, stop apologizing, and stop being so bloody tough on yourself,' orders Anna. 'You don't have to cope. But anyway, you are. Strikes me you're actually coping very well. Though you can let yourself off the hook a little – no one will mind if you cry. Least of all me.'

'*I* mind,' says Karen.

'Well, all right, you mind.' Anna laughs affectionately. 'But no one else does, honestly.'

'The children will mind.'

'No, they won't. What they'll mind is a mother who bottles everything up and pretends everything is tickety-boo. I'm sure that's much worse.'

'You are?'

'Yes. Tears are not a weakness. It's good to let it out.' Anna is convinced by this insight; she feels instinctively that Karen's unshed tears will only fill the well of her sadness more deeply in the long term. Yet at the same time she feels uncomfortable; she is aware that she is bottling stuff up too. This contradiction makes her feel uneasy, so almost immediately she rationalizes the situation: her circumstances are different; she's not lost a partner; she's got a living to earn; plus she needs to be strong for Karen. Then again, Karen believes she has to be strong for the children. Once more Anna has the sense that she and Karen mirror one another. Even now their reactions are similar; they both want to be strong for others. They are codependent, as if they are playing a game of Jenga. Pull the wrong wooden peg out of the construction and the whole lot will come down – quite who is going to blow it is anyone's guess.

'But it's all my fault,' wails Karen again. 'I should have done more . . .'

Oh, no, thinks Anna. She knows it is crazily soon after the event – barely forty-eight hours – but hearing Karen beating herself up is especially hard to bear.

'Karen—'

'I feel like I killed him,' says Karen, quietly.

'Oh, *honey.*'

'I do, though.'

'That's plain silly.' Anna wishes she was with her friend in person – she longs to give her a hug. It is so frustrating not being able to reason with her face to face, help her grasp how wrong she is to blame herself. Because here she and

Karen do not mirror one another – and Anna is reminded how different their situations really are. Karen is in another place entirely – a world turned upside down and inside out by what has happened. Karen's loss is of a magnitude that only she can feel. So however hard Anna strives, however much she wants Karen to, nothing she can say will persuade her friend to see events her way.

19:09

Anna is heading home after work when her phone rings once more. How weird; she has just transferred this particular number into her address book.

'Hello. It's Lou.'

'I know – I'd just put you into my mobile.'

'Spooky.'

'Indeed.'

'Are you on the train?' asks Lou.

'Yes, are you?'

'Yes.'

'Doubly spooky. But I only just caught it, so I'm at the back.'

'I'm up the front, so it's probably not worth finding each other now.' They are approaching Brighton. 'Still, I was just wondering, how are you? Was your day OK?'

'Fine, I suppose.' Anna laughs ruefully. 'Work's the least of my worries at the moment.'

'Mm. I understand.' A pause, then Lou asks, 'How's Karen?'

'Oh, er . . .' Anna doesn't feel she can lie to Lou, who was there when Simon died, after all, but she is loath to have an intimate conversation on the train where a great many people can hear every word. She thinks swiftly. Steve has some painting to finish for a client and will be home late; Karen is spending the evening with Simon's brother, Alan, so Anna is at a loose end. She'd been looking forward to some time alone, and had planned on having a nice warm bath and an early night. On the other hand, it would be good to talk to someone . . .

'Actually, you don't fancy a quick drink, do you?' she asks impulsively. 'Somewhere near the station?'

Another pause, then Lou says, 'Yeah, why not?'

'We could go to that pub on Trafalgar Street. I can never remember its name, but it's really nice.'

'The one down the far end? I can never remember its name either.'

They *are* in sync; they are even forgetting the same things.

'Yes. On the right as you're walking down.'

'That would be great. I'll wait for you at the ticket barrier.'

As the train clatters past the cleaning depot, freshly spruced carriages glisten shiny and bright in the fluorescent light. Then it slows to pass through signals and finally creeps alongside the station platform.

*   *   *

Lou rang Anna on a whim, because she had been thinking about her and Karen, wondering what she could do to help. She knows this is futile: what has happened has happened, and she also knows she should protect herself, because she has a tendency to give too much, and it's not as if she doesn't put a lot of herself into her job caring for people already. Nonetheless, she feels such empathy for them both she can't ignore it.

And there is Anna now, amongst the throng pressing towards the barriers. Lou waves.

'Hi, hi,' beams Anna when she comes through the gate. She kisses Lou on each cheek.

Anna seems warmer every time I meet her, thinks Lou. Funny, that. Some people, who seem so friendly on first impression, turn out to be disappointingly superficial, whereas the aloof ones, like Anna, emerge as affectionate and loyal.

Lou collects her bicycle and they start walking. It's chilly, and there's a bridge beneath the station that channels the wind, messing up Anna's hair. She is wearing shiny dark-green leather boots with high heels that drive her with a click click click down the hill, forcing her to take small steps. Lou's hair is unkempt regardless of the weather; her trainers are easy to stride in, well worn, comfy. We are an unlikely duo, she thinks.

'Ah, that's what it's called,' says Anna, when they reach the door. *The Lord Nelson.*

At the bar, Lou wedges in between a group of red-faced older men and a couple of young guys in duffel coats. 'What will you have?'

Anna peruses the wine list. 'A glass of this.' She points to a red near the foot of the page. 'But don't worry, I'll get them.'

Lou notes that Anna has expensive tastes. All the same, she says, 'No, get the next one.'

The girl behind the bar comes over, smiles. She's cute; quirkily dressed, with crazy-coloured spiky hair. She's younger than Lou – probably a student – and Lou knows at once she is gay. Lou orders Anna's red and a half of lager for herself. An impatient 'harrumph' indicates that one of the older men had been waiting for a while, but she decides to ignore it. So what if she is getting preferential treatment? It's often the other way round.

She looks about her. The room is broken into cosy nooks and crannies; the air is filled with beer, voices and laughter.

Anna echoes her thoughts. 'I like it here – it's just what I needed.'

'Shall we go there?' Lou gestures towards an alcove. Two high-backed leather benches face each other on either side of a narrow table.

Anna slips off her mackintosh and as she edges into her seat, Lou realizes it's the first time she has seen her without her coat on. She is dressed simply in a black skirt and polo-neck jumper, but it's the set of huge, polished stone beads around her neck that lifts the outfit from the mundane. It takes confidence to put together clothes like this, Lou thinks, and it's all the more impressive given what Anna has been through. Taking a seat opposite, Lou feels scruffy, conscious her outfit has been randomly flung together. Still, now is not the moment to fret about appearances, and Lou is more interested in what goes on inside most people anyway. Nonetheless, she doesn't want to launch straight in and stir up Anna's worries – that would be tactless. She wants Anna to take the lead. So she just reiterates, 'Work was OK, then?'

Anna nods. 'I guess I can't complain. I appreciate not being that taxed at the moment.'

'Sure.'

'And the people I work with are very nice, but I find it's easier sometimes not to tell them everything that's going on. Allows me to separate it off, if you know what I mean?'

Lou smiles. 'I do indeed.' If only Anna knew just how much I identify with that, she thinks. Yet she doesn't feel it's appropriate to explain everything that's been going on for her that week – Anna has enough to deal with. Instead she says, 'This was a really nice idea.'

'Mm . . . It's lovely to come to a pub and not have to worry—' Anna breaks off.

Lou is convinced she was about to reveal more, but is not sure what. She tries another route. 'So tell me, what brought you to Brighton?'

'Ooh, it's a long story' – Anna sits back – 'but I'll try to keep it short.' She takes a deep breath. 'Well, for many years, I was with the same guy, Neil. We lived in London – and it was nice, but a bit too nice. Safe, if you know what I mean.'

'Yes.' Lou understands completely.

'I mean, Neil was lovely – don't get me wrong. And he was very successful. In fact, he spoilt me rotten. I do miss that.' Just for a moment Anna looks bereft. 'To a large extent, I had a lot, materially. A beautiful flat, fast car, good job . . .' She drifts off, remembering. So that's where the expensive tastes come from, thinks Lou. 'But I guess I just got bored. Not that it manifested itself that way. To be honest, I began having panic attacks. I don't know if you've ever had them?'

'No.' Lou shakes her head.

'I didn't know what they were, initially. It was very alarming. I would feel like I couldn't breathe, go all dizzy, like I had vertigo or something – once I even fainted on the Tube.'

'How horrible.'

'Yes, and what was really scary was it seemed so random

– I could never tell when it was going to happen. Eventually, it got so bad, I went to see my GP, and he referred me to a therapist.'

'Did that help?'

'Kind of, yes. I won't bore you with all the detail, but together we worked out that I was claustrophobic, in the broadest sense. My life, my work, my relationship, everything – were constraining me. So I decided to make some big changes. I didn't want to have children with Neil – that must have been a sign – whereas by that stage he wanted them with me. But I just couldn't imagine it, living a pristine life in this big Georgian house, working in advertising and everything.' She shudders. 'It seemed heinous.'

Wow, thinks Lou. So I was right. Anna isn't what she seems.

'So I left him.' Anna shakes her head, as if still incredulous she did it.

'That must have taken some doing.'

'I guess so. But I thought I'd go mad, if I stayed. I'm sure I would have. Do you know what I mean?'

'Sure.' Again Lou comprehends only too well. But she can illuminate Anna later – right now she wants more. She leans forward, and Anna continues.

'Then I was left wondering where to go and what to do. When I started to think about it all, I decided to unravel everything. I was sick of London, that whole rat race thing. Everyone trying to outdo each other in the salary stakes, working stupid hours – you know. So I jacked in my job, went freelance. I decided I wanted a change of scene, too. I'd been at university here, years before, so I knew and liked the place. And Brighton's not so far from London, as you know, so it made it possible to get up there for work. But I guess in the end it was having Karen and Simon here that drew me back – they persuaded me. Karen has been in Brighton since college – she never left – it's where we met, and she and Simon got together soon after. So I bought a little house near them and the rest, as they say, is history.'

Now Anna has revealed this much, Lou is even more curious about her current partner. What kind of man would she go for now? she wonders. But she doesn't want Anna to think she's prying. Anyway, now it's probably her turn and if she opens up herself, then Anna might elaborate.

Anna gives her the cue. 'So what brought you to Brighton? I take it you didn't grow up here?'

She has been very frank, Lou thinks; I should return the compliment. But she's nearing the end of her glass and could do with another if she's going to dredge up the past. 'It's quite a tale, I suppose,' she says. 'Shall I get another round in first?'

'Sure,' agrees Anna. 'But it's my turn. I fancy some crisps, too. Do you?'

* * *

Several minutes later, Anna is back. Lou puts down her mobile – she's just been sending a text to Howie about Friday.

'Didn't seem to get served quite as fast as you,' Anna observes wryly. 'So, you were saying?'

Lou takes a deep breath. 'I guess, in a nutshell, I came to get away from my family.'

'Ah.'

'Maybe that's a bit strong, but to get away from my mother, certainly, after my father died.'

'That was a while ago, you said?'

'Nearly ten years ago now. Cancer.'

'I'm sorry.' Anna feels bad for having led Lou here. Death seems to surround them.

'Anyhow, I grew up in Hitchin, in Hertfordshire. Do you know it?'

Anna shakes her head.

'It's the sort of place England is full of. A market town, pretty, but, God – to use your word – claustrophobic as hell. Specially if, like me, you're gay.'

Aha, thinks Anna. I'm glad that's out there. She had known, but nonetheless, it will be easier now it's been said.

Lou scratches her head, as if it will help formulate the right words, and sighs. 'The last few months of my father's life, he was very sick. So I went home to help my mother look after him. And I stayed on a few months after he died, to help my mother get back on her feet. Actually, I suggested her that she set up a B&B, to take her mind off being alone.'

'Did she do it?'

Lou nods. 'Yes, she still runs it now.'

'That was very good of you to look after her, and your father, all that time,' says Anna. 'Have you no brothers or sisters?'

'A younger sister, Georgia.'

'So why were you the one to help?'

'Good question.' Lou laughs, sardonic. 'She's married, with children. And I'm the eldest; the one expected to be dutiful.' Single daughter becomes carer – it is a common pattern. 'I needed to get away, and after six months of living with her I was beginning to crawl the walls. Like you, I left. Obviously my reasons for choosing Brighton were a little different. But I'd friends here, like you. And I wanted to be somewhere with a scene I could be part of, feel at home. I never felt at home where I grew up.'

Anna wants to complete the picture. 'So what led you to counselling?'

'I did voluntary work with the homeless, initially. I dealt with a lot of addicts, especially alcoholics.' Anna blanches at the word; wonders if Lou has noticed, but Lou is either too involved in her story, or too polite, to register surprise at Anna's reaction. Lou carries on, 'I became fascinated by what led them down that path – made them so self-destructive. So I thought I'd train properly as a counsellor, which I did. I finished my training last year. Then I got the job at the school in Hammersmith at the start of the autumn term. I still work with the homeless, though, every Friday afternoon.'

We come full circle, thinks Anna. It's enough to make her believe in Fate. It makes her wonder if perhaps there are other reasons they have been brought together. 'I wish Karen could meet you,' she says suddenly.

'Really?'

'Yes.' She pauses briefly to consider. 'I think it would be really helpful for her to talk to you.'

'Do you – why?'

'I don't know.' Anna tries to explain. 'It's a gut instinct more than anything. But she feels so guilty, and what with your being a counsellor and all . . .'

'Maybe.'

'Would you mind if I suggested it?'

'No, not at all. I'd love to be able to help.'

'I think it's a really good idea.'

'But there's no rush. Now may not be the best time. Perhaps you should leave it a while.'

Anna is impatient to act. 'I'm going to call her.'

'Are you sure? She's got a lot on at the moment.'

'I agree, but it can do no harm to ask.' Anna opens her mobile. She has Karen on speed dial and the children will be in bed. Karen answers on almost the first ring and Anna gets straight to the point. 'Karen. I'm going to suggest something to you. And before you say no, hear me out.'

'OK.'

'Why don't you have a chat with the woman I met on the train I mentioned to you yesterday? The one who was sitting near you?'

'What good will that do?' Karen sounds mystified.

'Because. . .' Anna hesitates, half wishing she'd heeded Lou's advice to wait. This is not a conversation she's planned and she is still working out the rationale. 'Well, for several reasons.'

'Yes?'

'Mm. Firstly, because Lou, she's called, saw everything that happened.'

'You said,' says Karen slowly. 'Must have been awful for her.'

197

'That's not what I mean.' Anna is frustrated but struggles to mask it. She wishes her friend would stop putting others first, just for once. 'Of course, you're right – I'm sure it wasn't an easy thing to witness, and I don't mean to be hard, honey, but it's never the same, an experience like that, if you don't know the person. Lou didn't know Simon, obviously.'

'I guess,' Karen relents.

'Which is my point, really. Lou might help you be a bit more, well, objective about it.'

'Objective! Why would I want to be more objective about losing my husband!?'

Anna has blundered. Now Karen is even more upset – and rightly so: Anna must have seemed horribly uncaring. This is such a sensitive area, how can she explain herself properly? Surely it's best to be honest. 'I just hate the way you're blaming yourself so much.'

'I see.'

But Anna can tell Karen is still unsure. And really, that's no surprise. She has so much on her mind maybe Lou was right; maybe it is too soon to suggest this. Perhaps it would be better saved till more time has elapsed and Karen is through the worst. Yet Anna isn't ready to give up. 'Lou is a counsellor. And I'm not saying you need counselling, but she does know something about bereavement. And she works with kids, too. Who knows, she might even be able to help you with Molly and Luke.'

'Oh,' says Karen, her tone of voice changing.

Anna can hear curiosity now, so attempts to clinch it. 'I know she'd be happy to talk to you.'

But her enthusiasm seems to have the opposite effect. 'How do you know?' The doubt is back.

'I saw her on the train today,' Anna confesses.

'By coincidence?'

'No, actually, I texted her.' Anna realizes Karen won't want to feel as though Anna has been discussing her misfortune with a stranger, so she spells it out: 'I owed her some money for the cab we got into London.'

'Ah.' The tone is interested once more. 'But what makes you think she'd want to speak to me?'

'She offered,' says Anna, bluntly. She can't be circumspect any longer, though she doesn't think it appropriate to say they are out together right at that moment in the pub. She hopes Karen can't tell from the background noise. 'She asked after you, as anyone would. So I told her you were handling everything really well – which of course you are, magnificently. But – and I hope you don't mind – I did say that you felt it was your fault. And she said, no, it wasn't. In any way.'

'Oh.'

There is a prolonged silence. Karen is clearly absorbing it all.

'OK,' she relents. 'If it'll make you happy.'

Again Anna struggles to be clear. 'It would. But only because I think it might help you.'

'OK, OK. I suppose I've got nothing more to lose, have I?'

'No,' she acknowledges. 'I guess you haven't.'

Thursday

19:53

I'm not going home tonight, the note says, *decided to stay in Brighton. Fancy going for a swim and picnic on the beach?*

Hurriedly, Karen folds the piece of paper, before her colleagues can see. She looks around to check no one is watching, glances up at Simon.

He's grinning, eyebrow raised.

Her stomach lurches. She fancies him *soo* much – she is powerless to resist. How can she possibly? She knows it's wrong: he has a girlfriend – he lives with her, for goodness' sake – and what they're doing is unfair, cruel. She is not sure what he has said to his girlfriend to wangle a night away and she doesn't want to know. She would hate it if it was done to her – she has never seen herself as the kind of girl who would steal another woman's man. She and Anna have always been most disapproving about women who do that, arguing through college and beyond that there are plenty of available men out there, that it is quite unnecessary to go for those who are already spoken for. But she has liked Simon since the day she started this job, and he is the one who initiated this whole thing. He is the one who blew her away with a clandestine kiss at the office summer party just a week ago, who asked if he could come back and stay at hers afterwards; he is the one who doubtless made unconvincing excuses when he returned home the next day. And it only took that single night to open this Pandora's box of mutual passion; being together was far, far better than it should have been, were it only a one-night stand. Plus, from the way he has been since – more than just flirtatious, snatching moments to be with her that are quite uncalled for given they work in different departments, even once stroking her arm when they had a few seconds alone – Karen senses that he really likes her.

She nods, quickly, surreptitiously, and two hours later they are headed in his car towards Hove, several miles from their office in Kemptown, but risky nonetheless. She watches Simon's profile as he drives, concentrating, but he keeps turning to her, and every time he does so, he is smiling. He doesn't seem to care, and she wonders if, actually, he wants to be caught. In some ways she does, because she knows, already, albeit crazily swiftly, that she wants more of this man, that once was never, ever going to be enough.

They stop off at a Greek supermarket and run in to buy food and wine. In the cold light of day it is a grotty little shop, but this isn't the cold light of day, it is a magical July evening; the world is bathed in the warm peachy glow of seven o'clock sunlight, and everything, everyone, looks stunning, including this funny, down-at-heel grocery store. Inside, it is as if a haven of seductive delicacies is offering itself up to them. So what would normally seem a fairly conventional selection of staple foods and cheap alcohol becomes a cornucopia of delights – hummus, taramasalata, olives, stuffed vine leaves, pitta bread – and they are utterly spoilt for choice.

It will all, inevitably, taste delicious. Rapidly, they fill a basket, add a bottle of wine – they are agreed, it should be bubbly, chilled, and why not rosé? It seems to reflect the mood of the evening – heady yet light, harmless. Hardly the choice of immoral wrongdoers, surely: more that of two people enjoying the moment, caught up in such a forceful and unstoppable attraction that any implications their actions might have are pushed light years away.

Minutes later they are parked up on the roadside by a man-made lagoon on the west of the city: beyond it is the sea. It's as close to ideal as they are going to get without driving further than either of them has the patience for; distant enough from the most popular strip of Brighton beach to be relatively private. Simon slings a tartan travel rug he keeps in the back of his car over his shoulder like a Scotsman's cloak and, as they stroll along the edge of the purpose-built lake, plastic bags rustling, flip-flops flipping, the light catches baby waves – ripples that dance and sparkle blue and turquoise.

'Where shall we go?' Simon asks, when they reach the promenade.

Karen scans the beach; her chief priority is to be far from other people, second to that she wants to be in the sun.

'There,' she says, pointing to a spot on the shingle bathed in orange.

'Perfect,' says Simon, and he is right: it is.

They crunch across the stones, put down the bags and Simon flings the rug wide so it catches the breeze and lays out flat and square.

Karen stands for a moment, looking at the sea. It is windy,

but not too windy; the waves are enticing, not intimidating; gulls swoop down and up, round and about, playing in the breeze. Misty shafts of light illuminate the pebbles; tonight they are a million shades of pink and russet and yellow and gold, not grey, as they're so often pictured.

She can feel Simon watching her, and senses herself as he might see her; long, long chestnut hair spidering in the wind, white cotton skirt flapping about her shins, faded green T-shirt hourglassing her waist and breasts. She is, she feels at that second, womanly; even, possibly, beautiful.

'Right.' Simon lies down on his side. He props his head on one hand, and with the other reaches forward to the adjacent space. 'Come here,' he invites her, patting it.

Karen doesn't need asking twice; she turns, kneels, and slides alongside. Within seconds he is kissing her; her body is bending towards him, her back arching like a cat indulging in the heat, stretching out in ecstasy. She reaches up, strokes his hair; he has lovely hair – dark, thick, slightly wavy – it's one of the first things she noticed about him. And as he presses his body into her, she thinks how wonderful it is to be with a big man, a proper man, not one of these wispy poetic types that she's fallen for in the past. It makes her feel smaller, more feminine, and she loves that. She inhales his scent: the same smell that blew her away a week before, slightly lemony, fresh, oh-so-male, and, to her at any rate, incredibly, mind-blowingly sexy.

'Shall we swim?' he asks, breaking away a few minutes later.

Part of Karen is so enjoying the sensation of his mouth on hers, lips and tongues exploring, that she doesn't want to stop what they are doing; another part feels they should, as now he has his leg wedged between hers, pressing into her groin, and his hand up her top. If they don't halt, soon they will be doing far more than they should, given they're in a public space. Plus she likes the idea of going into the sea: it is balmy, very warm, and if they're not able to have sex here, then doing something alternatively sensuous appeals. She's wearing a matching bra and knickers; they could easily pass as a bikini. And if they end up wet, what does it matter? She can go home without them on and no one will know.

'OK.' She sits up. At once she slips her skirt down over her knees, her T-shirt over her head and she's there, almost naked, in front of him. Again she can feel him looking at her.

'You're gorgeous,' he says, running a hand down her back. The feel of his fingers on her flesh makes her tempted to resume kissing, but no, she is going to resist; the waves beckon.

'Last one in!' she says, jumping up and running, still in her flip-flops, down the shingle. She kicks off her flip-flops and splash splash SPLASH! – never mind the pain of the pebbles on the soles of her feet – she is in, up to her thighs, oooh, brrrrrr! Quickly-quickly, swiftly dipping so she is past the sensitive bit and up to her waist, and yeooow! further, up to her shoulders. But although the water is cool, it is nowhere near as chilly as she feared it might be – a mild spring and recent heatwave have warmed it. Her hair floats about her, but she keeps her face out, conscious her mascara will smudge and wanting to look her prettiest for Simon. She looks back to land: he is running down the beach in his boxers; within seconds he's in the water beside her.

She hooks her legs around him, frog-like, and leans back a little, paddling with her arms to keep herself afloat. Despite the cold, he has an erection; she can feel it. Cheekily, she rubs the outside of his boxers with her palm.

He raises an eyebrow again, smiles, and groans, 'Ooh.'

Then, *whoosh!* and he's let go of her, and ducked under, emerging with wet hair, face dripping.

Now she grins, flips over and swims off, teasing him. The sky above is breathtaking; wisps of candyfloss clouds in mauve and sugar pink over the elegant white art deco houses immediately to their west. She cannot think when she has ever been this happy.

Then she is back in his arms, he holds her against the waves, and, yes, mm, they are kissing, salt water mingling with saliva. She wraps her arms around his neck, he holds her waist, and now she doesn't give a damn it's a public place; no one else is anywhere near them, and no one can see what's going on beneath the surface anyway. So she scoops her legs around his hips once more and presses into him, gently gyrating her hips so she's rubbing him rhythmically, tantalizing.

It is too much – or not enough – for him, and he eases his cock out of his boxers, pushes aside her make-do bikini briefs and OH! He is inside her; she can't quite believe it, the audacity, the sheer pleasure of it: they are actually doing it, having sex in the sea.

They kiss constantly as he moves in and out of her; she has had a couple of lovers before, but honest to God, no one has ever felt as good, as perfect a fit, as Simon. It is surely the best sensation in the world; right now, she can't imagine one better.

That there are people in the distance walking along the promenade adds to the frisson; the feeling that they shouldn't be doing what they are for all sorts of reasons, but hell, yes, yes, they should, they really, really should . . .

Later, on the shingle, Simon cracks open the sparkling rosé and they drink it straight from the bottle.

He watches Karen swig; she knows it looks sexual, and doesn't care. If anything it turns her on, too, although actually she couldn't possibly be turned on any more than she already is.

'Hang on,' he says suddenly. 'I'm just going to the car.' And before she can ask why, he is up and off, at so brisk a pace he is almost running.

Shortly he's back, out of breath.

'I had it with me to shoot the project we're doing.' In his hand is an instamatic camera.

'Oh no, please don't,' protests Karen, holding up her palm. But he ignores her and takes several snaps.

'My turn,' she counters, and takes a couple of him. Then, 'Come here.' She yanks him towards her. 'I want one of the two of us.'

'How are you going to do that? There's no self-timer.'

'Like this,' she retorts, and holds the camera out as far away from them both as she can. She tilts her head into his, smiles, and CLICK! The moment is captured.

*

She is looking at it now, that photograph.

His hair damp, curled on his forehead, not a single wisp of grey; hers falling in tendrils about her shoulders, improbably youthful skin gleaming in the last rays of the day. She is nearer the lens; chin up, eyes slanted, her smile that of a woman who's just made love. He is grinning, cat who got the cream.

Even now, twenty years later, she can taste the salty tang of the seawater. But no. Karen is standing by the bedroom window, holding the picture frame in her hand; the salt is the salt of her tears.

She once read that memories are like rivulets of water on stone. The more they are replayed, the deeper they become etched in the mind, so the most powerful remain the most potent, forever.

That day is carved into her mind like a railroad cut through rock, and for a while it seems whatever else she tries to think of, she can't. It's as if the chemicals in her brain are determined to sweep her up and carry her to another place, like pebbles shifted by waves, gulls carried by wind, or a vapour trail dissolving into the ether.

Still, enough.

Focus, Karen, focus.

What was she doing?

Oh, yes, she was watching out for Anna. Karen lives on a hill; she can see down the whole street from the bay. Anna is due round with some woman she met on the train called Lou, but she is uncharacteristically late.

Hurriedly, angry with herself for giving in to such nostalgia,

Karen puts the picture back on the dressing table and roughly swipes away her tears.

*　*　*

It's happened again, and on the train too. Floods of tears, without warning.

One minute Anna is functioning fine, reading the evening paper. She kept it together all through work, then had a chat with Bill, her colleague, as far as Haywards Heath, where he changes for Worthing – she even managed to talk to him about Simon a little, without breaking down. She got through Wivelsfield and Burgess Hill by focusing on the crossword.

But then, at Preston Park, the dam breaks. And she has no idea when the suddenly rising river of tears is going to stop, where it is headed, what damage and debris it is going to leave in its wake. To make matters worse, she is due at Karen's in fifteen minutes. She doesn't want Karen to see her like this. She's even arranged to go on ahead of Lou so as to give them a little time together, the two of them. She *has* to be strong for Karen.

Anna gets off the train, eyes streaming. Though she is making no noise, she is conscious people are staring, but she is too distressed to worry what strangers think of her.

She turns right out of the station and up the hill, her vision blurred but she knows the way. She knows it is sadness about Simon but that doesn't help: she feels *everything* is so bleak. She has a desperate yearning to be with someone; she can't manage the upset on her own, she is so overwhelmed.

She has to go past her house en route to Karen's, and it occurs to her that perhaps Steve will be home. He'll have finished work, and what she needs right now is a hug – a great big hug that squeezes out all the tears, like wringing clothes in a mangle. Then, hopefully, she can go on to Karen's, restored.

She turns the key in the door and calls down the hallway. But unlike the other night, when she came in to the smell of spaghetti Bolognese and words of comfort, she is greeted by silence.

She goes into the kitchen.

No Steve.

He is probably at the pub. For a moment she is angry, not sad, but then she is gripped by misery again, so she sits down at the kitchen table, doesn't even take off her coat, and wails.

Now she is free to vocalize, she is almost scared by the force and depth of her anguish. It is as if she is crying herself inside out; she is roaring, the way a child roars, hiccuping. Presently, she is not crying for Simon and Karen and Molly and Luke, and Phyllis and Alan and everyone else; she is weeping for herself.

Anna always feels she has to be so strong and wise and funny and bright and right now she doesn't feel any of those things. She feels weak and needy and vulnerable, and she wants someone to look after her. Yet simultaneously she has a strong sense of foreboding: she is conscious Simon's death has cast a brutal light on her own circumstance and she is increasingly uncomfortable with what it has exposed. So, perversely, she decides to put her hunch to the test (it's not as if she could feel any worse, after all), picks up her phone and dials.

After a few rings, he answers.

'Steve?'

'Yes?'

'It's me, Anna.' She can detect people talking in the background, laughter, music.

'I know. Your silly little face comes up on my screen.' At once she knows he is tipsy. Not drunk, not yet, but on the way. She can hear it in his voice: he is speaking too slowly, as if he is having to think more than usual about what he says. And the phrase 'silly little face' is not one he'd use sober. Her suspicions confirmed, she is furious.

'Where are you?'

There is a pause. He knows she knows where he is: he doesn't want to admit it, but he has no choice. Eventually he concedes. 'The Charminster Arms.' Their local.

'Oh, right. How long have you been there?'

'Not long, just got here.' She knows he is lying. 'Why? Where are you?'

'At home.'

Another pause. Inebriated, information takes longer to penetrate. 'But I thought you were going to Karen's?'

'I was, but I came home.'

'Oh, why?'

'I felt miserable.' Might as well say it as it is. She wants to know how he'll handle this information – she is challenging him.

'Right.'

'I thought you might give me a cuddle.'

'I see.'

But he doesn't see. He can't. He won't see anything straight, if he's drinking. And once he's started he won't stop, so his cuddles will be worthless. They'll come at a price – the risk of verbal abuse – and it's not one Anna wants to pay.

Eventually . . . 'Do you want me to come home?' he offers. She knows he does not want to.

'It doesn't matter.'

'I will if you like.' Again she hears slowness.

'No, I'm fine.' She is brisk. 'I haven't got time to wait for you. It was only if you were here – and you're not. I'm late as it is. Don't worry. I'll see you later.' Now all she wants to do is get him off the phone. 'Bye.' She snaps down the clamshell.

For a minute or two she sits staring at it, as it lies on the kitchen table.

She was right. Where, in these moments when she needs looking after, *is* Steve? Yes, he is there sometimes, but not now and by no means always. And, increasingly, sometimes is nowhere near good enough.

She's exhausted by crying, and to compound that now she has to deal with her disappointment in him. Sometimes she wonders if being with Steve is against her better judgement: if her physical lust for him means she suppresses the fact he is bad for her emotionally, financially, and socially too, come to that. She knows deep down that several of her friends don't approve of him, and that they worry about her. Karen and Simon have intimated as much; others are too tactful to say, but she can feel it. Like a cold draught from an open window, it might not be visible, but it fills the air nonetheless. She has edged away from those who make her feel most uncomfortable; others she sees without Steve because she enjoys herself more without silent disapproval weighing down the experience. Yet people perceive one another differently; a few of her friends get on well with Steve, too. Certainly one or two of her girlfriends have said they find him physically attractive. And whereas she senses some believe she could 'do better' than pair up with a handyman, others envy the fact that he's several years her junior and can do useful work around the house.

It is all very complicated.

But she has no time to examine further: Karen will be worried about where she has got to, and Anna has arranged for her to meet Lou. The meeting was her idea; she can hardly bow out.

Anna gets to her feet. She makes herself look presentable again, and is soon on her way. As she nears the house, she senses Karen's presence. She looks up. Karen is standing at the window, waiting. Anna forces a smile, waves, and increases her pace.

20:23

Karen's house is on one of Brighton's many hilly residential streets. On either side of the road, late Victorian terraces stagger up the gradient, tired-looking in the orange glow of street lamps. At the top is a pair of 1930s semi-detached houses. From the outside, they are not especially attractive, but Lou supposes they offer more space for the money because of it, and she knows Karen has children. There is a built-in garage at the front, so Lou has to go round the side to locate the main door. She locks her bike to a drainpipe and rings on the doorbell. Its 'ding-dong' reminds her of the 'Avon calling' ads from her childhood.

She hears voices inside and has a moment of trepidation. Lou has arranged to meet Anna here as she has been getting behind with writing up her session notes from the school, and doesn't want to let her paperwork slip another week. She has such a full weekend planned that this evening after work was her only opportunity. It also seemed sensitive to allow Karen and Anna an hour or so alone before she arrived, rather than intruding on the children's bedtime.

But now the encounter is upon her, Lou is anxious about exactly what's expected of her, how she – if anyone – is going to help. It makes little difference that she's a counsellor;

she's still unsure of how to speak to the bereaved, especially a woman who has lost someone so very dear so terribly recently.

Footsteps come towards her down the hall, the door opens. It's Karen. She is dressed more casually than she was on the train that Monday morning, in faded jeans and a floaty top – but Lou recognizes her immediately. Her face seems different this evening, though: the appalled, frightened panic has diminished; instead her features are a picture of sadness. It is the same transformation that Lou noted in Anna the morning before, but a dozen times more marked.

'Hello.' Karen's voice is soft, gentle. 'You must be Lou.'

'And you're Karen.'

'Yes.'

'I wish we were meeting in happier circumstances.'

Karen gives a rueful laugh. 'Me too. But come in, come in.'

Lou steps over the threshold into a square hallway. Obviously it's a family home: there are pictures of the children in frames on the cream-painted walls; the coat rack is crammed with diminutive duffel coats, anoraks and scarves; on the parquet floor are several pairs of small boiled-sweet-coloured wellington boots and scuffed shoes, scattered higgledy-piggledy.

'Ah, Lou, hi,' says a familiar voice; it's bolder, more confident, a contrast to Karen's, and Anna comes through from the kitchen. Lou is relieved to see she has a glass in her hand.

Anna seems to pick up on the unspoken request. 'Would you like some wine?'

'Yes, please.'

'I'll get you some.' Clearly Anna is at home here. Lou wonders exactly how long she and Karen have known each other, where precisely they met.

'Dump your bag and come through,' says Karen.

Lou does as she is told, hangs up her parka and follows them both into the kitchen.

The kitchen is a generously proportioned room divided by a breakfast bar. At the far end are built-in painted units, a cooker, a sink and French windows to the garden. It is dark outside but Lou guesses it is just a patio; near the city centre this is the norm. Directly in front of her is a large oak table, battered and scored by use, to her left a fridge-freezer. Children's drawings are stuck with magnets to the top half; at child height magnet letters spell 'luke' and 'dog' and 'apple' in bright shades of plastic.

She's just absorbing this when Karen says: 'I remember you from the train.'

Lou is taken aback: in all the commotion, she hadn't expected Karen to notice her.

'Red or white?' interrupts Anna.

Lou sees they are both drinking red. 'Er . . .'

'Have whichever you want,' reassures Karen. 'There's plenty.'

'I prefer white,' she admits.

'No problem,' says Karen, and reaches past her into the fridge. 'Sauvignon OK?'

'Great.' Lou is struck by how Karen is making her feel welcome, even with so much else on her mind. There are some people whose nature it is to look after others no matter what, she thinks. And others, like Lou's mother, whose nature it is not to. In comparison, her mother's hosting is self-conscious and showy. She pushes her resentment away. She is not here to think about her mother.

'I didn't think I would recognize you,' says Karen. 'But you were really helpful.'

'Was I?' Lou is touched.

'Yes. I think you realized what was happening before anybody.'

'Maybe. Everything occurred so fast.'

'Yes.'

A couple of beats of silence. Lou is at a loss. 'I'm sorry,' is all she can muster. It seems hopelessly inadequate. She tries to recall her actions. She shouted, tried to get people to act swiftly; wasn't that it? 'I wish could have done more,' she admits.

'I wish I could have, too.' Karen twists the stem of her glass. Then her voice drops, and she says in a whisper, but with real ferocity, '*God*, how I wish that!'

Anna moves closer to her friend, reaches out, puts one arm around her shoulder. 'Sweetheart . . .'

Lou can feel such raw pain she is almost knocked sideways by it.

'I should have tried to revive him.' Karen closes her eyes, as if she's looking inwards, examining her failing.

Lou has a rush of guilt: she didn't try to save him either.

'I don't think you could have,' says Anna, quietly.

'But I'm his *wife!*' Karen cries. It's a fast track to her emotions, this conversation, and Lou has not been there five minutes. She's used to outbursts from her students, but she feels involved in this so personally that she cannot be as distant as usual, and it shakes her. To emphasize what she means, Karen says, 'I should have looked after him. That's what wives should do . . .' Her voice cracks. 'He was always so good at looking after me.'

'Yes, he was.' Anna is wistful; once again Lou has the impression she is bereft of being fully cared for. 'But you have been wonderful at looking after Simon, at looking after *everyone*, honey, including me. I can't bear for you to feel you're not. You're one of life's great looker-afterers.'

'I'm sorry, Lou,' Karen says suddenly, 'you're still standing. Please, do sit down.'

This illustrates Anna's point exactly. Lou pulls a chair back from the table. 'Thanks.'

'Have you eaten?' Karen reaches into one of the cupboards.

'Um—' Lou doesn't want to put her out, but she hasn't had anything since lunch.

'You haven't,' states Karen.

'No, but really – don't worry—'

'Well, let's start with these.' Karen pulls out a packet of Kettle Chips and empties them into a bowl.

'That's fine. I can eat properly when I get home, honestly.'

'Don't be silly.'

'I'll cook something,' offers Anna. She looks sternly at Karen. 'I'm worried you're not eating.'

'I'm not hungry.'

'That's not the point.' Anna is firm. 'You have to eat.' She edges Karen out of the way and starts rummaging in the cupboard. She's tall, reaches up high and retrieves a bag of pasta. 'Got anything to go with this?' Then she answers her own question: 'Don't worry, leave it with me.' She opens the fridge and pulls out a half-finished jar of pasta sauce, onions, courgettes and an aubergine. She seems so capable, assertive, it gives Lou a glimpse of what she must be like professionally. Thinking of work reminds her. She pushes back her chair.

'Ooh, I've just thought. I hope you don't mind, but I printed something off for you.' She heads into the hall and returns with a piece of paper, which she hands to Karen. 'It's all very obvious, I know, but sometimes it's easy to forget the common-sense stuff.'

Anna comes to read over Karen's shoulder:

Coping with Sudden Death

It is important to focus on the basics the body needs for day-to-day survival:

- *Maintain a normal routine. Even if it is difficult to do regular activities, try to anyway. Keeping structure in your day will help you feel more in control.*
- *Get enough sleep, or at least plenty of rest.*
- *It may be helpful to write lists or notes, or keep an agenda.*
- *Try to get some regular exercise. This can help relieve stress and tension.*
- *Keep a balanced diet. Watch out for junk food or high-calorie comfort-food binges. Drink plenty of water.*
- *Drink alcohol only in moderation. Alcohol should not be used as a way of masking the pain.*
- *Do what comforts, sustains and recharges. Remember other difficult times and how you have survived them. This will help you draw upon your inner strength.*

'See? Just what I was saying.' Anna taps the middle of the list.

'Thanks.' Karen starts to cry.

Lou feels dreadful – she's gauged it wrong. 'I'm sorry, I didn't mean to upset you.'

'You haven't.' Karen half smiles. 'I just find it almost worse when people are nice to me.'

Anna gives her friend's shoulder a squeeze. 'Well, you may have to get used to that.'

'It's weird,' sighs Karen. 'Everything feels so surreal. Even this. I can kind of understand it, I know what it's saying, but I just can't get my head around the words. I can't get my head round anything, right from the moment Simon – er . . .' – she stumbles – 'had the heart attack.'

'I think that's quite normal,' says Lou. 'It's all been a terrible shock. It's just your body's – or rather your mind's – way of dealing with it. When my Dad died, I remember, it was so incomprehensible, it was as if my head was lagging behind the rest of me. I spent ages trying to work it all out.'

'And did you?' asks Karen.

'Kind of . . . I mean some of it still doesn't make sense, or seem fair, rather.'

'What did your Dad die of?'

'Cancer. It wasn't the same, obviously. It was pretty quick, but still, we had some time to get used to the idea. So it's no surprise you can't get your head around stuff.'

'Sometimes I feel almost normal,' says Karen. 'When I'm organizing things, just briefly, for a few moments at a time. Then, next minute, it's like I'm free-falling through space.

There are no walls, no ceiling, no floor. I think I'll never feel normal again.'

'I'm sure that's really common too. You've been through a massive, massive trauma.' Lou pauses. 'Would it help if I told you what I remember from that day? Sometimes it's good to get another perspective.'

'Um . . .' Karen hesitates. Maybe she doesn't want to go back there. But then she says, 'Yes, I guess it might.'

Lou continues. 'I remember I was sitting opposite a woman who was doing her make-up. I was half asleep, almost, watching people out of the corner of my eye. Then I remember looking at you and your husband, Simon, isn't it?' She doesn't wait for an answer. 'And you were chatting. I couldn't hear what about – I was wearing my iPod, but I recall thinking – honestly, I'm not just saying this – how happy you looked.'

'Really?' Karen inhales sharply.

'Yes. He was stroking your hand, you looked so easy in each other's company. I thought you had a kind of intimacy that seemed very special.'

'Gosh, how funny you should notice that.'

'I guess I'm nosy,' Lou admits.

'But it's nice,' interjects Anna. 'Isn't it, Karen? It means Simon's last moments were really happy.'

'I suppose . . . I hadn't thought of that. It all seems such light years ago . . . What else did you see?'

'Well, everything seemed to slow down then, for me, but actually, the whole thing must have been less than a couple of minutes. I remember Simon being sick, first—'

'Me too, I remember that.'

'So I took off my iPod. Then I remember him clutching his chest, and I heard him say, "I'm sorry."'

'Really? He said, "I'm sorry"?'

'Yes, he did, definitely.'

'I don't think I heard that.'

'I'm sure that's what he said.'

'Bless him . . .' Karen chokes. 'What do you think he was saying sorry for? Probably for throwing up. How typical . . . Always worrying. And proud – he'd have hated that, being sick in public. Silly man, as if it mattered.'

'Perhaps he was saying sorry for leaving you,' observes Anna.

'Do you think so?'

'I do,' says Anna, reaching in her bag for a tissue. As she hands it to Karen, Lou notices it is already damp – presumably Anna too was crying, earlier. 'Were those his last words?'

'As I heard them,' Lou nods.

'I didn't hear him say anything else.' Tentatively, Karen agrees. She takes the tissue, mops up her tears.

'I think—' Lou pauses, trying to recollect. She can picture Simon clutching his chest, his head lolling. Yes, she is sure: 'He passed away immediately after that. It seemed like a very big coronary, and it was so fast.'

'That *is* what the doctors told me . . .' Karen says, slowly. 'But I still feel I could have done more.'

'So could I,' shrugs Lou.

'No, you did loads.'

'And you did loads,' says Lou. 'I saw you.'

Karen sniffs. 'I stood there and panicked. I was useless.'

'You didn't just stand there. You called for help. You knew which way the guard was—'

'Oh?'

'Middle carriage. I wouldn't have known that.' Lou laughs at herself. 'I'd have sent someone the wrong way, probably, and we'd have lost more time. How did you know where he was?'

Karen stops crying and sniffs. 'I had to buy a ticket off the guard once. I was travelling up with Simon and we were running late. He has a season, so I got mine on board.'

'There you are – perfect example of how un-useless you were,' says Anna.

'It was lucky the guard was there,' says Karen. 'I was in a complete panic so I just said the first thing that came into my head. He could easily have been somewhere else.'

'But he wasn't,' says Anna. 'And most people wouldn't think that straight, I assure you.'

'I think I understand a little of what you're going through,' Lou interjects. 'I felt similar in some ways about the death of my Dad. At first I got so cross the tumour wasn't found sooner, but then I came to see we don't work that way.'

'What do you mean?'

'Well, we only go to the doctor's when we're *ill*, don't we? Not before.'

'I do wish he'd gone to the doctor sooner,' admits Karen.

'Of course you do, that's only natural. But there you are – that's already one way it could have been different – and the fact he didn't go is much more down to him than to you.'

'I could have made him go.'

'When did Simon ever go to the doctor because you told him to?' asks Anna. She reaches for the bottle and tops up her wine, and Karen's, then goes to the fridge for the white to replenish Lou's, too. 'You know he wouldn't have, sweetheart, he just wasn't interested.'

'I can imagine,' nods Lou. 'My Dad was the same. He'd never have gone.'

'I guess you're right . . .'

'And anyway, I ended up thinking about Dad, yes, he could have gone to the doctor, but who's to say the doctor would have spotted his condition? He could have spent his whole life traipsing down to the surgery, but he wasn't a hypochondriac, and actually I'm glad he wasn't.' She takes a sip from her glass. 'I don't think hypochondriacs have much fun.'

'Simon had fun,' says Anna.

'But you didn't feel your Dad dying was your fault, did you?' asks Karen.

'Actually, in some ways, I did. He could have eaten better, exercised more, and *I* could have encouraged him, helped him – I love sport, I take care of myself, so I could have shown him, and I didn't. I certainly could have badgered him more to give up smoking.'

'Oh.'

'But now – and admittedly it's years later, so it's different – I can see that his death wasn't the result of one single thing; and therefore one single thing couldn't have changed it.'

'I don't quite understand what you mean . . .'

'It's like a whole lot of stuff came together to make my Dad ill; he smoked, he got stressed by my Mum, he ate rubbish, he worried, he hated the doctor . . .'

'And some of it was just sheer bad luck, surely?' prompts Anna.

'Yes. Some people get cancer, some people don't.'

Anna affirms, 'So you're saying it was wrong of you to blame yourself.'

Lou knows this is what Anna – desperately – wants Karen to believe, but as she's talking it through, she realizes her own take on it is more complicated. She chooses her words carefully. 'I don't know, I think it's what happens, this feeling of guilt. Certainly that's what happened to me. And it's quite understandable. With Simon, we were each involved in his death, I guess, in terms of how we reacted to it – you, me, the nurses, the doctors, and the other passengers. But no one single person is to blame, even if we – all – feel we could have done more. I'm really sure of that.'

Karen takes a deep breath and lets the air out, slowly. 'Thank you . . . That's really helpful.'

'I'm glad.' Lou has surprised herself: she has had more to say than she thought.

They are silent again.

'Do you really believe he was saying he was sorry to leave me?' asks Karen eventually in a small voice.

Once more Lou is pierced by the magnitude of Karen's loss. For all the echoes, it is not the same as losing her father: she had time to acclimatize. Although her father was young – sixty – he was not as young as Simon. Losing a partner – Lou can hardly imagine it. She is single and inevitably feels lonely from time to time, but the sense of being alone must be excruciating after losing your companion of twenty years. That's the tragedy of falling in love; it brings with it the potential for loss. Poor Karen: half a lifetime of loving, suddenly torn away.

Lou knows it is not necessarily what a trained bereavement counsellor would do, but then she isn't a bereavement counsellor; besides, she's not here in any formal capacity. And faced with Karen's grief and need for reassurance, Lou is keen to offer as much comfort as possible. 'Yes, I feel he was. And I truly don't think you could have done any more than you did.'

'No, maybe not . . .' Karen looks down. 'I just wish I'd got to say goodbye. I'd give anything to say goodbye.'

Of course, thinks Lou. Here her father's death offers no comparison: she did get to say goodbye.

Again they are silent.

Eventually, Lou can only reiterate what she is sure of. 'Above all, I think you should remember his last few minutes were really, really happy.'

'OK . . .' Karen blows her nose. The tissue is so sodden now that it is falling apart, tiny pieces of mangled white. Then she struggles, smiles. 'Thank you,' she says. 'You don't know what this means to me.'

23:41

Anna gets home after Steve; he is on his knees in the kitchen rummaging in the cupboard beneath the sink.

'If you're looking for that bottle,' she informs him as she walks into the room, 'I threw it away.'

He turns to look up. 'You did *what?*'

'I binned it,' she declares.

'What gave you the right to do that?'

Anna hasn't got it in her to be patient just now, or to moderate her language to mask her anger. She has used up her reserves during her evening with Karen and Lou. This keeps happening – now that she has someone else who needs her, she has little energy for Steve. There isn't the headspace to process the emotions required to manage him. Usually she would be soothing, deliberately non-confrontational, try to avoid being drawn into his irrational arguments. But tonight she simply cannot be bothered. If necessary, she will have a fight. Indeed, she almost *wants* a fight, not just because she is annoyed with him for letting her down, but because she is so angry with the world/God/Fate for taking Simon away. She wants to vent. So she says, 'I put the bottle in recycling.'

Of course, Steve is one of the worst outlets for hostility.

He is not an impassive punchbag, and intoxicated he is not remotely capable of handling her in a mood like this, as experience should have taught Anna well. But she is on a roll. 'There was hardly anything left in it, and you know I don't like you having spirits in the house.'

Inevitably, Steve rises to the bait. He gets to his feet. 'Oh, little Miss Bossy Boots. You don't like it, do you? I'd forgotten that, what a self-righteous madam you can be.' He takes a step towards her. Although Anna is tall, he is taller, and broader, and strong from years of manual labour. He is very intimidating.

But Anna is not as threatened as she might – or should – be, were she thinking straight herself; she's too furious. 'Don't be rude to me, Steve.'

'Don't be rude to you?' he mimics. His mouth twists. 'I'll be as rude to you as I want to be.'

'Not in my house, you won't.' She knows this will strike a nerve.

'*Your* house,' he sneers. 'That just about says it all, doesn't it? I thought it was "our" house. Isn't that what you said to me? "Come and live at my house, *sweetheart*, and we'll make it ours."'

'Oh, give over, Steve.' Anna goes to hang up her coat, then returns to the kitchen doorway. 'If you want it to be "our" house then try treating me – and it – with a bit of respect.' But this holds no sway with Steve. It is not an argument he can follow at present, or is interested in fathoming.

'You've always thought this was your house, haven't you?' He is shouting by now. 'That's the bloody problem.' It is true. She bought it long before meeting Steve and he pays her rent; she pays the mortgage. But his contribution is minimal – far less than half, so he does pretty well out of the arrangement. 'Me? I'm not good enough for you. I'm just the bloody in-house decorator.'

It's always the same. The inequality between them taps into Steve's insecurity, which fuels his low self-esteem, and, in turn, his drinking. Only, of course, this hatred doesn't get directed internally when he is drunk; it spirals out at anyone who gets in the way, like a cluster bomb. More often than not, the chief casualty is Anna.

They have had this row before, which makes it the more tiresome. 'I invited you to move in before I realized what a drunk you were,' Anna snaps, and thinks, what a *nasty* drunk. 'If I've changed my tune, you've only yourself to blame.'

'I am NOT drunk!' Steve yells.

She laughs. It's ludicrous; he so obviously is.

'You always say I'm drunk when I'm not.'

She shakes her head, then for want of comment, just spits, 'Fuck off, Steve.'

A red rag, of course. He comes right up to her, takes her chin in his hands, and, gripping her hard, says, 'You know what? You're a cunt.'

She flinches at the word, but he misreads her, thinks she's recoiling for another reason.

'Don't worry. You think I'm going to hit you? Well, I won't.'

'I don't think that, no,' she says. He's never hit her yet. The way he towers over her – shoulders braced menacingly, arm muscles taut with anger – is scary. But he has always stopped there, just before actual violence. It is as if he knows that if he ever were to hit her, he would be crossing a line from which he – they – can never return, because while Anna will put up with a lot, she won't put up with that.

'You're a fucking cunt,' he says again, and punches the wall with his fist.

Anna takes the opportunity to duck out from beneath his arm. At the bottom of the stairs she stops, turns, and says, 'Steve, just leave it. I'm going to bed.'

'No, you're not.' He tries to grab her, misses. 'I want to talk to you.'

'I'm sorry, but I don't want to talk to you.' She moves up a couple of steps. 'If you're not ready to come to bed, I suggest you watch some telly, and go to sleep down there.'

'TALK TO ME!' he bellows.

'I don't want to. It's nearly midnight, and I've got work tomorrow. I'm tired.'

'Why won't you talk to me?' he wails. She can sense his mood shifting. Sure enough: 'I love you, Anna.' Then, grotesquely, madly, he falls to his knees, pleading. The hall floor is quarry tile; it must be painful. 'I love you!'

Anna doesn't feel loved, or loving. She feels repelled by him, and is almost inclined to rebuff him completely. But her anger has ebbed, she wants an easy time of it, she needs sleep.

So she says, 'I love you too, but it's bedtime.' And while he is still on his knees, she turns back and mounts the stairs.

As she gets undressed she thinks, there is such a vast gulf between her relationship with Steve, and Karen's with Simon. The tenderness Lou touched on, that she was able to discern in a few seconds – that's love, isn't it? And the caring Karen talked of; she and Simon looked after one another all the time. But Steve had failed Anna earlier, and has failed her again now.

Steve.

Simon.

Similar names. Similar ages. Similar partners, in many ways. They even lived a few hundred yards from one another.

But they are a world apart.

*   *   *

'I do worry about her, you know.' Karen hangs up her blouse in the wardrobe.

'I know you do, love.' Simon is in bed already, sitting half up, propped by pillows. He leans to turn on the bedside light.

'Well, at least she's here tonight. But she'll go back to him in the morning, I know she will.'

'She's a grown woman,' says Simon.

'And stubborn.'

'Call it stubborn if you want. I'd say she knows her own mind.'

'She's in love with him, that's the trouble.'

'Don't get me wrong, I like the guy. But I don't think he's good for her.'

'You're telling me!' Karen reaches for her cleanser, scrubs her eye make-up more viciously than usual to remove it.

'She says he doesn't hit her. Do you believe her?'

'I think so.' Karen steps out of her knickers, unclips her bra, hurls them at the laundry basket. Frustration makes her do it with extra force, but the gesture is futile – they catch in the air and fall short of their destination. She picks them up. 'But how long before he does?' She sits down on the edge of the bed, naked, gloomy.

'If he did, he'd have me to answer to.'

'I love that you're so protective of her.' Karen gives Simon a kiss on the top of his head.

He shifts to reach her, starts to stroke her back. 'With any luck, it won't get that far.'

At his touch, Karen relaxes a little. 'You never know, maybe he'll get some help.'

'Maybe . . .' Simon strokes her some more. 'I could have a word with him, if you like.'

She turns to look at him. 'Could you?'

He shrugs. 'If you think it'll do any good.'

'What would you say?'

'I don't know. Take him to the pub?' He chuckles. 'Tell him man-to-man he has a problem with drink?'

Karen laughs too – going for a couple of beers is Simon's usual way of befriending men. Then she thinks of her friend, downstairs asleep on the sofa. She knows it has taken a lot for Anna to come over; things must have got pretty bad. 'No.' She shakes her head. 'On second thoughts, I don't think talking to him is a good idea. It might have the reverse effect. You'll make him defensive, and he could behave even worse.'

'Whatever; I'll take my lead from you. You've been friends such ages, but you know I'm really fond of her too.'

Karen smiles, rueful. 'I wish I'd never introduced them. But after breaking up with Neil I thought she could do with a boost and I liked Steve at first – he seemed so confident and down to earth. You know what she's like – give her a weak man and she'll run rings around him. Neil simply wasn't strong enough for her. And let's face it, Steve is very good looking.'

'He's nice, too – sober,' observes Simon. 'Even I can see that.'

'Well, yeah, I suppose. That's half the problem, though, isn't it? If he weren't, she wouldn't give him the time of day. She's stubborn and proud, but she's not a complete idiot.'

'No, she's not.'

Karen reaches under the pillow for her nightdress, stands up and pulls it on. 'I guess we've done what we can for now. My hunch is this isn't the first time he's been vile – I reckon she's just kept it from us before. But it won't be the last, either. All we can do is be here for her. It just makes me appreciate how lucky I am having a lovely man like you.' She gets into bed beside him. 'Light, hon.'

Simon reaches to turn out his bedside lamp. 'Spoon me,' he requests, rolling over onto his side.

It's not fair, she thinks, snuggling up to the curl of her husband's back as his breathing slows. Why should I get Simon and Anna get Steve?

But then life's not fair, is it?

Friday

08:06

From the way light is bleaching through the curtains, Lou can tell it's sunny.

Good-oh, she thinks, Friday. No work, no commute, plus today is tennis. She plays throughout the year, weather permitting. And that's not all – she has the evening to look forward to. She is meeting a new girl!

Lou knows her optimism is irrational. She may not even like this woman, let alone fancy her. But perhaps, this once, she could be lucky. Vic gets on with her; that says a lot. Vic thinks Lou will fancy her; Vic knows Lou's taste. If she is a director of a web company, she is likely to be bright. Then there is her name. *Sofia.* Lou likes that especially – it seems ripe with potential.

Yet there is a dull ache in the back of her skull, as if her brain has been parched of water.

Stupid me, she berates herself. I had too much wine at Karen's last night.

Lou knows why she did it, too. She was 'drinking on feelings', as they say in counselling; a clumsy expression used to describe often complex behaviour. And how stupid of her, when it even advised not to use alcohol like that in the list she gave Karen. But she'd been keen not to say the wrong thing, needed to relax and hadn't kept track as she would usually. Lou is not a big drinker, generally, so it doesn't take much before she feels the effects.

Ah, well, she decides. There's nothing else for it: best get busy. I'm out again tonight and may well drink then too – knowing Vic, we are sure to – so I need to get rid of one headache before acquiring another.

She throws back the covers, goes into the living room and opens the curtains. Sun streams in through her window, clear, bright, forcing her to squint.

She can see the old man opposite, looking out of his attic window too. He's there every morning at this time, drinking tea from a cup and saucer – the street is so narrow he can't be more than twenty feet away. His hair is uncombed, wispy, forming long, mad cobwebs like a character from a fairy tale, and he is still in his paisley pyjamas, which are buttoned wrong, asymmetric. She waves, but his eyesight is not good, and he doesn't see her. She's chatted to him, though, in the nearby newsagent on their street corner. He's lived in the same flat for over forty years, and there is something about this that pleases Lou. It might be wishful thinking, but she has a hunch he's gay, and she likes to think he has been there since the early days; she fondly imagines him being a homosexual crusader in the 1960s, coming to an area that was rougher round the edges, then. Whatever his persuasion, he is fragile and solitary now; she supposes he doesn't participate in much fraternizing these days.

Looking down at the street, Lou can see that the seagulls have been busy. Brighton's dustmen fight a losing battle against them, and today the birds have got into a couple of bags of rubbish, ripping them open and scattering debris. Briefly Lou is annoyed and wishes people would dispose of their waste in the communal bins. There always seems to be something left out on the pavement – a half-eaten take-away, old furniture, a rusting bike with bent wheels – but the city has such an itinerant population that many local residents don't seem to know what the collection arrangements are, or care.

Then she reminds herself that the mess, the scruffiness, the couldn't-care-less-ness, is all part of Brighton's rich but well-worn tapestry. And let's face it, she has it better than most. For there, twinkling at her from down the end of the street, is the sea. It is flat beneath a clear blue sky, a stripe of deepest azure at the horizon, paler by the shingle, so there can't be much wind. A perfect day. If Karen's bereavement has clarified anything for Lou, it is to be thankful for small blessings.

She does not bother to shower; she'll only get hot playing tennis, and anyway, she wants to make a ritual of it before she meets Vic and Sofia later. There's something about getting clean after exercise that is especially pleasurable. What she *will* do, however, is ring her mother.

'Hi, Mum,' she says, when her mother answers. 'Just thought I'd let you know when I'll be with you.'

'Oh, super. When?'

Lou knows they are likely to be out late and she doesn't want to rush her guests in the morning, and that's aside from any ulterior motives. 'I was hoping to be with you early afternoon. Say about two?'

Silence.

'OK?' she prompts.

'I guess so.'

I guess not, thinks Lou. If recent events are making her assess what's important, the flip side is that she is less tolerant of minor irritations. Immediately, she is riled. Her mother seems so petty. 'What's the problem?'

'Well, it's only I was expecting you earlier. Given you said you were coming for the weekend, Saturday afternoon is rather late.'

'I never said that.' Lou's response is clipped. She feels guilty, however: did she, maybe? She's fairly sure not, but such a lot has happened in the last few days, she can't be certain. 'I thought I said I'd head to you on Saturday morning—'

'Two o'clock is hardly morning, darling.'

Grrr! It's a perfect example of her mother's manipulation: 'darling' used to conjure up a sense of daughterly responsibility, not a term of endearment at all. Lou mutters, 'I meant I was *leaving* in the morning, not that I'd be there then.'

'Oh, right, my misunderstanding,' says her mother, clearly believing it isn't.

'It takes me over two hours on the train up to you,' Lou justifies.

'Hm,' says her mother. Lou can sense her calculating journey times – can almost hear the unspoken question down the line: what on earth is my daughter doing till midday? – not to mention the accompanying disapproval.

She is about to retaliate when the elderly man opposite shifts from his stance at the window, gazes in her direction. Suddenly, he sees her; she is caught in the sun. He waves and smiles; it deflates Lou's fury. It's not worth it; life, as she has so recently been reminded, is too short. She changes her tone.

'I'm sorry, Mum, I didn't mean to mislead you. I have friends coming down tonight, you see, and I can hardly shove them out into the cold before breakfast. You're such a good host yourself, you'd hate it if I did that, wouldn't you?'

The flattery works. 'Do you think I'm a good host, dear? Why, thank you.'

'Of course, Mum,' lies Lou. 'The best. And you know what? I've got some lovely photos to show you, when I come.'

'Oh, really, dear? What of?'

'Georgia and the children,' she says. 'I took them at Christmas, remember?' Secretly, she is proud of her ability behind a lens.

'That'll be nice,' says her mother.

'Great,' says Lou. The placation seems to have worked. 'Look, I have tennis now, so I have to go. We'll catch up properly tomorrow. I'm looking forward to it. See you then, between two and three. Bye.'

She sits down heavily, head in her hands. 'Looking forward to it' – as if! She needs to sort out these issues with her mother. She hates the way they are both behaving – there is so much duplicity and manipulation, so little integrity to their dealings. It is such a contrast to the openness of her conversation last night – and Karen and Anna are almost strangers. To be so false with the woman who gave birth to her; now more than ever, it doesn't feel right.

*   *   *

Little by little Anna pieces events together as she wakes from slumber. With a lurch she remembers; Simon is dead . . . Ah, yes; that is why her alarm has not gone off: she is not going to work today. She is helping Karen make food for the funeral. Yet she had a good evening with Karen and Lou the night before, given the circumstances. Lou seemed genuinely helpful. Introducing them has been a good thing.

I like Lou, she thinks.

Then, another lurch: Steve.

When she arrived home, he was vile. She'd actually thought he might hit her . . . just fleetingly. Didn't she? She'd denied it at the time; she didn't really acknowledge it. It's only with hindsight that she can recognize what he momentarily seemed capable of. Now she has slept on it, his drunken behaviour seems almost unreal. His moods are so extreme compared to anything else she has experienced that it's as if she can't find a place for them in her day-to-day existence. She knows that if she were to judge him by the same criteria she applies to herself and others, he would fall far short, yet she makes an exception. Perhaps because his conduct is often at its worst outside of normal waking hours, it creates a sense that the two of them occupy somewhere utterly foreign and other, a place where normal standards do not apply. A looking-glass world.

But maybe it is time she stopped making excuses. Simon was a man with principles; he was never excessive or self-righteous about them, but he always treated people well. Anna admired him for that. And now that Simon is dead, it has thrown her double standards into sharp relief. Living with compromise seems harder. For that is what she is doing, isn't it?

Her back is turned to Steve, but she can smell the alcohol, even from here. She is on the very edge of the bed, as if even in sleep she wanted to keep her distance.

She rolls over slowly, so as not to wake him.

At this moment, she does not love him. She doesn't even hate him. She *pities* him. And once pity has entered any relationship . . .

Fuck it, she thinks. Fuck him. Steve has taken too much of her energy already; since waking she has done nothing but think of him. Their issues can wait. He doesn't deserve it. Until after the funeral at least, Karen must be her priority.

*   *   *

The supermarket is crowded; Friday morning is a busy time. Karen is one of many mothers pushing a large trolley round the aisles, stocking up for the weekend. Unlike many, she is without the children; for this she is thankful. It is good to have this opportunity; she doesn't get it very often. But every Friday she has a few hours to herself. She doesn't go to work, Luke is at school and Molly is at Tracy's. Shopping might not seem a thrilling use of her time; nonetheless she is enjoying it. It is a relief to be without her offspring, wheedling to buy items she has no wish to purchase. So she allows herself to float round the aisles in an indulgent daze.

Close to the entrance, she spies a box of bright pink, scaly produce she does not recognize. *Dragon fruit*, says the label. She picks one up. It is cool, smooth to the touch, almost like plastic. She wonders how it tastes, what it's like inside. It is expensive, they don't need it, but Luke might enjoy it, and Karen tries to encourage him to eat more healthily. She puts it in the trolley along with her regulars: bananas, grapes, apples.

She finishes her round of vegetables and stocks up on staples: bread, dried pasta, fish, chicken. At the end of an aisle, she sees a wheat beer on offer. Simon has always said North European lager is best: does Belgium meet his remit? She's not sure, but she likes the design of the bottles, the intriguing mistiness of the liquid, and the price seems reasonable, so she scoops up a six-pack.

Past household cleaning and toiletries, she comes across a rack of children's clothing; all the items are winter stock, on sale. A turquoise corduroy dress covered in roses is reduced to 40 per cent of its original price. She rarely gets presents for the children on a whim, but this is a practical purchase. The colours will suit Molly and it's marked 'Age 4', so it will be a bit big for her and with luck will do for next year too, which makes it even more of a bargain. Karen puts it in the trolley.

That's it: three impulse buys, hardly wild behaviour.

At the till she packs sensibly. Baked beans, tins of tomatoes, puree, and sweetcorn in one bag; washing-up liquid, loo paper, a bathroom scourer in another . . . She pays by debit card and as she waits for her PIN to be verified, checks her watch. There is still a lot of the morning left before she has to collect Molly. She can go home and unload, ready for the weekend. They haven't got a great deal planned but she is happy at the prospect of family time, having Simon home.

It is these two days each week she looks forward to, especially.

*

'Wakey, wakey!'

Karen comes to with a jolt.

She is stopped in the entrance of the supermarket. A man is pushing against her empty trolley, struggling to get through the gate.

'Oh, er, so sorry.' She moves out of his way and with a sigh he wheels past.

She is at the supermarket she always goes to, in Hove. It's Friday, the day she usually does the shopping; once more she is alone.

Last time she was here, she was buying food for Simon.

A week ago that afternoon, Simon phoned her to say he'd got off work an hour early. A week ago that evening, Simon went to the fridge for a beer as soon as he got in, moaned that she'd bought the wrong kind, then felt bad about being ungrateful so came to kiss her while she was cooking. 'You're lovely,' he told her, to make up, and although she saw through his thought process, it made her smile. A week ago he and Luke sliced open the dragon fruit together, admired the exotic pale flesh inside, then tasted it, exclaiming 'Yuck!' and pulling faces, and they all laughed. A week ago he admired Molly in her new dress – 'You look so pretty!' – and gently chided Karen – 'Though I hardly think our daughter needs more clothes' – in a tone that said he forgave her.

A week ago . . .

Seven days, that is all.

And she is here again, preparing for his funeral.

She still feels as if this is happening to someone else; her real life is the one she had back then, this is an aberration. And what is she doing, anyway? She must be mad, thinking she can cater for dozens of people. She can barely function at the moment as it is. She should have let the staff at the funeral parlour organize it, as they had offered, and as Phyllis had suggested only yesterday. She has not been thinking rationally, using her basic common sense. It's as if aspects of her personality have vanished along with Simon, leaving her floundering, like a mountaineer on treacherous terrain, lost in fog.

12.21

'I feel I keep asking you to rescue me,' says Karen.

'You do not. I offered last night. So, where do you want these?' Anna holds up a couple of tuna tins bound together in cellophane. They are in Karen's kitchen, unloading the shopping. Half-unpacked bags cover the table and counter-tops. Boxes of wine and bottles of soft drinks are scattered at their feet. Toby the kitten is busy investigating, bounding in and out of the purchases, excited by all the different smells.

'Let's put stuff we'll need here.' Karen lifts the bags off the table to make room. 'The tuna is for vol-au-vents. The mayo is in there.'

Anna laughs. 'You don't make it easy on yourself, do you?'

'I wasn't thinking very straight. I'd even made a list, but I realize now it was useless. I've no idea what I'm doing most of the time.'

Anna places the mayonnaise alongside the tuna. They are silent for a moment, concentrating. Eventually she says, 'So how many people are you expecting?'

'No idea.'

'Roughly?'

'Well, I emailed nearly sixty, then there are the people I phoned, and our neighbours . . .'

Anna tries not to flinch. It's wonderful Simon was so popular. 'Do you think they will all come?'

'No, no, surely not.'

Anna hopes Karen has a plan of what to cook, as, from what she has seen so far, her friend hasn't a clue where to start. 'Did you have any recipes in mind?'

'Um . . . Kind of . . .'

'And when are Molly and Luke home?'

'Tracy has them this morning. Phyllis is bringing them here about half one.'

'Not that long, then.'

'No.'

'Never mind,' Anna says brightly. 'We'll just make the most of the time we've got. When they get here, they can help.'

'Right. They can help,' Karen echoes. They stand back. By now the table is piled high with ingredients – goat's cheese and tins of chickpeas, bags of frozen prawns, bacon, grapes, onions, olives, an aubergine . . .

Karen starts to giggle, hysterical. Soon tears are streaming from her eyes, she is laughing so much. 'I'm sorry.' She slows herself. 'It's just the idea of Molly helping with filo fucking pastry . . . Oh, dear—' She laughs even harder.

'Don't be sorry.' Anna is giggling too. Making canapés is a crazy undertaking; three-year-old hands will hardly speed matters. But there is something so cathartic about hearing Karen laugh again, properly, and swear, too, that however inappropriate it may seem, it is worth a dozen dumb suggestions.

Just then, the doorbell rings. They both jump, startled.

'You expecting anyone?'

'No.' Karen frowns. 'Probably someone local, dropping in a card or some flowers or something. The living room is rammed already.' She pulls a face and clearly doesn't relish the prospect. 'Shall we just leave it?' Her tone is illicit, colluding. It reminds Anna of their student days, when they would entice one another to go to the pub rather than studying.

'It's up to you,' she says.

'I can't handle any more sympathy from people I hardly know.'

Anna drops her voice. 'We'd best hide, then. They might see we're here.' The front door has stained and frosted glass panels. Press your face up close and it is easy to tell if someone is home – the line of vision is straight down the hall.

'Ooh, yes.' Karen quickly drops on all fours and scuttles under the table.

Anna crawls in to join her. They are at Toby's level – he scuttles over, purring.

'This is the second time this week I've been under a kitchen table,' whispers Karen. 'No wonder I'm going bonkers.'

'How come?'

'Molly hid under Tracy's when she had that tantrum.'

'Ah.'

After a while, Karen whispers, 'Have they gone yet?'

'I'll check.' Anna edges a chair out of the way and pokes her head out. 'Oh!' She rapidly pulls it back in. 'They saw me!'

'Shit.'

'They were peeping through the letterbox!'

'Whatever will they think of us?'

'That we've lost the plot completely?' Their shoulders shake with suppressed laughter.

At that moment a voice bellows towards them. 'Anna? What the hell are you doing?'

'Bollocks,' says Anna.

'Who is it?'

'Steve.'

'Did you know he was coming?'

'No.'

'We'd better let him in, then.' Karen scrambles to her feet. 'Hang on a sec!' she calls, then whispers, 'What's he doing here?'

'Don't know.' Anna shrugs. Tellingly, she is far from glad at the prospect of seeing him. 'He was asleep when I left,' she explains, dusting down her trousers and following Karen to the door.

Steve is standing on the doorstep. Anna observes at once, relieved, that he is sober. The reek of booze has gone; she can smell his deodorant. He is freshly shaved, too.

Moreover, he is brandishing a cardboard box. It takes her a moment to be sure her eyes are not deceiving her. But, no, they're not: it's full of kitchen implements; fluted quiche tins, baking trays, pie cases, a tartlet holder, her Delia Smith recipe book. He has even tucked her gingham apron into a measuring jug.

'Bloody hell,' she says.

'I thought you might need me,' he states. 'And I didn't know what you already have in the way of dishes. Can I come in?'

'Oh, er . . . yes,' says Karen. They both step back to make way.

Anna is puzzled. 'Didn't you have work today?'

'Mike called me this morning. The plaster needs to dry before I can paint the place I was supposed to. He said leave it till Monday.' Mike is a builder who often subcontracts work to Steve.

'You saw my note, then?' Anna had left one on the hall table earlier, letting Steve know where she was going.

'Yup. I thought I'd come and help.' He glances round. 'Looks like you need it.' Steve is so good at cooking, preparing food for lots of people won't faze him in the slightest. In fact, sober, he'll relish it.

'Gosh, darling, that's brilliant.' Anna kisses him. Now he's said that – and reminded her of how thoughtful and generous he can be – she is really happy to see him, and Karen is positively beaming. But this is not the only reason Anna is delighted. It is that she hasn't had to ask him. He has recognized her need – and Karen's – of his own accord. He is being truly helpful. And as he unpacks his box of supplies onto the draining board – the only surface where there is room – she thinks to herself that whilst this might not make up entirely for his behaviour of the night before, it does go some way towards redeeming him.

* * *

Steve pulls the apron over his head.

'Karen, I haven't said how sorry I am.' He stands back, looks at her.

'Thank you,' says Karen. She sees the compassion in his eyes, and sadness hits her again, right in the solar plexus, winding her. How could she have been *laughing*?

Steve opens his arms, as if instinctively gleaning that this is what she needs. Karen almost falls forward into them, and he pulls her in to his chest, tight. At once she is aware that this is the first time she has been held, properly hugged, by a man, since Simon died. Steve is not as big as Simon. He is not quite as tall, is less solid around the trunk. His apron is not as soft as Simon's jumper would be; he is not as cuddly. He smells different. But still, it takes Karen back, in a rush, to that feeling of safety, intimacy and protection that she associates with Simon, and triggers something deep within her. She starts to cry.

There have been so many, many words, but she has had very little physical comfort, and none like this. Every fibre of her being aches for Simon: the scent of him, the touch of him, the feel of him, his warmth. She would do anything at that moment for it to be Simon, standing here, holding her tight. Anything. Soon she is sobbing so hard that she is making the front of Steve's apron wet.

Steve says nothing, other than, 'Karen, our poor Karen,' very softly. And he strokes her hair, gently.

For several minutes they stand there, clutching one another.

Eventually Karen steps away, pulls out of his arms.

She smiles at him and says, 'Thank you.' There is no need for further discussion. He has given her something precious; they both know that.

'Right.' Steve takes a deep breath and ties up the strings of the apron around his back. 'Where shall we start?'

*　*　*

Lou cycles along the seafront; her muscles are warm, she is still hot from tennis. Just after the Palace Pier, she turns left into one of the side streets and, a few yards up, brakes, flips her leg over the saddle and locks her bike to some black iron railings. From the outside there is little to suggest that the Regency building – with once-grand ornate crevices and arched windows – is now a shelter for homeless men. It is here that Lou volunteers every Friday, leading a group counselling session.

She usually ends up with about ten people; half of whom change from one week to another, half of whom are more constant attendees. She tries not to allow those who come regularly to dominate, but it can be hard. It is much easier – and more rewarding – working with those who participate on a frequent basis. With newcomers she feels they are just getting used to the set-up by the time the session finishes, and there is often little she can do to help. These are men with complex histories, and, despite their similarities, they are individuals. They are homeless for very different reasons – there are alcoholics and drug addicts, men with mental health problems, men whose relationships have broken down, or who have lost their jobs or suffered some kind of trauma. She scans the circle quickly: there are eight today; only three regulars, and – she sighs inwardly – five people she has never seen before. Why are there so few familiar faces?

A wooden chair with a red fabric seat is empty. Scrawled across the back are the words, 'JIM'S CHARE. DO NOT USE!!!' in indelible marker. Lou knows Jim is not a hostile man; far from it: it is purely an indication of the struggle these men face every day to retain whatever material possessions they have acquired.

Jim has been coming to her group almost as long as she has been volunteering, which is nearly two years now. He misses weeks occasionally, and he never says very much, sometimes not a word, but there's something about him that Lou particularly likes. She first encountered him before he started coming to the centre, on a street corner near her home in Kemptown. He was sitting in a doorway, making himself sandwiches from sliced brown bread, butter and cottage cheese, using a white plastic knife. The painstaking way he was setting about it – while dressed in a cumbersome old woollen coat, back hunched against the wind and the damp – caught her eye. Later, when she met him properly, she asked if he was particularly fond of brown bread and cottage cheese. He explained he liked to eat well, that the sandwiches were better for him than the food offered by the hostel. Initially it struck Lou as incongruous, the notion that a homeless man should be so concerned about his health: she'd assumed they were mainly addicts, bent on destroying their bodies. But the longer she worked at the centre, the more she realized it wasn't odd at all. Her presumptions were wrong: Jim might be a lost soul, a loner, but he never, as far as she knew, touched drugs or alcohol. She would see him outside often, despite his place at the hostel, wandering around Kemptown, collecting rubbish from pavements. Yet he wasn't foraging for food, or amassing bags of stuff to carry round with him. He was tidying up. He would put the rubbish, bit by bit, into public waste bins, clearing the debris left by other, less thoughtful, people and the seagulls. His diligence, his perfectionism, touched her.

The circle is ready to begin.

'So where is Jim?' Lou asks. 'He wasn't here last week either.'

'Gone,' says Roddy. An older guy, he too is a regular. He is not that bright and his speech lacks frills, but he is well meaning and honest, friendly with most of the other guys.

'Gone?' Lou is used to transience; men pass through the centre all the time. Nevertheless, she would be very sad to see Jim leave.

Roddy nods.

'Last week you didn't know where he was,' says Lou. 'You said he might be coming back.'

'We know where he was now,' says Roddy.

There is something in his tone that sounds ominous. 'Where?'

'Sea.'

'Oh?' Another member of the circle starts rocking his chair violently as if to articulate that he is not getting enough attention. It bangs against the wall, distracting them: Lou struggles to focus. 'Shh, please, Tim. We'll be with you in a second. Please carry on, Roddy.'

Roddy clarifies. 'He took a walk. Into it.'

'The sea?' Lou shivers. It is February, the water is freezing.

'They found him, floating. Washed up by the pier, on Tuesday.'

'Oh, God.' Lou is winded. 'What happened?'

'He went on a bender.'

'But I didn't think Jim drank.'

'He didn't, not for years.'

'So what made him drink now, then?'

Roddy shrugs. 'He found out his wife got remarried.'

'Jim had a wife? I didn't know.' Lou feels dreadful: she has been seeing him for so long and yet was unaware.

'Yep. They split up a decade back. She kicked him out – that's how he ended up on the streets. I thought you knew that?'

'No.' She is choked. Jim kept so much contained. 'How did he find out she was married?'

'Bumped into her. She still lives in Brighton, Whitehawk. She told him.'

'Ah.' Lou is finding it hard to take it in.

'First drink he's had in a long time. They hauled him out, early morning. All grey, like a fish, apparently.'

Lou is shocked. It's not the first time one of her group has died, but previously there have been signs; increasing drug use or depression – she has seen it coming. But she thought Jim was different. She hadn't known he'd been a drinker in the past, but even if she had, she'd never have thought he would go down that road again. She had admired him, the way he managed to be clean, even when he had nothing: no family to look after him, no job, no home of his own. And she had thought that he, more than any of the men that surround her, would, ultimately, be OK. Yet he was as vulnerable as any of them, seemingly more so: they are here, he is dead.

Lou takes a deep breath and struggles to regain her composure. 'Perhaps we can have a few moments' silence to remember him.'

And as they sit, heads bowed, she thinks, so that was why he was so determined to keep healthy – he knew how fragile he was. It reminds her; it is never over, addiction. Addicts are never cured completely, because one day, in a few split seconds, something can happen that makes temptation impossible to resist, even after years of abstention. So they are always recovering, lives precarious; the potential for relapse hanging over them, like a guillotine waiting to fall.

17:02

Steve opens the oven door. 'Perfect. Pass me the gloves.'

Anna does as she is told. Karen's kitchen is his territory now; he has established his domain over the course of the afternoon – even the kitten has been banished to the living room. Anna feels a whoosh of hot air as Steve removes two quiches from the bottom oven and a third from the top, each swollen with baked egg and cheese and expertly browned.

'One tuna, one ham and mushroom and one mixed vegetable,' he announces, laying them on mats so they don't scald the worktop.

Anna feels a mix of relief and pride. Relief that they have come so far in the last few hours; pride in Steve's accomplishment.

'I think that's us done for today,' he says, looking around. The surfaces that were previously covered in tins, packets and jars are testimony to his endeavours. Almost miraculously, he has transformed an ill-matched assortment of purchases into an appetizing array. He has made vast bowls of salsa dip and hummus, from scratch. He has assembled trays of dates stuffed with Parmesan wrapped in bacon, and goat's cheese, grape and pistachio truffles. He has baked four pizzas and one caramelized onion tart, and made three giant salads – one cracked wheat and two bean – that will, he has assured Karen, get better as they absorb dressing overnight. Anna did have to head to the local delicatessen for extra ingredients, not once but twice, and they have both been barked at several times, but nonetheless, it is a truly spectacular spread.

'Now, all you need to do is stick the vol-au-vents and Brie in filo in the oven for a few minutes tomorrow,' he instructs. 'And make the green salads, put out the crisps and bread and bake some potatoes. You could reheat the quiches and pizzas and tart too, if you'd prefer them hot.'

Anna glances at her friend. Karen is nodding, but Anna can tell she is overwhelmed.

It is one of Steve's many inconsistencies: he can be so useless one minute and so capable the next, yet when he is performing well he forgets his own failings – and sometimes those of others – and can be brisk, even bullish.

Anna empathizes with Karen. When exactly is she supposed to do this? It is not as if she is throwing a party, where her only worries other than food are when to take a bath and what to wear. She's going to be at a funeral; her husband's funeral. Inevitably, it will be extremely tough for her. She can hardly leave early to switch the oven on and toss lettuce leaves. She will be a mess.

Anna doesn't want to say this, however, so simply points out, 'It is quite a lot to remember.'

'Doesn't seem that much to me,' mutters Steve. Anna can tell he's offended, as if they're saying that he has not been that helpful, and is setting Karen too big a task. He is so contradictory, she thinks, momentarily maddened. He can be overly sensitive himself one minute, insensitive to others the next. Yet he can be exceptionally considerate too, as this intricate preparation demonstrates.

She tries to ease the situation. 'We'll help though, won't we?' she says to Steve.

'Of course.' He pauses, as if he's only just remembered what all this food is in aid of. Then he declares, 'In fact, yeah, why not? Look, I don't really need to come to the funeral. I can stay here, if you want, do it for you.'

'Sorry?' Karen can't keep up with what he is saying.

'I don't really need to come to the funeral,' he restates. 'I hate them, to be honest. I know Simon was your husband and everything, but – well – I just can't really handle them – the coffin and all that crying and stuff.'

Karen sighs. 'No, I hate them too.'

'I mean, I'll come if you want, of course,' Steve adds quickly, clearly concerned he might have sounded callous. 'I liked Simon, obviously, and I do want to pay my respects.'

'No, no, don't come if you don't want to. I am sure there will be lots of people there.'

I want him to, thinks Anna, but perhaps it is not the time to express her own needs.

'Seriously, though, if you're not bothered, I really don't mind coming here first, if you like. You can let me in, and I'll – you know – sort this lot while you're out. Turn on the oven, cook the rest of the food, put everything out. I'll even serve if you like.'

'You wouldn't mind? Really?'

'Not in the slightest,' says Steve. 'It would be my pleasure, and my way of paying my respects to Simon.'

Anna can see him already, wearing her apron, serving generous portions and charming the guests. He will be in his element, enjoying the kudos of hosting without the stress of it being his ultimate responsibility. For a split second she worries that he might drink too much, but surely he wouldn't do that . . . Anyway, the funeral is late morning; that early in the day they should be safe enough. She *would* like him to go with her – or at least ask her if she minds that he doesn't – but she'll cope, she supposes; doesn't she always? And besides, he is doing this to support Karen. Anna allows herself to feel proud of him once more.

*　*　*

'Now, children,' says Karen, going into the living room once she has said goodbye to Anna and Steve. 'Telly off. You've had enough for one day.'

'No!' says Molly. Not that she appears to have been watching it anyway; she is dancing one of her many Barbie dolls along the back of the sofa on her perpetually pointed toes.

'So have you finished cooking?' asks Phyllis.

'Phew, yes, till tomorrow.'

'You look worn out. Do you want me to give the children their supper?'

Karen thinks she could do with sitting down, but is so out of touch with her physical needs she can barely tell. And Phyllis appears shattered – she has been looking after Molly and Luke the entire afternoon pretty much single-handed. 'No, don't worry, I'll do it. You relax. Can I get you a cup of something?'

'Tea with lemon would be lovely.' Yet instead of staying put on the sofa, Phyllis follows Karen into the kitchen and gently shuts the door. 'Um, I didn't want to mention this when the others were here,' – her voice is low – 'but I think you ought to know that Luke is saying he doesn't want to come tomorrow.'

'What, to the funeral?'

'Mm.' Phyllis nods. 'I didn't really want to push it, I didn't feel it was my place. I suppose it is a huge amount for him to deal with and understand.'

'Of course,' says Karen, reaching for a mug. Actually she wouldn't have minded if Phyllis *had* pushed it. She is not sure she has the strength to manage Luke quite as sympathetically as she would like. He's still being what Karen, in normal circumstances, would term difficult. He's been uncommunicative and sullen since the incident at Tracy's, and she's finding it difficult not to snap at him. Nonetheless, she can appreciate why Phyllis thought it wasn't her role. 'I think he should come, though, don't you?'

'I don't know, dear.' Phyllis frowns. 'Yes, I suppose I do. But he is adamant.'

Karen quickly dunks a teabag in the mug, slices a lemon and hands Phyllis her drink. 'Leave it with me.'

Luke could stay at home with Steve, she supposes, so it isn't a problem logistically, but instinctively she feels that if he doesn't come, she – and he – will always regret it. It is not as if he will get another chance, when he is older and more able to handle it. She returns to the living room, her mind made up.

'Before we have supper,' she announces, realizing she

sounds far more authoritative than she feels, 'I want to talk to you both. You know tomorrow is Daddy's funeral?' Molly nods, but Luke says nothing. 'Luke? What's the matter?'

'Don't want to go.' Luke is sitting on the floor, fiddling with the Velcro straps on his shoes, fastening and unfastening them with repeated ripping sounds.

It's an irritating noise. Karen stifles an urge to tell him to stop it. Instead she sits down beside him, crosses her legs so as to be able to get really close and says, 'Do you know what, sweetheart, I don't want to go much either, but I am going to. Why don't you want to go?'

'Just don't,' he says, looking down.

Sometimes Luke can be like this, Karen is aware. Although he is physically adventurous – unknown sporting and outdoor activities rarely intimidate him – he can be disinclined to venture into new social terrain. Unknown quantities and people unnerve him. Starting school was a real trial, for instance, even more than for most children.

She has to think, hard. Through the tangle of her own upset and anxiety it's a real struggle to work out what is going on for him; it's almost impossible, when she hasn't begun to process her own emotions. He seems as conflicted as she is; one moment apparently coping well – he wanted to say goodbye to his father, after all. Yet here he is, barely seventy-two hours later, refusing to go to his funeral. But wasn't she laughing one minute and crying the next with Anna, earlier? Maybe it's not so odd, after all. It's simply Luke's way of showing her how unhappy he is. He doesn't want his father to be dead; therefore he doesn't want to go to the funeral.

Perhaps if Karen explains again what to expect it will make it less overwhelming. 'I know we've never been to a funeral before, is that what's worrying you?'

Luke is silent. Molly has resumed dancing Barbie round the room, seemingly oblivious. Tip tip tip go her pink plastic toes, all along the edge of the fireguard, up and over the telly, down its side and along the window ledge.

'I know *funeral* is a bit of a strange word,' Karen continues, struck by the fact. 'It sounds very serious, and we've not ever been to one before. But it isn't strange, really. It's very normal when someone has died, like your Daddy. Pretty much everyone who dies has a funeral.'

'Why?' asks Luke.

Karen hesitates. Yet again she is making this up as she goes along, plucking definitions and answers from the muddle of her brain. She's not convinced they are good ones, but what choice does she have? 'It's a special chance for Daddy's family and friends to meet up, you see, and say thank you and goodbye to Daddy. You and Molly got to do that already, but not everyone did, and this is so they can say goodbye too. There will be lots of people you know, including some of your friends, like Austin and his Mummy, and Tracy and Lola – and we want to all be together.'

'Will everyone be crying?' asks Luke.

Maybe that's what's worrying him. But Karen can hardly lie. 'Yes, some people will cry, I'm sure. They will be sad that Daddy has died, just like we're sad.'

'Will lots of grown-ups be crying?'

Ah, so this is definitely a source of concern. Karen can understand. She can remember how awfully disconcerting it was seeing adults cry when she was little; it flummoxed her completely, it wasn't their role. Again, though, she feels she must be honest. 'I'm afraid some grown-ups will probably cry, because they will be sad, just like I am and you are and Granny is. But there will probably be lots of laughter too.' She pauses, wondering what else she can tell him. 'You might notice that some people will be wearing black, or dark colours too, which might look a bit odd at first, but you will get used to it. In fact, we'll go in a very big black car, you and me and Molly and Granny. It's very big and ever so shiny.'

'Really?' Karen can tell this has impressed him.

'Mm. You wouldn't want to miss out on that, would you?'

Luke places his bottom lip over the top one and sucks, a gesture Karen knows means he is thinking.

She can understand his trepidation. The rituals with which he is familiar – Christmas, Easter, birthdays – are focused on children, if not Luke personally; his part is clear. He is a key participant, his behaviour understood, appreciated, enjoyed. But funerals are different: Karen doesn't remember ever going to one as a child. Relatives died; adults marked their passing. Yet although part of her feels she should shelter Luke from this pain, she is determined not to baulk.

'Sweetie, I know it's a bit weird and a bit scary, but I do want you to come. It's a special family thing, and it is important to me that you are there with me. I promise that if you don't like it when we're there, or you feel a bit funny or anything, you can leave and go outside to play or go for a walk or something. We'll find a grown-up – maybe Godmother Anna or Tracy – to go with you. But as you're Daddy's special boy, and it's Daddy's special day, I want us all to be there, together.'

Luke doesn't say any more, and Karen can tell he is far from happy, but she decides to leave it there. She knows that Luke is best cajoled in stages, rather than all at once – not that she has ever had to deal with anything quite like this. And of course, usually, she has Simon to help her . . .

Still, *still*, she can't begin to grasp that she'll never be able to talk to Simon about the children again.

17:14

'They're coming! They're coming!' Karen charges down the stairs from the upstairs bay, flip-flops clacking. 'Back garden, everyone, this instant! Stop that, Phyllis' – she gently slaps her mother-in-law's knuckles to indicate now is not the time to be snipping chives to garnish a tomato salad – 'Anna, grab that bubbly' – and shoos them outside. She follows, pushing the back door shut behind her.

Nearly three dozen people are gathered in the yard. Those close to the window crouch down so as not to be visible from the kitchen. It's a squeeze – the space is barely thirty feet by twenty, and even in ordinary circumstances it's bursting with pots of flowers, garden furniture and toys: beach balls, buckets and spades, small plastic tennis bats.

'Where's Daddy?' Molly's high-pitched voice pierces the air.

'SHHH!' Excitement and nerves make Karen short. 'Sorry, Molster,' she whispers into her ear. 'Daddy and Uncle Al are walking up the hill. They'll be here any moment.'

A few beats' silence. Friends and relatives share expectant glances; children struggle to suppress giggles. Will Simon have guessed? Will he be happy to see them all? Some people hate surprises.

The only sound is Steve, who is stationed down the side return that runs the length of the house, softly turning coals on the barbecue. Karen frowns. He shouldn't have lit it yet. Simon might see the smoke from the street and wonder what is going on.

Through the open kitchen window, she can hear the key turning in the front door. There is the heavy stomping of two men on the doormat – presumably they are removing dirt from their boots – then they step into the hall.

'Karen?' It's Simon.

'That's strange,' says Alan, deliberately throwing his voice, 'I thought they were going to be here.' He's in on the act, of course. The brothers have been playing football together on Hove Lawns as they do most Sundays, but nonetheless it's a responsibility, getting Simon here on time. Karen imagines Alan will be keen to get the pretence over with so he can abdicate responsibility and relax.

'Blimey – what a lot of food,' Simon mutters. Evidently they are in the kitchen.

We should have hidden it, thinks Karen. He's expecting them to have lunch with Alan's family, but there's far too much for eight. It's clearly not a roast, either. But hopefully he won't have time to think about that. Sure enough, in seconds, the back door opens and the two men pause on the threshold.

'Karen?' Simon says again. Before he can take in the throng before him, up they all jump.

'**SURPRISE!**' they yell in unison, pressing forward.

Bang! Bang! go the party poppers. Pop! goes the champagne. At once there are coloured streamers and overflowing plastic glasses, squealing children and laughing adults every-where.

And, in the centre of the throng, Simon.

Looking at first stunned, then overwhelmed, then – Karen can tell – overjoyed.

'Oh, my GOD!' he is saying, his hand to his mouth to smother his emotion. 'You shouldn't have . . .' Men are slapping his back, women are kissing his cheeks; he struggles to turn round and take in who is there. It's almost everyone he knows: Alan's wife, Françoise, with their teenage children; Tracy, who looks after Molly and Luke, and a couple of families from up the road. There is his mother, of course, and his school friend Pete, with his new girlfriend, Emily. There are several of his colleagues – his boss, Charles, has come all the way from Hampstead – and even his fellow footballers, who only just made it to the house before he and Alan got there; Alan was under strict instructions to pull in for petrol en route. And these are just the people to hand. She can see tears glistening in her husband's eyes and he chokes, 'You shouldn't have.'

The children run towards him, released from their curfew. 'Happy birthday, Daddy!' they cry. Simon scoops them into a double hug; they are still small enough that he can lift them both in his arms.

Then more slowly, with measured steps, Karen comes forward. 'Happy birthday, darling.' She reaches round the children's heads to kiss him. His lips are soft and warm, heat radiates from him; he is still sweaty from the game.

'Wow.' He shakes his head. 'I can't get over it. Really, I had no idea.'

'You didn't?'

'Not a clue.' He turns to Alan. 'You sneaky bastard!'

'Fifty.' Alan raises a bottle of beer. 'You didn't think you'd get away with that scot-free?'

Simon shakes his head. 'You knew all along.'

Alan grins. 'Why do you think I said we couldn't stop for a swifty?'

'He *didn't* want to!' Karen chides.

Simon laughs. 'I said *don't* tell the wives.'

Karen reaches round his bottom, hugs him and the children tight. 'Seriously,' – she needs him to verify – 'you don't mind?'

'No, no, it's great. It must have taken heaps of planning. Whenever did you find the time?' Again he pauses to take it in; he is calmer now. 'I can't get over it. Tell you what, though,' – he puts the children down – 'I *would* like a shower.' Although he has removed his football boots and is in his sandals, he is still dressed in his red and white sweat-shirt and shorts and his legs are very muddy.

'Of course,' nods Karen.

'Here—' Anna interrupts to hand him a glass of bubbly. 'Take this with you.'

*

Karen looks round the kitchen. Who would have guessed, eighteen months back – whoever would have guessed – that the next time the surfaces would be covered in dishes prepared in her husband's honour, it would be for his funeral?

She still can't fully conceive of it. Back then, she had

assumed that they had twenty more years together, minimum. Fifty-one is no age for anyone to die, but Simon – *her* Simon?

Fifty-one . . .

It's all so unfair, so terribly, so dreadfully unfair.

Suddenly, Karen is overpowered by fury. And before she can stop herself, she picks up a plastic bowl, piled high with one of Steve's lovingly prepared salads. She doesn't pause to worry if she might break something or scare the children and Phyllis in the living room next door.

'**AAAAAAAAAAAAAAARRRRRRRRGGGGHHHH!**' she roars, a banshee howl from the depths of her gut, and hurls the bowl across the room.

The container bounces off the far wall, splattering beans, sweetcorn and vinaigrette all over the paintwork, and lands, with a useless clatter, on the terracotta-tiled floor.

*   *   *

Lou is sitting in her favourite cafe, overlooking the beach, watching teenage boys skid pebbles into the sea. She ought to go home, shower for tonight, but she needs to clear her head, blow away the sense of other people's tragedy that seems to cling to her. So she has come here, instead, a mug of tea on the table before her, steaming. The glittering and playful light of that morning has gone; the day is fading, fast. It has turned cloudy and chilly and windy, but a bright-yellow tarpaulin shelters her from the worst. Where the boys are playing close to the shore, the water is grey, tinged with orange from churned-up sand, and white horses run all the way to the horizon, a reminder of the power of the elements.

What a week, she thinks, and it is only Friday.

Simon's death touched Lou. And now, there is Jim. How strange, how appallingly sad, that his ex-wife remarrying seems to have been the catalyst that drove him to it.

Lou exhales, slowly.

Her emotions are moving, colliding, re-settling as a result of events; intensifying the sense of her own mortality, making her question her life, how happy she is. And perhaps more than anything, what she feels most strongly as she sits, hands wrapped round her mug of tea, is loneliness.

She first touched on it the night before, that feeling, when she compared her own situation to Karen's. And now, after this, with Jim, she feels it even more acutely: as she looks down at the pebbles in every shade and shape of brown and pink and beige, Simon's death, Jim's suicide, have made her feel gut-wrenchingly alone. Not just alone, but insignificant, as if she is just one tiny stone on an infinite swathe of shingle.

Shingle . . . Suddenly, she remembers: Tuesday. She casts her mind back to the day after Simon died. Wasn't that when she saw an ambulance near here, by the pier? She was on her way to the station, cycling: she had to swerve . . . There was a body, being carried from the beach . . .

Christ, she wonders, was that Jim?

She puts her head in her hands.

Poor Jim. The cottage cheese man. The bin man. And to have walked into the sea: what a brutal, desolate way to go.

Lou wouldn't have been in Jim's head that day for the world.

By contrast, in a way, she almost envies Karen. Seeing

Karen weep for Simon, hearing her talk of him, has made Lou all the more conscious that there is no one special in her life, that she has no partner. She might not be Jim, but still she has had no one to tell about what happened on the train the other morning. So far, other than Anna and Karen, no one she knows is aware that she has witnessed death, first-hand, that week. No one knows she has met with Karen, that they have talked, and Lou has tried to help. So she is carrying the experience on her own. And she is sick of it, having to bear everything alone. Absolutely sick of it. Will it always be this way?

Yet at once another emotion collides with this one: guilt. So she rebukes herself: how can she envy Karen? It is perverse of her, selfish. Her life, her problems, her loneliness; they are nothing, really. She is not homeless; she has not lost a partner. And if she is alone, then whose fault is it, whose decision, ultimately, other than hers?

*

'You know your problem? You're not out, Lou, that's what it is.'

Opposite Lou, limbs tense with fury, chin up, defiant, is Fi, her girlfriend of nearly two years. They are standing in the kitchen of Lou's attic flat, arguing. They are always rowing, but this is the worst yet; Lou can already tell that from here, there will be no going back.

'I am,' protests Lou.

'No, you're not. Not to your family.'

'My sister knows.'

'That's easy. She's our generation. What about your mum? Your aunt?'

'Why is it such a big deal?' Lou asks.

'Because it's *important*, Lou, that's why. I know you think it doesn't matter, but it does. It matters hugely, and the reason you don't think it does is because you can't face doing it.'

Ouch, that hurts. Because it's true. Lou can't face it, and Fi can't understand why.

'I'm fed up with it,' says Fi. 'Coming to stay with your mother, pretending. It's not the separate bedrooms – Jeez, I can live without sex for a night or two. It's the lies. "This is my *friend* Fi"' – she mimics a pathetic voice. 'It's the evasive answers when your mother asks if there's a man in your life. I'm not your friend; I'm your girlfriend, your lover. It's ludicrous at your age, to be telling her otherwise. You're over thirty years old.'

'You don't understand. She's not like your parents. She's not liberal and understanding. She doesn't read the *Guardian* and live in Kentish Town and lecture in politics. She's old-fashioned and prudish. She runs a B&B in Hertfordshire and reads the *Daily Mail*. She'd go ballistic.'

'I know. I've seen what she's like. I've frigging well met her. But that's not the point. You're making this issue all about her, but actually, it's about you. You're not being true to yourself, Lou, keeping it secret. Frankly, I don't give a fuck about her.' Fi shakes her head, despairing. 'It's you I give a fuck about. And so what if she goes ballistic? You'll live through it.'

It's at this moment, exactly, that Lou withdraws. She says

nothing, just shrugs her shoulders. She knows Fi is driven nuts by the way she closes down; that, especially coming on top of her refusal to tell her mother, it will push Fi even further away. Fi has said countless times she can't bear the way Lou does this, that it makes her feel shut out, rejected.

But Lou can't explain; she cannot go there. It is too complicated, too fraught. It is to do with losing her father, this whole issue. And it is not only that she promised her Dad, when he died, not to tell her mother. It is also – more, maybe – Lou's fear that if she does tell her, her mother will cut her off, and she'll lose her mother too. Losing one parent was bad enough, but losing both – no matter what she thinks of her mother   Lou can't face that. If she is forced to make a choice, and she does feel she is being forced, she would rather lose Fi, that is the truth of it.

19:35

Once more, Lou is by the ticket barriers on Brighton station, waiting, this time for Vic and Sofia. Her mood has lifted and she is more excited now: they are due any minute. Lou watches the platforms eagerly, not sure where the train will come in. In London – and every other place Lou has lived – trains always arrive on the same platform, day in, day out. But in Brighton, it seems far more ad hoc. It strikes her as appropriate, this lack of order and formality, as if irreverence has permeated the very infrastructure of the city. She imagines what consternation it would cause if trains to and from her hometown were to run like this. In Hitchin, everything is very orderly. Even the station flora and fauna are perfectly manicured all year round.

Lou sometimes indulges in a sort of 'watched kettle never boils' philosophy; she is superstitious that way. So she wanders into WHSmith nearby on the concourse, hoping it will precipitate the train's arrival. The newsagent is crammed, but Lou doesn't want to make a purchase; it's distraction she is after: she's trying not to admit it to herself, but she is nervous.

A train draws in, the doors open. Sure enough, there is her friend, striding down the platform, looking as incredible as ever. Vic is nearly six feet tall and part Jamaican. With a mass of frizzy shoulder-length hair and statuesque figure, she'd be striking in any event, but she never shies from creating an impression: today she is dressed in giant spike heels and a fake leopard-skin coat, wheeling a bright-red patent bag behind her.

Seconds later, Vic sees Lou, waves enthusiastically, and with confident strides cuts a swathe through the throng. Before Lou can quite work out what's happening, she is being kissed on each cheek with a flamboyant 'Mwah! Darling! Mwah! Darling!' and left reeling by an astonishingly strong musk perfume. As Lou emerges from the leopard-skin embrace, she looks around and realizes Vic has no one in tow: she is alone.

'Where's Sofia?' she asks. Perhaps she's not coming. No, Vic wouldn't do that to her, surely.

'She ended up on a different train,' breezes Vic. 'I said I was meeting you here, she should be here any moment.'

Just then a voice over Lou's shoulder interrupts. 'Vic, hi. Lou, er . . . hello . . .'

Lou turns, takes in short dark tousled hair, deep brown eyes . . . Attraction hits her in the solar plexus. For Sofia is not merely pretty: she's *lovely*, a gorgeous pixie, a girl Puck.

'Lou, Sofia. Sofia, Lou.'

Wow, thinks Lou, but immediately wonders, what on earth

is a girl like this doing, coming to meet me? She can hardly be short of offers.

They head to the taxi rank outside the station. The queue is short and in a couple of minutes Lou and Sofia are ensconced on the back seat of a cab.

'Budge up,' says Vic. 'Oh, sod it, never mind. I'll sit in the front.'

With a huff, Vic plonks herself next to the driver and shuts the door.

'Where in Kemptown?' asks the driver.

Lou leans towards him. 'Top end of Magdalene Street, please.'

Air escapes from the puffed plastic seat as she sits back, and she is acutely conscious of Sofia's presence beside her. It is as if the space between them is filled with static. She imagines it like one of those Van de Graaff generators; she had a small one in the early 1980s shaped like a globe: it shot sparks when you held your hand close to it, tiny forks of lightning connecting to your palm.

Vic swivels round. 'So what's the plan?'

'Are you hungry?'

'Bit peckish,' says Vic. 'I'm not sure I'll last the whole night without anything.'

It's as Lou expected; it takes a lot to fuel Vic's height and flamboyance, so she's thought this through earlier. 'We could go to that tapas place on the Lanes, if you're happy to, then everyone can have what they fancy.' There's lots of choice, and it's not expensive, so Lou won't have to create a fuss about being vegetarian or strapped for cash. She has one worry, nevertheless: 'If that's OK by you, Sofia? I think it's quite good – the owner is Spanish – but it still probably won't compare to the tapas you can get at home.'

'That's fine. I am sure even bad tapas are better than a lot of English food.' Sofia smiles and winks, teasing. It only makes Lou flustered – she's not sure how to react.

They dump their bags at Lou's flat and swiftly head out. The restaurant is a brisk ten minutes' walk away, and when they arrive it is already buzzing. Gingham tablecloths and wooden tables and chairs are packed tightly together; there is barely a seat free.

'Wonder if Howie's here? Save us waiting.' Vic scans the room. 'Ha! There he is.'

She is right: sitting at a table in the far corner, a bottle of wine open before him, is a familiar figure: goatee-bearded, bespectacled, close-shaven head, peering at the menu. Inevitably, Vic's leopard-skin presence distracts him and he looks up and beckons them over.

Vic eases her way through. 'Hiya. How are you?'

Howie grins. 'Fine. You?'

'I'm great. Blimey, though – you look totally different. Last time we met you were a pirate, and I was a Madame.'

'So you remember each other,' Lou interrupts. She is conscious Sofia is standing politely, waiting. 'Howie, this is Vic's friend, Sofia.'

'Sofia?' Howie raises an eyebrow.

Lou can detect innuendo in the gesture. Damn it, she thinks. I should never have confessed to him Vic is setting me up – it'll only intrigue him and make me more self-conscious.

Howie hands the menu to Sofia the moment she is seated.

While she is perusing he directs her: 'The chorizo is very good.'

'Sofia's Spanish.' Lou feels protective. Howie can be full on at times; that's why he and Vic got on so well previously – two drama queens together.

'I don't eat meat,' Sofia explains.

Lou is surprised, and pleased – more common ground.

'That's pretty unusual for a Spaniard,' observes Howie, filling their glasses. 'How did that go down at home?'

'One of the reasons I left,' says Sofia wryly.

'So, been here long, then?'

'Seven years.'

'You should move to Brighton,' says Howie. Like many who have adopted it as their home, he is evangelical about the city's allure. 'It's full of vegetarians.'

'I do love it here.' Sofia glances up, catching Lou's eye.

That was a sign, wasn't it, Lou thinks, approbation of my city? Or am I imagining it? She half wishes Howie would talk to Vic, instead; after all, they've met before. But of course Howie is more interested in Sofia – he knows Lou may fancy her. She couldn't have created a more titillating opportunity for him if she'd tried.

'So tell us about yourself,' Howie continues. But his inter-rogation could be useful: he might get her to reveal what Lou is too diplomatic to ask.

'What do you want to know?'

'Let's start with what brought you to England.'

'I'm a designer. My firm were doing a big project here, and they wanted someone who could speak both Spanish and English to oversee it. So they sent me. I've probably been there a bit too long now, but I love the people and they are very good to me.'

'So where are they based?'

'East Croydon.'

Howie makes the leap in a flash. 'So you *could* move here! Where do you live now?'

'Dalston.'

'Good God, woman – it must take you an *age* to get to work from there.'

'It's not that bad – just over an hour. And I have lots of friends nearby.'

'But if it's friends you're after, then where better than here? It's full of dykes.'

'I like my friends. They're special.'

Lou is glad. So far, it's looking rather promising. Sofia seems to have similar priorities: friends are important to her, too. And it sounds as if Sofia's company rates her highly – she must have talent. But Lou mustn't get ahead of herself. She reins herself in; if Sofia is as attractive and accomplished as she seems, Lou is concerned she's out of her league.

'Well, clearly we'll have to work on you.' He turns to Lou and Vic. 'Won't we?' Then he reaches over for the wine, tops up their glasses, signals to the waiter and hands him the empty bottle. 'Same again, please.'

As the waiter turns back to the bar, he nearly collides with a fellow diner, on her way to their table.

'Hello,' she says.

Lou gulps. Crazy-coloured hair, quirky clothes, cute face: it's the student from behind the bar in the pub on Trafalgar Street.

Well I never, thinks Lou. What are the odds of this? I don't get so much as the bat of an eyelash in months, then I meet two nice-looking women in one evening.

She's just thinking romantic possibilities seem like buses when the girl says, provocatively, 'Fancy seeing you here.' She flashes that same flirtatious smile she gave when she served Lou at the Lord Nelson.

'Indeed,' says Lou, taken aback by her directness. 'Small world.' Again she feels herself blushing.

The girl says, 'Didn't know you ever came to Brighton. You should have said.'

And Lou realizes – the girl's flirtatious smile is not for her at all.

It's not Lou she's recognized: it's Sofia.

21:44

Anna and Steve are watching television. A comedy quiz where the guests comment on current affairs, it is one of Anna's favourite programmes. She associates it with winding down after a busy week; she enjoys the ironic humour and banter. The lights are low, the fire is lit, flames flicker on the ceiling, and Anna, snuggled under a rug on the sofa, is the most relaxed she has been in days. Then Steve gets to his feet.

'Where are you going?' she asks.

'To buy some fags.'

At once Anna braces, suspicious. 'Oh.'

He doesn't look at her; he doesn't have to. She knows. But before she can take issue, he is gone.

Anna pulls her knees in tight, wraps her arms around them. They have done so well today, Steve has been wonderful; why must he do this? It's no better because she can see it coming.

He is gone slightly longer than he should be; she is just beginning to worry when the door slams. He enters the room again, clutching a plastic bag. 'Fancy a glass of red wine?' He removes his cigarettes, puts them on the mantelpiece, along with a bottle.

She shakes her head.

'I'm going to.'

She sighs. 'It's a bit late.' It's not, of course, but Anna doesn't know how to voice the fact that she understands a glass of red won't be his first drink of the evening. Those extra few minutes have betrayed him: he will have bought some vodka, with luck a quarter bottle, but more likely half; downed it, perhaps with a can of Red Bull, while he was out. Yet Anna can't accuse him of that without precipitating a scene, so instead protests about the hour, even though she knows it's pointless and makes her sound a killjoy.

'It's not even ten!'

It is like being struck, this tone – he is both defensive and aggressive in one. And whereas in days gone by she would have let it go, she is now increasingly conscious of how important honesty is within a relationship. She can't get her head around what compels him to head off into the cold, make his sneaky purchase, then swig it on the street corner, furtively. She has never seen him do it – he hides it from her – but she knows. It is so seedy, so desperate.

She shudders.

This is all it has taken – a few centilitres of spirits, a few moments of time – to destroy the tranquillity. The television is still on the same Friday-night show, but now the laughter seems canned and forced; the fire still flickers, but its flames no longer seem to warm the room. Anna still has a rug wrapped tight around her, but now it is to provide protection, not comfort; a shell she wishes was harder, more resistant.

*   *   *

'So,' says the girl. 'What brings you to this neck of the woods?'

'Oh, er . . .' Sofia is stumbling – is she blushing, now, too?

Lou is quick to assess. This is no straightforward platonic encounter, she is certain.

'My, um . . . friends,' mutters Sofia, eventually.

The girl looks round the table. Sees Lou, does a mild double take. 'Don't I recognize you as well?'

'Mm,' Lou nods, wishing she didn't.

'So where do I know *you* from?'

Lou catches Howie's eye. She can tell he's filling in the gaps at a thousand miles per hour. Doubtless he's given the three of them a very fruity past history already.

She struggles to set the record straight at once. 'I saw you in the Lord Nelson, a couple of days ago.'

'Yes, that's it!' The girl laughs, clearly unfazed by the situation.

'So you here with friends too, then?' asks Lou, hoping to appear cooler than she feels. Not that she's really interested in why the girl is at the restaurant; she's far more concerned with what her relationship is to Sofia, how they know each other. There is such a frisson in the air, she can't suppress a stab of jealousy.

The girl nods at a nearby large group. 'It's my mate's twenty-first. We're nearly finished' – Great, thinks Lou – 'but we're going on to the Candy Bar later, if you want to join us.' Lou's heart sinks again.

'Ah . . . right,' nods Sofia. 'Um . . . yeah. Maybe . . .'

Lou can hardly keep her emotions under control: one minute she's buoyed, thinking the girl is hitting on her; now

– only seconds later – she's hitting on Sofia and Sofia's responding. Her whole evening seems to be disintegrating, but of course she's powerless to object. As the girl saunters off seductively, she suppresses a shudder.

Suddenly, Vic pipes up. 'I hate the Candy Bar. It's way too young for us.'

'And they won't let me in,' says Howie.

Lou wants to cheer. She is just relaxing slightly when the girl turns, comes back and says to Sofia, 'Oh, before we leave, you did promise me your number before, remember?' Lou can't believe her audacity.

'Um, er . . . yes,' responds Sofia, all of a dither. Hurriedly, she gets out a pen from her bag, scribbles the digits on a napkin, and hands it to her.

* * *

Anna and Steve sit in silence. The television is on, but Anna is no longer watching. She can't focus; she can't speak. She is so enraged with Steve, so disappointed in him, she knows if she were to say anything, she wouldn't be able to disguise her anger. That would only provoke the hostility that inevitably accompanies his drinking, so it's better to say nothing. But then containing her fury only turns the pressure inwards; she feels like a can of fizzy drink that's been dropped on the floor, a cylinder stretched so tight that liquid will spray everywhere the moment the top is unsealed.

For half an hour she sits like this. Eventually she can't bear it any more. So she lifts the blanket from round her knees, picks up her mobile from the coffee table and gets to her feet.

'Now where are you going?' asks Steve.

'To make a cup of tea.' She can't resist spitting, 'Why, do you want one?'

'Of course I don't.'

'Right, then.'

'Why are you taking your mobile?'

'Because I want to make a call.'

'It's a bit bloody late for that.'

She checks her watch: he's right. It is half ten. The only person she would normally feel able to ring at this hour is Karen, and she can hardly phone her tonight of all nights – not with the funeral tomorrow.

She pauses in the hall, considering. Perhaps there *is* someone she could speak to, or at least text . . . She heads to the kitchen and puts on the kettle. Whilst she is waiting for it to boil she taps:

Hi Lou, hope you're having a nice evening, whatever you're doing. Sorry to bother you so late, but perhaps you could give me a ring when you get a moment? Tomorrow, or whenever. I'd like to ask your advice. Nothing to do with Karen – it's my stupid boyfriend this time. Take care, Anna x

She takes a moment to re-read it. Even at this hour, the professional writer in her won't permit a reprieve. She presses the backspace several times, deletes '*my stupid boyfriend*' and amends it to '*me*'. In so doing she is absolving Steve, but she also figures that it's unreasonable to dump her frustration on Lou at 10.30 on a Friday night. She presses 'Send', drums her fingertips on the countertop.

She wishes she could speak to Lou right now, but the odds of her having her phone switched on, or hearing it if she does, are negligible. For the time being Anna must wait, contained.

*   *   *

'So now where?' asks Howie. They are huddled together outside the restaurant. 'How about the Queen's Head? It's open late.'

'Sure,' says Vic, and Lou is relieved to see that Sofia nods in agreement.

On one hand, she and Sofia have been getting on very well so far. Sofia has given Lou the low-down on much of her life – and somehow Lou has found herself confiding much more than she meant to in return. She has told Sofia not just about her job and friends in Brighton, but has touched on what brought her to the city, her political beliefs, and more. The signals would all be good, but . . .

Lou is niggled by the way Sofia readily handed the girl in the restaurant her phone number. She's not sure exactly what it means, but she isn't comfortable with the implications. Is Sofia going to get together with the girl on another night? Sofia is so attractive, Lou reasons, she could easily be seeing several women. And however much Lou likes her, she doesn't want to be just another notch on Sofia's well-chiselled bedpost.

Once inside the pub, Sofia offers to buy the first round.

'A bottle of Becks, please,' says Vic, then announces, 'I need the loo.'

Lou follows her down there to have the chance for a tête-à-tête.

'*Well?*' says Vic, immediately.

Lou nods. 'She's nice.' She does not want to give too much away.

'Nice?' squawks Vic. 'Of course she's bloody nice! She wouldn't be my mate if she wasn't nice. Do you fancy her, though, or what?'

'Oh, honestly, Vic,' Lou shuffles her feet, looks down. She can feel other women in the queue for the cubicles listening in.

'Aha!' Vic peers at her face, then claps her hands. 'I knew it!' Clearly she is thrilled, though whether she is more delighted to have brought two good friends together or with her own matchmaking ability Lou cannot be sure. 'I reckon she fancies you, too,' Vic nods sagely.

'You do?'

'She's definitely got the hots for you, I can tell.'

'Really?'

'Sure, all that probing about your life, she's keen.'

'But what about that girl?' asks Lou.

'What girl?'

'You know, the one Sofia gave her number.'

'Oh, *her.* That's nothing, I'm sure.'

But Lou can't dismiss it so easily. Vic has got a vested interest in bringing them together, and as yet Lou doesn't trust the situation.

At that moment a cubicle comes free.

'You go first,' says Vic, and Lou takes her up on the offer. As she is sitting inside, she hears Vic, evidently unaware

291

that tipsiness has made her even louder than usual, say *sotto voce*, 'Go on, then, what do you think?'

It can only be Sofia she is talking to. Once she bought the round, she must have come downstairs, too.

Lou waits, breath bated, for the answer.

'She's lovely,' says Sofia.

Lou smiles. So she does like her, then! But she can tell from Sofia's voice that she knows Lou is listening. She may simply be being polite: she is not as tipsy as Vic, and is more self-aware.

'But do you fancy her?' prompts Vic.

'Isn't she still in here?' Sofia points out. 'I didn't see her when I came down the stairs.'

'Yes, but she won't hear.'

'I think she will,' Sofia says firmly, and Lou can't help but laugh to herself.

'I *can* hear,' she says, emerging from her cubicle.

And as Vic heads into a cubicle, Sofia grins at Lou and knowingly shakes her head.

* * *

Karen is lying in the bath. She looks down at her body, distorted by perspective. She has added bubbles to the water; she lifts a leg: bubbles slide down it, a miniature avalanche. She turns her thigh, critical. Her skin is pale, any hint of a summer tan long gone. She could do with toning up, losing a little weight. As if that matters now. She focuses her attention nearer: her breasts, once her pride and joy, are not what they were after breastfeeding two children; they've lost their firm roundedness, and sag, slightly forlornly, to each side, lifted a little by the water.

'*But I love them,*' she can hear Simon say. He has put the loo seat down so he can use it as a chair and chat to her while she baths. And she nods, knowing this is true; he still gives them ample attention. Not just when they make love, either; sometimes he'll sneak a swift grapple when no one is looking, taking her by surprise in the kitchen and grabbing her breasts from behind, whispering 'Phwoar!' in her ear.

Besides, his body has changed too; in two decades he has put on nearly two stone, his midriff is not as taut as it was, his tummy boasts more than a hint of flab, his pectorals are no longer hard, even his biceps are softer. Does she mind that, either? No, of course not, it makes her feel better; allows her to feel sexy in spite of her own faults. She'd hate a twenty-something Simon now; it would intimidate her, make her feel vulnerable.

'How could your body have let you down so?' she whispers. His imperfections were so minor, so *normal*, they were the flaws of almost every middle-aged man. There were no signs that anything was seriously wrong.

'*Don't ask me,*' he says. '*Do you think I meant for this to happen?*'

'*Of course not.*' She likes it here, with her back to the loo; she can't see him, but she knows he is there. '*We've got your funeral tomorrow,*' she tells him.

'*You poor thing,*' he replies. '*I hope you haven't got yourself in a stew about it.*'

Her pre-hosting nerves are legendary: she gets irritable

and tense, and even Luke has noticed it. 'Mummy wasn't very nice before my birthday party,' he once soberly told Anna. Karen had laughed at the time, touched by his perception.

The phone rings, breaking her train of thought. She can't be bothered to get out of the bath; she doesn't feel like answering it, and anyway, she probably won't make it in time. The answerphone clicks on automatically.

'You have reached Karen and Simon and Luke and Molly's house,' says Simon. It is the first time Karen has heard this announcement since his death. She gasps; it heightens the sense of his presence. She closes her eyes, absorbing the timbre of his voice, sucking it in, as if it were nourishment and she were starving. The words might be commonplace: 'I'm afraid we're not here right now, so please leave a message after the tone,' but each one is rare and precious.

'Hello, darling, it's Mum.' The familiar voice takes her by surprise. It is late for her mother to be calling. She and Karen's father live in the Algarve, where they are an hour ahead; it must be nearly midnight there. 'I'd just thought I'd let you know I'll be arriving at Gatwick at nine tomorrow morning, so I should be with you by eleven or so,' she says. 'I've managed to find someone to look after your father for a few days too, so I can stay until Tuesday, at least, or if he seems to be doing OK without me, Wednesday or Thursday.'

As she hears the phone click down, Karen sighs with relief.

The moment her mother says she is coming, Karen realizes how dreadfully she has missed having her there. There is no substitute for maternal love at a time like this, but her parents are in their seventies and live a long way away. Moreover, Karen's father has Alzheimer's disease and can't be left for any length of time without a carer. It is a role her mother fulfils round the clock, and finding a substitute is never easy. Since her father's diagnosis Karen has got used to putting her own needs second – it has been several years since she has made many demands of her mother, let alone her father. Even this weekend just gone she'd said she would be OK with Phyllis and Anna to support her until the day of the funeral, and that despite her mother protesting she'd like to come sooner. But now she realizes that however supportive others have been, it is not the same. Phyllis has her own grief, Anna is not her mother.

Bizarrely, having her needs met at last makes Karen feel sadder. She starts to cry.

'I want my Mummy,' she sniffs.

She can sense Simon, who is still sitting behind her, nod in understanding. Momentarily, she feels no older than Luke, or even Molly, and, with a childlike gesture, wipes her cheeks with the back of her hand. In the damp atmosphere of the bathroom, she doesn't know where condensation begins and tears end.

Saturday

01:07

It's gone one in the morning by the time they stumble out of the pub.

'Fancy a coffee at ours?' suggests Howie.

Lou is keen to prolong the evening as long as possible and Howie lives close to her place. 'I'm up for it.'

'Me too,' say Sofia and Vic.

It's all going swimmingly, but Lou has yet to ascertain what exactly to make of Sofia. Given Sofia's body language, Lou is pretty certain she *is* physically attracted to her. Sofia has been sitting in the pub with her arm resting on the back of the bench they were sharing, for instance, almost around Lou's shoulders, for over two hours. She's been laughing a lot, too. But there has been no opportunity for either one of them to do more with the others so near, making it hard to gauge for sure. And Lou still can't shake her concern that Sofia may have several women interested in her – good-looking ones at that – and vice versa.

Aargh! She would *so* like to know how Sofia feels! Why is it so complicated? She mentally kicks herself. When merely meeting someone is ridden with angst and open to mis-interpretation, is it any wonder she is so hopeless at relationships?

Lord, she realizes, she has been so wrapped up in her thoughts that the others are way ahead of her. But Sofia has paused at the corner to wait. Lou runs to catch up.

'So sorry,' she says, breathless. 'I was in a world of my own.'

'No, it's good,' says Sofia. And before Lou can stop her, or pull it away, she grabs her hand.

Sofia's palm feels lovely; indeed, the gesture seems so genuine, so affectionate, so intimate, that all at once Lou can't bear the suspense any longer. She might be confused, but she's attracted to Sofia so she has to know, before things – they – go any further.

'Um . . . Can I ask you something?' she says.

'Yeah, what?'

Lou is filled with trepidation – she finds this hard. But it's dark and they're a bit drunk – with luck her embarrassment is, at least slightly, hidden. Eventually she says, 'That girl, in the restaurant . . .?'

'What about her?'

'You gave her your number,' says Lou, quietly.

Sofia is about to laugh, but then seems to hear the anxiety in Lou's voice, and turns to face her.

'You didn't think I was interested in her, did you?'

Lou is silent. She feels so exposed, awkward, she can't admit it explicitly.

Sofia continues, 'I met her at a party in London a few weeks ago.'

Lou's heart begins to pound. Her reaction might seem excessive, but she can't help it; her hopes are up, yet she's bracing herself for disappointment.

Sofia continues, 'And I think she fancies me a bit, yes . . .'

Lou can hardly bear to hear more, yet she has to know.

'. . . Though frankly, I don't think she's that picky.'

Lou's mind races back to the Lord Nelson. That figures, she thinks; she came on to me a little, too.

'Anyway, she's going to Spain soon.'

'Ah . . .'

'And I said I have a friend in Madrid who is looking for a room-mate,' Sofia finishes. 'She wanted my number so I could put them in touch.'

'Oh.' All at once, Lou feels really, really foolish.

Sofia adds, 'Actually, I left the party without giving it to her originally because I found her a bit full on. Then I felt caught – what is the phrase? "on the hop" – by her at the restaurant just now. I was embarrassed.'

'I see,' says Lou.

They carry on walking, in silence, but the air is full of Lou's thoughts. She's happy there was nothing in it, but dismayed nonetheless.

I've made a *total* prat of myself, she thinks. And now Sofia knows just how keen I am; how mortifying! When will I ever learn?

They're nearly at Howie's and she's blown it completely.

But then Sofia turns, sweeps her into a doorway and kisses her.

Lou is astonished at first – it seems to be happening so easily, so fast. Yet in seconds she's far too caught up into the experience to analyse. She just gives in to it, and my, what a kiss it is. It's everything Lou has been yearning for, and more. Sofia smells gorgeous – gorgeous! – and her mouth is delicious, all soft and wet and warm; Lou never wants it to stop. They kiss for ages. *Ages.* She had forgotten how fantastic it can be.

'I've been wanting to do that all night,' Sofia says eventually. 'But I couldn't get you on your own.'

'You have?' Lou's heart skips.

'Mm,' Sofia nods. 'Hours.'

'Me too.' Lou smiles at her. 'But they'll be wondering where we are – I suppose we'd better go.'

'Yeah, I guess.' Sofia wrinkles her nose, indicating she doesn't want to.

They start walking, but a few paces later Sofia catches the collar of Lou's coat and guides her to a lamp post.

'I think it's so cute you were jealous!' she says, and kisses her again.

This time, Lou feels her whole body melt: it's as if she is carried up and away by waves of pure physical pleasure, out of her head entirely. As Sofia presses her body against hers, she's hit by a surge of lust so strong she thinks she would fall over were it not for the post supporting them.

That second kiss seals it: if Lou had any doubt that they were attracted to one another before, now she has none.

* * *

Anna hates nights like this, when sleep eludes her. It is as if the more she thinks about sleeping, the more she can't, until eventually she's in a whirl of panic. Worries turn over and over; worries she has no ability to sort or ease. They are like yellow cream in a butter churn, a great slopping unformed mass. Worry about Steve. Worry about work. Worry about Karen. Worry about Molly and Luke. Even worry about Lou, from whom she's heard nothing since she sent her that text. Worry, worry, worry . . .

And now she needs a pee.

Up she gets, heads to the bathroom. From there she can hear the TV is still on, loud, downstairs. Steve must be in the living room: he's not come to bed with her. Whether he has fallen asleep with the telly on, or is awake and watching some awful film; she doesn't know. She hopes it is the former. If she goes to check and he is awake, she's almost afraid of what she'll encounter. His mood could be beyond appeasement; she can't face taking that on again.

But if he *is* asleep, she would like to turn the television off. The noise might wake him later and she would rather he slept off the booze, right through till morning. She pads softly down, tentatively pushes open the door.

The only light comes from the screen flashing in the corner; the saturated reds and blues of a 1960s horror movie reveal a pitiful scene. Steve is indeed asleep, splayed out, no blankets, no cushions, fully clothed, shoes still on his feet, on the wooden floor.

She feels like kicking him.

Instead she tiptoes round him, turns off the telly. He murmurs something about not doing that, then resumes snoring.

She doesn't even put a blanket over him or a pillow beneath his head, because she doesn't want to wake him. She just pulls the door to, and goes back up the stairs.

In the bedroom, she opens the curtains a little, just to check what's going on outside.

Diagonally opposite her house is an office block with a wide porch where a homeless guy sometimes sleeps. She used to see him there a lot, but recently it's only been occasionally.

When Steve first moved in with Anna, he asked her why she didn't complain about the man to the people in the offices. She said it didn't bother her, he was doing no harm.

'He's very tidy,' she'd said. 'He puts his cardboard away, neatly, each morning – I've seen him. I don't think he's an addict or anything like that.'

He was even there one Christmas, so Steve decided to take him a glass of brandy.

'He didn't want it,' said Steve, bewildered, returning with the glass not drunk.

'See?' said Anna. 'I told you.'

'You won't believe what he was doing.'

'What?'

'Making cottage cheese sandwiches. I offered him some Christmas dinner, but he didn't want that either.'

'Oh, well, each to their own.'

He's not there tonight. I wonder what's happened to him? Anna thinks, pulling the curtains closed again and returning to bed. She hopes he has found somewhere else, permanent, to stay.

She thinks of Steve downstairs; how much more aware

of his drinking she is now than she was when he moved in. What would happen if she finished with him? Would he be able to look after himself, drinking the way he does? She is not sure he would; though he managed OK before he met her. Would he end up on the streets, too? It is yet another worry she can't work out, adding to the yellow gloop in her brain.

*   *   *

Lou undresses, conscious of Sofia in the room next door. Respecting Vic's request that she and Sofia do nothing in earshot, and not wanting to be presumptuous with Sofia, she has given them her futon.

Now, inhibitions freed by the fact there is no one watching, Lou shimmies out of her jeans with a sexy wiggle of her bottom. To hell with neatly folding them; she can't be arsed. She hooks them onto her ankle, kicks out, and gleefully watches them fly across the room. They land with an unexpected clunk, and Lou's mobile shoots out of the pocket across the wooden floor. Best check it has not come to any harm. It seems fine, and she is poised to put it on the table and get into her sleeping bag on the sofa, when the little envelope icon catches her eye. Who has texted her? She clicks, opens, reads.

Oh dear, she thinks, Anna needs to talk.

Lou checks the time the text was sent: 22:33. That's

pretty late to have tried to get in touch. Damn it. If she had heard her phone beep, Lou could have called back there and then, but the pub was so noisy. Though perhaps it was for the best – Lou wouldn't have given Anna her full attention.

She will ring Anna the next day, just as soon as she can.

* * *

Karen wakes, all of a sudden. She is freezing, shivering so hard her teeth are chattering. She's had a nightmare; she was caught in a whirlpool, being sucked down a vortex into a deep, dark pothole, gasping for air.

She turns on the light.

It's OK, she tells herself, looking round. You are here, in your room. It is fine.

She has been in a cold sweat. Her nightdress is drenched; she gets up, pulls it over her head, swaps it for a clean T-shirt and gets back into bed. But she can't stop shivering; if anything she feels even colder. She pulls the duvet right round her, tight and snug, like a tortoise shell.

Karen has always liked the sense of something protecting her as she sleeps, warm and cosy. When she was little, she used to get all her stuffed toys and lay them along the length of the bed, between the sheets, in a line. She'd get in afterwards and wedge them in, tight against her spine. Only then could she drift off.

'That's a bit cruel,' she remembers Simon saying, when she had told him.

'They weren't *real* animals, darling,' she'd laughed.

She might be grown-up, but still she likes the sensation of something snuggled close behind her. So in winter, Simon would wrap his body round her; he would become her tortoise shell. At the very least, their bodies would be touching somewhere: their legs would be intertwined, or they would be holding hands; she would know she was loved, and vice versa.

So that's why she can't stop shivering. It isn't OK: Simon isn't here.

Shake, shake, shake, go her muscles, contracting involuntarily. She tries to keep them still, to no avail. Judder, judder, judder, go her teeth.

She pulls her knees into her tummy, foetal.

Perhaps the shivering is another symptom of shock: a physical reaction to trauma. She is reminded of a cat she found once, that had been knocked over. It was in its death throes, by the side of the road outside the house. Juddering, as she is now. She had made Simon go and break its neck, out of kindness. She couldn't do it herself, but he had managed to.

Part of her would like someone to break *her* neck, put her out of her misery. But they can't; that is not a choice she has. She must go on, for Molly and Luke. There is simply no way she could leave her children; they need her more than ever. She focuses on them, her babies. And as she thinks of them – how small they are, how vulnerable, how much they love her, how much she loves them – gradually, gradually, the shivering subsides.

08:33

'Why don't you wear your red T-shirt? It really suits you, and you might be a bit hot in that, doing the barbecue,' says Anna. Steve is pulling a navy sweatshirt over his head. She flings open the window to get a sense of the temperature – inhales. Smiles. Ah! How she loves this view. The house is near the top of one of Brighton's several hills, and rows of pastel-coloured terraces spread before her like a toy town. Compared to London's endless sprawl, the city has clearly discernible boundaries, and in the distance, fields swoop up, green and brown, onto the South Downs. Above, the sky is hazy blue. 'It looks like another real scorcher.'

Anna pauses as she puts on her make-up to watch him. Steve's back is broad and strong, his skin tanned deep gold from outside labour, and, as he reaches into a drawer, she can see the definition of his muscles. He is blessed, she thinks, to have such a beautiful body.

'Well, madam.' He turns to face her. 'This all right for you?'

The scarlet top offsets his straw-blond hair – he looks his very best. Anna has a new dress herself, bought especially for today. It shows off her figure; they will make a hand-some couple at Simon's fiftieth.

Who cares that she has just put on her lipstick? She is so proud of Steve; he looks irresistible. She *has* to kiss him that moment.

*

Well, that dress won't do, Anna decides, returning it to the wardrobe. It is too summery, too revealing – it would be disrespectful; the likes of Phyllis might be offended. Yet being in black from head to toe seems too sombre for Simon. How about the skirt and polo neck she wore earlier this week with her dark-green boots and pebble necklace? She loves those boots and at least she'll feel like herself: she is sure Simon would have wanted that.

It feels so strange – thinking in terms of what Simon would have wished for, when he won't be there. She can't remember the last time Karen had a gathering on this scale where he wasn't around. Anna can hear him now, in full sociable mode, chuckling at some crass joke, arguing about politics, chasing children round the house with a monster roar . . .

Once again Anna is struck by her mother's words: life isn't fair.

If it was fair, why should Steve live on, his physique his blessing, a vessel for endless mistreatment, whilst Simon – whose only transgressions seem to have been that he worked too hard and stressed too much – be cursed with a body that let him down so?

Whereas Steve is astonishingly resilient physically, which

invites abuse: it is hard to motivate him to curtail his drinking when he recovers so fast.

My, how her feelings for him have altered since that barbecue.

She still loves him, for sure, but she no longer worships him so blindly. She can't, because if she is honest with herself – which she has frequently failed to be – Steve's consumption has been gradually escalating since he moved in, and with it, his temper.

Anna recalls the evening when he first really alarmed her. They'd just finished eating, and she'd tried to prevent him drinking more wine. He – they – had had enough already, she'd thought. Certainly she had.

'You can't stop me,' he'd said, provocatively.

Swiftly, she'd grabbed his glass from the kitchen table. Steve – reactions slowed – carried on pouring; wine had gone everywhere. And he'd gone ballistic, snatching the glass from her; the stem had snapped in the tussle. He had then taken the bowl of the glass, thrown it on the floor and stamped the pieces into the quarry tiles.

'There,' he'd snarled. 'Satisfied?'

Frightened of what he might do next, she'd fled to Karen and Simon's, even though it was late. They'd comforted and calmed her, but she'd remained shaken and upset for days. Of course, afterwards Steve was full of remorse, pledged to make amends. They'd both given up alcohol for a month as a consequence: Anna has never had a problem herself, but she'd hoped her abstention would make it easier for him. Yet when the month was up, he was back to where he had been before within days.

Since then he has had many, many chances; she has borne countless promises of sobriety. The words sound hollow these days, his humility a pretence. He has let her down repeatedly, run her ragged.

And where is he now? Exactly. Crashed out downstairs.

Viciously, she shakes out her skirt.

Damn him.

This morning Steve can choose his own outfit. She will save her energy for Simon. It's his day, after all.

* * *

'What's the matter with this one?' Karen holds up a navy velvet pinafore.

Molly stamps her foot. 'Want to wear my new dress!'

'But your new one isn't a party dress,' says Karen patiently. How can she explain that turquoise and pink flowers are too jolly for a funeral? It seems ironic, as Simon liked Molly's new dress. 'This is your Christmas dress,' she lures, and before Molly can descend into a full tantrum, pops the pinafore over her head. 'There.' She turns her daughter to face her and tugs down the hem. 'You look really pretty. Can we brush your hair next?'

'Noooooooo!' wails Molly. Her hair is soft and fine, like candyfloss, and forms knots at the slightest opportunity.

'You can't go to Daddy's special party with a great big tangle in your hair.'

'Ow!'

She carries on, despite her daughter's protestations. 'Right, you're done.' She kisses the top of Molly's head. 'Good girl.'

What's the time? she wonders, and checks her watch to see how long they've got.

*   *   *

'It's nearly nine,' says Lou, poised at the bedside with two mugs. 'You wanted me to wake you.'

'Did I?' mutters Vic. She rolls over and snuggles under the covers.

'Yup. I've brought you a cup of tea.' Lou edges a cup onto the bedside table. 'You've got your party today.'

'Bloody hell, so I have.' Vic flings her arms out over the duvet. 'My house is a wreck.'

'Never!' Lou teases.

The noise causes Sofia to stir. 'Hello . . .' she says sleepily, and smiles up at Lou.

She looks adorable, Lou thinks, all ruffle-haired and bleary-eyed. But she simply says, 'Tea.'

'Thank you.' Sofia manoeuvres herself to a seated position and reaches across Vic for her mug.

Lou perches on the edge of the futon. 'Don't feel you have to rush.'

Vic takes a noisy slurp. 'I thought you were going to your mum's?'

'I am, but I don't have to leave till just gone midday.'

'I need to get home, tidy up.' Vic pouts. 'Why did you let me get so drunk?'

'I think you did it all on your own,' Lou laughs. She finds

bantering with Vic enjoyable anyway, but this morning Sofia's presence adds a special thrill. 'How are you feeling?' she asks Sofia, her heart aflutter. She has been awake since six, consumed by hope and trepidation. Sofia said some lovely things last night, but was it the wine talking? Lou can't be sure Sofia will want to see her again.

'I'm good. A bit hungover, maybe . . . but yes, really good.' Sofia opens her eyes wide, locking her gaze with Lou's. 'I had a *lovely* evening.'

That is a signal, surely it is! Inside, Lou jumps for joy. 'Me too.' Once more she can feel herself blushing.

Vic coughs pointedly. 'Great,' she declares loudly. 'I am glad you two had such a good time. I feel fucking dreadful.'

'Ooh, you!' Sofia knocks Vic's elbow, nearly spilling her tea. 'I tell you what. I'm not busy today. Why don't I help tidy up your place?'

'Have you seen it?' warns Lou.

'No . . .'

'She's not wrong when she says it's a pigsty.'

'I don't know what you mean,' protests Vic. 'It's only a few papers and stuff.'

Lou shakes her head. 'It's a tip!'

'It's fine,' shrugs Sofia. 'I come from a big family, I'm used to mess.'

'I'd *love* you to help me.' Vic kisses Sofia's cheek.

Lou has a pang of envy. She wishes she were alone with Sofia; she would like to be the one spending the day with her; she wouldn't even mind if they had chores that needed doing. Silently, she curses her mother.

313

She switches focus. 'What do you want for breakfast? I've lots in.'

*   *   *

I wonder how much of this they grasp, thinks Karen as she follows Luke's forthright stride and Molly's more careful bottom-sliding down the stairs. They seem to dip in and out of understanding; one minute connecting with surprising perspicacity, the next distracted by more immediate issues. So, 'Did Daddy die because he did something bad?' and, 'Is he coming back after the special party?' or the heartbreaking, 'Was it my fault?' jostle alongside, 'Will there be cake?' and, 'When are we going in the shiny car?'

She has had to repeat some answers again and again. They seem to take in as much as they can manage, then change the subject abruptly when they've had enough.

Yet, in a less obvious way, isn't she doing this too? Connecting and disconnecting, facing grief then turning from it? One minute she is caught up in minutiae: Will her feet get sore standing in heels at the church? Have they made enough food? Will the kitten get scared by dozens of strangers in the house; should she shut him in a room upstairs? The next moment she is weeping uncontrollably, taken over by pain so profound she can barely move. Then there was the salad bowl incident; her own fury scared her.

But maybe these are different ways of dealing with events, for all of them. Molly and Luke are infantile echoes of her; their emotions pared down, their reactions simpler but similar, for if they have difficulty taking in what has happened, then so, too, does she.

Why is she dressing up, for instance? Why can't she wear clothes to reflect the fact that she is at her lowest ebb – a tracksuit, a jumper full of holes, dirty jeans? Why can't she leave her hair a mess, her face unmade-up? The crazed and grieving Karen doesn't care about her appearance. Yet she must go through with this charade, polish herself and her children to perfection: she, in particular, must hold it together. Oh, she can cry, yes, that's allowed, people expect that, they will sympathize. But what about screaming? Howling and hurling plates like she did yesterday? She imagines the shocked faces as she shouts and swears and smashes everything. But she is so angry, surely others must feel the same. Maybe a plate-throwing ceremony would be a more fitting ritual than church. Then everyone could have a go, smashing crockery up against the back garden wall.

10:23

'I'm off,' Anna tells Steve, keen to get out of the house before she explodes at him.

'Oh, right.' He is surprised. 'I thought the funeral wasn't till half eleven.'

'It's not. I fancy a walk. But you need to hurry up, or you'll be late for Karen.'

'Sure, sure.'

'In fact, you ought to ring her, check when she's leaving, in case she needs to put the keys somewhere for you.' Here she goes again, sorting out his mess: if he had not got drunk the night before, he wouldn't have overslept, wouldn't be so slow and bleary now.

It is bad enough that is he not coming to the funeral with her – she is privately very hurt about that; but if he lets Karen down too, she won't be able to control her fury, and it's not the moment to lose her temper.

Steve says cautiously, 'I haven't got her number.'

'Christ!' Anna snatches her mobile from her bag. '*I'll* ring her. You're useless.' She marches to the front door, yanks it open.

'Where are you going to tell her to leave the keys?' he cowers.

'I don't pissing know. Under a pot or something. Look for them!' She stops herself: it's actually important to Karen that Steve is able to fulfil his pledge to take care of the food. She presses speed dial and while she waits for Karen to answer, says, 'Sorting keys for you is the last thing she needs an hour before her husband's funeral.'

'Sorry.'

'No, you're not!' she snaps. 'If you were really sorry, you'd stop getting drunk the whole fucking time!'

'I can't stop,' he says, quietly.

*　　*　　*

'I suppose we'd better get going shortly,' says Vic.

'So soon?' asks Lou, disappointed: she doesn't have to leave for over an hour to get to her mother's.

'I've heaps to do,' Vic sighs. 'It's not just that the flat is a tip; I need to get booze in, and food.'

'Right.' Lou can't help but feel a little miffed that Vic's disorganization will curtail her time with Sofia. She's also conscious of Vic's presence. How can she and Sofia arrange to see one another again, or even swap numbers, with Vic sitting there? Vic is her oldest friend, but nevertheless Lou is shy about it.

Just then, Vic demonstrates genuine sensitivity. 'I'm going onto the roof terrace, I need to make a couple of phone calls before we go,' she says.

Lou wants to hug her. *That's* why she is my friend, she reminds herself. For all her bluster, self-centredness and lack of tact, Vic has Lou's best interests, and happiness, at heart.

*   *   *

Jesus, who's ringing me now? thinks Karen, snatching up the phone. Oh, it's Anna.

'I'm so sorry,' Anna opens without preamble. 'It's just I suddenly thought – you're probably about to go, so Steve will need you to leave keys.'

'OK . . .' says Karen, catching up. She had not thought about that one – she'd assumed he'd be round any minute. Stupid of me, she thinks. Since when has Steve ever been reliable?

There's no time to make her exasperation explicit, however, and anyway, this is not top of her concerns. She's finding it hard to keep Molly and Luke focused – they are both rest-less and need to go and *do* something, not sit and watch telly, which is how she is trying to occupy them. And her mother is due any minute – she's called to say she has made good time through customs, and will come to the house to drop off her case first.

'I'll put them under the box tree pot by the door,' she says.

'Great, thanks.' There is a moment's pause. 'How are you?'

'Frantic.'

'Do you need me to do anything?'

Karen considers for a second. At once she feels a surge of gratitude. She would not have got through the last week without her friend, yet she has barely given a thought to the fact that Anna has lost someone dear to her too. Steve won't have been much support, either; she could place a bet on that. Anna will be largely shouldering her grief alone. Karen's voice softens. 'No, no. I don't. We'll see you at the church. But thank you so much for asking.'

* * *

Vic has no sooner pulled the door to the roof terrace to behind her when Sofia says, 'Do you have a busy week next week?'

'Quite. Though I think I'm free a couple of evenings. Why?'

Sofia plunges straight in. 'Would you like to go out, then?'

Lou nods. 'That would be nice. I work Monday to Thursday in town, if you'd prefer to meet up there.'

'How about Thursday? Then you won't have to worry about getting up the next day.'

Well I never, thinks Lou. Either she is being very considerate, or she is planning on us having a late night. Either is good, though she would prefer the latter. The very idea makes her flustered and excited. She can't believe how swiftly this is falling into place.

'How about coming round for supper?' says Sofia, as if she has sensed Lou's desire to be somewhere seduction will be easy. 'I'll cook for you.'

'That would be lovely,' says Lou. Inside she's turning somersaults and cartwheels and head-over-heels all at once.

'Do you have email? I'll send you directions.'

'Of course. Hang on a minute – let me give you my card.'

This is good too: maybe they can chat more online between now and Thursday.

She is hunting for her purse when Vic comes back into the room. 'That's me sorted. Well then, Sofia, I guess we'd better get on our way.'

Five minutes later, Lou wishes Vic a happy birthday for the next day, then they are gone. Initially Lou is in something of a daze, she is so affected by Sofia. She allows herself to enjoy it for a while. Then she remembers, with a sudden pang of guilt: Anna. Perhaps now would be a good time to call.

'Hi,' Anna answers. 'Thanks for ringing me.'

'Not at all.'

'Sorry for texting so late last night. I hope I didn't disturb you.'

'No, I was in the pub, I didn't hear it. Is everything OK?'

'Well—' Anna snorts. 'Hardly. I'm on my way to Simon's funeral.'

'God, I'm sorry.' Lou comes back to earth with a thump – how could she have forgotten? 'Do you want me to call you later?'

'Actually, it's not a bad moment to talk. I've a bit of a walk to the church and I'm ahead of schedule. Otherwise I won't get to speak to you till tomorrow at the earliest, and I was kind of wanting your advice – um – quite soon.'

'Of course. How can I help?'

Anna takes a deep breath. 'It's – er – my boyfriend, Steve.'

Lou suspected as much: she's had such a strong sense of Anna holding something back that it had to involve someone major in her life. 'Oh?'

'He's drinking too much.'

320

Lou waits.

'Actually, more than too much. I think he's an alcoholic.'

'Ah.' Lou's heart reaches out to her. If ever she has experienced an almost insurmountable issue in her line of work, addiction to alcohol seems to be it. Haven't events with Jim tragically underlined that? And the repercussions on the nearest and dearest tend to be profound – they invariably get the brunt of it. But telling Anna this won't help her at this point, so instead Lou asks, 'Is he not with you now?'

'No. He offered to help with the food, so he's going to Karen's. He's missing the funeral.'

Sounds like emotional evasion, thinks Lou, that's typical addictive behaviour. But she keeps her opinion to herself.

* * *

The doorbell rings. Karen runs to answer it.

'Darling,' says her mother, holding out her arms. 'My poor darling.'

'Hi, Mum.' Karen returns the hug swiftly, then breaks free, remembering. 'Hang on—' She reaches for the spare keys on the hall table and slides them under the pot by the door. 'Sorry, just worried I might forget.'

'It's OK. Now,' – her mother grasps one of her hands – 'stop.' She stands away to look at her.

Karen exhales, closes her eyes with exhaustion, leans against the wall for support.

'Come here again,' her mother orders, and pulls Karen to her. Just as when Steve hugged her, the physical contact makes Karen cry. Yet her mother's embrace feels different;

far from reminding her of Simon, it reverberates back decades. She inhales her mother's familiar scent – the Rive Gauche she has worn since Karen was a girl – and clutches her mother's lambswool cardigan tight in her palms. It is soft and comforting. Their relationship might have changed in recent years; her mother needs caring for more now, she moves more slowly than she did, she has shrunk a little, too – yet she is still Karen's mother, her rock.

For the first time since Simon died, Karen feels safe.

* * *

'I don't know what to do,' confesses Anna. 'I've tried everything.'

'It's not up to you to do anything,' Lou points out gently.

'What do you mean?'

'It's his problem, not yours, if he's drinking too much.'

'I know, but—'

Lou cuts her short. 'I hope you don't mind my being honest, but I've worked with quite a few addicts, so I have some idea of what you may be going through.'

'I thought you might have, that's why I wanted to talk to you.'

'The temptation can be to think you can cure him.'

'Yes.'

'But I'm afraid you can't.'

'Oh?'

'He has to do it for himself.'

Anna is silent. Her head feels so full she can barely see straight. Simon's funeral is in less than an hour, and although she's said it's a good time, now she and Lou are talking, the subject is more than she can cope with. She can feel her mind shutting down, blocking things off. Even the motion of walking seems separated from her, her feet miles below her. It is as if she is heading through mist, everything looks so foggy. 'No, you're probably right,' she says, but her voice sounds distant; it could be someone else who is speaking. Then, suddenly – 'Oh, I'm sorry, hang on—' she rushes for the gutter.

She is violently sick.

It is mainly coffee; she has barely eaten. She is hot and clammy, shaking all over.

A few seconds later she hears a muffled voice. 'Anna? Anna?' It is Lou, still on the phone.

Anna picks her mobile up from the pavement where it has fallen, her hands trembling. 'Yes, yes, I'm sorry.'

'I think you should find somewhere to sit down.'

'Right, yes.' Anna sways over to a low garden wall nearby. 'Found somewhere.'

'You OK?'

She laughs at herself. 'Um, I think so.'

'Were you just sick?'

'Mm.'

'That's not good,' says Lou. 'Do you want me to come and meet you?'

'Oh, no, don't worry.'

'It's fine – I could do. I'm going to my mother's but I could be a bit late. And I wouldn't stay, I could just see you were all right—'

'Honestly, no, I couldn't ask that of you.'

'Yes, you could.' Lou doesn't pause for her to argue, 'I'm going to. In fact, I'll come with you to the funeral. I think you could do with some support.'

'No, no – you can't do that.'

'I can. You've no one to look after you. You need it. Give me a few minutes. I've just got to gather my stuff. Then I'll jump in a cab and come to you. I can head off to Hertfordshire from there. Really, it's fine. Um . . .' Anna senses she is considering. 'In fact, I'd quite like to come to the funeral anyway. Pay my respects. In a funny way, I feel I sort of knew Simon a bit, too.'

Anna feels a bit better on hearing this: maybe she won't be putting Lou out so much. 'If you're sure . . .'

Lou has evidently decided. 'Where are you?'

'On a wall.' Anna looks around her, helpless. The street is lined with trees, detached 1930s houses are set back from the pavement by generous front gardens; she is outside one such property now. She can't see a sign anywhere. She feels just like she did when she was small and got separated from her parents at the village fete once: panic, fear and helplessness mingle. Her voice trembles. 'I don't know the name of the road.'

'OK . . . Don't move, but see if you can find a landmark.'

Anna spies trees on the opposite side of the street ahead of her. 'Ah yes, I'm by the park between the Dials and the beach. I can see a bench. I could meet you there.'

'I know where you mean. And where's the funeral, and what time?'

'At a church round the corner from here, at half eleven.'

'That's good, we've nearly three-quarters of an hour. What

on earth were you doing leaving so early? It's not that far from you, surely?'

'I wanted to get away from Steve.'

'I see. Well, it's better, actually – it means you don't have to rush. Take it slow.'

'Thanks,' says Anna. The fog is lifting: not fully, but slightly, so she can function. Having given in to being rescued, she is extremely grateful. Through the haze, she can see why Lou is such a good counsellor. 'I'm going over to the gardens now.'

'Stay talking to me. I don't want you keeling over. What shall we chat about?' Lou's tone is light.

'I don't know.' Anna doesn't feel she can initiate anything.

'Then I'm just going to talk to you. It won't be scintillating, because you're going to have to listen to me while I tell you what I'm going to pack, so I remember everything, but you'll have to put up with me.' She begins, 'Toothbrush, toothpaste, shower gel, comb . . .'

And although she isn't really taking in what Lou is saying – there is no room for further information in her brain – the very ordinariness of the items she is listing calms Anna, giving her a distinct sense of solace.

10:54

How tough to have a boyfriend who sounds such hard work, thinks Lou, as the taxi crawls through the traffic of central Brighton.

Beside her is a hastily packed overnight bag. She checks her hair in the driver's mirror; she looks a bit rumpled, but it could be worse, considering the time she got to bed and the rush just now. Right: next. She had best let her mother know her plans have changed.

'Hi, Mum.' She tries to keep her voice positive.

'Hello, darling. You just setting off?'

'Kind of. I'm really sorry, but I'm afraid I'm going to be a bit later than I said.'

'Oh.'

That pause laden with meaning, *again:* her mother is peeved. Yet Lou is damned if she's going to be made to feel guilty: Anna's is a genuine need, surely her mother will understand that. But as often happens, her mother's aggrieved tone makes her defensive, less inclined to soften her words, or explain herself fully. 'I'm going to a funeral,' she says bluntly.

'A funeral?'

'It's a long story, I'll tell you when I see you.'

'Who's died?'

'It's no one I knew very well, a guy I met on the train.'

'What?'

'Mum, I really can't go into it now. It's something that happened earlier this week.'

'Ri-ight.' She can detect confusion – and, she suspects, scepticism – in her mother's voice. How dare she! Lou seethes. Why can't she just trust my judgement? Realize I wouldn't be doing this without a very good reason?

'Look. I'm sorry. I know it's important to you that I am there. I'll be with you as soon as I can. The funeral's in half an hour, I'm just staying for that, then getting a train. I'm not going to be very late, I promise. I should be there just a couple of hours after I said. That's all. OK?'

'Er, yes,' says her mother. Lou can tell she is reeling from trying to keep up, but she doesn't care.

'Good. I'll see you then.' And to make the point that she is annoyed, Lou cuts the connection without bidding her farewell.

* * *

Anna takes a seat and curls her legs up under her to try to relax.

It is quite mild, for February, and the mist seems to be clearing – whether it is real or imaginary, she can't tell. She is surrounded by crocuses: swathes of yellow and mauve adorn the patchy grass, their trumpet heads pointing optimistically upwards to the sky. They give off a faint smell too; she didn't think they did, but in such hundreds she is aware of it: sweet, honeyed, and – what else? That's it: saffron.

Spring is here. In the few days that have passed since Simon's death, the season has turned over.

And here comes a taxi, edging slowly down the road; the driver must be looking for her.

She gets to her feet, waves.

'Sit down,' Lou orders, the moment she has paid. She fishes in her rucksack. 'I brought you some water.'

'Thanks.'

They sit without speaking on the bench, taking it in turns to sip. Their silence makes way for the sounds of recreation to be heard: children shouting, birds singing, dogs barking, owners calling them.

'It's beautiful here,' says Lou, after a while. 'I don't really know this park. It's quite a way from Kemptown so I've never had reason to come.'

'It's my favourite,' says Anna. 'It's got so many different bits. There's a rose garden there' – she gestures one way – 'with a big stretch of lawn that's perfect for sunbathing. Up that hill, it's woody, and people come with their dogs. All those leaves to tear through and squirrels to chase . . . And tucked behind is a magical enclosed garden, with a dovecote and giant tree; they do yoga classes in its shade in summer. And over there, you can see, it's rather a good playground. Karen and Simon bring Molly and Luke a lot.' She flinches. 'Used to, I mean.' She sighs. 'Well, I'm sure Karen will still bring them, but—'

Lou touches Anna's hand. 'It's OK. I know what you mean.'

From where they are sitting they can see older children swinging down a giant pulley from the top of the hill to the bottom. Two smaller ones on a roundabout: 'Come on, come on! Faster! FASTER!' they are yelling. One is on all fours, head lifted up at the sky, hair flying, hands gripping the metal bars, eager; the other sits, more sedate. On the ground, passing the bars from right hand to left, right to left, right to left, are their parents, spinning them obediently.

After a while Anna says, 'Thank you so much for this. I really appreciate it, you know.'

'It's my pleasure,' says Lou.

It's an odd choice of words, but Anna knows what she means. For what is life about, if not meaningful moments like these?

'Are you feeling strong enough to go, then?' Lou asks.

Anna takes a deep breath and gets to her feet. 'Yes,' she nods. 'Ready as I'll ever be.'

* * *

The church is already quite full. It is a large space, not especially attractive, with cream walls and rows of highly polished wooden pews. Rather functional stained-glass windows rise up on either side of them, and the air is several degrees chillier than outside.

Anna heads up the central aisle.

'Do you think it's OK if I sit with you here?' asks Lou. 'There might be other people wanting to be close.'

'Of course.' Anna is certain. 'We won't sit in the very front, we'll go back one,' and she slides herself into a pew.

I wonder why Karen chose this? Lou muses. There must be prettier churches nearby. But she doesn't say so. Instead she asks, her voice low, 'Was Simon a regular churchgoer?'

Anna shakes her head. 'Hardly.' She smooths the back of her skirt, sits down and opens a guide to the service. Then she leans into Lou, whispers, 'Apparently everyone has the right to a funeral in their parish church, even if they haven't been churchgoers.'

'I didn't know that.'

'Me neither. Simon went sometimes, but not very often – Christmas, usually, and sometimes Easter.'

Lou thinks of Simon; the man she never knew. He lies a few feet away: there is the coffin, draped in white cloth, a simple bunch of lilies the only adornment.

Behind them people are still streaming in; Lou can scarcely believe the numbers. Maybe that's why this particular church, she realizes: it's big. There are all ages; some in black, others not, though most look smart and soberly dressed. She is conscious of her own casual attire – a parka, jeans – she didn't have time to change. She hopes no one minds, or thinks her unseemly.

Here comes Karen and these must be Molly and Luke – Lou has not met them before. Luke, she observes at once, is the spit of Karen, with his thick chestnut hair and delicate, pointed features. She wonders if Molly, with her blonde curls, rounder face and rosy cheeks, resembles Simon as a child. Poor loves, she thinks, to lose their father when they are so tiny.

They take a seat directly ahead, in the front pew. Karen turns round and smiles at Anna, and sees Lou next to her.

'Thank you for coming,' she says.

Lou can see she has made an effort: her hair is glossy

and washed, she has make-up on, and she is wearing an elegant dark-grey dress. But she also looks as if she hasn't slept for days, and her eyes are bloodshot; she must have been crying, moments ago.

Then, almost from nowhere, Jim comes to her mind, and Lou wonders if he had a service to mark his passing. It is tragic that Simon has died leaving behind so many people to mourn him, but perhaps it is even more tragic to leave this world with no one special to miss you.

* * *

Minutes later, the service begins.

The vicar steps forward and welcomes them with a few words. He reads 'The Lord Is My Shepherd', just as Karen has asked, and then utters some prayers. There is a rustling of papers as the congregation reaches for the words, then an almost unanimous 'Amen'.

Karen is struggling. She is biting back tears; everything seems too much, yet she wants to take it in, treasure these minutes, not cry. She is also aware of Molly and Luke beside her, doesn't want them to cause a disturbance, though so far they are being surprisingly good.

The vicar nods at her. This is her moment.

Karen gets to her feet, walks over to the lectern. She is conscious of her heels clicking on the flagstones and the children watching her, wide-eyed.

In her hands she holds two pieces of A4, folded together in quarters. She opens them and leans into the microphone.

'I started out not wanting to say anything,' she admits.

Her voice booms high up to the rafters, disconcerting her. She steps back a little, not wanting to be too loud. 'And then I thought I couldn't do that; it might be something I would regret not doing for the rest of *my* life.'

She is aware of row upon row of familiar faces, watching her. In each the emotions are transparent: she can see concern and expectation, people willing her to get through what she is about to say. She can see exhaustion, confusion, scores of unanswered 'why?'s. Above all, she can see sorrow for the man they, too, have lost. She has never seen such grief, head on. It chokes her; for a few seconds she cannot speak. But she must do this. She *must*. She gulps.

'So then I thought I'd tell you what I loved about Simon. And I began to make this list.' She looks down, and reads: 'His thick, lustrous hair.' She smiles, and looks for Alan. 'I know, I put that first, it's ridiculous, but it's the first thing I thought of. For those of you who didn't know, Simon was very proud of his hair.'

Alan rubs his balding pate; his wife leans her head against his shoulder and squeezes his hand.

'The list goes on. His laugh. His sense of humour. His ability as a father . . . Then I realized it was too good to be true: it didn't really explain everything that Simon was about. You don't want to hear just a list of his best qualities, do you? They're not only what made the man. He wasn't perfect. Far from it.'

She hears some people chuckle.

'So then I started writing down his faults, and as I wrote, I realized; they're what I loved about Simon, probably more than his virtues. It's his failings that made him who he was.

The vulnerable, kind, generous, funny, sociable, lovely man who is' – she coughs and corrects herself – 'was – my husband.'

She picks up the second piece of paper.

'So, here goes. I loved that he was always late for everything. Not really late, but a bit late, all the time. But he would really beat himself up about it, constantly scold himself, when actually he wasn't that bad a timekeeper. I mean, yes, he was often ten minutes late, sometimes twenty. But it was rarely anything more than that; not like some people, who keep you waiting for hours, or who cancel at the last minute. Instead he was very reliable; you always knew he'd turn up – he just operated several minutes behind everyone else. So, being with him, I soon learnt to make allowances: to add a quarter of an hour or so to when I'd expect him. Lord knows, the silly man never worked out how to do that himself, and just say he was going a few minutes later, but – well,' – she shrugs – 'he never did.'

Again she glances up; she can see Phyllis sitting between Molly and Luke, smiling and nodding in agreement.

'Another thing,' she continues, in the flow. 'He spoilt the children.'

She sees her mother beam broadly.

'He was utterly useless when it came to Molly and Luke – putty in their hands. He wouldn't set boundaries. He'd give them second helpings when I wanted to save food till the next day; he'd let them off finishing when I wanted them to learn to eat up, and when he took them shopping, they'd come home with all sorts of things that he'd been persuaded to buy. Our house is full to bursting because of it. That, I'll admit, often drove me mad. I was left to be the big bad discipline wolf. I rarely bought them presents on a whim because Simon did it far too often. But then a while ago, I realized how lucky I was. No parent is perfect, and the thing about Simon was he let Molly and Luke get away with a lot because he loved them so much. And isn't it better to have a father who loves you too much, than not enough? He absolutely adored them.' She looks down at Molly and Luke, and again wonders how much they are taking in. They are looking up at her, eyes wide. She is surprised, she had expected them to be distracted; it is not as if they are used to church. Phyllis leans around to give them each a hug.

'Which brings me on to another of Simon's flaws. He worked too hard, at least for his own good. Let's be truthful: that commute, the stress, the hours, weren't great for his health. But he did love his work.' Now she looks for his colleagues, and spies a cluster of them, near the back. 'He was rarely happier than when he was planning out some new landscape design. All that detail, all that potential of the plants. Though that's not what made the job for him: it was that he loved the people he worked with; he often said so. He even – the creep – liked Charles, his boss.' She laughs and nods towards Charles, who looks a little embarrassed. 'He was, it's true, thinking of changing his work, so he could spend more time with us and didn't have to carry on commuting – you may not have known that. But regardless, he was planning on carrying on the same line of business, setting up his own practice – he was absolutely, one hundred per cent dedicated. And it was his choice to work that hard; no one forced him to do it. He was simply very conscientious, and wanted to do his best and provide the best for us, his family.'

She glances again at the children. By now Molly is in a world of her own, swinging her legs to some abstract rhythm where her feet don't reach the floor. But Luke is still watching her, quizzical, as if he is trying to take on what she is saying, and is half getting it. He's clutching Blue Crocodile in the crook of his arm; it's as if the toy is listening too.

'Goodness.' She checks her paper. 'Here I am, only on his third fault, and I've got heaps to go. Let me move on apace. There was his weight too – an imperfection, for sure. In fact, his health generally was not something he looked after as well he might. Well . . . he certainly paid the price for that.' She bites her lip, holding back tears once more. 'But again, there were things about even that I loved: his appetite, for starters – the way he just loved, enjoyed, his food. And I rather liked his size, it gave me more to cuddle . . .'

She catches her breath to steady her voice. 'What else is there? Hmm, yes, his mess. He was pretty untidy, Simon – I spent a lot of effort clearing up after him. It never ceased to astonish me, given the neat architectural drawings he could do.' She smiles ruefully and moves on to his taste in literature. 'Dreadful, sometimes. Best-sellers, they were Simon's weakness. He devoured them on the train; one, two a week. That awful code book, for instance. You know the one – it was out a few years ago. I'm sorry if some of you liked it. Though you're in good company, because Simon absolutely raved about it, and, to my embarrassment, recommended it willy-nilly. To Anna, for instance. She's a writer, if you didn't know.' She grins at her friend, who is shaking her head in recollection.

'It wasn't *that* bad,' mutters Anna.

'You said it was rubbish!' says Karen, and laughter reverberates round the church. 'That's it, I suppose. I've got some more written down here, but I'll leave this list out so you can all have a look later, if you want, when you come back to the house. Thank you, Vicar.' And she gets down from the steps and returns to her seat, careful to take the folded pieces of paper with her, tidy to the end.

12:39

Anna is the first to arrive back at Karen's. She is keen to make sure Steve has fulfilled his culinary pledge, so when Karen asks her to go ahead and welcome guests while close members of the family go on to the cemetery, she is thankful to have an excuse. She has Molly and Luke with her too; Luke got tetchy after the service and wanted to go home, so Anna offered to escort him, then Molly wanted to come as well. They have been very good, and Karen decided the burial might be a bit much for them. Anna is secretly glad not to have to go through the 'ashes to ashes' stuff herself.

Steve opens the door and Anna knows immediately that he is on form. Once more he is clean and well presented, and there is a mouth-watering aroma of baking; once more she is relieved. But it's a dance she is tiring of: one step forward, two steps back.

He reaches to embrace her, and she shies away.

'Aw, come on,' he pleads, and she lets go of the children and allows him to wrap his arms around her.

Yet after a few seconds she begins to feel suffocated: the rough wool of his jumper makes her hot and chafes her cheek; the clinch feels more like imprisonment than condolence, and she wriggles free.

'I'm sorry,' she says. 'I just can't do that at the moment.'

He drops his arms, helpless. 'OK,' he says, but she can tell from the way he stomps down the hall that she has offended him. Yet even this antagonizes her: compared to Steve, Lou was so generous in her support, asking for nothing in return; she just gave. And when the funeral was over, she slipped away without fuss to the station.

I suppose it is easier for her, Anna reasons. She is not bound up in this; she is not my partner, she didn't really know Simon.

Still.

She follows Steve into the kitchen, ushering Luke and Molly with her. 'It smells great, darling,' she says brightly. 'Well done.'

Then she sees what he is doing. At first she can't believe it, but, yes, he has a corkscrew, and glasses.

She is incredulous. 'You're not drinking, are you?'

'Of course,' he says, sounding as incredulous as she.

'It's a *funeral*,' she mutters, trying to keep her voice low so Molly and Luke don't hear.

'People will want wine.' Steve is confident.

'Yeah, they might, but not the moment they walk through the door.'

Guests are coming down the hall and into the kitchen as she speaks.

'Glass of vino?' offers Steve, blasé.

'Er, yes please, I suppose, why not?' says the first arrival. It's Charles; he is a little taken aback, but seems happy to be offered it.

Steve grins at Anna sarcastically.

338

Anna is gobsmacked by his audacity. 'It's not even one o'clock,' she growls, watching through narrowed eyes as he hands a glass to Charles and pours a second for himself.

'I'd prefer a cup of tea,' requests one of Simon and Karen's neighbours.

'Sure,' Anna says, tight-lipped, 'let me make you one,' and she elbows Steve out of the way to reach for the kettle. 'Actually,' – she changes her mind – 'perhaps you could do this, *darling*. I'm going to see if Molly and Luke would like a bite for lunch. They normally eat quite early,' – she leans to ruffle their hair – 'don't you, my loves?'

* * *

The sign at the end of the carriage tells Lou the lavatory is engaged, but she wants to be first in the queue: must be all the water she drank in the park, earlier. She makes her way in the same direction the train is headed, catching the handles on alternate seat backs in broken rhythm, endeavouring to steady herself as the train speeds and sways.

She stands in the concertina gap between carriages, waiting. The train unexpectedly lurches and Lou loses her footing for a moment, staggers, triggering the automatic door open and closed, open and closed. Eventually the black lettering on the lock rotates to 'vacant' and a woman and small boy emerge. 'Sorry,' mouths the woman, as she guides the child ahead of her, hand on head. Lou smiles, sympathetic.

She enters the cubicle with a sense of trepidation: they can be grim, train loos. Afterwards, as she battles with the defective hand dryer, she hopes her mother appreciates what

339

she's putting herself through. Lou spends vast tracts of her life commuting anyway; a train is the last place she'd choose to be on a Saturday. And today she is forgoing both Vic's birthday party and seeing more of Sofia.

Lou's mother irritates her at the best of times; she's not sure she's going to have the patience to deal with her. It has been a full-on twenty-four hours following a particularly demanding week, and Lou is both physically and mentally worn out. It won't take much to rile her, yet she knows in advance that her mother is likely to find it hard to comprehend why she wanted to go to Simon's funeral. If she is expected to justify her decision, that will annoy Lou all the more because she's seen it coming.

And that is the easy bit, believe it or not. She certainly won't be able to explain to her mother that she is tired because she met a potential new girlfriend the night before and they were up till the small hours.

Once again Lou wonders just how much longer she can carry on living what is essentially a lie. Time and time again recently, with increasing ferocity, it just doesn't feel right.

* * *

'Don't worry,' says Karen, brushing away Anna's apology when she gets back. 'I'd probably have offered wine myself, in due course.'

'He's opened six bottles!' hisses Anna. The kitchen is full of guests; she has observed Steve serving glass after glass, noting he fills them close to the brim – then topping up his own to the same level.

'It's fine,' Karen reiterates, 'he's helping people relax. Don't worry, honestly.'

But Anna *is* worried. What Karen doesn't realize is that, first and foremost, Steve's generosity extends to himself.

With a Herculean effort Anna tries to shift her focus elsewhere: it is an endless cycle, this, creating the headspace for Karen – or indeed anyone – when Steve is clamouring for her mental energy. If only being with him weren't such a see-saw emotionally, leaving her bursting with pride one minute, the next wanting to curl up with embarrassment. The best thing to do, she decides, is leave him to it for the moment. So she grabs a paper plate, loads it with food, and takes it through to the living room.

* * *

'Hello, Lola.' Lola is Tracy's seven-year-old daughter. Karen crouches down slightly to speak to her so they're at the same height. 'Do you know who's upstairs?'

Lola shakes her head.

'A kitten.'

Lola gasps.

'He's called Toby. I wonder if you might like to go with Molly and her friends to meet him? Not too many of you, mind, he's still very small.'

'Can I?'

Karen nods. Lola is sensible and, because Tracy is a childminder, used to being around younger children – she seems to enjoy the natural superiority that goes with the role.

'WHO WANTS TO COME AND MEET THE KITTEN?'

she yells now from the kitchen doorway, and within seconds a cluster of small girls and boys are following her to Molly and Luke's bedroom. Just before they disappear from earshot, Karen hears Lola dictate, 'We've got to be very gentle.'

'Don't let the kitten out of the room!' Tracy yells after her daughter. She turns to Karen. 'Will he be OK?'

'He's used to Molly and Luke,' says Karen. She checks for her son outside. He seems happy enough; he's trying to score goals against the back wall with his friend Austin; Uncle Alan is keeper. Their patio is hardly built for such an enterprise, and Karen is fleetingly concerned about the kitchen windows, but surely Fate must owe her a few after this week. It is far more important that the children are enjoying themselves; she doesn't want them to remember their father's funeral as a totally morose affair.

'So, how are you doing?' asks Tracy, then immediately corrects herself. 'Silly question, I guess.'

'No, it's fine,' Karen smiles to show she is not put out. 'To be perfectly honest, the last couple of days I've hardly had a moment. Organizing this has taken so much time. I've had people phoning me, or I've had to phone them, nonstop; and there's been a constant stream of visitors on top of that. I've had Simon's mother Phyllis here, or Alan and Françoise; yesterday Steve and Anna were round to help with the cooking; now my Mum's arrived . . . When all this is over, I expect that's when it'll sink in.' She stops. 'Though, frankly, I'm absolutely dreading having time to think.'

'I expect you are.'

'There's so much I haven't considered yet.' It seems easier to talk to Tracy about these issues, perhaps because their relationship has always had the children as its focus, and Tracy didn't know Simon well; Karen doesn't feel she has to tread as carefully.

'I can imagine you get so caught up in the aftermath, you can't think further ahead.'

'Exactly,' Karen sighs. Her fear is that once the funeral is over, it will simply make space for her new reality to crush her. She tries to explain. 'There's the house move, for a start: I mean, I'm not going ahead with that now, obviously, but I'm sure there will be lots of bits and pieces to sort out there, even so. And I know that Simon had life assurance, for instance. But I've done absolutely nothing about it. I don't even know where the paperwork is.'

'It's a blessing he had that,' observes Tracy.

'Mm, though I've no idea what it means to us financially.'

'There's plenty of time.'

'I suppose . . .' Although Karen feels it is pretty pressing; the mortgage and bills still have to be paid, regardless. Charles has made a point of saying that she is not to worry, but she can't help sensing that people will gradually expect her to start functioning more normally, and it might be way before she is ready. If she is ever ready . . .

Tracy seems to read her mind and want to help. 'Anyhow, I just wanted to say that, over the next few weeks, I'm here. I can have Molly and Luke whenever you need me to, in addition to when I normally have them. And – you know – that's for you, I mean, as a friend, not something I expect you to, um, pay for.' She looks suddenly awkward.

'Thank you.' Tracy's generosity moves Karen, especially because she knows Tracy has relatively little income and even less time on her hands. Her eyes well up. 'Sorry.' She reaches for a hanky.

'And don't *ever* say sorry to me for being tearful, either,' Tracy admonishes. She takes Karen's arm to guide her. 'Now, you know what I'm going to suggest you do next? Come with me and let's each have a plateful of this incredible-looking food. I don't know about you, but I fancy some of that onion tart and maybe a piece of this pizza . . .'

16:29

Neither Lou nor her mother owns a car, but their reasons could not be more different. Lou is motivated largely by environmental concerns. She actually enjoys driving, and, when she was younger, had a Beetle. But these days she is more aware of the damage cars do, and she doesn't really need one in any case. Brighton is a compact city, she lives centrally and it is easy enough to get around on foot or by bicycle, and commuting to London by train is relatively cheap, quick and straightforward.

Lou's mother, on the other hand, has never even learnt to drive, and now she's pushing seventy, it's unlikely she ever will. This means she's pretty much housebound, and has been since Lou's father died. She's heavily reliant on the goodwill of others to ferry her from A to B – Lou's brother-in-law is called on far more often than he is happy about. (It's significant, Lou thinks, that she rings him over and above Georgia, her daughter. But therein, Lou reckons, lies a clue as to her mother's real motivation for not driving: she believes it is a man's role to be behind the wheel.) And when the B&B is empty, as is often the case during the week and especially in winter, Lou's mother ends up rattling around an empty home growing increasingly lonely and neurotic.

The lack of car also means that there is no one at the station to meet Lou, so she is forced to get a taxi. She hardly feels that she can ask her aunt and uncle to scoop her up, when her uncle has been unwell, and they are guests, too. Nonetheless, it is another few pounds that she resents paying on top of her fare; and when she doesn't want to visit anyway, this only increases her feelings of resentment as she marches up the garden path, hungover, under-slept and braced for a grilling about her tardy arrival.

*   *   *

'How's Dad?' says Karen. She realizes she and her mother have been together several hours and she has not even asked.

'Oh, you know,' replies her mother.

Karen does know. The last time she saw her father was at Christmas, when she and Simon and the children went out to Portugal for a few days. He knew who Karen was, and Simon, but he couldn't remember Molly and Luke's names. His mind can't retain them. Old memories, people etched deep in his brain, remain; more recent experiences pass like cars on a motorway, *whoosh*, and they are gone.

'I'm sorry he wasn't up to coming,' says her Mum. 'But you know how travelling fazes him.'

'I understand.'

It pierces Karen's grief to think of her father like this. Little by little she is losing him as well. Her mother is losing her husband, just as Karen has lost hers. The bereavement may not be as swift, as sudden or as shocking

– Karen's father is eighty; nonetheless it is breaking her Mum's heart.

*   *   *

Lou is welcomed in the usual way: with tea, in the lounge. While she waits for her mother to come through from the kitchen, Lou makes small talk with her aunt and uncle, Audrey and Pat. Eventually her mother arrives with a dark wooden tray covered, as is her custom, with a pristine white linen napkin placed so the corners hang over the edges in a perfect diamond. On it tinkle four elegant pink floral cups and saucers edged with gold, a matching teapot, a small jug of milk, a bowl of sugar cubes with an immaculately polished pair of silver tongs and a spread of biscuits carefully arranged in a flower shape.

'Tea, darling?' says her mother.

'Why don't you do the others first?' suggests Lou. 'I prefer mine strong.'

Her mother does as requested; nonetheless when Lou is handed her cup she can tell it is not as she likes it, even after all these years of the same request.

'Choccie biscuit?'

Lou is hardly a child. The use of the diminutive phrase grates, even though she knows she's being unfair. She reaches over, taking not one but two. She is very hungry.

'Leave enough for the rest of us,' says her mother.

Lou restrains from observing there must be at least a dozen biscuits on the plate still and murmurs an apology.

'So.' Her mother sits up in her chair, spine impressively straight for her age. 'Tell us about this funeral you went to at such late notice, darling. Did you go dressed like that, by the way?'

Lou struggles not to rise to it. 'Yes. It was a very informal ceremony.'

'I see.' Her mother makes it plain that she doesn't. 'Whose was it, did you say?'

Lou had hoped she would at least be given a few hours' respite before the interrogation: that it is happening within minutes of walking through the door aggravates her further.

She takes a deep breath. How is she going to explain swiftly and clearly, so they can drop the subject and move on? She doesn't want to get drawn into the details; it seems tasteless. Even though she didn't know Simon personally, she is loyal to the sense she has of the man as Karen's husband and Luke and Molly's father. Lou doesn't want this contaminated by her mother's curiosity or judgement.

'It's just this guy I, um, well, sort of met on the train.'

'Oh?' Her mother leans forward, all ears.

'I didn't really know him that well, but, there was something about him . . .' Lou fumbles for words.

'Yes?'

She decides to omit the details of Karen and Anna and their subsequent meetings. This will only complicate affairs; maybe keeping it short and simple will satisfy her mother.

'He died suddenly, really unexpectedly, you see. He was still, um, fairly young. We used to chat from time to time,' – this is a bit of a lie, but Lou is making it up as she goes in an attempt to get her mother to leave the matter be – 'and I, er . . . I liked him, we got on, so when I found out he had died, I decided to go to his funeral, pay my respects, you know, say goodbye.' Phew. Hopefully this will suffice and she is out the other side.

But . . . 'Ah, I *see*,' says her mother. Her tone is full of innuendo.

At once Lou realizes the conclusion she has drawn: that there was some kind of romantic involvement. How could she get it *so* wrong? It's almost laughable.

'No, no, it wasn't like that,' Lou corrects. 'He was just a friend.'

'If you say so,' says her mother, and glances knowingly at Uncle Pat and Aunt Audrey. She smiles sympathetically at her daughter. 'No wonder you wanted to go to the funeral.'

Rather than argue, or clarify, Lou decides the simplest thing is to let it be.

*   *   *

By early evening Steve has used all the alcohol in the house. He seems to have made it his mission to spend the afternoon getting everyone sozzled: he has been topping up glasses before it's even occurred to anyone that they might need a refill; Anna has been keeping an eye on him. The gathering turns into a riotous affair as a result. The stereo goes on in the lounge and some middle-aged parents even start dancing – to their teenagers' mortification; younger children are allowed to run shrieking round the house playing sardines without supervision; conversation flows between strangers with ease. People are laughing – celebrating – and Anna is glad; Simon would have liked that. Nonetheless, the whole experience makes her uneasy. She is aware, as other guests aren't, that this is a mask for Steve. It allows him to drink freely himself and hide his own intoxicated state, and Anna suspects that for every measure everyone else has, he's had several.

'We're out of booze,' Steve says now to Karen, grabbing her in the hall as she passes him on her way upstairs. 'Do you want me to go and get more?'

'Are we really?' asks Karen. 'I bought loads, and we had a couple of cases in the hall cupboard.'

'They're finished,' Steve tells her. Anna is watching him from the lounge doorway.

Karen is disconcerted. 'Mm, yes, er – I suppose we do need some more then.'

'I'll go,' Steve offers again.

'Thanks. That would be great.'

But he stands there for a moment before adding, bluntly, 'I'll need some money.'

'Of course, sorry.'

Anna cringes. Cash is not at the front of Karen's mind today, nor should it be. This is one reason she resents Steve for not earning much and for spending what money he does have on himself. It means he never treats anyone to anything, even a recent widow to a few bottles of wine. 'I'll sort this,' she declares. 'Let me get my bag.'

'No, that's fine. I should get it.' Karen is evidently uncomfortable with Anna's generosity.

'We'll work it out another time,' she says, hoping Karen will not remember at a future date.

'Sure.' Karen smiles, and heads on up the stairs.

Anna goes into the kitchen, locates her purse and hands over two twenty pound notes.

'Why don't you just give me your card?' suggests Steve.

Anna doesn't trust him with her card, not after several drinks. He is quite capable of sneaking in a bottle of something stronger for himself.

'Nope,' she says. 'This'll be enough. I think you ought to take someone else with you. Help carry it.' If he's not on his own, then, with luck, he'll be too self-conscious to buy himself anything.

'Why don't you come?'

But Anna does not want to go to the off-licence. She doesn't want more alcohol, it's nearly ten minutes' walk in the cold, and actually, she doesn't want to be alone with Steve. 'Why don't you ask a bloke to go with you? The bags will be heavy.'

'I'll go,' offers Alan, and the two of them set off.

19:21

Half an hour later, Alan and Steve return, with six carrier bags between them.

'Thank you,' says Anna, greeting them as they put down their load. But her appreciation is really directed at Alan, and she kisses him on the cheek.

'What, no kiss for me?' asks Steve, but she ignores him. She has gone a couple of paces down the hall when Steve grabs her shoulder and spins her to face him. 'You didn't say thank you to me.'

'Pardon me,' she says sarcastically.

'What's up with you?' he asks. He is almost shouting; he has lost the ability to gauge his own volume.

A few guests peer into the hall to see what's going on.

Anna lowers her voice in the hope it will encourage Steve to drop his. 'Nothing's up. I'm fine.'

But – 'Don't lie to me!' – he's louder still. A couple who have been chatting in the kitchen doorway break off their conversation and glance at them, wary.

'Just leave it, will you?' Anna hisses.

'I WILL NOT LEAVE IT!' Steve bellows, and everyone in the vicinity falls silent. 'Why did you kiss Alan and not me?'

Drinking always brings out jealousy in Steve. The sober

Steve is confident, sexually; it was one of the first things that attracted Anna to him. But yet again the drunkard is a different beast: the archetypal green-eyed monster.

'I didn't mean anything by it,' Anna says, conscious of the disturbance they are causing and wanting to ease the situation, fast.

'Yes, you did.' His lips are taut, eyes full of malice.

She shakes her head. 'I was just saying thank you.'

'Hey, mate,' Alan interrupts, gently easing Steve's shoulder away from Anna: he is towering over her. 'Take it easy, eh? She didn't mean anything by it.'

But his intrusion only exacerbates matters. 'GET OFF ME!' And with force Steve elbows Alan sharply away.

'Whoa.' Alan steps back, palms raised to indicate he wants no violence. 'There's no need for that.'

'You would say that, wouldn't you?' Steve rounds on him. It is all happening at such speed that Anna is powerless to prevent it.

Karen appears at the top of the stairs to see what the fuss is about.

Steve looks up, sees her, realizes he has an audience.

'Why don't you just say it?' he jeers.

'Say what?' Alan is mystified.

'You'd rather it had been me!'

'Sorry?'

Steve takes in the couple in the kitchen, watching; people in the living room open-mouthed, horrified.

'You'd rather it had been me!'

Karen speaks from halfway down the stairs: – 'I think you need to quieten down, Steve,' but to no avail.

He stares at Karen; Anna sees the venom in his eyes –
the venom she normally sees directed at her. 'YOU'D
RATHER IT HAD BEEN ME, TOO.'

Then he rotates, directing his fury a full 360 degrees.
**'YOU'D ALL RATHER IT HAD BEEN ME WHO
DIED THAN SIMON.'**

There is an appalled silence.

Then Karen says, her voice calm: 'Do you know what,
Steve? I don't know about everyone else, I can't speak for
them. But actually, as far as I am concerned, you are right.
I *would* rather it had been you than Simon. Now, I want
you to leave my house, this minute. You've caused enough
trouble. Go home, and sleep it off.'

Steve is so shocked that she actually said this that for
several moments he says nothing.

'Just sort him out,' Karen mutters to Anna over the banis-
ters as she returns upstairs. Anna can see she is shaking;
beneath her composure is fury.

'I'll take him home,' she nods. She's vaguely aware that
around her people have started talking again; the dialogue
is a combination of forced brightness as if nothing has
happened, and muted discussion of how awful Steve has
been.

By now he is leaning against the wall, barely standing.

'Will you be all right?' Alan asks her. 'I can see to him, if
you want. At least let me come with you.'

'Please, no.' Alan has done – and put up with – enough
already. 'I'll be fine.' Frankly, if she were in his place, she
would have socked Steve one. But Alan, like his brother, is
essentially gentle; it's not in his temperament to be physically

aggressive anywhere other than on the football pitch, and he is caught up in grief, too. 'I'm sorry,' she says to him now.

'It's not your fault,' replies Alan.

But Anna feels it is.

Steve has enraged Anna countless times before, but nothing compares to this. How *dare* he? It is utterly beyond her ken, but that doesn't make her any less upset. When she gets him home she doesn't care how drunk he is, she is going to give him a piece of her mind; but first she has to get him there.

'Come on,' she says, through gritted teeth, and tugs his jumper towards the door.

'Whereurewegoing?' slurs Steve.

'Home. You're not welcome.' She takes his arm, even though contact with him at this moment revolts her, and leads him outside.

'Bye,' she says to Alan, over her shoulder.

Steve can barely keep upright; he lurches against the porch, then staggers down the path.

'Why don't you put him to bed and come back?' Alan suggests, from the doorway.

'I might just do that,' Anna nods, although she suspects it is unlikely.

She steers Steve through the gate and to the left. It seems to take an age to get him to the end of the street. He trips several times, giggling and saying 'oops' with each stumble. Anna doesn't find it remotely funny; it tries her patience still more.

'Why are you so cross?' he asks as they veer across the main road dangerously slowly.

'I can't believe you have to ask.' But of course he has to: in this state, he has lost virtually all memory, and certainly reason.

'I only had a few glasses of wine.'

'Yeah, right,' she snorts. 'I'll get you home and then I'll tell you what you've done wrong.' She doesn't want to yell at him in the street.

'Ooh, dear, Anna's cwoss with me,' he says, pulling a naughty-little-boy face. Perhaps if he was sober she might find it engaging: now it's simply pathetic.

Eventually, she gets him to Charminster Street. He falls up the garden path and stops at the door, expectant. She reaches in her bag for her key and opens it with one hand, keeping him upright with the other. Then she shoves him over the threshold.

'You pushed me!' he protests as he pitches forward onto the stairs. He braces his arms, just catches himself.

'Yup,' she snarls. 'I did.'

'Why?'

'To make sure you got inside.' She kicks the front door shut behind her. 'But if you weren't so slaughtered you wouldn't have fallen over. Don't make such a big deal of it.'

'But you hurt me,' he whines, precariously returning to standing.

'I did not hurt you. But anyway, if we're talking about hurt, what do you think you do to me?'

'Huh?'

He won't keep up, and she knows it is a waste of time, but she has to vent regardless. She is too enraged to contain it. 'Your behaviour today was very hurtful. To me, and lots of others. In fact, I have never seen, or known, anything like it.'

'Eh?'

'For Christ's sake, Steve! People were grieving, you bloody idiot. It was a funeral. A man had died. A man had suddenly, out of the blue, with no warning, DIED. A relatively young man. A man we all loved very much. A man who left a wife, children, and countless friends and relatives, in mourning. And you were abusive first to his brother, of all people, then Karen, his wife, then pretty much everyone who was there!'

'Sorry.'

'Don't bother with sorry. It's too late for sorry. I'm sick of it. You even managed to make the whole thing about you. But frankly, Karen was right. Simon is worth ten of you.'

'What did you say?' He steps towards her, shoulders braced.

Anna edges back towards the front door. She's seen it before – this ability to switch not just emotionally but physically too – from a clumsy, embarrassing drunk to someone cruel and threatening. Nonetheless, even though she knows it will lead to trouble, she reiterates: 'I said that Simon is – or I suppose I should say was – worth ten of you.' She is so filled with rage that she doesn't care what happens next.

'Bitch.'

The insult barely touches her. She lifts her chin, defiant. 'I am *not* a bitch. I am simply telling you the truth. Today you turned a circumstance that was going to be tough enough for everyone anyway, into a disaster. We were at a funeral, Steve, remember? *My friend's funeral.* Yet you were aggressive. Rude and utterly, one hundred per cent insensitive. Why? Because you got drunk, that's why.' Steve may not be articulate at the moment, but boy, Anna is. Rage has sharpened her tongue, wised up her mind.

'I am NOT drunk!'

'Do me a favour. You were – are – absolutely shit-faced. *You* are the one with the problem – if that's what you meant by "bitch" – because your behaviour took absolutely no account of anyone other than yourself. You are completely incapable of putting yourself in anyone else's shoes, Steve. And' – she reaches what, for their relationship, is the crux of it – 'that means *my* shoes, too.'

'Eh?'

'Try to keep up. I have just lost a friend, a very, very dear friend. I am deeply, deeply upset. But ever since Simon died, which is now – what? Five days ago – you have done nothing, yes, *NOTHING* to support me.'

'Yes, I have—'

'What, you made me spaghetti Bolognese? Oops, sorry. I forgot.' She gives a mock gasp of apology. 'Oh, of course, you made all that food yesterday too. That was good of you, I grant you. And actually, you enjoyed it. But it also gave you the perfect excuse not to come to the funeral. Whereas I wanted you, *needed* you, there. Though that didn't even seem to cross your stupid, narcissistic little mind.' He jerks his head up; the insult seems to have penetrated. 'You think of yourself first and foremost, and you don't like funerals. Well, get this. *No one likes them!*

'I think – *hope* – you also thought of Karen. But I'm your girlfriend, and you didn't think – not *once* – to check it out with me.'

She stops, looks at him. He seems to be sobering up a

358

little, keeping abreast of her tirade, just. Then she says, 'You know what I want right now?'

'What?' They are standing, like two boxers squaring up to each other, a couple of feet apart.

'I want you to go to hell.'

Then she leans in close, and spits in his face, literally, a horrible stringy lump of gob. It lands on his cheek and slides down, gradually.

Watching it is immensely gratifying.

There's a pause – he is slower because of the alcohol – then he reacts. He lunges towards her and shoves her, viciously, with considerable strength, so she flies backwards.

She bangs her head on the front door, slips to the floor.

But although she is winded and shocked, in a split second she is galvanized. Now she is in full fight mode, adrenaline coursing. Part of her is aware Steve is bigger than she is, more powerful, but she doesn't care. He has threatened her once too often. Reason about her lesser strength plays no role in this. She wants him to feel – physically – the force of her fury. So, like a wild animal, she pushes herself up onto her haunches. Before he has a chance to move, she kicks out with all her might. Her legs are long; she reaches high. Her boots – those evil, high-heeled, pointy-toed, dark-green leather boots – are effective weapons. And as she kicks she catches him right between the thighs. Right, *right* where it hurts.

He doubles over, in agony.

She does not stop. She scrabbles to her feet. And, while he is still bent over, cursing, she opens the front door. Then she grabs him, before he has a chance to realize what she is doing, and shoves him, with every ounce of energy she has, outside.

He falls backwards onto the path, lands on his arse, but she doesn't pause to see if he is badly hurt: her own safety is paramount. She steps back inside the hallway and: BANG! slams the door. Then she puts the chain across and bolts it.

* * *

'Do you think Anna's OK?' asks Karen.

'Hope so,' says Alan. They are both still reeling from the encounter.

Karen bites her lip. 'Perhaps I'd better ring her.'

'I think you've enough to deal with. Françoise and I can drop round there, if you like, on our way home. We'll be going soon, I expect.'

'Would you mind?'

'No, sure, that's fine.' Alan and his family live a couple of miles away; Anna's house is en route.

'Steve's a pillock,' observes Alan.

'Sure is,' Karen nods. 'I feel terrible for introducing them.'

'She'll dump him.' Alan is confident. 'You'll see.'

'I hope you're right.'

'Here.' Alan opens his arms; they embrace. He leans back, pushes her hair away from her face, looks into her eyes. 'You mustn't blame yourself. Not about Steve, or Simon either, come to that.'

'I'm not!' protests Karen.

'You *are*.' His voice is firm, but soft, kind; her heart lurches, it reminds her so of Simon.

'OK.' She nods. 'But will you text me when you get home, let me know Anna is all right?'

* * *

Shortly, Anna hears Steve getting to his feet, dusting himself down. Then he opens the letter box, peers in.

She moves away from him, sits on the stairs, stares at him.

'You going to let me in?' he asks.

'You fucking kidding?' Then she realizes what she has wanted to say since the argument started; maybe for days before that, perhaps even from the time she found out Simon had died. 'You are never coming back in here again.'

'What?'

'What do you mean, "what?" You heard me. I said, you are never coming back into my home, ever again.'

'You can't do that.'

'Try me.'

The letter box flaps shut. She braces herself: she knows what he is going to do next. Sure enough: BAM! She can feel the door, indeed the whole hall, house, vibrate, as he thows his full body weight against the wood. And again: BAM! And again: BAM!

She is worried; will the bolts hold? But she is still too full of adrenaline to give in to anxiety: she runs upstairs, opens the bay window in the bedroom, leans out.

He is down below her, in the dark, his whole body twisted sideways. He takes a few steps back, then lunges towards the door again. He doesn't seem to care that he might hurt himself.

'Oi!'

He looks up.

'You carry on doing that, and I'll call the police.'

'You wouldn't.' His jaw is clenched, unbelieving.

'Of course I would.' She goes inside, gets the cordless landline phone from the dressing table, and returns to the window. She holds it up for him to see: 'I think this probably warrants 999, don't you?'

He whines, then. 'Let me in, Anna. Please.' She is reminded of the Three Little Pigs.

She laughs, incredulous. 'No way.'

His face has that same expression she has seen so often before when he is drunk; his mouth is slack, his brow furrowed with confusion. Despite his aggression, his posture is lazy, his limbs ill-co-ordinated. And, at last, it is as if the last vestiges of mist have finally cleared from Anna's vision. She can see him for what he is.

A sad, pitiful drunkard.

And she understands the message Karen's speech at Simon's funeral had for her. That while Karen loved Simon for his faults, Anna doesn't love Steve for his. She can't and never will. How can she, when Steve's worst fault – his addiction – leads to this? She is being terrorized in her own home. It is untenable. *They* are untenable.

'You've got to let me in,' wails Steve.

'No.'

'Where am I going to sleep?'

'That's your problem.'

'Aw, Anna . . .'

He sounds about five years old, but it fails to touch her.

She is resolute. 'No, don't "aw Anna" me. I've had it. We're through. Over. You don't think of anyone as much as yourself. You even made the whole funeral about you. And over the last few days, you've acted as if I have to choose between you and my closest friend. So, I'm choosing my friend. And there's no point you standing out here and arguing. If you yell or bang on my door once more, I'm calling the police. Now go, sleep where the hell you like, I don't care. I'll leave your stuff outside for you tomorrow.'

She moves away from the window, goes into the spare room, grabs a couple of old, worn blankets. Then she returns to the bedroom window, leans out.

Steve is sitting on the path, looking sorrowful.

'Here,' she says.

He looks up.

'You can have these,' she says, holding out the blankets. 'Catch.'

And she throws first one, then the other down to him. The first lands still folded, heavy, but the second opens, catching in the air like a parachute.

For several minutes, Steve lingers by the front door, swearing. Then he quietens, but Anna can still hear him pacing outside. She doesn't respond in any way, but then he starts ringing her. First, on the landline. Repeatedly. Until she unplugs it. Then on her mobile. She turns that off, too. Eventually she hears him pick up the blankets and shuffle away.

21:45

That's it, then, thinks Karen, closing the front door. All the guests have departed. Now, she must check her mobile.

Alan has been true to his word.

All quiet on the western front, says his text. *Been round, couldn't hear anything untoward, so didn't bother disturbing them – reckon they were both asleep and didn't want to wake them. Rest easy.*

Still, something is niggling her. She has had the sense all week that things between Anna and Steve have been increasingly tense, in spite of the Friday they spent happily cooking together. She has been so consumed by events that she has not given it much thought, but this evening's frightful row has brought her fear to the fore, and she shudders to think what Steve is capable of when he is pushed to the limit.

She decides to ring Anna herself, to be sure.

But Anna's mobile appears to be off; it goes straight through to voice message. Karen tries the landline. It just rings and rings, with no answer.

'Leave it, darling,' says her mother. 'Anna is old enough to look after herself.'

Karen shakes her head. 'I'm worried, Mum.' How can she

explain that she and Anna have a connection that goes beyond the bounds of many friendships; that sometimes they seem virtually linked by a sixth sense, psychically, especially when emotions are running high, as they have been lately? Her mother will think she is being melodramatic.

'I know you're anxious, and you're a good friend. But given everything else you've got happening, I think you should let yourself off the hook. Let someone else help if need be.'

'I'm her closest friend,' Karen protests. 'And I live round the corner. What if something has happened to her?'

'Nothing will have happened to her. Alan's text told you: they've gone to sleep. She's probably just unplugged the phones so they aren't disturbed. I think you've got so used to worrying and being upset about everything this week that you can't switch off, which is quite understandable, but I am sure they are fine. I'll look after the children and you can pop round and see her in the morning, if you like.'

'OK . . .' But Karen is still unsure.

* * *

Lou is sitting in the lounge with her mother, Aunt Audrey and Uncle Pat. Uncle Pat has a wing-backed armchair pulled close to the television; along with his other ailments, he is deaf, and otherwise – as he has explained loudly – he can't hear the chat-show host. Audrey and Lou's mother are sharing the settee, their poker-like spines testimony to their rigorous ('Sit up straight!') upbringing. Lou is lounging, feet slung over one of the arms, on the one chair she finds remotely comfortable – a saggy recliner that has only escaped being deemed too scruffy and jettisoned by her mother because it was her father's favourite.

Uncle Pat is actually blocking Lou's view of the chat show, but Lou isn't really watching anyway. Instead she is picking at her nails, a displacement activity for the aggravation she is feeling following the earlier discussion regarding Simon.

Can't my mother see I wouldn't be interested in a man? she thinks, as she pulls at a particularly resistant bit of cuticle. Yet she can observe fast enough that I wasn't dressed appropriately for a funeral. I haven't had a boyfriend in years, yes, *years*. Not since I was fifteen. What does she think I have done for all this time? Abstain?

Lou thinks of Sofia and their kiss the night before. Then she glances over at her mother; her helmet of grey hair with its Thatcher-like precision waves, her lips lined from decades of being held in an almost permanently pursed position. But in spite of her uptight appearance, her mother has produced two daughters close in age. She must have conceived them somehow. Lou even recalls her father implying her mother was surprisingly passionate sexually, and after all, there must have been something that kept two such different people together for over three decades.

She must, therefore, be in denial.

It's a situation that has eaten away at Lou all her adult life. And how perverse it is. Here she is, virtually spread-eagled on the armchair, her body responding to the mere recollection of kissing a woman.

'I'm gay,' she murmurs quietly.

But her mother is so engrossed in the television that she does not hear.

*   *   *

'You go to bed, Mum,' says Karen. 'I'll be upstairs in a minute.'

'Why don't you leave that till tomorrow?'

Karen is emptying the dishwasher. 'I'm fine, honestly. I'd rather do it now. Then I can put on another load. Why don't you have a bath, help you unwind?'

'That's a nice idea. Would you like me to leave you the water?'

'Yeah, why not?' They haven't done this for years; it reminds Karen of her childhood. Her mum is of the generation where such frugality was commonplace. Karen has often thought people could do with acting more like that again.

It is peculiar, isn't it, she thinks, as she removes dishes and stacks them on the sideboard; the way the past makes its presence felt at unexpected moments. Here she is, handling crockery laden with her own history.

There is the chipped cast-iron casserole Phyllis passed to her a few years ago, saying Karen would have more use for it than she did, now she had children. There are eclectic mugs from a range of sources: promotional ones Simon has brought back from work, a couple of finely shaped porcelain ones that were a gift from Anna, a jokey one from Alan about hirsute men being better lovers. There are the flan cases that were her grandmother's, offered up when Karen went to college. It was the same autumn her grandmother went into a home; Karen recalls her saying she'd not be cooking any more but maybe Karen could use them to equip her own place? Karen had been blasé back then; now she finds the memory deeply affecting whenever she uses them.

Next, she removes one, two, three, four, five, six matching dinner plates from the service she and Simon asked for as a wedding present. How many meals has she served on these? She runs her finger round the edge, tracing the single line of blue glaze round the rim. They are nothing showy, just plain white china. Their friends weren't awash with money at the time; she and Simon were married when she was relatively young, and she and her peers had only recently graduated. An extravagant wedding list would have seemed greedy. Anyway, they've lasted well enough; only two have been broken. And what would have been the point of something so precious and fragile they could never eat from them? Whereas these have had years of good use, taking them right through from their first dinner parties as a couple, when pretty much the only dish she knew how to cook was shepherd's pie, to the children's birthday parties. Their flat base makes them ideal for cakes, just as they have been ideal today for the quiches, pizzas and tarts . . .

And so it comes, like the plates themselves, full circle. At the heart of almost all these memories is Simon. For so long he has been intrinsic to her existence: almost every piece of crockery relates in some way to the two of them. Even the items that pre-date their relationship he has used, shared with her, time and time again.

It is too much to assimilate. Karen has shed every tear she can today. She is wrung out, numb.

Instead she empties the cutlery basket and refills the machine with one last load. Then she clips a tablet in the soap container, shuts the door, and rotates the dial to start.

*   *   *

Once more, Anna wakes after only a few hours' sleep. She is surprised, relieved, that Steve has not caused any further disturbance. Perhaps he has gone away.

She returns to the bay, peeks between the gap in the curtains. If he's still in the garden, she doesn't want him to see her and cause another scene.

There's no one there.

Then something catches her eye. In the doorway of the office building up the road are her blankets; she can't see him, but from their rounded shape she deduces that Steve must be curled up underneath, asleep. It is where the home-less guy used to shelter: the man with the cottage-cheese sandwiches.

Sunday

08:23

Karen stirs; someone is by her side in the bed.

Could it be?

It can't be.

It isn't.

It's Luke. He sneaked in under the covers in the night; now it comes back to her.

Is every morning going to be like this? A punch to her stomach, every time she opens her eyes?

She closes her lids, in the hope it will all go away. Wraps herself tight round Luke; whether she is protecting him or he her, she doesn't know. But he feels warm and soft, and, while he still slumbers, at peace. Maybe for a few fleeting moments, some of it will rub off on her.

*   *   *

First thing on waking, Anna checks out of the window. Steve has gone from the doorway, taken the blankets with him. She pushes up the window, leans out, scans the road.

No sign.

She is still rattled by all that's happened, but, ever practical, swiftly assesses. She can't leave the house at the moment, lest he return. Steve has keys. So, before she does anything else, she must call a locksmith. She plugs in the landline phone once more and eventually gets through to one.

It transpires it will cost double because it is Sunday. 'Can't you wait till tomorrow?' says the man. 'If you're in the house already?'

'No,' says Anna, baldly. Thus, within an hour, she is up, dressed, and watching a guy chisel away at the front door.

She is scared Steve will come back before the man has finished, but rather than sit around jigging her feet, she decides to put her agitation to good use. She gets a roll of bin bags from under the kitchen sink and takes them upstairs. There, she takes every item of his clothing from the hangers in the wardrobe and lays them out on the bed. Then, with a half-hearted attempt at folding, she places them one by one into the bags. Within twenty minutes she is done.

She is hunting for boxes for his books when she remembers: her mobile is still switched off. Perhaps she can risk turning it on. At least she can vet the calls. No sooner has it sounded its start-up jingle than it rings. She jumps, nervous.

It's Karen.

'Thank God! I've been trying to get through for *ages*.'

'I'm sorry. I turned my mobile off. Why didn't you try the landline?'

'I tried last night. It just rang and rang. Then I tried again this morning and it was engaged. I thought there must be a fault on the line or something.'

'No, I unplugged it. And then this morning I must have been on the phone to the locksmith.'

'A locksmith? Why?'

'Steve and I have split up.' There seems little point in prefacing it.

'Oh.' The surprise in Karen's voice is evident.

Anna waits for it to sink in.

'Really?' Karen asks, after a moment.

'Yes.' Anna knows that Karen is probably not saying too much, lest she change her mind in the near future. It's always a hazard when couples part – declaring swift allegiances can easily backfire should they get back together. She wants to make it plain this is terminal. 'We had a massive fight when we got in.'

'God, I'm sorry.'

'It's not your fault.'

'No, I suppose.'

'He was being an absolute twat. I should be the one apologizing to you.'

'It's not your fault, either.'

But again Anna feels that it is. 'I should have seen it coming.'

'Anna, with Steve you can never see it coming. One minute he's utterly charming, the next – well, I hope you don't mind me saying this – but a, um, drunken bore.'

'That's putting it mildly.'

'Last night he surpassed himself.'

'You're telling me!' says Anna. 'You didn't see the worst of it. When he got back here he was awful.'

'He didn't hit you, did he?'

'Not exactly . . .' Then Anna laughs. 'I think I probably hurt him more than he hurt me.'

'Oh?'

'I kicked him in the balls.'

'Well done!' applauds Karen, and finally Anna has a sense of how her friend truly feels about him. 'Where is he now?'

'I threw him out.'

'What, this morning?'

'No, last night.'

'Ooh, dear, the poor bugger. It was a bit cold.'

'I gave him some blankets.'

It is only as she is retelling this that Anna can see just how bizarre the whole experience has been. The mirror is shattering on her looking-glass world.

'So now what?'

'I've changed the locks.'

'Bloody hell,' Karen gasps. 'You haven't wasted much time.'

'Only four years,' observes Anna dryly.

'Well, I am sorry,' Karen repeats. 'I did like him, in a way.' Then she adds, 'The sober him, anyway.'

'That's the problem: it's only half of him.'

'Mm . . .' She can sense Karen thinking. 'What are you doing today?'

'Packing up his stuff mostly, I expect. Why?'

'Mum offered to keep an eye on Molly and Luke for a bit, later. Shall I come round, lend you a hand?'

'That'd be great,' says Anna.

*   *   *

It has been a long week and Lou needs to catch up on her sleep. This, together with the fact that it is Sunday, justifies her staying in bed an hour or so longer than usual. Half awake, half dozing, she listens to the sound of people moving about the house. The buzz of the water heater as her aunt takes a shower, the faint strain of classical music from the radio in the conservatory, the clink of dishes in the kitchen.

Eventually, she knows she can't get away with it any longer: her mother will be pacing, keen for Lou to have breakfast. She throws back the bedcovers, pulls on her dressing gown and makes her way downstairs. She can hear voices: but it's not Uncle Pat talking to her mother: her sister Georgia is here. Georgia often drops by at the weekend; she and her mother are in the kitchen.

'Elliot is rather like your father,' her mother is saying.

'Do you think so? I thought he was more like Howard.' Howard is Georgia's husband, Elliot her son.

'No, see here? His chin? That's your father to a T.'

Lou frowns and pauses on the bottom stair. Damn Georgia, showing her mother the Christmas photos – *she*'d wanted to do that. She was the one who'd taken them, after all, and she is pleased with what she'd captured with her camera. She is disappointed at missing an opportunity to gain her mother's praise. Then again, she should have known better than to send her sister a set: when it comes to snaps of her offspring, of course Georgia is going to want to show them off at the first opportunity. Lou tells herself not to be churlish and goes to join them.

'Good morning,' says her mother.

Lou takes a cup and saucer from the dresser, lifts the tea cosy, pours herself a cup of tea from the pot. She likes it strong but this is stewed and – she dips in her little finger – cold.

'I think I'll make a fresh one,' she mutters.

'Oh, yeah, sorry, we made that a while ago,' says Georgia. 'I get up so early, with the children. It's automatic. I am jealous of you, able to sleep so late!'

Just for a split second Lou feels like saying, 'No, you're not.' But instead she takes a seat next to them, reaches for the photos. Her nephew Elliot licking a spoon of cake mix with most of it around his mouth; Elliot taking his first bandy-legged steps; Elliot splashing in the bath – to be anything less than enthused would be horrid of her. Then there is her niece being breastfed; her niece's face scrunched up and scowling; her niece grinning and playing with a rattle Lou herself gave her.

Lou adds milk to her tea and immerses herself in the moment, gazing and laughing and cooing along with her mother and sister, and she is pleased with the pictures after all, even though her mother doesn't once say how good they are.

Then, as they come to the last one, Lou has an inexplicable rush of emotion. Suddenly, she feels like crying.

She gets up, walks to the window, trying to place what it is that has affected her so. Tears prick behind her eyes. Then the cause comes to her, as she brushes them away. It is envy. Not of her sister's life: she wouldn't want her marriage, or her house, or even, come to that, her children. But she does envy her sister's relationship with their mother.

It seems so easy, so clean, so honest, in comparison with her own.

*　*　*

Anna is midway through sealing up the third box of Steve's books with a noisy length of gaffer tape, when her phone rings again.

It's Lou. 'Hi,' she says. 'This a good moment?'

This time, Anna feels more confident that it truly is OK to chat. The hurricane has passed. She is picking up the pieces, but not caught up as she was, mid whirl. 'Yes.'

'I just wondered how it went, yesterday.'

Where should I start? thinks Anna. It has been one almighty twenty-four hours. 'The gathering back at Karen's was wonderful. On the whole.'

'I am so pleased.'

'Where are you?' Anna wants to verify before she launches into the full version of events.

'At my mother's. Well, actually, I've come out to buy the papers. Wanted the excuse for a walk.'

As she says this Anna hears a car swish by. 'You get there OK?'

'Yeah, fine.'

Anna doesn't know Lou that well yet, but nevertheless can detect an undertone to her voice; Lou does not sound fine, really. 'Everything all right?'

Lou exhales. 'I'm just having a shit time with my mother. She's driving me insane.'

'Ah.' Anna just knows, from the way Lou says this, and from what she has intimated before, when they were out earlier in the week, that there is history there. 'I'm sorry to hear that.'

'Same old, same old, I guess. I didn't really expect it to be otherwise. Still, sometimes you hope it will be different. You can't help it.'

'Yes.' Anna thinks of Steve. How often did she hope against hope that he would be different, that he would change? She decides to confide. 'Actually, Steve and I split up last night.'

'Oh.'

Anna gives her a few seconds, as she did Karen.

'That's a shame,' says Lou, eventually.

'Do you think so?' Anna is surprised Lou would feel this way. She wouldn't have thought Lou would have judged them an ideal couple.

But Lou clarifies, 'It's always a shame, when people who care for each other split up. I got the sense you cared for him a lot.'

Considering how short a time they have known one another, Lou has her sussed. 'I do, I did.'

'But it's awfully hard, living with an alcoholic, that I do appreciate.'

'I just couldn't do it any more.' Anna looks round at all the boxes. It *is* a shame. There were things she and Steve had in common like this – reading – that she will miss dreadfully.

'I did mean what I said though, you know, in the park.'

'Oh?'

'That you can't sort it out for him, cure him.'

'No.'

'He'll probably have to hit rock bottom, you know, before he does that. That's what they say. In some ways you may have helped him, made him face it. With you there to support him, you were enabling him; he was bound to carry on drinking.'

Anna has heard this reasoning before, but not till this

morning has it resonated with her so strongly. Steve at rock bottom; it is a tragic thought. She feels for him. 'Do you think he'll be all right?' She wants Lou to say he will. She can't take him back, she knows that; nonetheless she feels concerned for him, guilty. She has left him – or some might say he has left himself – with no home.

'Probably,' says Lou. 'There is help there for him, if he seeks it out.'

'You mean like Alcoholics Anonymous and so on?'

'I do. Has he ever tried anything like that?'

'No.'

'You never know, he might do now. Meanwhile, has he somewhere to stay?'

'I don't know.' Anna is frank. The guilt grows. She still feels responsible for him – she can't shake that off overnight. But counter to this is another feeling, new, but she treasures it: a recognition she must, first and foremost, look after herself. 'I don't want him here,' she reiterates.

'No.'

'He might stay with the guy he works with sometimes, Mike, or something, I hope. I don't even really want to speak to him. But I would like to know he is OK.' She is torn. 'I haven't heard from him yet, this morning.'

'Has he got his mobile with him?'

Anna recalls the ceaseless calls the night before. 'Yes.'

'I could ring him, if you like,' offers Lou, unexpectedly.

'What do you mean?'

'Check he's all right. I work at a hostel for the homeless, too. So if the worst comes to the worst, and he's not with Mike or anyone, I could direct him there.'

Anna feels a mix of emotions: the idea of Steve in a hostel churns her up again inside. Nonetheless, she would like to know he is warm and cared for, however basically. It would be better than nothing. She can't bear to think of him sleeping in a doorway for another night.

'Would you mind?'

'Of course not. I can withhold my number so he can't ring me back. We'll just check he's OK.'

Anna wouldn't want Lou to get embroiled in endless calls; she doesn't want a mediator. But Lou has evidently experienced behaviour like Steve's before – not that surprising, given her work – and thinks practically as well as generously.

Anna is grateful, especially when Lou is having such a difficult day herself.

Lou's mother doesn't know how lucky she is, thinks Anna, as she waits for Lou to call her with news. She shouldn't give her daughter a hard time; she should be proud.

* * *

No time like the present, thinks Lou. She doesn't really know what she is going to say, but there is little point in rehearsal. She has been out for a while now, walking round the village green. Her mother will be wondering where she is.

To her relief, Steve answers straight away. 'Hello?'

'Oh, hi,' she says, still gathering herself. 'I, er, you don't know me, but I'm Lou, a friend of Anna's.'

'Yes. She has mentioned you.' Lou detects an Antipodean twang. 'What do you want?'

'I'm calling on her behalf. She just wants to know that you're all right.'

'I'm OK,' he says. He doesn't sound drunk, Lou concludes. Good. 'Just a bit of a bad night. Is Anna all right?' She hears his voice soften.

'Yes, she seems to be.' She cuts to it. 'Where are you?'

'At my mate Dave's. He says I can stay here, just for a bit.'

Ah, so Anna was right. That is also good. To some degree, he is someone else's problem now. But something in Lou doesn't want to leave it right there: she wants to steer him, give him hope. Not for him and Anna, but for himself.

'I'm glad to hear that,' she says. Then she adds, 'Look, Steve, you don't know me, you can tell me to piss off, and you might never use it, or do anything, that's up to you. I know you drink a lot – Anna has told me.' She pauses, waiting. If he is going to do it, this is when he will put the phone down on her. But no, he is still there; she can hear him, breathing. So she continues, 'In a bit, when I've looked it up, I'm going to text you a number. Some people that might be able to support you if you feel you want to stop. OK?'

'Whatever,' he says. Then adds, 'Thank you.'

13.00

Lunch is served bang on one; in fact the carriage clock on the dining-room mantelpiece strikes just as they take their seats: Lou's mother, Lou, Pat, Audrey; Georgia has left to cook for her own family.

Nonetheless, Lou's mother has unfolded an extra leaf of the oak table in honour of Pat and Audrey. She has cooked roast beef for them, too; Lou, as usual, must make do with the vegetables.

'Are you still one of those vegans, then?' asks Pat.

'Vegetarian,' corrects Lou. 'I eat dairy.'

'Thought you'd have grown out of it by now,' he says, carving the meat with relish. Blood oozes down the side of the joint and onto the platter. He scoops it into a spoon and covers his helping.

'It's not something you *grow out* of,' Audrey corrects him. 'It's something you believe in.' She smiles at Lou, to show she understands – sort of.

Lou nods, appreciative. She has long observed that Audrey is more liberal than her husband, and, come to that, her sister, Lou's mother. Her mother is the one who has children and grandchildren, yet her sibling seems more, not less, in touch with the younger generation.

384

For a few moments the only sounds are the scrape of polished silver on bone china. Then Audrey attempts to make conversation. 'So,' she says innocently, 'do you have a boyfriend at the moment, dear?'

Lou nearly drops her fork. She is not used to such direct questioning; her mother avoids it.

'*I* think there was something going on between Lou and that man on the train,' says Lou's mother, arching an eyebrow. Evidently, with Audrey and Pat to back her, she is prepared to probe more deeply than usual.

Lou grates her teeth. 'No,' she insists, 'there wasn't.'

She looks down, concentrating on spearing a carrot. Really, this meal is unbelievably bland; she can't even have gravy because it has been made with the fat of the meat.

'It's all right, dear, you can tell us,' says Uncle Pat, with the same overly sympathetic note in his voice as Lou could hear in her mother's yesterday.

But I can't! Lou protests inwardly. That's the whole point.

'I don't think she wants to talk about it,' Audrey realizes. 'Sorry, dear, I didn't mean to intrude. It's only you're such a nice girl and—'

' – getting on a bit,' says Uncle Pat, helpfully.

'Pat!' chides Audrey: 'That wasn't what I meant.'

'I was married at twenty-one,' Lou's mother points out.

'I know.' Lou reaches for the mustard. She needs something to give this wretched food flavour.

'And your sister was married at twenty-four.'

'I know that too.'

'So you don't want to have babies, then?' asks Uncle Pat.

Lou feels herself being stretched by this conversation, like the string of a kite being pulled by the wind.

'I, er, don't know,' she mutters.

'You'd make a lovely mother,' says Audrey.

Lou knows she means it kindly, but honestly . . . Audrey might have made a lovely mother too, but Lou wouldn't contemplate saying so. She has no idea why Audrey hasn't had children – miscarriages, infertility, her husband's impotence – any of these could be the reason why. There might be all sorts of nerves it could touch. Why can't they leave her alone?

'You know what? I don't think I really want children,' she says, hoping to shock them, just a little. It is not even completely true – the reality is she hasn't found anyone she would consider co-parenting with. But at least it might stop them prying.

'Oh,' says Lou's mother.

Lou can read the disappointment in her face. Yet why should she be so let down? Aren't two grandchildren enough? This reminds Lou of the photographs, earlier, and she feels the string inside her tautening.

Maybe it's because her mother sees herself reflected in Lou's circumstance: they are both single women, living alone. And even though she won't admit it, Lou's mother is lonely, her existence so circumscribed that she cannot believe Lou's life could be otherwise.

Lou shudders. She can't have her mother believe they are alike, not for a second. They are different, totally different. She has to make it clear.

And then she thinks of Simon, and all that has happened in the last week, and how she only has one life, which she has to live well, or at least, as best, with as much integrity, as she can. She recalls her father's plea to keep the truth from her mother, and, at last, she sees it for what it was.

Cowardice.

Well, her father might have spent his life avoiding confrontation with his wife, but it killed him and Lou is sure as hell not going to let it kill her. She realizes that if she carries on denying who she is, then she really might end up like her mother; suffocated. If not immediately, then eventually.

She cannot pretend any more.

Once she has acknowledged this, the string can no longer take the strain. It snaps.

And—

'I'm gay,' she says.

This time there is no television to drown them out; they are there, in the middle of the table. The two most powerful words she has ever spoken, eclipsing the overcooked vegetables, undercooked meat and rapidly congealing gravy.

*   *   *

Warmed-up pizza, bean salad, couscous: Karen gives the children, herself and her mother a lunch of leftovers from the day before. Then, while Molly is having a nap and Luke and her mother are quietly practising Luke's handwriting together, she slips away to Anna's.

The short walk is the first time she has been alone – completely alone – for days. She has always had people upstairs, in the room next door, somewhere near.

It is a miserable afternoon. It doesn't warrant an umbrella or pulling up the hood of her anorak, but dampness hangs in the air, permeating her hair and clothes, sitting on her skin. In many ways it is a day like a thousand others, though as she walks she grows increasingly aware: today is different. It is the first day of her life fully, properly without Simon.

He is buried, gone.

As she passes white terraced house after white terraced house, some with peeling paint, some newly decorated, some with scaffolding, she is struck: not all, but so many of them, are family homes. Inside, behind their whitewashed exteriors, are people with partners, children. They will be laughing, playing, arguing, sulking, serving Sunday lunches, snoozing on the sofa.

It seems unreal that her world no longer mirrors theirs.

* * *

'I knew it,' says Uncle Pat.

'If you knew it, how come you never asked me?' Uncle Pat appears not to know how to answer, so Lou helps him. 'Because you were afraid to, maybe?'

'I, er, don't know . . .'

'Well, I think so,' she says. 'And who can blame you? I was frightened to say so myself. The truth is, you've all known for years, but never admitted it out loud.'

She looks at them each in turn. Aunt Audrey is studiously examining her plate; it seems Royal Doulton has never been so fascinating. Uncle Pat is watching her, head cocked to one side, as if unexpectedly confronted by a strange animal in a zoo and trying to appraise it. But it is her mother who Lou really wants to read, and can't.

Her face is blank, expressionless.

'You know what, Mum?' she says. 'I haven't got a boyfriend not because I can't get one, but because I don't want one. I like women. At the end of the day, it is that simple. Dad knew and he asked me not to tell you. So I haven't: not for all these years. I've protected you – kept it from you – because he was so worried it would upset you. In fact, he said it would destroy you. But I'm thirty-two, for fuck's sake.' She can see her mother recoil at her swearing, but Lou is no longer able to restrain herself. It must – she must – come out.

She turns to her uncle. 'And you're right, Uncle Pat, I *am* getting older.' Then she says to her mother, 'So what I've come to realize is that it's all very well, protecting you, Mum, but what is protecting you doing to ME? If I carry on like this, living a lie, I'm the one that's going to end up destroyed, eaten away. I'm telling you. I'm gay.

'There's no going back, no changing it, no "oh-she-just-hasn't-met-the-right-man". I am never going to be Georgia. I am never going to be married, with two point four children, live in a nice little house in the country, with a nice little husband, close to you. I am never going to drive a nice little Golf round Hitchin while my husband goes to work to pay for my frigging children's clothes from Boden and my designer handbags like her. I don't give a monkey's for any of it.

'I live in Brighton, where there are lots of other people just like me. I earn my own living. I have my own friends. And I'm going to sleep with women.'

She stops, breathes out, braces herself for the onslaught. Waits . . .

But instead, her mother just says, 'Has everyone finished?' and rises to her feet.

They pass their plates to her as implicitly requested, her mother collects them, and, without another word, she leaves the room.

The three of them sit there, awkwardly, Lou listening to the clock ticking on the mantelpiece, marking the passage of time.

Eventually, Audrey coughs, then says, 'Well, then . . . Does that mean you've got a girlfriend, dear?'

Lou laughs, slightly manic. 'No.' Sofia comes to mind, but it is far, far too soon to give her that title, and anyway, Lou doesn't want scrutiny about a specific relationship to add further heat to an already explosive situation.

Audrey smiles sympathetically and Lou feels that, ever so subtly, she is offering her support.

'I'm not really seeing anyone,' she volunteers.

She can feel Uncle Pat squirming, as if the very mention of her seeing a woman conjures up every kind of sexual freakery.

Lou returns her aunt's smile, then takes a deep breath, reaches over, tips the remaining vegetables into one dish, places the empty container underneath, picks up the gravy boat and heads out into the kitchen.

Her mother is standing at the sink, elbow-deep in soap-suds.

Lou goes over to the draining board with the dishes.

Her Mum is crying.

Lou fights down anger, leans round to look her in the eye. 'You OK, Mum?'

Her mother won't meet her gaze. With her eyes studiously focused on the garden straight ahead, she says, 'I don't understand, Lou. What did I do wrong?'

'It's nothing you did, Mum,' Lou replies. Inside she is screaming: what makes you believe you have to do something *wrong* for me to be gay?

Her mother finally turns to her, and Lou can see it: pain. A muscle twitches in her cheek; her eyes are full of sorrow.

'You were always your father's favourite,' says her mother, as if she is struggling to find an explanation.

'But not yours,' observes Lou.

'It's not that I didn't love you.'

Lou is shocked; her mother has never used the L-word with her before. She waits. Her mother's hands rest on the edge of the sink; suds drip, unchecked, to the floor.

'I just didn't understand you, that's all.'

'I know.' Suddenly Lou appreciates something of her mother's point of view. It must have been hard, having Lou as a daughter: a girl who was so easily, so firmly connected to her father. Maybe she felt excluded, disempowered. 'I'm trying to help you understand me more now.'

'Mm.' Her mother looks back out of the window, pensive. Outside, the garden is immaculately tended: the lawn gleams green with neatly manicured grass; pots of primulas and pansies edge the path in height order, smallest near the front, like a line-up of pupils for a school photograph.

'It's not too late, you know.' Lou reaches over, places her own hand on top of her mother's, gives it a squeeze. She is not used to touching her; they do so rarely. Through the wet and the soap, she feels her mother's bones, her fragility.

And although her mother doesn't respond, still doesn't look at Lou, she doesn't pull away, either.

For the time being, Lou is aware, this is as much as her mother can give.

* * *

'Coffee, that's what we need,' says Karen. 'I'll make it, you carry on.'

She knows where Anna keeps the grounds, how the percolator works; and presently, she carries the mugs up the stairs, being careful not to spill anything on the cream carpet.

'Stop for a minute,' she suggests. They both take a seat on the bench in the bay window. Karen puts the mugs down on the floor close by.

For a moment they sit in silence, looking out.

It is not a smart street, and it is unlikely that it ever will be. There is litter on the pavement: a plastic bottle, a carrier bag, an old newspaper, wet from the rain. A car drives past, slowly, looking for a space to park; a young man walks up the road, side-stepping puddles. In the distance, on the hillside, a new office block is going up; next door, the house has lost some roof tiles.

'Here we are, both of us without our men,' says Anna, then adds, apologetic, 'not that I mean it's the same for me as you.'

She looks different today, Karen thinks. Then she realizes why. She has left her make-up off: a sure sign, if one were needed, that events have forced her, as they have with Karen, to abandon her routine. But Karen likes seeing Anna exposed this way: she seems younger, more vulnerable, real.

Karen leans forward, takes her hand.

'Courage,' she says.

Sunday

11:43

The sky is the bluest of blues, cloudless. It is high summer, hot. The car window is fully wound down; Lou is leaning her left arm on the door, resting her head on her elbow, enjoying the breeze. They are in Sofia's battered MG, roof folded back, headed along the seafront; Sofia is driving. Lou watches Sofia's profile as she looks ahead, concentrating, and her heart soars up, up, to meet the cloudless sky.

It is one of those oh-so-rare times when Lou can't, in any way, imagine how she could be happier. She loves her job, for all the pain-in-the-neck students she has to deal with. She loves this city, for all its down-at-heel mishmash of buildings and people and shingle-not-sand. She loves her flat, albeit small and imperfectly formed. She loves her friends, both old and new. She even – in a weird way – loves her mum. She knows her mum is trying – she can hear the effort in her voice when they speak. And although she can hear the disapproval too, it is nonetheless out there, in the open, who Lou is. At last, it is more her mum's problem than hers. And her mother can deal with it, slowly, at her own pace. For, finally, Lou has a different focus: she has shifted, she has let go. Perhaps she needed to witness death in order to realize how much she wanted to meet someone, to make herself available, to free herself from the shackles of her past. Whatever the reason, Lou is in love, and, as of last night, it is official. She'd said it first, softly, while she and Sofia were in bed – 'I love you.' And Sofia had said, louder, with undoubted force, 'I love you, too,' and then they had both giggled, and kissed, and soon after that first Sofia, then Lou, came.

They are nearing a set of lights. 'You need to go right here,' instructs Lou.

Sofia indicates, makes the turn, and as they drive up away from the promenade through residential Hove, Lou has a sudden thought as to what would make this moment even more perfect.

'Let's stop and get ice creams,' she says.

* * *

Karen is on her hands and knees, weeding the allotment, listening. Molly and Luke are chatting to each other, playing nearby. The earth is wet from rain the night before; they are making mud pies. A little further away someone is banging wood with a mallet: erecting a fence, maybe, or mending a shed. And further away still, she can hear chanting in the playing field across the road: 'Go! Go! Go!' It's the weekend, so it must be the school baseball or rounders team, cheering on one of their members to complete a circuit and score.

Karen can feel the sun on her back, warming.

'Children,' she says, getting to her feet. 'You need lotion.'

'No, no, no lotion!' Molly stamps her feet on clumpy grass. She hates this ritual.

'Yes lotion.' Karen walks over to the big wicker basket she has brought out with her and rummages for a plastic bottle. 'Come here.' And before Molly can protest further, she squirts the blue-white liquid onto her palms and squelches it over Molly's limbs, sliding her hands round the plump flesh of her arms; down the front, then up the back of her legs. Then smear, smear, on either cheek – Molly is in full recoil mode by now, feet stamping one-two, one-two with increasing ferocity, and Karen can sense she's right on the verge of a wail when – 'Right, you're done' – she releases Molly to her game.

Phew, scene avoided. Molly's tantrums have eased again lately – they reached a crescendo a month previously, but just when Karen really thought she might not be able to stand any more without doing something she'd regret, they'd decreased. Now they appear to be more of a once-a-day event, and that she can just about manage.

'Your turn, Luke.' He stands there, compliant, the barrel of his chest braced. His colouring is hers, but his physique is just like his father, thinks Karen, and his talents are his dad's, too.

She wishes Simon could see them. He is missing these changes, the nuances of their growing up. The way Molly is less difficult, Luke's body is changing from child to boy . . . She feels lonely, watching them sometimes, thinking about them like this: although she has friends and family who are glad to hear about her children, only their father would have appreciated these subtle differences just as she does.

Then she feels a gust of wind, hears the leaves rustle high in the trees, the buzz of a bee close at hand. And, for the first time since that dreadful, dreadful day in February, she has a real sense that she might, she will, get through this. It is not over yet, she knows, and in countless ways it never will be. She is taking it day by lonely, numbing day, and she will never be fully OK with what has happened. But she is learning to live differently, in this world where Simon is gone. Her emotions are being played out on a new terrain; she is gradually unearthing her grief so she can rebuild herself from the ground up. As much by instinct as design, she is finding what gives her solace and leaning towards it, like a flower to sunlight. She can continue.

'You're finished,' she says, clipping shut the bottle top and giving Luke's bottom a gentle pat.

*　*　*

Anna clicks round the dials of the padlock until the code is in a line and yanks it apart. She pushes open the big metal gate; it swings wide. She is laden; a waxed cotton bag containing sandwiches, water and shortbread over her shoulder, a large garden fork in one hand, a rug in the other. She locks the gate behind her and heads along the path.

As she turns the corner, she sees that Karen, Molly and Luke are there before her.

Molly runs to say hello. 'It's Godmother Anna!'

Karen is bent double, weeding. 'Hiya.' She lifts her head, beams.

'Hello.' Anna puts everything down on a patch of rough grass and admires Karen's pile of wilting green. 'You've done heaps already.'

'Look at my patch!' squeals Luke, stopping his pies to yank Anna's T-shirt with muddy hands. She has no choice but to follow him to the smallest bed. And sure enough, lo, the sunflowers have shot up in the week since she was last here; they're over two foot tall, a fine row of big, healthy leaves drooping a little in the heat, beginning to bud flowers.

'Wow!' she says. 'Soon they'll be as big as you.'

'I know.' Luke is proud. 'And see, here, my seeds have grown too.'

'Ooh, yes. What are they called?'

'Candytuft.'

'How lovely. Let's see how the vegetables are doing, shall we?'

Luke marches her to the bed where Karen is working. 'The runners have grown, haven't they?' Anna observes. Twirling around a frame of bamboo poles, they are in flower, zinging bright red beads of promise. One or two have turned to beans already.

Karen nods. 'The lettuces need picking. Take as many as you can; they'll only go past their best.'

'Great. So what do you want me to do?' asks Anna.

Karen knows more about this than she does, having read up on it extensively, and consulted Phyllis. 'There's no point in watering now. It's too hot. We'll do that just before we go. Perhaps if you could clear the bed around the rhubarb?'

'Sure.' Anna gets her gardening gloves from her bag. Soon she is on her knees, tugging weeds from the soil.

Shortly, there is a 'Hello! Hello!' from the path.

It's Lou, and, close behind, Sofia. They look the part somehow, more than Anna feels she does, dressed in cut-off jeans and cotton vests. They complement each other, symmetrical, like bookends. There is something particularly delightful about them as a couple.

'Ladies, welcome,' she says, getting to her feet.

'We brought ice creams!' announces Sofia.

'Yay!' Up jumps Molly. She's been concentrating hard, laying flint stones in size order, in a row next to her mud pies.

'They need eating now. This *minute*,' orders Lou, rummaging in a white plastic bag. Anna notes, not for the first time, that she's a natural with children. No wonder she does what she does, work-wise. 'Do you want chocolate or strawberry?' Lou asks Molly.

'Strawberry!'

Lou hands her a lolly. 'Luke?'

'Chocolate!'

'I'd like chocolate too,' says Anna, 'if that's OK?'

'Sure. Karen?'

'I'll have whatever's left,' offers Karen.

'No, you choose next,' insists Lou.

Anna smiles. Typical Karen. But typical Lou, too: Karen has met her match in terms of generosity. They are mirrors, the two of them. And yet in other ways she, Anna, and Karen mirror each other; and, equally, so do she and Lou. Their friendship reminds her of the three-panelled mirror on her mother's dressing table. When she was little, she used to angle the three panels to see reflection after reflection of herself, growing fainter and fainter ad infinitum. She loved the way it presented a different perspective on the world.

Anna tears open her wrapper, takes a lick. Mm, white chocolate. Wicked, delicious.

'We have an announcement,' says Lou.

Anna can tell from her expression that it is something good.

'Sofia's moving to Brighton,' Lou says, grinning at her girlfriend.

'That's wonderful,' says Anna.

'Congratulations!' Karen smiles.

Lou reaches out, pulls her girlfriend to her hip. Sofia blushes.

Anna has a stab of jealousy – she is thrilled for them, yet can't help but envy their happiness. Don't be ungracious, she tells herself. It is not your time; it is theirs. Lou is so lovely; she deserves to be happy.

'Does that mean you'll be doing the commute?' she asks.

'Yes,' says Sofia.

'Another one on the seven forty-four,' says Lou.

'Great,' says Anna. She feels a twinge of sadness; her one-on-one chats with Lou will vanish.

'I go to East Croydon, though,' explains Sofia.

Ah, thinks Anna, so we'll still have some time on the train, just us. She wishes she could be less churlish: hopes they are unaware. But it is not yet six months since that day in February; a week less still since she split with Steve. She has no regrets; she knows now he could never have made her happy, even though he has, apparently, joined AA, is doing better. But sobriety is his journey, not hers: he needs to do it for himself, alone. Still, she misses him hugely, doesn't feel ready for another relationship yet. But as time passes, she hopes that she might be, eventually, with someone new, easier, kinder.

Maybe.

Probably . . .

What she does know for sure is that it has not been easy. Not for herself, for Karen, or the children. Karen still cries daily, Anna knows, though she tries to hide it. Luke still sleeps with his mother every night; Karen admits she is indulging herself as much as him, but must at some stage encourage him back to his room. She will do it too, soon; Karen is like that, brave.

Some day, eventually, Anna hopes, Karen will also meet someone new. It will doubtless take her longer, because she and Simon were together for ages, but again, perhaps not.

Who knows?

Until then, and after that, they have each other. God/Fate/Fortune willing, she and Karen will have one another for many years to come. And other friends, like Lou, and now Sofia.

Suddenly Anna feels like crying, looking round at them all. Four months ago, when the women took on this allotment, it was just a patch of rough land. No beds, no flowers, no vegetables; just a wilderness of brambles and couch grass, badly in need of some TLC. They have forked over the soil and planted it. They have sweated and laughed, been driven mad by excess rain and not enough water, moaned about slugs until Karen relented and succumbed to pellets, and struggled (and failed) to keep it free from weeds. Molly and Luke have helped, as well. Today, there are eight beds in total, each edged with planks of wood. And they have exotic purple and frizzy green lettuces ready, and traditional floppy-leafed ones on their way. They have had rocket a while, and they have ripe raspberries and almost endless rhubarb. Soon they will have beans and broccoli, cabbages and kale, gooseberries, blackberries, pumpkins and plums from a tree that was there already. It may not be the big garden in Hove that Karen so yearned for, but it is more than a viable alternative. Nature has a way of healing the soul; the allotment has been a bridge back to the outside world. That they do it together fills Anna with joy.

So why does she feel like weeping? She stops what she is doing to consider, then realizes.

It is Simon.

Simon would have loved it. The allotment would have been just his kind of place, with its feeling of community and burgeoning life and its vast stretch of sky. And he loved plants so, and planning, plotting space; he would have been in his element.

Then again, maybe he is here. He has returned to the soil, after all. Life, death, the seasons, day, night: it is a pattern, a cycle.

Anna has finished her ice cream, picks up her trowel. Soon she is back on her knees, struggling to edge a particularly tenacious dandelion from the earth.

Acknowledgements

First off, a massive thank you to Vivien Green, my agent. When Fortune dealt out the cards of my life, she dealt me an ace; words cannot express my gratitude. Secondly, thank you to Sam Humphreys from Picador, who right from the off was 110 per cent behind this novel. Two aces; I am blessed. Not forgetting everyone else at Picador, Gaia Banks at Sheil Land, and all the folk at Digital and Direct.

I would also like to thank the friends who read as I wrote. They are Alison Boydell and Clare Stratton, who helped me hone the first draft and told me when they thought I'd got it wrong. Also Clare Allison, Jackie Donnellan, Patrick Fitzgerald, Hattie Gordon, Emma Hall, Katy Holford, Alex Hyde, Niccy Lowit, Kate Miller, Aiden and Ginette Roworth and Joanna Watson, who all read the draft once I was done and whose insights were invaluable. There's Diane Messidoro too, and John Knight, for the author photograph. And of course my mother, Mary Rayner, who is my inspiration. Plus thank you, Tom Bicât, not just for reading it even when he doesn't 'do' novels, but for not minding if I got snappy when I was in the throes of creation, and for just being, well, lovely.

Finally, this book is dedicated to my women friends.
In a way, I wrote it for all of you.

* * *

For more information on Sarah Rayner, visit
www.thecreativepumpkin.com.